IN MAGIC'S SHADOW

BOOK 2 OF THE FOUR SISTERS SERIES

ANAYA MACLEOD

❦ Created with Vellum

TO DREAM

No-one truly knows what they are capable of until they take a chance and believe in themselves. It is then they discover what it means to follow a dream and uncover the secrets that give their life meaning.

Anaya MacLeod

THE STORY SO FAR

In this series, the story takes the reader to various sites on both Earth and a planet called Eratus. Eratus is in a star system not far from Earth's solar system.

Connell (**Adopted Son of the High King Of Eratus**) and Laela (**Enchantress of the Four Sisters**) prepare for a healing ceremony to heal the **Shield** that protects the life on the planet of Eratus. The magic in the healing also renews the barriers around a series of magical prisons which lock away an enemy of Eratus – **The Ancients**.

What **Connell** didn't expect was for the healing ceremony to be sabotaged, resulting in the tragic deaths of most who were present at the healing. The sabotage allows a **Darkness** to enter the Shield. The **Darkness** has a specific objective – to release the **Ancients** by changing the magical composition of the Shield so that the **Ancients** can remove the barriers surrounding their prisons.

Drakon (Son of the High King Of Eratus) is aware of the dangers Eratus faces with the **Ancients** and the **Darkness** but his focus is on finding hidden caches of **Ancient**

Weapons which he believes will give him all the power he desires to destroy his enemies and rule over Eratus. **Drakon** has a lover called **Reya (who is also his General)** and she helps locate the map and records for these ancient weapons. She is also charged with the responsibility of finding test subjects (people) for Drakon to use when he is ready to test the weapons—once he finds them. Not much is known about these weapons, except that they're ancient and therefore they must be powerful.

Owain (The High King of Eratus) has made it a priority to heal the Shield and to ensure the **Ancients** do not escape their prison. He implements a plan to destroy the **Darkness.** But there is a catch. **Sascha, (Adopted daughter of the High King Of Eratus)** is the only one who can carry out the plan and she was evicted from Eratus and sent to Earth with any memories of her life on Eratus removed. It was done as a punishment for attempting to kill him—**Owain (The High King of Eratus)**—and he had sworn that day he would never allow her to come back.

Marco (Connell's lifelong friend and Sascha's Ex Fiancée) along with **Sascha's** bonded pet, **Soleil**, are given the task of convincing **Sascha** to leave Earth and to return to Eratus to help save their planet. But considering the fact that she was evicted, there was a question around whether **Sascha** would ever want to return to her home planet.

When **Sascha** was first sent to Earth she was kidnapped and brutally tortured. She was eventually rescued and after she recovered from the kidnapping she managed to build a new life on Earth as a vet. But she constantly struggled with not being able to remember her past.

As fate would have it, she ended up becoming a foster mum for three girls **Lee, Ella and Kira**, who supposedly lost their parents when they were young. Like **Sascha** the girls had no memories of their past. One afternoon, after a series of unusual events, they discover they have all been tortured by a nightmare where they see themselves murdering an old man and a young woman. They decide to work together to search for a meaning to the dream, and discover the old man is called **Eham (A Dark Mage)** and the young woman is **Jenny, (His Granddaughter)**—and they are very much alive. On the surface it appears there is little that connects the **Girls**, **Sascha, Eham and Jenny** but time reveals their connections are a lot more significant than any of them had realized.

While **Sascha** and **The Girls** start on their journey of discovery, to learn more about each other, and their pasts, **Connell** is also on a road to discovery. **Reya** visits him in his chambers and reveals the truth about her connection to **Sascha**, shares some secrets about who **Drakon** really is, and poisons Connell with black lyrium. She then sends one of her creations, a **pit hound,** to kill him.

Meanwhile, **Sascha** agrees to heal the Shield and destroy the **Darkness** but the only way she can do that is by regaining her memory and renewing her powers. After a series of trials, with the help of **Athena, (Goddess of Wisdom)**, they persuade **Zeus, Ruler of Olympus** to give his permission for her memory and powers to be returned. This permission comes with a price.

Once **Sascha** regains her memory and her powers she journeys to Kalurth's Peak where, with the help of **Athena**, two **Master dragons—Zinnath and Kalurth**—and a pair of blades called the **Blades of Light**, **Sascha** destroys the **Darkness** in the Shield after battling an **Ancient** with sparkling blue eyes. Together Athena, Zinnath, Kalurth, and Sascha, then heal the Shield.

Throughout the novel **Sascha** renews her bond with

Soleil and meets many creatures: a gibleree (creature of darkness) called **Bibacr**; a manticore called George; and monsters such as **pit hounds**.

And along the way **Sascha** falls in love with **Marco** all over again.

MAP OF THE ANCIENTS

ERATUS: THE YEAR 2650 (AGS), 150 YEARS AGO

*A*tticus sat in his ebony rocking chair on the porch outside his workshop and stroked the silky fur of the baby manticore lying in his arms. The pungent smell of the coming storm wafted around him as he studied the ominous black wall of cloud. The dark mass raced across the crimson skies, its underside writhing and twisting as if desperate to begin the destruction it had been created for.

The wailing alarms had finally fallen silent and everyone was as ready as they could be for what was to come. Atticus glanced down at Kan as the creature yawned, stretched, and snuggled into Atticus's robe. The sleeping draught was already taking effect. Whatever happened next, Kan would sleep through it. His heart ached when he considered the possibility that Kan's life—all of their lives—could be about to end, and all because of the perverted mind of a long-dead High King. But there was still a chance that they would survive this.

"Kan," Atticus whispered, "I have one more thing to do before we return to the castle."

He leaned down and gently placed the manticore on a

silk, purple cushion underneath the ebony table beside his chair. "Rest now, little one."

Kan pulled his leathery wings closer to his body and snuggled deeper into the cushion, resting his heavy head on his paws.

Atticus took a moment to relax back into the rocker and savor what was probably the last chance he would ever have to sit here. He still remembered the day he had first placed this chair on the porch, the pride he had felt as he had admired his handiwork. And he still enjoyed the thrill that raced through him when he sat in it and surveyed the picturesque castle gardens where he asked Rochelle to become his queen. Though his official duties as High King of Eratus consumed most of his waking moments, he still managed to find time to disappear into his workshop to do a little carving or polishing.

A loud boom cracked through the skies, leaving an eerie silence in its wake. Atticus glanced at Kan to see if the sound had woken him, but he was still asleep. In the ensuing quiet, Atticus could hear the clock in his workshop ticking down the last hour before the magic was to be released. He leaned over and picked up the map from the table next to him. Atticus shuddered as his hand grasped the rough paper. So many had died trying to preserve this map, keep some record of where the weapons had been stored. But it was his job to destroy it. It and the chronicle. The magical storm should destroy all the weapon caches hidden around Eratus, but if not, at least the likelihood of anyone ever finding them would be about a trillion to one. But if by some chance they did find the weapons, without the chronicle they wouldn't have the instructions on how to release it.

Atticus bowed his head. "Athena, Goddess of Wisdom, I pray I do not fail you."

He raised his head and glanced at the roaring furnace

carved into the stone platform next to his workshop. The gauge on the wall of the furnace indicated that it wasn't yet hot enough to melt the gold cover protecting the chronicle. A few more minutes would do it.

Atticus placed the map back on the table next to his dagger and the chronicle and picked up his mug of prumble ale. He wasn't superstitious, but he certainly believed that this map was cursed. Everyone who had tried to destroy it thus far had failed. But this time would be different.

He pushed his curly gray hair off his face and took a sip of ale. The crunch of gravel from the pathway warned him that someone was approaching and instinct had him putting his ale on the table and reaching for his blade. He surreptitiously glanced toward the sound, then breathed a sigh of relief.

"Leeron," he called out. "You should have stayed in the castle. Careful. The ground isn't steady."

"Duty comes first, Sire," Leeron replied.

Atticus smiled to himself. Despite what they were facing, the aide-de-camp still looked impeccable in his uniform of black pants, white shirt, silver cufflinks, and white gloves. In his hands was a tray of cookies.

Seconds later, the ground rumbled and, in one violent roar, split in front of Leeron. He stumbled over the long, thin crack, regained his balance, and continued toward the workshop as if nothing had happened.

"Leeron, what in Athena's name are you doing out here?"

"Sire," Leeron said, striding up the stairs. He bowed before Atticus. "If it pleases you, I brought some of the queen's dragon berry cookies for you to have with your ale."

"You came out in this storm to bring me cookies?" Atticus shook his head. "You are crazy."

"Sire—"

Atticus stretched out and placed his hand on Leeron's

skinny shoulders. "There is no need for formalities, Leeron. Especially now."

"Formalities are even more important now, Sire. With our world disappearing around us, it is good to have something to hold on to." Leeron placed the plate of cookies on the table next to the High King's chair and then stood in silence as he studied Kan.

Atticus put his dagger back into its scabbard, broke a bit off one of the cookies, and popped it into his mouth. "Is there something else you wanted to say, Leeron?"

Leeron cleared his throat and raised his head. Tears filled his eyes. "You have a compassionate heart, Sire. No matter what happens, the sacrifices you have made for your people and your creatures," he said, nodding at Kan, "will never be forgotten. It has been a real honor to serve you."

Atticus swallowed the lump in his throat. "We may still survive this. The shields may work."

"Yes, Sire. I believe that, too, but I needed you to know, just in case they don't."

Atticus nodded. "Thank you, Leeron . . ." The rest of the sentence stuck in his throat.

Why do I find it so hard to say something nice, even now, when there's every chance we won't survive?

He shook his head in frustration. When he looked up again, Leeron was wiping tears away from his eyes with the back of his hand.

"Will you join us before the defensive shield is put in place, Sire?"

"Yes, we will be down there soon." They had all placed so much hope in the protection the shields offered. Atticus prayed their faith would be rewarded. The shields should be in place soon, but there were still those who refused to come in under their protection. Those unfortunate souls had no chance of surviving what was to come.

Leeron turned on his heel and walked back down the pathway as the skies opened. Black rain raced toward the ground, drenching everyone and everything that hadn't found shelter. As Leeron put his hand up to cover his face from the stinging pellets of rain, the ground beneath his feet shifted. The thin crack across the pathway opened and Leeron tripped over its edge and fell into the gaping maw, his screams muffled by the sound of the pelting rain.

Leaping out of his chair, Atticus raced to the stairs and headed for the spot where Leeron had been standing before he had fallen.

"Leeron, hold on. I'm coming."

The ground shook again and the sound of rock grinding against rock filled the air as the gap closed, swallowing Leeron.

"No," Atticus screamed. "Leeron!"

There was no reply. Leeron was gone.

Atticus finally arrived at the spot where Leeron had disappeared and stared at the scarred ground. "Leeron," he murmured. "What a waste! To have made it this far and then die delivering me cookies." He shook his head.

Atticus stood for a moment, grieving silently. When the ground shook again, rousing him from his trance, he turned and scanned the castle balconies to see if anyone else had witnessed the tragedy, but they were empty. "Rest in Athena's grace, my friend. Depending on how things go, I may join you soon."

He took a deep breath and trudged up the stairs, back to the furnace. The gauge showed it had reached the right temperature. It was time to finish this and return to the castle.

The rain eased to a light shower as he picked up the map and the book, and returned to the roaring flames. He gave the map one last look, then stepped forward and threw it into the fire. He watched as the paper curled and turned to ash. It seemed such an easy end for something that had caused so much destruction.

He ran his fingers over the book's ornate golden cover. A dark red-brown stain—the blood of the consul who had spent so long compiling it—marred the book's delicately carved trim. After spending so many years putting the chronicle together, the consul's last act had been to try to destroy it. It was the Ancients who had stopped him.

Atticus opened the book and trailed his fingers down the first page. He recognized the familiar twinge in his stomach as he struggled with what the chronicle repre-sented. It was the story of their past. If High King Taolis had realized what devastation the weapon he designed would create, would he have thought twice about the direc-tion he was taking?

Atticus closed the book with a snap. His stomach churned as he lifted the book, threw it into the furnace, and watched the fire devour it.

Maybe now the consul's spirit would rest. Future king-doms would be safe.

Once the book was nothing but ash and melted gold, Atticus turned and faced the horizon, searching for the signals that would show that the defensive shields had been placed over the villages. It wasn't long before the sky exploded with rockets the colors of fire and ice. He exhaled slowly.

The shields are up. May Athena protect us all.

The ground shuddered beneath him. It was time to join the others. He walked over and locked the doors of his workshop.

Atticus tutted at himself. "How stupid are you? Locking the workshop? This will probably all be destroyed in the next hour."

He leaned down and picked up Kan and carried him to the castle.

"You decided to join us," the queen called out when he arrived in the great hall. "We are relieved. Put Kan with his family over there in the corner."

"Have they all . . ."

"Yes," the queen answered. "They have all been given the draught."

"Did you see what happened to Leeron?" Atticus asked.

"Yes," she said, walking over to embrace her husband. "It was a tragedy."

"I didn't think anyone saw it," Atticus replied. "I looked up here—"

"We saw it but the heavy rains forced us inside." She shook her head. "I know it is the wrong thing to say, but I'm glad it wasn't you. I'm glad you're here with us."

"I had to be here," Atticus said. "I couldn't leave the love of my life to face this on her own."

The queen handed him a glass filled with a sweet, fruity liquid. "Take this. The drink will help to ease the pain of losing Leeron." She glanced over at Atticus's brother. "It has certainly helped Crypto relax."

Atticus took a sip. "It's as potent as ever, My Queen."

"And change your clothing," she answered. "You're soaking."

Atticus entered his chambers, stripped off his wet robe, and then put on a pair of black pants and a blue tunic. When he rejoined his queen, she was standing at the balcony rim. She looked beautiful, her long onyx-colored hair blowing in the winds, her fitted navy gown showing off the trim figure that so many women of the court envied. He took her hand in his and together they watched as the mages gathered outside the main tavern in the courtyard. They were dressed in red, gold, and silver robes, which glistened in the light of the flickering torches set up behind them. The burning torches filled the air with the aromas of beeswax and eucalyptus. The mages tilted their heads back, stretched out their arms, and began to chant. A sizzle of electricity filled the skies and a blue shield enveloped the castle grounds.

"Raise your cups, everyone," Crypto said. "Let us toast to a new beginning."

"Hear, hear." There was a murmur of agreement as glasses clinked together.

"Now, Sire," Crypto said, turning to face Atticus, "I don't want you to get mad at me, but I thought now was the right time to tell you."

Atticus's stomach twisted as a sense of dread flooded through him. "What is it, brother?"

"As the court's historian," Crypto said, "it is my duty to protect the documents that record our story so that future generations can learn from our mistakes."

"It's too late, brother." Atticus glanced in the direction of the furnace. "I'm sorry, but I destroyed them."

"Then it's fortunate I knew what you had planned."

Atticus gulped. "What . . . what have you done, brother?"

"I had the map and chronicle copied. I kept the originals and sent them to the Four Sisters for safekeeping. You had the copies."

Atticus felt the blood draining from his face. "No. Tell me you didn't do that."

"Our people deserve another chance," Crypto replied.

"But the—the blood on the chronicle . . ." Atticus stammered.

"Easy to fake," Crypto replied.

Atticus's mind raced as he tried to work out how he could get to the Four Sisters, order them to destroy everything his brother had given them. But then the skies opened and the world shook violently as the war against the weapons began.

He dropped to his knees. "Athena, I'm sorry. I failed you. Please give me a chance to undo what my brother has done."

His last thought before the darkness descended was that he had to somehow survive what was to come. He had to fix this.

THE SEASON OF THE THREE MOONS

ERATUS: PRESENT TIME, 2801 (AGS)

*D*rakon, still dressed in the leather pants and vest that he wore for training, left the warmth of his war room and sauntered along the ramparts to where he could get a good view of the courtyard. The suns hadn't risen yet and the two half-moons provided the only light. He shivered as the chilly winds whistled along the top of the castle walls.

It's still nearly two months to the season of the three moons. It shouldn't be this cool.

As he stretched himself to his full height, his hand dropped to the bollock dagger tucked into his belt. His shoulder-length dark hair blew around his face in the cool winds. There was a click of talons on the edge of the ramparts wall and the faint whiff of sulfur. Drakon's hand reached out automatically to stroke the smooth neck of the leader of his golden fire dragons. Kalamar's tough, shiny scales, the colors of amber and molten gold, glinted in the moonlight.

"Hello, Kalamar."

Kalamar sidled up to Drakon as they surveyed the scene

below. Kalamar was half the size of his more powerful cousins, but that was because he was from the Kingdom of Breyth whereas most dragons originated from the Kingdom of Brun. Drakon wished, and not for the first time, he could speak to Kalamar in the same way he could talk to his cousins but Kalamar had his own, very clear, way of communicating and that was enough.

The air was filled with whispered conversations as soldiers and mages tried to finalize the packing of their supplies on their pyrans, without waking the rest of the castle. The pyrans clicked their beaks and constantly shifted their talons on the clay surface as they adjusted their positions to balance the weight of the loads their riders were putting on their backs. The scent of pine floated on the winds blowing around the courtyard.

Pyrans always seem to smell of the forest, which is surprising considering they spend most of their lives in the castle.

Mage Isabella stood next to Lieutenant General Chiane at the castle gates, her fingers and arms moving clumsily as she cast a protection spell over the group. Drakon's lips curled into a snarl as he stared at her—a plain-looking redhead with empty green eyes.

That creature is all talk. How could I have ever thought she might rival Reya?

For all of Reya's faults, he missed her. She was a graceful creature and a demon in bed. Isabella was weak, insipid, and a great disappointment. His serving wench brought him much more pleasure. If not for Isabella's magical skills, he would have sent her away.

Drakon's attention turned to Lieutenant General Novo who was dressed in silver chain mail which jangled as he stormed around the courtyard barking orders at the group preparing to leave.

"If this is the fastest you can load up your pyran, lad,"

Novo snapped at his young aide, "perhaps we should take your missus instead. She at least seems to understand what I mean when I say hurry."

Novo turned to walk back to his pyran and crashed into a couple of the mages. "And if *you* get under my feet one more time," Novo exploded, "then I will personally show you how that staff of yours should be used. And it won't be a magical experience for you."

Drakon smirked as the mages skittered away from Novo and positioned themselves at the back of the group. Novo had often said how much he hated mages, believing they had been planted in the castle by the Four Sisters and were only there to avenge Reya's death.

"Mount," Novo yelled out.

Each of the mages and soldiers clambered up onto the back of their pyran, now loaded for their trip to Brun. Pyrans had proven themselves in battle, with their long talons and sharp beaks, but their strong backs and powerful wings had given them a unique role in transportation on Eratus. While the feathered creatures came in various colors Novo climbed up onto one of the drabber looking pyrans. His was a dumb beast, unlike the others, but its broad back, strong loins, and powerful hindquarters made it a perfect beast of burden.

"My Prince," Novo called out. "We're about to leave. Any final commands?"

"You know what is expected, Novo. Do not fail me. Find that cache of weapons."

"Let's—"

Novo was drowned out by a loud whirring sound that echoed around the grounds. A large circle of spinning air opened next to the staircase leading up to the ramparts, not far from where Drakon was standing. It spat out a bloodied body, shimmered, and then disappeared.

The grounds fell silent as the body tried to stand, then collapsed.

"Help him, you fool," Chiane barked at the soldier closest to the wounded man. The soldier leaped from his pyran and raced over to the bloodied body. His face lost all its color as he stared down at the man at his feet.

"In Athena's name, tell us who it is," Chiane demanded.

The soldier whipped off his cloak, draped it over the man's shoulders, and turned back to Chiane. "Sir, I think you should see this."

"Chiane, bring him to me," Drakon ordered. "Novo, you're dismissed. You have work to do. I expect results before the two moons set a second time. Go. Now!"

"Soldier," Novo called out. "Take your position."

The soldier kept glancing back at the body as he raced toward his pyran. His family tossed him a cloak to replace the one he had used to cover the injured man.

"Check your transportation chips before we enter the portal." The group raised their right hand and tapped it. Novo glanced around as each person confirmed their chip was working. "Now, let's fly."

The pyrans hunkered down, stretched their wings, then leaped up into the air, the whoosh of their powerful wings causing bystanders to take several steps backward. Seconds later the small group flew over the walls of the castle and were on their way to the Kingdom of Brun. Quiet descended on the courtyard once again.

Chiane and one of his men moved forward, picked up the wounded man, and carried him up the stairs to Drakon.

They placed him so he was sitting with his back leaning against the wall of the stone ramparts. Chiane leaned down to reposition the cloak and they all gasped at the sight of the mutilated body. It looked as if the man had fallen into a pit of spikes.

"How are you still alive?" Chiane spluttered. He retrieved a leather water flask from his jacket pocket and, squatting next to the man, offered him a drink. As the man took a sip, he started coughing, blood splattering on the ground next to him. He gasped for breath and then looked up at Drakon. "My Prince, I came here to warn you."

"Where are you from?" Drakon asked.

"The Kingdom of Ta—Tasuna," the man stammered.

"Tasuna?" Drakon repeated.

"Yes. We have seen akhult tracks, lots of them. There were a group of us that came to warn you but we were attacked as we entered the portal. I was the only one that survived."

"Akhult." Chiane stood, his hand gripping the hilt of his sword.

"You must be mistaken," Drakon said. "Those creatures don't return until the storms during the season of the three moons, and that is at least two months away."

"What attacked you?" Chiane asked.

"Ice ghouls."

"But it's been centuries since the ice ghouls attacked the living," Chiane said.

"These ones did, and they had these . . . spikes. They looked like ice spears." The man coughed again. He grunted as he tried to breathe.

"We need to carry this man to the healer," Chiane said.

"It's too late for me," the man replied. "But I need you to believe me. What I say is true. The season of the three moons is near. The ice ghouls killed the others and destroyed the portal."

Chiane leaned over and rested his hand on the man's shoulder. "We believe you. Where were the guardians that guard the portal?"

"Those grotesque creatures left weeks ago."

"So if the guardians have moved on, they know the storm

season is near," Chiane said. "You were very brave to come and warn us. What is your name?"

"I'm Sinar—" The man sagged against the wall and fell silent.

Chiane pressed his fingers to the man's neck. "He's dead." Chiane mumbled a quiet prayer before he turned to Drakon. "I'm sure the man speaks the truth, My Prince?"

Drakon stared at the body. "I agree."

"We need to move fast then," Chiane said. "We need to start readying for the storms."

Chiane was right. They needed to start preparing, and fast. But Drakon had other work to do first. He walked away from Chiane's soldier and signaled for Chiane to join him.

"We must not say anything to anyone," Drakon muttered. "If the High King finds out, he will shut down all the portals. We need to keep the portals open until we have the weapons."

"What about Marco?" Chiane asked.

"We can't let him know about this either. He will side with the King. And who was appointed as our telepath, when the old man finally passed on?"

"I don't know," Chiane said, "but I'll find out."

"Whoever it is must know the portal has been destroyed, which means they will be seeking an audience with the King to find out what they should advise the kingdoms. The telepath must never meet with the King."

A spine-tingling howl echoed through the forest that surrounded the castle.

"The akhult," the soldier whimpered.

Drakon glared at the soldier. "It was a wolf, that's all. Are you a man or a hurly?"

"My Prince," Chiane murmured. "You won't do these young soldiers any favors by comparing them to those furry little creatures."

"Then he needs to act more like a soldier." Drakon studied the soldier for a few seconds before turning back to Chiane. "Have the body taken to the furnace. Then make sure you"— Drakon glanced at the soldier—"tie up any loose ends. We cannot afford for your man to tell anyone what we found out today."

"My soldiers are loyal," Chiane replied. "He will not share what he heard with anyone. I can guarantee you that."

"In normal circumstances I would leave it with you, Chiane, but these are not normal circumstances. You have my orders."

"Yes, My Prince."

Chiane walked back to the soldier. "Take the body to the furnace. It's important we keep what happened here today to ourselves. We can't afford to cause panic."

"Yes, sir," the soldier said. "But shouldn't we give him a burial, let his family know of his death? After all, he came here to warn us. We owe him—"

"We owe the people here," Drakon said as he joined them. "It's our job to protect them. There's no need to create panic, not until we know more. Once you have disposed of the body, report directly to Chiane. He has a task for you." Drakon turned to Chiane. "Isn't that correct, Chiane?"

Chiane nodded.

"Good, we understand each other. I will see you in my war room as soon as you have finished here."

"Yes, My Prince," Chiane answered.

The soldier picked up the body and, with the help of Chiane, positioned it on his shoulder. He turned and headed for the staircase that led down to the furnace.

"Come, Kalamar," Drakon called out.

Kalamar flew ahead of Drakon and landed elegantly in the corner of the war room. He curled up with his family, who were still fast asleep.

Drakon stood in the doorway and breathed in the warm smell of pine and honey—the scent of the woods that made up the dragon's nest. He clapped his hands softly so as not to wake the sleeping dragons, and the lights in the overhead beams started to glow.

A soft blue light surrounded the carved marble table that stood in the center of the room. Shapes emerged from the table as the map—a three-dimensional representation of the site of the ancient weapons in Brun—came to life. Drakon walked toward the table and strode around it as he examined the map of the site that had, thus far, proven inaccessible.

Drakon had finished reviewing the site map when Chiane walked into the war room and joined him at the table.

"Chiane, have your men left for Earth yet?"

"Yes. They left before the first sun rose yesterday."

"Sokentash!" Drakon cursed. He stopped walking and glared at Chiane. "Only yesterday?"

Chiane cleared his throat. "Yes, My Prince. The mages have only just found a way to open the portals again, including the two portals to Earth. Whatever happened at the healing ceremony did a lot of damage to them."

"I don't understand how that happened," Drakon snapped. "It's never happened before. Damn dragons probably did it deliberately."

"The good news," Chiane said, "is that the portal guardians have finally gone into hibernation, except for the ones at the first portal—the smaller Earth portal. But we will be using the second portal to travel to Earth, so they won't be an issue for us."

Drakon grunted. "I wouldn't get too excited about that news, Chiane. What's ahead of us is a lot more dangerous than a couple of monsters." Drakon glanced at Chiane in time to see him rub the back of his neck before he rested his hand on the hilt of his sword.

Good, the man is starting to realize what we're up against.

"Anyway," Drakon continued, "even if Novo finds a way to open the weapons site in Brun, I will still want a detailed sketch of the site on Earth." He pointed at the table. "The same sort of detail as this one. Find someone who can do the drawings and send them to Earth to join your men."

"Yes, My Prince. Do you still intend to go to Earth?"

"If Novo's attempt to open the site here doesn't work, then yes, we will still be going. And make sure the men have had their transportation chips checked. This is the Earth portal, after all. Only a fool would travel through the portal to Earth without his transportation chip fully charged."

"I will do that. But is it worth leaving for Earth at this time? What if the akhult—"

Drakon glared at Chiane, who lowered his head and nodded.

"Yes, My Prince."

Drakon rested the palms of his hands on the edge of the table. "If what this man said is correct, then I agree that we don't have much time. We will escalate our plans. If the storms of the three seasons arrive and the portals cease to work, I cannot be stuck on Earth with the ancient weapons. Keep in contact with Novo and let me know if he is successful . . . or not."

"I will."

"And one more thing." Drakon rubbed the armband he was wearing. "I need you to use your contacts to find me someone who can organize a replacement band for this one. If Athena finds out I'm wearing this to stop the Ancients from controlling me, she will think I owe her. She might try to demand my obedience in return for allowing me to wear it. I cannot let that happen."

"Right away, My Prince." Chiane bowed, turned on his heel, and left.

Drakon stepped over to where the fire dragons slept and leaned against the wall as he studied the creatures. A few minutes later, he pushed himself upright. He had work to do.

"Kalamar," he whispered, "keep your family safe. I may need you all very soon."

Kalamar raised his head and stared at Drakon. He emitted a soft purring sound as he moved his body closer to his mate's and rested his head on her back.

Drakon pushed down the warm glow that flooded through him.

Since when do I care about dragons?

Something had changed when he had returned from the Peaceful Valley after killing the Master. He had never heard them sing to him in the way they did that day. When they circled him, moved closer and lay down at his feet . . . it was like he was a god. And the dragons were his people. The bond they formed that day seemed to have changed him. He wasn't quite sure what it meant. Or why their actions had reached a part of him he'd kept hidden for so long. But time would reveal whether his bond with these creatures was real.

Drakon turned and walked out of the war room.

Let's see how loyal Fenix is.

Last time the fire dragons and Fenix had met, Kalamar had reacted to the pyran's presence in a way that worried Drakon. It was almost as if he was warning Drakon about her. But then again, fire dragons and pyrans had never liked each other.

When Drakon arrived at his chambers, he turned to the guard standing by his door. "Ask my aide to find Fenix and send her to me."

"Yes, Prince Drakon." The guard brought his clenched fist to his chest in salute.

Minutes later claws clicked along the balcony rim.

Fenix is here. Good.

Fenix warbled as she dropped to the floor and trotted into Drakon's chambers. Her silken ebony and scarlet feathers glistened in the filtered light of the suns, while her onyx-colored eyes watched Drakon's every move.

"I have a job for you, Fenix," Drakon said. "I need you to fly Sascha to my encampment in Cirrone near the Jaynor River. I don't care how you do it, but you must not try to take her through the portal."

"But . . . but what if she doesn't want to go there?" Fenix stammered.

"Capture her, do whatever you need to do, but get her to that encampment. Novo has already prepared a . . . welcoming party . . . for her. She'll be safe. But no one can know how she was taken or where she has gone."

"Soleil is Sascha's protector. He won't let me take her."

"Keep this a secret from Soleil," Drakon said.

Fenix stared at Drakon.

"This will be good for you, Fenix. You have become too attached to Soleil and forgotten who it is you serve."

Fenix lowered her head in acknowledgment.

"Does Soleil know about your children? Does he know he's their father?"

"No, I can't—"

"See? You can keep secrets from him. And if you don't do what I ask . . . well, you know I can't let disobedience go unpunished. What if I told my fire dragons where to find your children? What do you think would happen?"

"You can't! They would kill them."

"Then you need to find a way to capture Sascha and take

her to Cirrone. But remember, no one can know where she is, including that damn Soleil."

"If Soleil ever finds out, he will never forgive me," Fenix said. "Not after everything they've been through."

"That's not my problem. And if I was you, I wouldn't let it bother me. Unless, of course, your children don't mean as much to you as Soleil does."

Fenix went quiet as she studied the ground. "Yes, My Prince."

"Good. There is every chance I'll be going to Earth before the second moon sets tomorrow. I'll be gone a couple of days. When I get back I expect to find her safely locked up in the quarters in Cirrone. And you to be there, waiting with her."

"Yes, My Prince."

Drakon smiled to himself as Fenix trotted out to the balcony, leaped onto the balcony rim, and flew off in the direction of Sascha's chambers.

She won't fail me. And once it is done, I will make sure Soleil finds out Fenix was responsible for it.

He laughed.

"Let's see their relationship survive that."

THE NIGHTMARE

ERATUS

*T*he stench of warm copper and the gargled groans of the dying filled the cave. Sascha ignored the scene around her as she studied the old man.

"Eham, begging is a waste of time."

Eham bowed low, the torchlight glinting on the blood splattered over his hooded robe.

"Please, Sascha, spare him."

Jenny stood silently next to Eham, tears rolling down her face. Gripping her tunic was the child. It stood there, head tilted to the side, a smile upon its face. Olive skin, dark hair, and sparkling, bright blue eyes—a smaller version of the creature that had tried to destroy Sascha during the healing ceremony.

Anger sizzled in Sascha's blood as she pushed past Eham.

Eham grabbed at her arm as he tried to slow her down. "Everything is not what it seems, Sascha. Please."

Sascha pulled her arm free and shook her head as she continued to stare at the child. "You know what I pledged. I swore to destroy the darkness on Eratus. The child must die, and if you—or Jenny—get in my way, I will do what I need to do. But the child will die a quick death. It will not suffer."

Sascha pushed her hands into the pockets of her black cloak, grasped the tips of the Blades of Light, her thumb on one side of the blade and her fingers on the other. She bent her wrist back, swung her arm forward, and released the blades.

The blades spun in circles, becoming brighter and brighter as they spun faster and faster.

"They're pretty," the child cooed. He let Jenny's tunic drop from his hand and dashed across the gravel floor with surprising speed in an effort to catch them.

"No," Jenny screamed as she raced after the child to stop him from touching the blades. He frowned as he reached out to the light. A second later his body shimmered and disappeared. The blades changed direction and headed for Jenny and Eham. Eham tried to raise a magical shield to protect them, but his magic wouldn't work. Seconds later, they were both engulfed in the magic of the blades. Their bodies turned to dust and the blades fell to the ground with a soft thud.

A chuckle echoed around the cave. Sascha twisted around to see where the laughter was coming from. The child sat, seemingly unharmed, next to a silver box. There was a picture inscribed on the box, but it was faint. Sascha squinted as she tried to work out what the marking was. There was a picture of a small vial with a cross through it, and another picture of a larger vial, but there was no cross on the larger one. Next to the design was a circled V symbol.

"You amuse me, mortal. Mortals will try to interfere in the plans of the gods, but the heavens will never let a mortal win. You will never be free."

A distant voice was repeating her name. She stared at the child for a few more seconds before turning and walking toward the voice. Somehow, she had to win this fight.

But how can I defeat a god?

"Sascha, wake up. It's only a dream." Marco shook her gently as his voice called her back to consciousness.

Sascha pushed his hand away and covered her eyes with her arm. She needed to get her bearings. "Give me a second, Marco."

Sascha let her arm drop from her face, flicked her eyes open, and stared at the beams above her bed. She was back in her chambers. She breathed in the familiar smell of honeywood, pine, and cinnamon. But the nightmare was back. And this time it was different. It had morphed so many events together.

But that creature was dead. How could it appear to me as a child?

She turned to Marco. He was sitting in the bed beside her, his back resting against a couple of pillows. The sheet was down around his waist, his broad shoulders and dark shoulder-length hair adding an air of appeal that was hard to ignore. But she could see the deep lines under his eyes. He needed sleep, and she needed time to recover from that dream.

"Sascha? Are you okay?" Marco asked.

Sascha shoved back the white silk sheets as she pushed herself up and swung her legs off the bed. "Yes, I'm fine. As you said, it was only a dream."

"You were crying out, Sasch, but I couldn't understand what you were saying. Do you want to talk about it?"

Sascha glanced at him. His dark eyebrows crinkled together as he studied her. She stood and walked over to the window. The cool, peppermint-scented breeze relaxed her and the knotted muscles in her neck began to unwind. She needed time to think this through.

"Marco, did your brother say anything to you about Jenny having a child?"

"You mean Alex?"

"Yes. Did he say anything? He did spend a bit of time with her in Scotland."

"No, nothing. But, Sasch, wouldn't you have known if she had a child? How long did she work for you?"

"She was with me for over two years. You wouldn't think it was possible to keep a child a secret for all that time."

"Has this got anything to do with the nightmare?" Marco asked.

"Yes, it does. When are Jenny and Eham expected to arrive back on Eratus?"

"This morning," Marco said. "They're returning this morning."

"I need to talk to them when they return," Sascha replied. "If you see them, would you ask them to come and find me?"

"Sure. But what happened in the nightmare? Is it the same as the one you had when you were on Earth?"

"I thought the nightmares had finished," Sascha whispered. "But they're back. Though it was different this time."

The sheets rustled as Marco climbed out of bed and joined her at the window. She rested against him and he wrapped his arms around her. "But the dreams are still about Eham?"

"Yes," Sascha said.

"Did you see yourself killing him, like you did last time?"

Sascha stared out at the crashing waves of the ocean as she tried to work out how she was going to answer the question.

This is Marco. I need to be honest.

"Everything keeps coming back to the healing ceremony,"

Sascha said.

"So what happened in this nightmare?" Marco asked.

She had tried to forget the harrowing memories of the burning, red magic the Ancient had used when he'd tried to destroy her. But nothing seemed to work. The memories refused to go away. The fact her skin still felt tender, as if it had been badly burned, was a constant reminder. And the sound of the dragons' singing being replaced with those loud, piercing cries of agony still haunted her. How the four of them managed to complete the healing ceremony, heal the Shield, and protect Eratus from the darkness was something she would never fully understand. But if the nightmare was a warning, she was going to have to find that same strength to deal with whatever evil this child represented.

"Yes, I did kill him. But this time I saw Jenny standing with him, and she was protecting a child. The child looked so much like that evil creature I killed in the healing ceremony."

"And did you kill Jenny . . . and the child?"

"Yes, I did." Tears stung Sascha's eyes. "I killed a child. Am I truly capable of such a vile act?"

"No, Sasch. You're not. Unless . . . there has to be more to this nightmare."

"At the end of the dream, the child did come back to life," Sascha said. "He was sitting on a pile of crates marked with these strange symbols and he was gloating. He said that he was a god and couldn't be killed. But I think he was lying. I think he was one of the Ancients and if he was . . . I will never let the Ancients get a grip on Eratus again." She paused for a moment, chewing her lip. "There is one more thing. The blades I used to kill them, I don't have them anymore. They disappeared during the healing ceremony once they destroyed the darkness in the Shield."

"You killed them using the Blades of Light?"

"Yes."

"The dream can't come true then. It can hardly come true if you don't even have the weapon you used."

Sascha's stomach churned and she felt nauseous. "You wouldn't think so, but I have this feeling that I can't shake. A feeling that the real battle is ahead of me. And a darkness even more evil than the one we encountered is lurking, waiting for the right time to reveal itself."

"Sascha, it was only a dream. You can't let it get to you."

"Don't lecture me, Marco. I know what I saw in the dream and I know what I saw at the healing. When I realized how close I was to losing everyone I loved . . . I will never let that happen again. I just pray that I am not faced with what I saw in my dream."

Marco and Sascha stood quietly for a few minutes, Sascha wrapped in Marco's arms, Marco's hand gently rubbing her arm.

"Those symbols on the crates, did you recognize them?" Marco asked.

"No, I didn't. The symbols were faint, but it looked like some kind of picture of vials. But that doesn't make sense. Does it?"

"No, it doesn't," Marco said. "But none of the dream makes sense. Do you think this child is Jenny's?"

"I don't know. I don't know what the connection is to Eham and Jenny. That's why I want to talk to them."

"I'll get them to come and see you." He kissed her bare shoulder. "As long as you promise not to kill them."

"This isn't a joke, Marco."

"Sorry, Sasch."

"That child worried me," Sascha said. "I know it's not possible, but that child could have been the creature's son."

Sascha turned and hugged Marco. It was tempting to stay wrapped in his arms, but she pushed herself away. "I'm going to have a bath. You rest. I know you haven't been home long."

Marco released a heavy sigh. "The whole exercise took so much longer than we expected. But we ended up receiving updates from all the camps on their progress in preparing for the season of the three moons." He scrubbed his face with his hands. "There's still a lot to do, but at least we have time on our side. Which reminds me, did you go out early this morning?"

"Why?"

"I thought I saw you. That's all."

"Yes, I couldn't sleep," Sascha said. "I thought some fresh air would help. Go back to bed now and get some sleep."

"Are you sure you'll be okay?"

"I'm fine. Rest! We can talk more about it later. After I've met with Eham and Jenny."

Marco staggered back to bed and pulled the sheet over him. "I'll bring them to you as soon as they return."

On the way to her wardrobe Sascha walked past Soleil's nest. The nest had been decorated with vines dyed in various colors so that it looked like a bonfire. It hurt to see it empty, but things were different now that Marco was back in her life. She picked up a sheer jade top with a white camisole, pants, and boots, and pressed a button in the wall beside her. The bathroom door swung open revealing a large room with a gleaming white stone floor and a large oval-shaped mirror. Petite emerald-green vines covered in yellow and orange flowers cascaded down from baskets placed at several points along the top of the bathroom walls. Sascha glanced over at the mirror. Almond-shaped amber eyes fringed with large dark lashes stared out from the center of the mirror. The sparkle of the glass reminded her why she had named the mirror Crystal.

"Crystal, run me a warm bath, and order me a mug of coffee—sorry, I mean vimberry." Vimberry didn't taste the same as coffee, but it was close enough.

"Yes, Sascha," Crystal replied.

"And don't play any music today. I just want some peace and quiet."

"As you command."

It had become second nature to speak to the mirror as if it were a maid. In some respects, she supposed that was exactly what it was, though she still felt uneasy when its amber eyes studied her. Sometimes it seemed as if the mirror was alive. At least the eyes weren't blue. She shuddered. The child's blue eyes couldn't be a coincidence. But how could Jenny possibly be connected? And if Jenny had a child, why would she hide it from them?

Perhaps there was something wrong with it.

Sascha pushed the thought aside. Surely she or one of the girls would have noticed something.

You never noticed anything different about Ken and Pat, and look how that turned out.

She shook her head. There was no point in speculating.

When the bath was full, Sascha stepped into the bubbling water. The soft scents of honey, pine, and cinnamon wafted around her. The room darkened, and the candles around the edge of the bath popped as they burst into life. Her shoulders relaxed as she allowed the warm water and the sweet aroma to work its magic.

As she leaned back against the bath, she lifted her hand and studied it. The mark had changed color since the healing ceremony. Much of the coffee color had gone and it now looked more like a faded scar. The dragon stone ring on her index finger glittered in the candlelight. She gave a silly grin.

"It's not an engagement ring," Marco had said, "because we don't have engagements on Eratus. We have ten-day wedding affairs instead. But with all the traveling you are doing, you need something to remind you of me."

She had laughed. "If I didn't forget you in the five years you were gone, I don't think I ever could."

"Sascha." Soleil's voice echoed in her mind.

"Soleil, where are you?"

"I'm with Fenix. Did you still want to go to the Four Sisters headquarters today?"

"Yes, thanks, Soleil. I need some time with my girls."

"Will they be back yet?"

"I think so. Lee and Ella were due to return from the time with their families early this morning. And Kira's already messaged me to say she's back from the college retreat. Give me half an hour and then come and get me. It'll be so good to see the girls again."

Of course! The girls. Perhaps they had the same dream, like last time.

Twenty minutes later, Sascha had bathed and dressed and was finishing her mug of vimberry. She pulled her long blond hair into a ponytail and applied a touch of dark green eyeshadow that matched the color of her eyes. She walked over to her desk that sat in the corner of her bedchamber and wrote a brief note for Marco, telling him where she had gone.

The bite in the air surprised her as she stepped onto the balcony to wait for Soleil. She tiptoed back into her bedchamber to get her jacket. When she returned to the balcony, she shut the doors behind her. She didn't want to wake Marco.

The happy whistles of the pyrans as they called to each other, and the cheery squeals of the furry little hurlies that played in the gardens below, lifted her spirits.

The powerful thumping of wings announced Soleil's arrival. Sascha smiled when she saw that Fenix was with him.

Those two seem to be building up a special friendship.

The two pyrans landed on the balcony and twirled

around to face her, Soleil's fiery golden feathers contrasting beautifully with Fenix's ebony and scarlet ones. Their talons were a similar rose-colored gold.

"You both came," Sascha whispered.

"Why are you whispering?" Soleil asked.

"Marco is asleep," Sascha replied. "Let's leave him to sleep a little longer. It's good to see you two together."

Fenix lowered her head and stared at the stone floor. "Soleil is a difficult creature, but we've both survived so far."

"I'm difficult?" Soleil clicked his beak.

"Did you want to come with us, Fenix?" Sascha asked.

"I offered to take you today, but Soleil said no."

"Now that Marco has moved in," Soleil said, "I don't see enough of Sascha as it is."

"I just thought . . . never mind," Fenix said as she jumped up onto the balcony rim.

Sascha caught Fenix sneaking a glance at her. Goose bumps skittered across her skin. "Fenix, is there something you want to ask me?"

"No, no. I . . . nothing." There was a loud whoosh of wings, and warm air whipped around Sascha as Fenix launched herself into the sky. "I'll see you both when you return."

Sascha watched Fenix fly away before she turned back to face Soleil. "Do you know why Fenix offered to take me, Soleil? Is there something we need to talk about?"

"I don't know what that was about," Soleil replied. "Perhaps she just wants to feel useful. Her relationship with Drakon has always been difficult, but things are worse now that Drakon and those fire dragons are getting on so well. Maybe she's worried that Drakon will want to get rid of her, send her to the fifth dimension."

Sascha flinched. "I know I haven't had much luck with

remembering how to save Fenix, but I will find a way. I promise you, I will."

"I know," Soleil said, "but that might not even be it. I just wish she'd trust me enough to tell me what's bothering her, what's wrong. She might talk to you. Would you help me?"

"I'm happy to try. Next time I need to go somewhere, perhaps I should ask Fenix to take me. Then I would have some time alone with her."

"If you can find out what's bugging her, I'd be grateful. Time for us to go."

Sascha climbed up onto Soleil's shoulders and strapped herself into the harness.

"Sascha, where do you think Laela is?" Soleil asked.

"What made you think of her?"

"I guess because we're going to the Four Sisters."

"I have no idea where she is," Sascha replied, "but I'll find her. Some people seem to think she died during the attack at the dragons' cave, but I don't. I'm sure she's alive and still working with the Ancients. Until I find her, find out what she's planning, I won't rest."

"I thought you and the others destroyed the Ancients during the healing ceremony," Soleil said.

"It seems we didn't destroy them. Over the past few weeks I've sensed a darkness, a power which I believe is connected to the Ancients. But whatever the darkness is, wherever it is, this time I will destroy it . . . completely."

"You should start with that Bibacr creature," Soleil spat. He hunkered down, stretched his wings, and then leaped up into the air heading northwest toward the Four Sisters headquarters.

Sascha was silent. Could she have been wrong about Bibacr? But he had become a good friend, and she liked him. She refused to believe that he had anything to do with the Ancients.

THE BODY

ERATUS

he buzz of conversation and the faint smell of ale followed Marco as he climbed the stone staircase to his chambers above the tavern in the castle grounds. He stuffed the note from Sascha into the pocket of his leather jacket and zipped the jacket up so that it hid the dagger he had strapped to his right thigh. Sascha's nightmares about Eham and Jenny worried him. It could just be a reaction to everything that had happened to her over the last couple of months, but . . .

That child. What was the deal with that child? And would those symbols she mentioned have any real meaning?

He raised his hand to open the door to his chambers when footsteps and heavy breathing sounded behind him.

"Colonel, I mean, My Lord," a voice called out.

Marco turned to see the captain of the Fire of the Phoenix racing toward him.

"My title is Colonel," Marco said. "This isn't the Kingdom of Brun. What is it?"

The man halted a couple of feet from Marco and saluted.

"The Lieutenant Colonel has asked to see you. He said it is urgent."

"Where is he?"

"In the furnace room."

"What's he doing there?"

"I'm not sure, Colonel."

Marco followed the captain down the stairs, out of the tavern, and across the training grounds to the entrance to the dungeons. Instead of going straight ahead to the prisons, they turned left to the furnace room. The captain opened the door and stood aside to allow Marco to walk past him. Marco rubbed his nose to ease the sting from the unpleasant hot metallic odor that wafted around the room. The air tasted of charcoal. In the center of the room Lieutenant Colonel Zabir was standing next to a soldier dressed in the armor of the Awakening. A covered bundle rested on the ground in front of a roaring furnace.

"Lieutenant Colonel, what is it?" Marco asked.

"I was walking past and saw this soldier about to throw this bundle into the furnace. It's not only that this soldier was breaking protocol . . . I think you need to see this."

"I . . . ," the soldier stuttered, "I am doing this by order of Prince Drakon and Lieutenant General Chiane."

Marco nodded at the bundle on the ground. "What's under the cover?"

Zabir squatted by the bundle and pulled back the cloth. He stood up quickly and backed away.

Marco moved closer to get a better look. An unnatural stillness filled the room. "Cover the poor man up. What happened to him, soldier?"

"I've been told to keep what happened this morning to myself," the soldier said. "Lieutenant Gen—"

"You have a choice," Zabir said. "Tell us now and you can leave here, or keep your secret and I will lock you up in one of the deepest dungeons where your body will never be found."

The soldier's eyes bulged as he wrapped his arms around his belly. "You can't . . ." The soldier's shoulders hunched forward as he sighed. "He came through a portal from the Kingdom of Tasuna early this morning. He said he came to warn us the season of the three moons was nearly here."

"But that's not possible," Zabir said. "It's still a couple of months away."

"He said he had seen the tracks of the akhult, and that he was attacked by ice ghouls. In the battle against the ice ghouls the portal in Tasuna was destroyed. Prince Drakon and the Lieutenant General ordered me to burn the body because they were worried that the news would cause panic."

"Chiane and Prince Drakon ordered this?" Marco asked.

"Yes, sir."

Marco stood and stared at the soldier, who was wringing his hands together. It wouldn't be a wise idea to stop this and involve Owain, not when he didn't have definite proof of Drakon and Chiane's involvement. The soldier's words wouldn't be enough. Drakon would say the soldier acted on his own. And Marco knew what Drakon did to those who failed him.

"Thank you, soldier. Do what you were commanded to do. We will make no mention of this."

"Thank you, sir," the soldier said. "Thank you."

Marco looked at Zabir and nodded at the door. When they arrived outside in the fresh, cool air, Zabir sagged against the castle wall. "The poor soul. His body was a mess."

"I know. But it's good we saw it. We must take this warning seriously. What confuses me is why Drakon would want it kept a secret from us and the High King. I can understand not telling the people, but he should have told us. And where is our telepath? He was supposed to have messaged the destruction of the portal to all of us. Our telepath is supposed to be an example to the others. Find him and remind him of his role."

"As you command, Colonel. It could be possible that he was stopped from telling anyone about the portal if Prince Drakon wanted it all kept a secret."

Marco ran his fingers through his hair. "True. But find out. If the telepaths don't notify their people the moment we shut down the portals, then the kingdoms will not have time to activate the shields before the akhult attack." Marco took a deep breath and released it slowly. "If this warning is real and the storm season is closer than we think, then we must escalate the preparations. The reports I received early this morning were worrying. We still have a lot of work to do before we're ready for the storms. Zabir, take a small group with you and go to each of the regions. See what you can do to help them speed up preparations, but don't let them know why we're pushing them. And while you're doing that, look for proof of whether any of this is true."

"Yes, Colonel," Zabir said.

"And as a precaution, only use pyrans. Do not use the portals."

"Yes, Colonel." Zabir pushed himself away from the wall, saluted, and walked away.

Marco glanced toward the furnace room. Drakon was up to something. But what? He needed to discuss this with Connell, but he had to talk to Jenny and Eham first.

He strode back to the tavern, but instead of going to his chambers, he entered the tavern and signaled to the bartender.

"Marco." The bartender nodded. "You're after a drink?"

"Not a bad idea," Marco said, "but I want to catch up with Eham and Jenny. When are they due in?"

"Prince Connell sent his healer to follow up on them,

too," the bartender replied. "When the healer found out they were late he organized for some mages to return to the first portal to locate them. But it seems Eham and Jenny have disappeared. Hopefully the guardians didn't get them."

"Eham and Jenny could protect themselves from the guardians. But it is a mystery why the guardians would stay at that portal and not go into hibernation like the others. Did the healer say why Prince Connell was following up on them?"

"No, but he said something about them being in danger. He said it was important they were safe."

"In danger?" Marco stepped back from the bar.

It can't be a coincidence that Sascha had that dream, and the two of them have now disappeared. But what was it that made Connell think they were in danger?

He walked back out of the tavern. He needed to talk to Connell.

CONNELL'S CHAMBERS

ERATUS

*C*onnell clenched his jaw as he used all his strength to push himself up in bed. His muscles burned and perspiration dripped down his face. George grunted as Connell's movements disturbed her. "Sorry, girl. I need to get comfortable."

The bed shifted beneath him as George pulled her leathery wings closer to her soft golden-colored body and nuzzled into him, positioning her heavy fur head neatly under his hand. Connell stroked her, his heart filled with love for the gorgeous animal. George was a gift from Athena, of that he was certain.

"I'll be okay, George. You're a good girl."

"Ar-ruf." Rusty stood in the middle of the room, tail wagging.

"And you're a good girl too, Rusty."

Connell smiled to himself. Who would have thought a manticore and a boxer dog would become such good friends? George was twice the size of Rusty and a lot deadlier but that didn't seem to make any difference to the way the two of them romped around together.

George lifted her head as a knock sounded on the door.

"Come in," Connell said.

Ciara opened the door and walked in. "My Prince." Rusty raced toward Ciara and launched herself at the woman. Ciara squawked as Rusty's full weight landed on her. "Easy, Rusty. You're not exactly light. I've only been gone a couple of hours. Anyone would think it's been years."

Connell grinned at the petite young woman with fiery red hair as she hugged Rusty before she pushed the dog off her. "I think that creature misses you."

After giving Rusty one last pat, Ciara turned toward Connell. "You don't realize how lucky you are to have the only boxer on Eratus. And one that gets on with manticores and pyrans. Rusty even seems to like the healer's pyran, much to everyone's surprise. I would have sworn there wasn't a creature alive that would get on with his pyran. Anyway, it's time for your treatment, but Marco is here to see you, too. Do you wish to speak to him first?"

"Yes, thank you, Ciara. Send him in. And I need you to organize someone to help me with an exercise routine. I need to build up my strength. Simple things are becoming increasingly more difficult."

"The Master Healer said we need to make sure the pit hound's venom is out of your system first," Ciara said. "If you start exercising before it's fully gone, it could kill you."

"Well, tell him to come and see me. It's been days now. The venom must be gone. I'm a Prince. I want to start doing my job, not hiding out in my chambers all day."

"He'll be back this afternoon. I'll get him to come and see you as soon as he returns to the castle. But people know you were attacked by a pit hound and that you nearly died. You're allowed time to heal." Ciara plumped up a couple of pillows behind Connell before walking to the door to let Marco in.

"Marco, Connell wants to talk to you before his treatment."

Marco moved past Ciara and ducked out of the way of Rusty's exuberant welcome. "Thanks, Ciara."

Marco did a double take as he stared at Connell but tried to hide it by sitting on the edge of Connell's bed and making a fuss of George. Connell knew he had lost a lot of weight and, having not been out in the sun for several weeks, knew he looked pale.

All I need is exercise and sun.

"Master Healer has asked that visitors don't stay too long," Ciara said as she glanced at Connell. "He said he would be angry with me if we tire Connell out. And Sascha has already been to see him this morning."

"Ciara, would you stop fussing," Connell snapped.

"Sascha has been here?" Marco asked.

"Yes," Connell said. "Is there anything wrong with a sister visiting her brother?"

"No, it's—it's nothing."

"And she looked at me the same way you just did."

"What do you mean?" Marco asked. "You . . . um . . . you look like you're improving."

"Liar," Connell said. "That's not what you were thinking at all."

Marco smirked. "That's not a nice thing to call a friend." He stared at his hands. "I'm sorry that things worked out this way and that you had to face Reya and that monster on your own."

Connell clenched his fists. "I don't need your pity, Marco. Or Sascha's. And I don't need your twenty-four-hour protection either. I may not be a warrior but I—"

"Okay, okay," Marco said, raising his hands in mock surrender.

Connell patted George. "Anyway, I had George. She saved

me. I don't know why everyone forgets manticores have wings. When Reya opened the windows to allow the pit hound to escape, it also gave George a way into the room."

"Do you mind me asking how you let that creature get so close to you? Why didn't you use your magic to protect yourself?"

"Reya gave me black lyrium."

"Black what?"

"I hadn't heard of it, either, but it takes a person's magic away for a period. Reya came to me with a sob story about Drakon using it on her, but it was a trick." Connell glanced over at George. "But George knew. I should have trusted her."

"Did you ask Sascha about the black lyrium?"

"Yes, she said she hadn't ever heard of it."

Connell sagged against the pillows. Sitting seemed to take so much energy.

"I need to leave you be," Marco said. "I'll come back later today."

"Not yet, don't go yet. Talk to me. Is Drakon still chasing after Sascha?"

Marco raised one eyebrow as he studied Connell. "What do you mean by chasing? She's his sister."

"No, she's not. Drakon's father was marked in the register of mages as unlisted which means Owain is not his father after all. And we know the mothers are different. So, there is no family connection between him and Sascha at all. You need to be careful. Drakon is in love with her. I've warned Sascha too."

"You've been in this room too long, Connell. You're becoming as gossipy as the maids."

Connell didn't say anything else. He could see it would be a waste of time. Marco had already dismissed it as nonsense. One day he would find out the truth but for now he was too tired to argue. "On another subject, what happened with Laela. Was she in the dragons' cave? Sascha said she heard her voice."

"We think she was there," Marco said. "But we haven't seen any sign of her since that day."

"Sascha said you both believe there's a strong possibility she's a member of the dragon hunters."

"We still have a lot to learn, Connell, but we are investigating. And searching for Laela."

"I was hoping that everything would settle down once the Shield was healed," Connell said. "But I don't think that's going to happen. And Sascha has become fanatical in her hatred for the darkness. Have you noticed?"

"She went through a lot. She needs time to forget. That's all. I wouldn't describe her as fanatical though."

"I'm worried about how it will all end," Connell said.

Marco repositioned himself on Connell's bed. "Talking about being worried, I hear you're worried about Eham and Jenny."

"I don't know if it's the sickness talking or a vision or what, but I think Eham and Jenny are in danger. I just don't know how or who from."

"Did Sascha tell you about her dream?" Marco asked.

"No. What dream?"

"Oh, nothing. I—"

There was a knock on the door and Ciara entered.

"I think we should let Connell rest now," Ciara said to Marco.

"You're not my mother, Ciara," Connell snarled. "I'll make the call when it's time for me to rest."

Ciara narrowed her eyes as she glared at Connell. "I'm doing what I was told to do. But if you think you know best—"

"I need to go anyway," Marco said as he stood up and walked to the door. "I'll come back later today. Okay?"

Connell nodded.

"You're doing a good job, Ciara," Marco said. "Don't worry about grumble guts over there."

Ciara smiled and walked over to a small table in the corner of the room to prepare Connell's treatment.

"Marco, next time you come to visit," Connell said, "I'll get you to help me escape this room. Being cooped up in here is not helping me at all."

Marco stood in the doorway and glanced at Connell and then Ciara. "I'll take you down to Ocean's Mouth. It's a great place to switch off from everything."

"Now that would be perfect." Connell snuck a sly grin at Ciara, who was grinding fresh herbs in a mortar and pestle. "Don't you think so, Ciara?"

Ciara grunted. "You wait until I talk to the healer."

George jumped up and stared at the door, a low roar rumbling in her chest. Connell's grin faded as he turned to the doorway. Standing behind Marco was a tall elegant-looking woman. Connell rubbed his eyes and looked again. The woman was still there. She was dressed in a fine silk gown that skimmed her lean, delicately carved body. She had perfect porcelain skin and flowing raven-colored hair that gleamed in the light. Connell's mouth dropped open. "No. It . . . it can't be," he stammered.

Marco twisted around, dagger in hand, ready to defend Connell. "What is it, Connell? What can you see?"

"It . . . it's Reya," Connell stammered.

"It can't be Reya, Novo killed her. She's dead." Marco took a step into the corridor. "Guards, did you see anyone?"

"No," they replied.

Marco took one last look down the passageway. He

sheathed his dagger and walked back to Connell. "Whoever it was has gone."

"Marco, it was Reya," Connell said.

George gave a final rumble, turned in a circle, and then lay down at the end of Connell's bed.

"I will place a couple of extra guards," Marco said. "Just to be on the safe side."

"Marco, I don't think . . . " Connell shook his head. "Thanks, Marco."

There's no point in telling him that extra guards will be a waste of time. If Reya is alive, and wants to get in here, she will. Nothing seems to stop her, not even death.

THE ARMBAND AND ISABELLA

ERATUS

*D*rakon rested against the balcony rim and pulled the sleeves of his blue shirt down so that they covered the armband. The suns were up now and it was easy to forget the events of the early morning, to list them as an aberration.

A flock of pyrans carrying supplies from the local farms flew past him on their way to the rooftop on the western tower of the castle. It was times like this that Drakon missed Reya. This was the time of day when they had sat together and discussed their plans for the day ahead. She had been a beautiful creature, but she had also been a traitor and had received a traitor's death.

He glanced up at the skies. He hoped it wouldn't be long before Novo sent him news of the site on Eratus. With any luck it would be good news. But there was every chance Brun wouldn't work out and they would have to put all their energies into retrieving the weapons from the site on Earth. He would do whatever he needed to do to get his hands on those weapons.

Drakon picked up his mug of vimberry and dropped into

the chair in the corner of the balcony. A chained fist banged on the door to his chambers.

"Enter," Drakon called out.

Chiane strode out to join him on the balcony, a cloaked figure in tow. The cloaked figure bowed before Drakon.

"My Prince," Chiane said. "This is Archmage Pealack. He is the one who helped me find the potion that killed the Master. He says he can make a replacement for your armband, but he needs to see it to determine the magic that was used to create it."

"Archmage Pealack. I feel I've heard that name before. Where are you from?"

"The Archmage can't speak. Not so that anyone can understand anyway," Chiane said. "He lost his tongue."

"Lost his tongue? How did that happen?"

"His last master removed it as a precaution to prevent the Archmage sharing any of his court's secrets."

"His last master didn't trust him then?"

"He didn't trust anyone. He was a brutal man with no redeeming qualities."

Drakon tilted his head to the side as he studied Chiane.

If he thinks that was brutal, how is he going to react when he finds out what I have planned for the weapons?

Drakon placed his mug on the ground next to his chair. "So you despise him for what he did, Chiane?"

"It was unnecessary. And foolish."

"So where is this master now?"

"Dead," Chiane said. "The stories of his death are sketchy."

"Interesting," Drakon said, leaning forward. He formed his hands into a steeple and looked directly at the Archmage. "What does he need to do to assess the magic that is used in the band?"

Chiane glanced at Pealack and nodded. Pealack shuffled over to stand next to Drakon and held out an open palm.

"He asks that you show him the band," Chiane said.

"I'm not taking it off," Drakon answered.

"You only need to rest your arm in the palm of his hand."

Drakon glanced quickly at Chiane and then raised his arm and rested it in Pealack's open hand. Pealack traced his finger over the design—an olive tree and an owl, the symbols of Athena—and then closed his eyes. He rested his free hand on the top of the band and mumbled a few words Drakon couldn't understand. A zap of electricity sparked between the two of them. Pealack released Drakon's arm and stepped back, his eyes still on the band.

"Have you been able to determine what magic is used?" Chiane asked.

Pealack nodded.

"And you can organize a replacement?"

Pealack nodded again.

"Good, that's good," Chiane replied as he walked over and patted Pealack on the back.

"So that's it then?" Drakon asked.

"Yes, it is."

"How long will it take?"

"Three or four days. I will return with the band as soon as it is finished."

"That long?" Drakon said.

Chiane nodded. "It is important to get it right, My Prince."

"Yes, it is. And he is still searching for more of that potion I used to kill the Master?"

"Yes, he is. It is an extremely rare potion, and he can't openly search for it but he won't give up until he finds more. He's sure there are other supplies . . . somewhere."

Drakon hadn't realized the potion created white fire until he used it. The bloodcurdling screams still echoed in Drakon's mind as the white fire destroyed the Master and his creatures and then roared its way toward him. The agony of the fire wouldn't easily be forgotten but he had plans and the potion would be useful.

"I'm sure the Archmage knows there are penalties for failure."

"He does," Chiane replied.

"Perhaps you could tell him I, too, am a brutal master. But I have no intention of dying like his last master."

Chiane gulped. "Yes, My Prince." He saluted, turned, and left, the Archmage following silently.

Drakon stood at the balcony rim and watched as Chiane and the Archmage walked out of the castle and toward the gates.

I need to be careful that I don't tell Chiane too much. For now, though, I need him. I will have to play this one carefully. But there may come a time—

"My Prince," a soft voice called out from the doorway to his chambers.

That voice sounded so much like . . . Reya. He turned quickly. It wasn't Reya. It was Isabella. Reya was dead, so, of course, it couldn't be her. He hadn't realized how alike their voices were, though that was where the similarities ended.

"My Prince," she called out again.

"Mage Isabella," he answered. "I'm busy. What do you want?"

She walked up to him, trailed her finger down his arm, and rested her hand on top of his. "I was hoping we could spend some more time together. I've missed you."

He flicked her hand off his. "I've too much to do. When I want you, I will summon you. Do not presume to approach me like this again. You won't want to pay the price if you do."

"I will do anything to please you, Drakon."

He gritted his teeth. "Drakon? Have I given you permission to use my name?"

She circled the room, taking in the various items of furniture. She strolled over to the ornately carved steel bed and ran her fingers along the frame. "Reya is gone. I know you have needs. And I know just how to satisfy them. I'm sure you remember how much I pleased you in the past."

"You were adequate, Isabella, but only adequate. Reya, on the other hand . . ."

"Adequate?" she snarled. "There was nothing about the way you reacted last time that suggested my performance was adequate. And of all the women to compare me to! That bitch is a traitor. She betrayed you." Isabella stood in front of him, her legs planted wide and her hands on her hips. "Do I need to be a traitor to get your interest?"

Drakon drew in a slow, steady breath, barely controlling the growing anger. Unlike Reya, Isabella had never seen how he punished those who displeased him. Perhaps now was the right time. But rather than watching the punishment, Isabella was going to get a taste of what it felt like. He walked over to the door.

"Guards, ensure we're not disturbed under any circumstances."

The men's eyes flicked toward Isabella. "Yes, My Prince."

Drakon turned and closed the door behind him. As he twisted around to face Isabella, he saw a smirk of victory pass across her face.

You think you have won this, you foolish woman.

"Would you like a drink of wine, Isabella?"

"Yes, please," she answered as she leaned against the side of the bed. Drakon filled a glass with wine and then opened the top drawer of his desk and pulled out a little vial. He positioned his body so that his body was shielding his hands from Isabella's view and poured the contents of the vial into the wine. He walked over and handed the glass to her.

"Aren't you having one?" she asked.

"No, I don't like to drink wine this early, but drink up. I'll wait. But not too long, so do hurry."

She gave him a simpering smile and gulped down her wine.

She was about to walk out onto the balcony when he put a hand on her arm and drew her back inside, closing the balcony doors behind them.

"I think it's time for some fun, don't you?" he said.

He clicked his fingers and a glowing chain appeared in his hand. His arm moved forward and the chain whipped around her wrists and leaped up and over the roof beams. He pulled the chain tightly, stretching her up so her feet just touched the floor. Isabella cried out in pain as the chains bit into her wrists. He walked around her, studying her, then walked over to a cupboard from which he retrieved a gag and a whip. He walked over to Isabella and kissed her roughly. As her mouth responded to his, he pulled back, and reached up and tied the gag over her mouth.

"I can't have you making too much noise. Who knows what the neighbors will think. So, you want to please me," he said, stepping behind her and ripping the back of her dress open.

"Mmph," she called out as she struggled to escape the chains.

The whip cracked through the air. He delighted in the muffled scream as the lash landed on her soft white back, drawing blood. She moved her wrists in a desperate attempt to use her magic to free herself, but nothing happened.

Drakon smirked. "I guess I should have told you. The wine wasn't just wine. There was something in it, something that, let's say, stops your magic from working. You're helpless." He laughed, the sound of it echoing off the walls.

The lash landed a second time and then a third. Her muffled screams lessened and were replaced with whimpers.

"You aren't very strong, are you?" Drakon said. "I know many women who could take more of this than you."

He sauntered around to face her. "Now, I will remove the gag, but it wouldn't be a good idea to scream. Who knows what that would make me do."

He pulled the gag down from her mouth.

"Please stop," she whimpered.

"What? Stop? You're not interested in playing anymore? But I thought you said you were interested in pleasing me." He held the butt of the whip under her chin. "You did say anything. Okay, so maybe you would prefer to play with my pets. They love to play with their food."

"I didn't mean this," she whimpered. "I meant in bed."

"But you don't satisfy me in bed, so what else is there?"

"Please, no more."

"I will stop," he promised, "and allow you to live, but only on one condition."

"Anything," she pleaded.

"Anything? There's that word again. You must stop being such an easy mark, Isabella. But I will overlook your mistake this time. You will never call me Drakon again. You will come to me only when I summon you. You will never talk about what happened here. I don't care how you explain your injuries, but it will have nothing to do with me. Is that clear?"

"Yes, My Prince," she whispered. "I'll do whatever you ask of me. I am your servant."

"And if you ever think about betraying me, I'll make you pay. Today's events will seem like a happy memory."

He flicked his fingers and the chain disappeared. She crumpled to the floor. "I'll give you a few minutes to compose yourself." He pointed to a door set into one of the walls of his chambers. "I want you to leave through that door. It will take you down to the dungeon. I can't have you wandering through the castle only half-dressed. Not a good look."

He walked over to his desk and wrote a short note. Drakon twisted away from his desk and smiled as he watched Isabella struggling to her feet. She whimpered as she fumbled around in a halfhearted attempt to straighten her ripped clothing. When she finally stood silently, cowering before him, he moved toward her and handed her the note. "This note has instructions for the guard you'll find in the dungeon. Show it to him and he will escort you to your room. It's been a pleasure, Isabella."

When she was gone, he locked the interior door behind her and strode toward the door that led out into the passageway. He opened it. "Guard, bring me my serving wench and some wine. I feel like celebrating."

"Yes, My Prince. Right away."

*S*oleil flew over the lush green fields of Aynor's Stone, over the buildings that made up the magic academy, and landed in the open paddock in the front of the headquarters of the Four Sisters. Sascha released herself from the harness and climbed down from Soleil's shoulders. The high-pitched whining of drills, the bang of hammers, and the sounds of revving engines filled the air as construction on the Four Sisters headquarters was well under way. Workers from each of the kingdoms of Eratus were providing a helping hand to upgrade the buildings and prepare for the coming storm season.

Sascha walked up to one of the tall ashberry-skinned workers from the Kingdom of Breyth.

"Hi, Brontu. How's the work going?"

"Hello, Enchantress." Brontu stopped hammering on a wooden door frame and flicked his hammer into the belt at his waist. "Everything is progressing well. Construction is easy compared to the job the cleaners have to do." He nodded toward the front of the main building where people were carrying buckets and emptying them into an electrical fire in the middle of the porch. "I feel for the poor cleaners."

"Why?" Sascha asked.

"Rats have been the only things living in many of those smaller buildings for years now. They're everywhere and they bite . . . hard. It's the cleaners' task to kill them and clean out their nests. It must be a revolting job."

"Can't they just destroy them with magic?" Sascha asked.

"Normal rats perhaps, but these ones seem to be immune to magic. The cleaners have to kill them the old-fashioned way using physical force."

Sascha shuddered. "In that case I agree. That is a revolting job."

Brontu stretched his back as he studied the magical fire on the porch. "That fire has proven to be an effective way of disposing of the bodies."

"It's a good idea. Who thought of it?"

"My wife," Brontu said as he stood taller and puffed his chest out.

"I must make a point of thanking her," Sascha said. "Thanks for telling me." She studied the construction workers as they finished building a retaining wall around the front of the headquarters. "Do you think everything will be ready in time?"

"Yes. We will be much safer than last time, and we'll have plenty of supplies. I honestly didn't think we would survive last year, but we did. I took it as testament to our magic and our ability to survive on very little food."

"We must never allow that to happen again," Sascha said.

Children's squealing laughter echoed from the playground in the center of the paddock. Brontu glanced over at the children and smiled. "And thank you for allowing us to bring our families here. It's hard to be separated from them for so long."

"I get it," Sascha said. "I know what it's like to be separated from those you love."

"Duck!" Soleil called out as a flock of pyrans flew in low with food supplies from the farms in Aynor Woods.

Sascha ducked just in time to miss a collision with two of the creatures.

"They load the poor beasts up with way too many supplies," Brontu said. "I'm sure they must be exhausted when they get home."

"I'd better go, Brontu."

"Athena bless you, Enchantress," Brontu said as Sascha waved goodbye.

She walked toward the front of the building and stopped to watch a group of students from the magic academy. They were experimenting with their magic by moving goods from where the pyrans had dropped them off in the paddocks to storage rooms at the back of the academy. A loud, booming crash brought a moment of silence. Everyone turned to see a red-faced mage standing in the middle of a mess of crates that had split apart.

"I told you to take one at a time," the supervisor called out to the young mage. "Stop trying to show off."

Sascha laughed. She remembered doing the same thing when she was young. She headed inside through the large carved ebony doors, which had been left open. The foyer was cool, with polished amber stone walls and a slate-tiled floor. Variously shaped cream-colored sofas and glass tables were set up around the foyer, creating little private pockets of space where a person could go to relax and read a book or enjoy a quiet drink.

"Sascha," a voice whispered from a dark corner in the foyer.

She walked toward the sound. "Bibacr? Bibacr is that you?"

A spindly, monkeylike creature with glowing red eyes and large red talons stepped out of the shadows. "Bibacr here to help Sascha."

"Help me? How?"

"Bibacr worried. Bibacr see bad things coming. Bibacr want to help Sascha."

"You can see the season of the three moons coming, Bibacr. That's all. And we will be ready for it." Sascha glanced out the front door. "Although it doesn't look like it at the moment."

"No, Bibacr worried Sascha in danger. A darkness is coming for her."

Sascha's skin prickled as she studied him. "What darkness? What are you talking about, Bibacr?"

"Bibacr doesn't know. Bibacr stand watch over Sascha. Make sure Sascha stay safe."

"I'll watch over Sascha," Soleil called out as he flew in through the front doors and landed on the floor next to Sascha. "You go away, Bibacr. The only darkness around here is you."

Bibacr pulled at Sascha's jacket. "Bibacr is friend. Bibacr not hurt Sascha."

Sascha glared at Soleil, who looked away from her, pretending not to notice the look in her eyes. Sascha turned back to Bibacr. "I know you're my friend. I'll be okay. But because you have warned me, I'll be extra careful."

Bibacr's head bobbed up and down. "Sascha be careful. Bibacr worried."

"If I need you, Bibacr—"

"Sascha," Lee screeched as she ran full speed toward her. "You're here!"

Lee's raven hair flowed around her shoulders and for once, her pale skin had some color. Sascha's heart warmed. She looked happy.

Lee pulled Sascha into a hug. "It's so good to see you. We missed you."

"I've missed you, too. I've come back here a couple of times and it has seemed so empty without you girls. How did it go with the family?"

"That's a long story. What are you doing in the corner?"

"I was talking to Bibacr about—" Sascha turned around to include Bibacr in the conversation, but he had gone.

"He's gone," Soleil said. "And that's good. If you want to destroy the darkness on Eratus, you should start with that creature. Giblerees are evil. They have you tricked. When your memory returns properly, you will know, you will understand."

"Kalurth didn't agree with you," Sascha snapped.

"Kalurth only sees the good in everyone. She doesn't see the evil."

"Don't underestimate Kalurth. Dragons see a lot more than we think they do. I trust their counsel."

"And you don't trust mine?" Soleil clicked his beak at her and then flew outside.

"That's not what I meant, Soleil, and you know it," she called after him.

"Don't worry," Lee said as she put her arm around Sascha's shoulders and guided her farther into the building. "Everyone has been told for years that giblerees are creatures of the darkness. It isn't surprising Soleil is finding it hard to accept Bibacr. He's worried about you."

"How did you understand what Soleil was saying?" Sascha asked.

"I guessed. It's easy to see when he's angry and when you mentioned Bibacr's name, Soleil's reaction made sense."

"You girls are too smart for your own good," Sascha said. "You may be right about Soleil's attitude when it comes to

Bibacr. I only hope that one day the two of them can get to a point where they can tolerate each other."

"I don't know how likely that is," Lee replied. She stopped for a moment, her arm dropping from Sascha's shoulders as she turned and stared out the front doors. "Sascha, do you think we could find a way for Ella and I to understand Soleil? It seems like everyone else can but us. Even Bibacr can talk to him."

Sascha felt for Lee and Ella. It would have been difficult to see others having conversations with Soleil when they couldn't. "I hadn't thought about the fact that Bibacr can talk to Soleil. It's strange but perhaps all creatures can talk to each other. Unfortunately, for us mere mortals, you have to be related to someone who has bonded to a pyran or bond to one yourself. Unless one day we find another way."

"When this is all over perhaps Ella and I should look into what is required to bond with a pyran," Lee said. "It would be nice to have our own pyran and it would be wonderful to be able to speak to Soleil and Fenix."

Sascha leaned over and hugged her. "We'll do some research into it. You never know what is possible. So where are the others? Apart from saying hello and catching up, I wanted to talk to all of you."

They walked toward the door to the study. "That sounds ominous. Is it about the dream?"

Sascha stared at Lee. "Have you girls started having the dream again?"

"Yes," Lee said, "but it has changed."

"So has mine," Sascha said.

"Ella has gone out for about an hour, but I'm in the middle of preparing our first lunch together, as a sort of reunion feast. I was hoping you'd be here in time. You are staying for lunch, aren't you?"

"If you're cooking, absolutely!"

Lee chuckled. "Kira will be so pleased to see you." Lee pointed at a pile of books sitting next to a wall lined with carved ebony shelves. "She's somewhere over there in that pile of books. Alex is with her."

"Alex is here?"

"Yes. Between you and me, I think he likes Kira. She is a bit young for him though, so he might have to be patient and wait."

"Isn't Alex twenty-three?" Sascha asked.

"Yes, he is."

"He's too old for her," Sascha said. "Kira's not even sixteen yet."

"She will be sixteen soon," Lee said. "It's only seven years older. And you're only reacting this way because it's Kira."

"It's more than seven years. And that's a big difference when you're as young as Kira."

"Well, you wait and see, Sascha. I wouldn't be surprised to one day see her and Alex become an item."

Sascha grunted as she headed off in the direction Lee had pointed. "Fifteen is too young to be thinking of that sort of thing," Sascha said over her shoulder as she moved closer to the mess of books.

Sitting cross-legged in the middle of a pile of books was Kira, one pencil tucked behind her right ear, another pencil tapping the page of the book she was studying. Her fiery strawberry-blond hair was tied back into a single plait that fell halfway down her back. Sascha looked over at the two-seater lounge that stood beside the pile of books and found a sleeping Alex curled up there, his long legs hanging awkwardly over the edge of the chair.

"How can you study in this mess?" Sascha whispered to Kira.

"What?" Kira squinted as she looked up with a pair of bleary eyes. "Sascha!" she cried, as she leaped up and hugged

Sascha, books spilling everywhere. "Ella told us not to expect you because you were busy at the castle."

"Of course I'd be here. How did you enjoy returning to Earth for the retreat?"

"It was the ultimate," Kira said. "Thanks for letting me go."

Sascha pulled Kira into another hug. "After smashing your college exams, how could I say no?"

"The exam seemed so much easier than I expected it to be," Kira said.

"Only because you had studied, and your marks showed your dedication." Sascha released Kira and rested her arm on Kira's shoulder. "The highest marks in the college's history. I'm so proud I could burst. Are you ready to begin your studies at the academy tomorrow?"

"It will be full on, but, yes, I'm ready. And before I forget, when the retreat finished I dropped in to visit Marcie at your clinic, as I promised."

"Thanks, Kira. I've been worried how the clinic is going."

"Well you don't need to be worried. Business is booming, and Marcie has them all working together as a team. She seems to have a knack with people, in the same way she has a knack with the animals. They were happy, and flat out. They said to say hello and they miss you."

"I miss them, and my clinic," Sascha said. "One day soon I will return to Earth and spend some time with them all. Catch up."

"I think they would like that, Sascha."

Sascha looked at the pile of books on the floor. "What are you studying?"

"The ritual practices of the people of Brun. I can't help wondering what it was that made them start believing they had to sacrifice healers to the Fire Gods. There had to be something, some reason. And maybe once we know that reason, we can convince them to change."

"Hello, Sascha," Alex mumbled as he rubbed his eyes and stretched. "Have you brought my brother with you?"

"No, I let Marco sleep. He didn't get home until late. He had to wait for reports on how the regions are going with their preparations for the season of the three moons."

"Well, in that case, I might leave you girls to catch up and go and help out with the building work outside."

"I'm surprised you've turned handyman, Alex," Sascha said.

"I need to keep busy until I get back to Earth, and that seems the best way to do it."

"Perhaps you don't need to return to Earth," Sascha said. "Marco needs help to rebuild the Fire of the Phoenix. They were devastated after the disasters, and I'm sure he would love to have you with him."

"Family working together can be a bad thing," Alex said. "Especially the two of us. We disagree on things . . . a lot."

"But you could help protect the girls," Sascha said.

Alex glanced over at Kira. "I'll think about it."

Perhaps Lee is right. Perhaps Alex does like Kira. Maybe I should remind him of the age difference. Or maybe not. Since when did I become this prudish?

"Girls, lunch is ready," Lee called out.

Kira put her arm through Sascha's and led her to lunch. As they walked into the large open dining area, Sascha realized Ella had arrived and was sitting at the oval-shaped ebony table with a bottle of wine. "Ella," Sascha said, "it's so good to see you." Ella's long white-blond curls had grown even longer, and her dark tanned skin was darker than ever. She was an exotic beauty.

Ella made no move to get up from the table and refused to meet Sascha's eyes.

"Lee told me you were here," she replied.

"Is something wrong, Ella?" Sascha asked.

"No. Why?"

"It's just that—oh, no reason. Anyway, it's good to have all of you together. I have something to ask you." Sascha wandered over to the marble benchtop where Lee was making a salad, and Kira followed.

"It's about the dreams," Lee said. She glanced over at Kira. "Not about her wedding, Kira."

"Ha ha," Kira said as she tried to smother a smirk.

Sascha picked up one of the cherry fruits from the kitchen bench and popped it in her mouth. "Yes. The dreams have started again, and I need to know if you girls are having them, too."

"I have, and so has Lee," Kira said. "But Ella hasn't. Have you, Ella?"

Ella shook her head, finished her glass of wine, and poured herself another one.

"We were wondering if we should come and see you, but we were hoping you would come today. It's worked out well." Lee glanced over at Ella. "After spending time with our . . . families we don't want to return to another castle too quickly. Castle walls seem to have ears."

"Didn't you enjoy your time with your families?" Sascha asked.

Lee poured a dressing into the bowl of salad and stirred it through. "Can we talk about it another time?"

"Sure," Sascha said. "Anytime you want to talk, send me a message and I'll come here. I'm not far away."

"Send you a message," Ella muttered. "That'll work."

"I promise, Ella," Sascha said. "I will come to you."

Lee moved closer to Sascha and put her hand on Sascha's arm. "Ella has a few things going on at the moment. She needs a bit of space."

Sascha peered over at Ella. "Okay." She turned back to Lee and Kira. "These dreams you're having, are you both dreaming the same thing?"

"Exactly the same," Lee said.

Sascha flashed a look at the table. "And you haven't been having any dreams at all, Ella?"

"No," Ella replied as she picked up her glass and swilled down the wine as if it was water.

Ella is drinking a lot. What is going on?

"What happens in your dream, girls?"

"Well," Kira said as she fiddled with the pencil she had taken from behind her ear. "We watch as Eham and Jenny are killed. We don't see ourselves killing them this time. The face of the killer is in shadow. But we also see a child standing with Jenny. It turns to us and pleads for its life, as if we can somehow save it. But we wake before anything else happens."

"Did you see any crates?" Sascha asked.

Lee tilted her head. "Crates? That's a strange question. No, I didn't see anything. Did you, Kira?"

"No, nothing. Why are you asking about crates?"

Sascha glanced over at Ella in time to see her quickly look away.

Ella is interested in the crates? But why?

Sascha shook her head. "I saw crates in my dream, and I thought you might have seen the same. Did the child have blue eyes?"

"Yes," Lee said. "So what was your dream, Sascha?"

Sascha took a deep breath.

There are some similarities in the dreams but why is there a difference? There wasn't this sort of a difference last time. I can't say I killed them.

"I see . . . Eham, Jenny, and the child being killed."

Lee and Kira stared at her. Ella poured herself another wine and drank it down in a couple of mouthfuls.

"That must have been tough," Lee said. "It would have

been hard to see the child die and not be able to do something about it."

Sascha's stomach knotted.

What would they say if they knew it was me who killed the child?

"It's made me more determined to find out what's going on."

"You're making a big deal out of nothing," Ella snapped. "Nothing bad happened last time we had the dream."

"But we never saw Jenny again after we met Eham," Lee said. "Perhaps it's different this time because we will be seeing them both."

"You seem scared, Ella," Sascha said. "You're sure you didn't have the dream?"

Ella jumped up, sending her chair flying backward. "Are you calling me a liar, Sascha?"

"No, of course not."

"Ella," Lee said, "Sascha wasn't having a go at you. Chill out."

"What else was she doing if she wasn't having a go at me?"

"Girls," Sascha said. "Ella, I'm sorry. I shouldn't have asked you that again. But I know something is—" Sascha glanced at Lee and remembered what she had said about Ella needing space. Now was not the time to argue with Ella. "Please, sit down, Ella. We need to work together, not fight each other."

"When are Jenny and Eham supposed to be arriving on Eratus?" Kira asked. "I assume we are still expecting them to return to Eratus."

"Marco said they're expected today," Sascha said.

"Today?" Kira repeated. "Do you think that's why the nightmares have started again?"

Sascha shook her head. "I don't know. And the child . . . do any of you know if Jenny had a child?"

"There's no way she did," Lee said. "We would've known.

You can't keep a child secret from your friends for all that time."

Lee opened the oven. "Let's forget about the dreams for now, at least until we see Eham and Jenny. Time for lunch. I'll carry these dishes to the table if you two set up the knives and forks. Ella, would you get some wine? I still have some bottles from Earth. They're in the fridge."

"Good idea," Sascha said.

"Can I have some wine, too?" Kira asked. "Please, just half a glass."

Lee raised her eyebrows as she turned to Sascha. "What do you think, Sascha?"

"Okay. Half wine and half sparkling water." Sascha wagged her finger at Kira. "But only one."

"Yes!" Kira said, fist-pumping the air.

By the time Ella arrived back with the wine, sparkling water, and glasses, lunch was on the table. The aroma of fresh salad, hot meats, and savory stews floated around the room.

While everyone else helped themselves to food, Ella sat down and poured herself some more wine.

"Sascha," Lee said. "We wanted to talk to you about how we can get our powers back. And our memories."

"Are you still finding it tough?" Sascha asked.

"We feel like outsiders in our own homes," Lee said. "Our families look at us as if they don't know what to say, as if they should apologize. They're worried about whether we will forgive them when our memories return. We feel more alone with our families than we ever did without them. I know that doesn't make sense, but it's true." Lee reached over and put her hand over Kira's. "Sorry, Kira. I should have been more sensitive. We shouldn't complain. At least we have our parents."

"I have Sascha," Kira said. "I have a mother."

Tears stung Sascha's eyes as happiness flooded through her. It was no wonder she loved Kira so much. The girl had such a generous spirit.

"And when she and Marco get married, I will have a father, too."

Lee laughed. "You'd better have Kira as your bridesmaid, Sascha, or she will never forgive you."

"When are you getting married?" Kira asked. "Have you set a date yet?"

"Marco and I were talking about it yesterday. We plan to get married when the preparations for the season of the three moons are complete, so next month. Which reminds me—"

"Yes, of course I will be your best woman, bridesmaid, or whatever they call them here," Kira screeched as she bounced up and down in her chair, clapping her hands together.

Sascha chuckled. "I didn't even get to ask you."

"I need to start planning," Kira said. "And we need a hen's party. Do they have parties like that here on Eratus?" Without waiting for an answer Kira took a breath and continued, "And at the wedding we need music and dancing—"

Sascha raised a hand to stop Kira. "You won't have enough time to plan a wedding that's too extravagant. And we still have a lot to do to prepare for the storms."

"That's okay. You and Marco sort out what you need to and I'll plan the wedding. The girls will help me."

"We could use the distraction," Lee said.

"Sascha," Soleil called out. "We need to leave now if you want to get back before dark."

"Soleil's calling," Sascha said, pushing herself away from the table and standing. "I want to meet with the dragons and Athena and be back on Eratus before dark if possible."

"If you're meeting with the dragons and Athena," Lee said,

"do you think you could talk to them about us getting our memories back? Maybe before the season of the three moons?"

"It's on my list of things to talk about. Before I go, girls, there's one thing I wouldn't mind your help with. See if you can find out how we can save pyrans from being sent to the fifth dimension when they separate from their masters. I have a feeling Fenix might need some help, and soon. Soleil said that before I was sent away to Earth I knew of a way to save the pyrans, but as I'm only getting fragments of my memory back, I might not remember in enough time to save Fenix. I need to find some other way to get an answer for her."

"How come Soleil didn't go to the fifth dimension when you left for Earth?" Kira asked.

"Before I left I specifically ordered him to stay, which meant he had a reason for not going. And I didn't die. But if Drakon decides he wants to send Fenix to the fifth dimension and orders her to go . . . "

"We will definitely help," Kira said. "There must be something in the library here. It's massive. You know, a couple of times I thought I saw Laela in the library. I'm sure she wouldn't be foolish enough to come here, but I would swear it was her."

"Don't be stupid," Ella slurred. "She'd hardly come here."

"Ella!" Sascha snapped. "That's enough of your attitude. Whatever is bugging you, do something about it. Kira, no one has seen Laela since the battle in the dragons' cave, so if you see her again, would you let me know? Everyone seems to think she's dead, but I don't. I'm sure she's alive and is still trying to work out how to release the Ancients. But we need to stop her. The Ancients must never get a hold on Eratus again."

"Laela had the power of the Four Sisters behind her last

time," Lee said. "This time she doesn't. She doesn't carry the same threat as before."

"But she's a threat," Sascha said. "And until we know exactly what she's up to, we cannot afford to let our guard down."

"Perhaps the dragons or Athena have some insight into what Laela is up to," Lee said.

"You could be right." Sascha went around the table and hugged each of the girls in turn.

"Sascha," Lee said, "I meant to tell you this before. We're building a secret gateway into the defensive shield. When we are given the signal to turn our shields on, no matter where you are you will be able to get in here to see us. It will be at the fork entrance in the Ohork River. Apart from Kira, you'll be the only one that can use the gateway because it will be hidden in magic's shadow."

A warm glow flowed through Sascha as she realized that no matter what Ella's reaction had been during her visit this time, they were still family. "Everyone will probably need to have their shields up soon. Will the gateway be finished in time? I don't want you jeopardizing your safety for this gateway."

"It's nearly complete," Lee said. "We will be testing it out tomorrow. Everything seems to be going smoothly."

"Thanks, Lee. I'll sleep better knowing I can get to you girls if I need to." Sascha moved on to Ella and tried to hug her but she pulled away. "Ella, if you need someone to talk to, I'm here for you," Sascha whispered.

Ella gave a hard, bitter laugh. "I don't need you." She nodded her head in the direction of the other two girls. "And neither do they. The only way you can help is by staying away."

Sascha stared at Ella, unable to form a response.

"Come on, Sascha," Soleil called. "It's time to go. We still need to make it through the portal to Earth."

"Coming, Soleil," Sascha said as she walked out of the building and toward the paddock.

What's happened? I thought Ella was in a bad mood but it's so much more than that. Ella hates me. But why?

OWAIN'S VISIT TO DRAKON

ERATUS

*D*rakon stood on the ramparts and sipped prumble ale as he watched Chiane direct their men in training maneuvers. Shields clashed and swords rang as the men tried to outdo each other. The stale smell of sweat drifted on the breeze, forcing Drakon to take a step back from the edge of the balcony rim.

He had spent the last couple of hours sparring with Chiane and, as usual, he was impressed with how tough and fit a warrior Chiane was. Though Drakon had trained earlier that morning, he hadn't been able to turn down the opportunity of training with Chiane. He was a worthy competitor.

Chiane may be a successful warrior, but he is too soft to be made general. I made a mistake in thinking he could replace Reya. And Novo is too arrogant.

What he needed was a cross between Chiane and Novo. Perhaps that was why Reya had been such a good general. It was a pity she had lost her focus, not to mention turned traitor.

I wonder how long she'd been plotting against me.

He shook his head. There was no point trying to work

it out.

But I'll be thinking carefully before I appoint anyone else to the role of general.

"Lieutenant General Chiane," Drakon called out.

Chiane looked up at Drakon and nodded. Drakon turned and walked into his war room and stood in front of his war table.

There was a soft trill from the corner of the room. Drakon glanced over to where his fire dragons were resting, their eyes glowing red in the dark. "Hello, my beauties."

Kalamar answered with a swish of his tail.

"Are you hungry? Mirror, some food for my dragons."

"Yes, My Prince," the Mirror answered.

Moments later, the ravenous creatures were feasting on a mischief of rats. Heavy boots thumped along the battlement and a chained fist knocked on the open door.

"Enter," Drakon said.

"My Prince." Chiane's eyes flicked toward the fire dragons before he joined Drakon at the war table.

"Have you received a report from Novo yet?" Drakon asked.

"Nothing so far."

"Have you sent anyone to follow up with him?"

"Novo knows he has until the second sun sets tomorrow," Chiane said. "I know he won't let us down."

"I expect more from you, Chiane. You can't afford to rely on the goodness of others. You need to doubt more, not be so trusting."

Chiane nodded. "I do have something to report. Pat has been following Jenny. Jenny met up with Eham in Brisbane, but they don't seem to be in a hurry to return to Eratus. They're staying in a hotel not far from the first portal. Pat asked what you would like her to do."

Drakon stared at the table as he decided whether he

would bring the two of them to Eratus by force or allow them to return when they were ready. His mind made up, he turned to Chiane. "Tell her to continue to keep an eye on them and report back as soon as they return to Eratus. Perhaps then we'll find out why Reya was so interested in Jenny. I thought it was something to do with the healing ceremony, but now I wonder if it might be more than that."

"I will advise Pat," Chiane said.

"I have another task for you, Chiane. I have ordered Fenix to take Sascha to my encampment at Cirrone. I need to check that everything is in place for when she arrives. Given everything that is supposedly happening in Tasuna, I'm concerned that the family who . . . gifted . . . us the land for the encampment might try to take it back. I can't let that happen, or rather, *you* can't let that happen. And since the main portal to Tasuna has been destroyed, you'll need to get some mages to activate the smaller portal that has been set up in the center of the encampment."

"Right away."

"Under no circumstances is anyone but Sascha or me allowed to use that portal. If any other poor, unfortunate souls think they can use it, show them they are wrong. Is that clear?"

"Yes, My Prince. It will take an hour or two for my men to get there without the main portal working. We'll have to rely on pyrans."

"That's not my problem. All I care about is that everything is in place when Fenix arrives in Cirrone with Sascha. You want to be a general? Then sort it out."

"I will."

"Cirrone is your hometown, isn't it?"

"Yes, it is."

"You should have no problems organizing everything for me then."

"I'll do as you command, My Prince." Chiane brought his fist to his chest in salute, turned on his heel, and left.

Drakon looked over at his pets as he prepared to leave.

"Drakon."

Drakon's head snapped up as Owain entered the war room. "Father, I didn't hear you."

Owain choked at the sight of the fire dragons feasting on the rats. "Do you have to feed those creatures indoors, Drakon? Our grounds are large. Surely there's somewhere else you can feed them."

Kalamar stopped eating and stared at Owain, his eyes following the man's every move.

"Why are you here, Father? That is, apart from sharing your wisdom on where I should feed my pets."

"You haven't been to see Connell. I'm worried about him and I wouldn't mind a second opinion."

Drakon laughed. "You think seeing me will help Connell? I'm afraid you don't know much about us, do you, Father? He won't want me intruding on his private sanctum."

"He's your brother, Drakon. Show some brotherly love."

"He's my *adopted* brother, and I'm showing some brotherly love by not visiting him."

Owain gave the dragons one last glance before turning and walking away. "I hope you will reconsider," Owain called out. "He's your brother and he would visit you if you were ill."

"I have a busy life, Father, or have you forgotten what I do around here?" Drakon replied.

Owain kept walking. "He's in his chambers, if you change your mind."

"Sokentash!" Drakon said as he stormed out of the war room.

You're going to regret this, Father. You want me to talk to Connell? Well, I will, but you won't like what I have to say.

THE DRAGONS AND ATHENA

* EARTH

*I*t seemed an age before Sascha heard Soleil's whisper. "We've arrived at the first portal so it won't be long now until we arrive at the dragons' cave. And, by the way, we're right. This is the portal the guardians are still protecting."

"Of course it would be," Sascha muttered.

"And they're awake and fishing in the river."

"I didn't realize guardians eat fish," Sascha said. "They don't look like the sort of creatures that eat fish." They watched as the hulky, hairy creatures lumbered around in the water, splashing about and scaring off any fish before they had a chance to capture them.

"They're not," Soleil said. "They prefer meat. They must be desperate if they're trying to fish."

"Which means they'll be desperate to catch us." Sascha shivered. The last time they had flown through this portal, Soleil had been clawed by the revolting creatures.

One of the guardians stopped searching, sniffed at the skies, and then roared.

"They've seen us," Soleil said. "Hang on. I'm going to have

to circle high and fly hard and fast into the portal so that we can get through before they catch us."

The wind blew by fast, then faster. Sascha felt the powerful beats of Soleil's wings. Minutes later, Soleil sailed through the portal.

"We made it." Sascha whooped as she caressed Soleil's neck. "And you didn't get hurt."

They flew toward the rooftop of Marco's apartment complex but instead of landing there, like they normally did, they headed directly for the dragons' cave.

"Soleil, remind me to ask the dragons about how we can save the pyrans from going to the fifth dimension. Perhaps they're the ones who told me what needs to happen."

"I will," Soleil answered.

It wasn't long before Soleil flew through the trees and scrub that hid the dragons' cave from view and landed neatly on the stone floor. Several of the large torches set into the cave walls were alight.

"Do those torches ever go out?" Sascha asked. "They always seem to be lit."

"I don't know," Soleil said.

The polished black stone walls of the cave glistened in the torchlight. Sascha glanced up at the arrow loops that lined the top of the walls. She swore she could still hear the screams as Kalurth sent white flashes of lightning crackling along the walkway behind the sloops, killing the soldiers hidden there.

"There was so much death last time we were here," Sascha whispered.

Sascha unfastened the harness and climbed down to the ground. She walked over to where Reya had been killed. All that remained was a dark stain from where her blood had pooled.

"Soleil, what do you think happened to Reya's body?"

"I don't know. I have a feeling the dragons know something, but they don't seem to want to share it with us."

"Maybe," Sascha said. "Speaking of the dragons, where are they?"

Wings pounded in the air, and trees and bushes were blown aside as a large majestic creature of gold and bronze flew into the cave on a breeze of pine and honey. "Zinnath," Sascha muttered. "Still as stunning as ever."

Seconds later, Kalurth flew in. She was smaller than Zinnath, and the color of emerald and diamonds.

"Zinnath and Kalurth," Sascha called out, "it's good to see you again."

The dragons pirouetted in the air and then landed with the grace of ballet dancers. Turning to face Sascha, they stretched their wings and then tucked them in by their sides. The clicking of their sharp talons echoed in the cave as they settled themselves down on the polished stone floor. Zinnath turned to the candles positioned in a semicircle around them, gave a short burst of fire, and grunted approvingly when the candles popped into life.

"You're looking well, Sascha," Kalurth said. "Life on Eratus must be agreeing with you."

"We're getting used to it," Sascha said. "Having Marco, Soleil, and the girls there makes all the difference."

"We were worried about you for a while after the ceremony," Kalurth said.

"I won't lie," Sascha said. "It's been hard. The pain, the fear, the face of the Ancient—they have all kept replaying over and over in my dreams."

Kalurth lowered her head. "We are sorry we couldn't help you as much as we would have liked to. It was all so quick, and you had only just been through the ceremony to get your powers back."

Sascha nodded. "The timing wasn't in my favor. But somehow, we did it."

"Yes, we did," Zinnath said. "Has your memory returned?"

"Fragments are coming back. I must admit that I find it very frustrating, but I'm hoping it won't be long until I remember everything."

Zinnath twisted his head to the side. "We were planning on coming back to see you. To be honest, we didn't think you'd come back to this cave. Did you want us to return your staff to you? We did secure it with the other ceremonial artifacts as you asked."

Sascha shuddered. "I'm happy to leave it with you until the next healing ceremony. The last thing I want to see at the moment is that staff."

"I can understand that," Zinnath replied. "So why are you here?"

"I need your counsel, and as far as this cave is concerned, it's time for me to put everything in the past."

"What do you need our counsel on?" Kalurth asked.

Sascha pushed her hands deep into the pockets of her jacket as she worked out how she was going to mention Eham.

"Out with it," Kalurth said. "We can't read minds."

"I need to talk to you about Eham," Sascha said.

"Eham?" Zinnath repeated. "He's a good man. A bit whacky, but a good man. He's been through a lot—"

"My heart, let the girl finish," Kalurth said. "What is it about Eham?"

Sascha took a deep breath. "There's no easy way to say this, so I'm just going to say it."

"I've found that's always the best way," Zinnath said. "In fact—"

"Zinnath!" Kalurth muttered. "What's wrong with you? Let the girl finish."

"She's taking so long," Zinnath muttered. "We could have raised a brood of dragons by now."

"Do you remember how we talked about the nightmares I used to have about killing Eham?" Sascha asked. "They've returned."

"Is it the same dream?" Kalurth asked.

Sascha shuffled her feet. "No, it's changed. I see him with Jenny and a child."

Kalurth lowered her neck and snaked her head in Sascha's direction. "A child. Did you say a child?"

"Yes."

"It's true then," Zinnath whispered.

"What's true?" Sascha asked.

"The child," Zinnath said. "We've heard rumors of a child, but what is the connection with Jenny? Surely the child doesn't belong to Jenny?"

Fifteen minutes later, Zinnath and Kalurth sat quietly as they digested everything Sascha had told them. The cave was silent except for the crackle of the burning torches and the calls of the birds outside as they settled in the trees before the night fell.

Sascha strode to the edge of the cave and stared out at the setting sun for a few seconds before she turned back to face the dragons. "You both seem more worried about this child than Eham or Jenny."

Zinnath glanced at Kalurth before turning his attention back to Sascha. "Your dream concerns us. Eham is loyal and we trust him completely. Jenny is the one who helped us save Eham when he was going through a very difficult time, so we feel fairly sure she can be trusted. But this child . . . we've only heard rumors. We can't see anything about this child in the stars, which worries us."

"I know there is a darkness that still exists on Eratus," Sascha said. "I don't know if it is another Ancient like the one

I battled at the healing ceremony or something else. But I thought it had something to do with Laela. Now, with this dream I'm having, I'm not so sure."

"Laela may be involved," Zinnath said, "but what you sense is much more powerful than her. If she is involved, she is nothing more than a pawn."

"How do you know what I sense?" Sascha asked.

"We sense it, too," Zinnath replied.

"My heart, do you think the gods are involved this time?" Kalurth asked.

Zinnath flexed his wings. "Let's hope not."

Sascha took a deep breath and released it slowly.

Should I have told them what the child said—what he implied about being a god?

"What is it you think is happening?" Sascha asked.

"We can't say anything yet," Kalurth said. "Not until we know more. If we tell you the wrong thing, it could be devastating for us all. When we're sure, we'll let you know."

"Do you know the meaning behind the symbol on the crates I saw in my dream?" Sascha asked.

"No," Kalurth said. "But it's intriguing why that specific detail would be in your dream."

"Perhaps Athena knows how it all fits together," Sascha said. "And what the crates or the symbols mean."

"She could do," Kalurth answered. "Have you spoken to her since the ceremony?"

"She came to see me to make sure I had recovered from the battle with the Ancient, but we had an argument. I told her I would visit her when I was ready, but I—the truth is, I can't remember where I can find her."

"She does have a cave on Eratus," Kalurth said. "But she will need to take you there. Where are you planning to go to meet her?"

"I thought I'd go to the cave at the back of the Fire of the

Phoenix headquarters. That was where she helped me heal Soleil."

"Zeus may not be happy," Kalurth said. "That's his cave."

"His cave? I'm only going there because I need to go where I know her power is strong. What difference does it make if I go to his cave, rather than hers?"

"Zeus likes protocols," Kalurth said. "You'll be breaking protocol by approaching Athena in this way."

"And in what way am I supposed to approach her?" Sascha grumbled.

"Don't get snarky with us, Sascha," Zinnath said. "It's different for everyone. Athena is not worried about how people approach her. Zeus, on the other hand, believes everyone needs to know their place when talking to gods. And you are going to his cave."

"And what is my . . . place . . . exactly?"

"It's not for us to answer that," Zinnath said. "Go and talk to Athena. The two of you have had a good relationship in the past. I'm sure she will help you with Zeus."

"That cave . . ." Soleil ruffled his feathers.

Sascha moved closer to Soleil and rested her hand on his neck. "I know it doesn't bring back happy memories for you, but I must do this."

Soleil nodded. "I know."

Sascha climbed up onto Soleil's shoulders and positioned herself in the harness. "This darkness. Do you think this . . . child is the darkness we've been sensing? And if that child is connected to the Ancients . . . "

"There will always be darkness, Sascha," Kalurth said. "Every creature has both good and bad in them. Life is a constant battle of good against evil."

"But we must even the odds," Sascha said. "Where we find evil, we must destroy it. It's that simple. Anything else is weakness."

"Sascha," Zinnath said, "you've been given a fresh start. Don't let yourself be consumed with the same need for vengeance you had before you left Eratus. Even if it seems like it is the right thing to do. It is that need for vengeance that got you addicted to green lyrium. And it was your need for revenge against Owain that started off the events that ended up with you being sent to Earth. Don't let it be the same with whatever you think this child is . . . or Jenny and Eham."

Sascha knew Zinnath was right but it was too hard to say so.

"You were going to ask about saving the pyrans," Soleil whispered.

"Oh, that's right. Kalurth and Zinnath, did I ever say anything to you about how to save the pyrans from being sent to the fifth dimension?"

"No. I don't even know if it's possible," Kalurth said.

"I mentioned it to Soleil before I left Eratus and I wouldn't have done that unless I was sure."

"I'll see what I can find out," Kalurth said.

"Thank you. I have a feeling that Drakon is planning to send Fenix there. Soleil and I want to make sure that doesn't happen."

Kalurth nodded. "We'll see what we can do. And please, let us know what Athena says. It may be that what we faced in the healing ceremony was just a sample of what we are facing now."

TRACKING JENNY AND EHAM

* EARTH

*T*he war pyran swooped out of the portal and landed neatly on the concrete rooftop of Marco's apartment complex in the middle of Brisbane City. The golden glow of the setting sun warmed Marco's back—a stark contrast to the freezing winds in the portal. Marco yawned, unstrapped himself from the harness on the pyran's shoulders, and climbed down to the roof. He rubbed his legs to ease the cramps from the trip.

"Meet me at the Fire of the Phoenix headquarters," he said to the pyran. "Hopefully it won't take me too long to track down Jenny and Eham."

The pyran lowered its head in acknowledgment, strutted to the edge of the building, and then flew off.

Marco reached into his jacket pocket and retrieved his phone. No messages. He walked to the stairwell door and made his way down to his apartment. As he opened the door, he was hit with a blast of warm air that smelled of George. It seemed so long ago that George was here. Marco removed the keystone from the pocket in his jacket and placed it in the top drawer of the cupboard near his bed. He enjoyed the fact he didn't have a transportation chip embedded under his skin. He needed the protection the chip gave when he traveled through the portal, which is why he wore the keystone, but he didn't like the fact that you could be traced once you had the chip implanted. Although admittedly the tracking part of the chip didn't work on Earth—which was a pity because he could have pinpointed Eham and Jenny easily if it did.

He changed out of his leather travel gear and into jeans and a white T-shirt. Marco strapped his Fitbit to his wrist and pressed the button to activate it. He had enough time for dinner at his coffee shop before he started the hunt for Eham and Jenny. They were staying at one of the hotels in the city, but no one seemed to know which one. He walked over to his travel satchel and retrieved a golden key, which he placed in the back pocket of his jeans, picked up his laptop, and left the apartment. Marco arrived at the traffic lights at the intersection at the end of his road, pressed the button, and waited for the lights to turn green.

A short, squat woman stood on the opposite side of the street, staring at him. Feeling slightly uneasy under her stare, Marco smiled at her hoping she would stop looking at him. It worked and she quickly started focusing on the traffic lights. Seconds later she turned around and headed toward the shopping center. There was something about her, something familiar, but what was it?

The lights turned green and he crossed the road and walked into his coffee shop. The solid timber counter gleamed. The bubbling water fountain sat in the middle of the shop and soft music floated in the air, creating a relaxing atmosphere. This time he would sit at one of the tables and get table service. Though the coffee shop was full, he managed to find a table next to one of the corner windows.

"Marco," a voice called out. Marco turned to see Mike waving at him.

"Mike, how are you?"

Mike strode toward him, leaned over, and gave Marco's hand a firm shake. "I'm good, and business is good, too. We're doing a roaring trade."

"I can see that," Marco said. "It's a credit to you and all of your hard work."

"And what are you doing—acting as the customer?" Mike asked.

"I wanted dinner and where else would I go for a good feed?"

Mike laughed. "Absolutely. Are you back again then?"

"Only for a day or two."

"And how is Eratus?" he whispered, glancing around to ensure no one had overheard him.

"Busy," Marco said. "I must admit it's good to be back here."

"What can I get you then? Your usual pasta and wine?"

"That would be brilliant. Thanks."

As Mike hurried off to organize the order, Marco took his laptop out of his carry bag and plugged it into the power point below the coffee table. There were too many hotels to visit every one of them. He had to narrow the field somehow. He doubted Jenny and Eham would have used their real names and he had no idea what story he was going to use to find out where they were staying. But he was sure something would turn up if he kept his eyes open.

He stared out of the window as he waited for the laptop to start up and saw the woman he had seen at the traffic lights sit down at one of the shop's outdoor tables. Instinct had him pulling back into the darkness as he studied her.

She is so familiar. Where have I seen her before?

It was when he was looking at the picture of Sascha, the

girls, and Rusty on the laptop screen that he remembered who she was. It was Pat.

"Pat," he mumbled. "What's she doing here?"

Marco was convinced that Pat was behind the murder of Ken. And if she could murder her partner, someone she had lived with and supposedly loved, what else was she capable of doing? Pat had disappeared, but he remembered the paperwork that he and Sascha had found on Pat and Ken's fridge. It suggested that Pat had taken off to Scotland to find Jenny, but when Jenny returned safely Marco didn't give Pat another thought.

As Marco planned what to do next, Mike delivered his order.

"Mike, don't look now, but a short, squat woman just sat down at one of the outdoor tables. Would you go and serve her? Then come back and tell me if you've seen her here before."

"Sure," Mike said. "You're being a bit cloak and dagger, but I'm happy to help."

Minutes later, Mike and the woman were laughing. He took her order down, strode into the coffee shop, logged it onto the computer, and then walked up to Marco.

"Yes, I know Pat. She's been a regular over the last week."

"You know her name then?"

"Sure do. She's been getting coffee every morning. Sometimes staying for breakfast. She's not usually here for dinner though."

"Has she ever been with anyone?"

Mike shook his head. "No, not that I'm aware of."

"Do you know if she's staying around here?"

"No, but she did ask about a nearby motor inn. The one in Greenslopes."

"I know the one," Marco said. "It's not far from here. I wonder if she's staying there?"

"I don't know. She's never mentioned it since."

Maybe Jenny and Eham aren't in the city after all. Maybe I was right, and Pat was after Jenny. And if Pat is interested in this area perhaps Jenny and Eham are around here, too.

He decided the best thing to do would be to follow her, see where she went and what she did. He packed his laptop away, sat back in his chair, and enjoyed his pasta and wine, all the while keeping an eye on Pat. When Marco was drinking his coffee, Pat put some money on the table, picked up her bag, and left.

Marco stood up, stretched casually, and then waved at Mike. "I'll catch up with you later. I have something to do. The food was perfect. Tell the chef for me."

"Don't we get a tip?" Mike called out.

"It's on the table."

Pat had crossed the road.

"Time to play detective," Marco murmured.

OWAIN'S VISIT TO CONNELL

ERATUS

Connell sat in his bed and listened to the waves crashing against the shoreline.

I have to get out of here, get out of this bed.

Desperation for a few moments of fresh air forced him to use all of his strength to swing his legs off the edge of the bed. "Ciara, would you help me? I'd like to sit on my balcony for a while."

"The evening is cool, Connell. I don't think it is a good idea."

"If you don't help me, I'll do it myself," Connell snapped.

Ciara stood in front of him, hands on her hips. "Okay. I'll help you out there as long as you use a wrap and keep yourself warm."

"Deal," Connell said.

A few minutes later, Ciara had him covered with a warm thick wrap and sitting on the chair on the balcony. "I'll take George and Rusty out for a walk," she said. "We'll be back in half an hour. I'll help you back to bed then."

As the door closed, Connell rested back into his chair and breathed in the faint peppermint scent of the ocean. The soft breeze and the ocean's scent began to work their magic, and Connell felt himself start to relax.

A loud thump sounded on the door as Owain strode into the room. "And what are you doing sitting outside in the cool night air?"

"I needed a change. I'm tired of looking at four walls all the time."

Owain looked him up and down. "You don't look much better. I hope you're doing everything the healer is asking you to do."

"Thanks, Father! You really do have a way with words."

"Sorry. I guess I shouldn't have said that."

"I feel better than I look," Connell lied. "How is everything going?"

"Are you allowed a glass of silkar?" Owain asked.

"I'd prefer a glass of prumble ale."

"Done." Moments later, Owain stepped back out onto the balcony and handed a glass of ale to Connell.

Owain stood at the balcony rim and stared down at the dark ocean. "Has your brother come to see you?"

"You mean Drakon?"

"Do you have another brother I should know about?"

Connell smiled. "No, he hasn't. Why?"

"I hoped he would, that's all. I wish the two of you would put your troubles aside and try to get along. One day I'll be gone and the leadership of Eratus will be left to you and Drakon."

"You mean left to Drakon," Connell said. "He's your true son." Connell wondered if he should tell Owain what Reya had said about Drakon's father being marked in the register of mages as . . . unlisted . . . but decided not to. It would look like he was trying to undermine Drakon so he, Connell, could be the next High King.

Maybe when I'm well and I have the register in my hand . . .

Owain turned to stare at Connell. "You're my son too, Connell."

Connell looked down and fiddled with the glass in his hand. "Drakon is to be the next High King. I accept that. But the chances of him accepting me as part of the court are pretty slim."

"He must. You're his brother."

"His adopted brother."

"Sweet souls and angels. Is it truly impossible for you two to put this matter of adoption aside and be friends? Your hate for each other could tear this planet apart. How can I die knowing what it is I'm leaving behind?"

"What's all this talk about dying, Father? Are you ill?"

"No, no, of course not," he growled. "I just wish you two would at least try to get along. If you two worked together . . ."

The breeze blew Owain's long gray hair about his face. Though Owain was half a head taller than Connell and broader across the chest, there were more similarities between the two of them than there were between Owain and Drakon. It almost made him believe that Reya had been telling the truth when she had said that he was Owain's true son.

"Father, I love you. But Drakon and I are entirely different people. You need to realize that. We'll never be able to get along the way you want us to."

There was a knock on the door. George exploded into the room, raced up to Connell, and nudged him. Rusty loped over to Owain, but changed direction when he grumbled at her, settling instead for saying hello to Connell. Ciara wasn't far behind them, a cup of Connell's evening medicine in her hand.

"Has half an hour gone by already?" Connell said. "That was fast."

"I'd better go," Owain mumbled. "I just wanted to see how you were. I'll visit you again tomorrow, sometime after lunch."

Connell watched as Owain shut the door behind him. There had been gray bags under Owain's eyes, and Connell was sure he had lost weight. There was something troubling him, but what? And all this talk about who would rule when he was gone.

Ciara helped him back into bed, gave him his medicine, and then left. Connell sagged back into the feather pillows.

I need to find out what's going on with Father.

Connell punched the bed. "This damn illness. Father needs me and I'm just lying here like a lump." George leaped up onto the bed and snuggled into Connell. "I'm okay, George. You go to sleep."

He glanced over at Rusty. "And you go to sleep too, Rusty."

She curled up in a ball on the mat next to Connell's bed, gave a loud sigh, and promptly fell asleep.

Connell yawned. The medicine was beginning to work.

Tomorrow I'll speak to my spies. I need to know what's going on. Something isn't right with Father.

ATHENA

* EARTH

*S*ascha studied the scarred landscape below them on which stood the Fire of the Phoenix headquarters. She repositioned herself on Soleil's shoulders as his muscles started to tense, making it hard for her to sit comfortably. She leaned down and stroked his neck. "I'm sorry to make you come here again, Soleil. I hope Athena is here and this isn't a wasted trip."

Soleil circled in low above the headquarters. "I needed to come back here and face my fears. You've done me a favor."

Though a lot of repair work had been completed around the grounds, the devastation caused by the battle with the hoard of pit hounds still showed. The funeral pyres for the dead men were gone, but the charred marks remained, and the stench of battle still soaked the air. The water fountain had been demolished and a new one was under construction. A pile of rubbish stood where the guard boxes had once been. What remained of the pit hounds' bodies was bundled on top of the rubbish, the light cast by the setting sun giving the bones an eerie glow.

They flew across a pathway covered in golden pebbles,

over a lattice fence covered in grapevines, and into the cave. Sascha clambered down from Soleil's shoulders. The walls glistened gold like the pebbles that formed the pathway. The sound of water bubbling in the creek at the back of the cave echoed around her.

"You go ahead, Sascha," Soleil said as he stood in the maw of the cave. "I'll wait for you here."

"We'll go soon," Sascha said.

Soleil ruffled his feathers. "Can we get out of here before nightfall?"

Sascha nodded. "I can sense the magic. It's strong. Hopefully I won't be long."

She wandered toward the creek at the back of the cave. Her stomach churned. The last time she had been here with Soleil, she had nearly lost him. Sascha wasn't sure how things would have turned out for her if he had died that day. She swallowed the lump in her throat as she sat cross-legged on the sand next to the turquoise-colored water.

Sascha closed her eyes and concentrated on the murmuring of the water as it glided across the smooth pebbles of the creek bed. She breathed in the scent of cinnamon and pine and visualized the filtered light of the sun setting in the west.

"Athena. If you're here, I need to talk to you."

There was no response.

"Athena?"

She waited in silence for what seemed to be an age.

She's not going to come. It'll be dark soon. I should go.

Soft music suddenly drifted around her—haunting, gentle sounds. Sascha opened her eyes. A misty figure appeared in the distance. It moved closer and started to take shape. It was a woman with olive skin, flowing dark brown hair, and sparkling gray eyes. She was dressed in a gown of white and gold.

"Hello, Sascha."

Sascha bowed her head. "I'm sorry I didn't come before now, Athena."

"Don't apologize," Athena said. "I understand. People often forget about the gods until they need them. I assume that is why you're here. You need me."

Sascha flinched. "Yes, I do." She stood up and stretched her legs. "So you're not a genie in a bottle. That's disappointing."

Athena laughed. "I do like the idea of being a genie. But I must admit I thought you were angry with me after the ceremony, especially when you didn't come and visit like you said you were going to."

"To be honest, Athena, I'm still struggling with my memory and I couldn't remember how to make contact with you. I guess I could have come here, like I did this time, but I wasn't sure this was going to work."

"I hadn't realized you didn't remember where my cave was. Let's start afresh. So why are you here?"

"I need to speak to you about the girls."

"They want to get their memories back?" Athena asked.

"Yes. They know the dangers, but they still want to go through the ritual. I can't help but worry about them."

Athena strolled toward Soleil. She studied Sascha as she stroked Soleil's feathers. "I will talk to Zeus for you and see what's possible."

"Is there any way we can convince Zeus to give them back their memories without forcing them through the ceremony?"

Athena took her hand off Soleil and folded her arms across her chest. She tilted her head to the side. "You probably should know that the girls' parents have already contacted me. They want to petition Zeus to send the girls back to Earth, put them through the process again."

"They want to what?" Sascha snapped. "Do they have any idea what it is they're asking?"

"They're angry at you, Sascha. They think that you have placed the girls in real danger by bringing them to Eratus. They say they want them safe, and safe means back on Earth with no memories of their past."

"Back to Earth? *Real* danger? The girls don't want to go back to Earth. They want to stay on Eratus. And it doesn't matter where they are—they're in *real* danger if they aren't given a chance to remember who they are and develop their powers."

"I agree with you, Sascha. But the parents have as much right to petition to have the girls sent back to Earth as you do to ask Zeus to give them back their memories."

Sascha stood in silence as she stared out the maw of the cave.

Something isn't right here. Are they worried about the safety of the girls, or is there another reason?

She took a deep breath.

Relax. You won't help them by blasting Athena.

"They have no say over what happens to Kira."

"You're right," Athena said. "You're Kira's mother. They have no say over her."

"The parents need to talk to the girls before they do anything. They're not children. Lee and Ella are eighteen years old. No one should decide their fates for them."

"Including you?"

Sascha sighed. "Yes, including me."

"So if the girls choose to return to Earth?" Athena asked.

"They won't. But if they tell me that is what they wish, I will . . . I will accept what they decide."

A loud voice boomed across the cave. "Athena, what are you doing in my cave?"

"Sascha, be careful," Soleil called out. "Zeus is here, and he's angry."

A figure appeared next to Athena—a regal-looking giant of a man with a beard and thick curly hair. He was dressed in a white toga with a golden sash around his waist.

Athena nodded. "Father."

"Zeus," Sascha said, "I wanted to—"

"Shush, Sascha," Athena whispered.

Zeus twisted around to face Sascha. "Since when does a mortal think she can address me without permission?"

"Sascha," Athena whispered, "you need to—"

Sascha's fingernails bit into her palms as she clenched her fists. "Athena, if you're going to tell me to apologize for being *rude enough* to talk to Zeus without permission, then forget it. What good is a god if every time we see them, we must act as mutes until they give us permission to speak?"

"I could destroy you with a flick of my finger, mortal," Zeus growled. "Take care how you speak to me."

"You would have a fight on your hands, Zeus. I'm not that easy to destroy."

All movement in the cave stopped; even the bubbling waters seemed to have stilled. The silence weighed as heavy as a winter's fog.

Zeus drew in a long breath, then chuckled, then laughed. Soon the cave was filled with the roar of his laughter, and the usual noises returned. "Mortal, you are either incredibly brave or a fool."

"I'll do what I need to do to help Lee, Ella, and Kira," Sascha said. "They're seeking permission for an audience with you to plead their case for their memories to be returned. And," Sascha glanced at Athena, "I understand Lee's and Ella's parents want them to be sent back to Earth."

"What do you expect me to do?" Zeus asked.

"I'm hoping you will meet with us and talk to the girls. Help us."

"I'll think on it. In the meantime, Athena, remind this . . . mortal about the appropriate protocols." He wiped a hand over his face in an attempt to hide a smirk. "Next time, I might refuse to talk to her."

Sascha held her chin high. "Assuming I want to talk to you, Zeus."

Athena glared at Sascha. "Thank you, Father. May we use your cave for a while longer? I need to talk to Sascha alone."

"Tell this mortal to go to *your* cave next time. Remind her this is *my* cave." There was a thunderous crack, a flash of white, and Zeus disappeared.

"That was fun . . . not," Sascha said.

"Don't worry about him," Athena said. "He's battling with his council over matters of the court. But you held your own. Which brings me to a point I wish to discuss with you. The Ancients have gone quiet. Too quiet. I know the healing ceremony wounded their power base, but it didn't destroy it. There should be some signs of activity, but there's nothing. It makes me nervous. We need to work out what's going on."

"But I've sensed the Ancients," Sascha said. "Well, I've sensed the darkness that seems inextricably linked with them. They're still there all right, though I can't determine whether it's Owain, Laela, or the child who is the source."

"Child?" Athena asked. "Have you seen the child?"

"Only in a nightmare. Why? Do you know anything about it?"

Athena shook her head. "No. And it's odd that I haven't sensed something if you have. I have a friend within the Ancients. He calls himself the Master and he lives in the Peaceful Valley. He's been quiet lately, too. You and I need to visit him, see if he can tell us what's going on."

"A friend within the Ancients? But how do you know you can trust him?"

"It's a long story. I'll let the Master tell you when we see him. But first, I need to check on Ares. He has a castle in the Peaceful Valley and I don't want him to see us visiting the Master."

"Ares? You mean the God of War?" Sascha asked.

"Yes, there is only one Ares. Thank the heavens. And somehow, he is connected to all of this. I'm sure of it. Wait here for me. I may be a while, but I'll come and get you when it's safe to go."

"You'll have to let Zeus know I'm staying here," Sascha said. "He didn't worry last time when I was here with Marco and the girls, but it seems this time he might."

"He'll be fine," Athena said. "Don't worry about it."

"I thought we were going to get back to Eratus before dark," Soleil said. "It'll be dark soon."

Athena turned to Soleil, cupped his head in her hands, and bent down to kiss him on the beak. "Soleil, you return to Eratus. This place makes you nervous and I understand why. It's going to take time for you to forget what happened here, so I'll take Sascha and deliver her back to Eratus when this is all done."

Soleil pulled his head away from Athena's touch. "I'm not going to leave Sascha here on her own just because you tell me to."

"Soleil, I'll stay in the squad bay," Sascha said. "I'll be safe. Fenix is the one who really needs your protection. I need you to keep an eye on her, ensure her safety. Take that worry off my mind."

"Fenix?" Soleil said. "You're going to use her to try and persuade me to abandon you?"

"Not abandon me. I need you to act as my spy. Make sure Drakon doesn't do anything to hurt Fenix. I couldn't live with myself if something happened and we weren't there to help her. We do owe her our lives."

"I still think I should stay. Fenix is a pyran. She can look after herself."

"Soleil, if you're worried about leaving Sascha alone," Athena said, "I'll provide her with my own personal protection."

Soleil grunted. "I guess that's okay but—"

"Soleil," Sascha whispered with a breath of frustration. "It is Fenix who is unprotected, and I know you love her."

Soleil glared at Sascha. "Love her? I don't know where you got that idea. I don't love her. She's all right but . . ."

Sascha smirked. "All right? That's what she is to you—a bit of all right? I think she deserves more than that."

"Why do you twist everything I say, Sascha?" Soleil said. He clicked his beak at her. "If you don't return before the first moon rises tomorrow, I'll be back here to get you." He turned toward Athena. "No matter what Athena says."

Athena chuckled. "A pyran with spunk. That warms the heart."

"Okay, agreed," Sascha replied, remembering what she had wanted to talk to Athena about. "Athena, did I ever talk about a way to save pyrans from being sent to the fifth dimension?"

"No, you didn't. If there is a way and if you found it, you did so without my help. Assuming you were right. I didn't think it was possible."

"Kalurth said the same thing, but I'm hoping you are both wrong. I can't lose Fenix, not that way."

∼

* EARTH – THE CAVE
The screeches of lorikeets and the monotonous caws of

the crows flying overhead woke her. Earth's sun was peaking above the horizon.

Athena still isn't here. How long am I going to have to wait?

Sascha had a quick shower, changed into some fresh clothes she'd left behind last time they were here, and prepared herself some bacon, eggs and toast, and a strong coffee.

It is so good to have normal coffee again. I've missed the coffee and the vegemite scrolls.

The squad bay was a great setup with a fully equipped kitchen, bathroom, and sleeping area. Sascha could understand why some of Marco's troops would use the squad bay as a base of operations whenever they were planning any major events.

As she walked back into the cave, cool air blasted around her legs and a portal opened. Athena stepped out of the portal and into the cave.

"Sorry you had to wait so long. Ares insisted on staying at his castle for the night and has only just left. Are you ready to go?"

Sascha zipped up her jacket and pulled the hood over her head. "Yes, I'm ready."

"Good. Follow me," Athena said, beckoning Sascha to follow her into the portal.

IN THE MOON'S SHADOW – PEACEFUL VALLEY

Sascha stepped off a transporter onto rocky ground. She was surrounded by near darkness, the only light a sliver of sunlight bouncing off the side of a large moon.

Where am I?

Sascha sniffed at the air.

And what is that smell? Blood and bone?

Sascha rubbed her nose. "It stinks here."

"It does. Let's go." Athena waved her hand in an arc and a winding trail began to glow with an iridescent white light. The trail was devoid of any vegetation but littered with skeletons.

"What is this place?" Sascha asked.

"It's called the Peaceful Valley, but it is anything but peaceful."

Sascha pointed at the skeletons. "What happened to them?"

"Black desert serpents spit up the bones of their victims," Athena said. "Once they've consumed all their flesh."

Sascha shuddered as she glanced around her. "Where are these serpents?"

"They live beneath the sands on either side of the trail. I'd suggest you don't leave the pathway."

They had only been walking for five minutes when they heard the first cries of huens circling above them. The sound sent shivers down Sascha's spine.

"Don't look up at them," Athena said. "Just walk."

Sascha adjusted the hood on her jacket. She'd heard stories about huens—how they attacked the eyes of the unwary, blinding them before going in for the kill. "Is there anything here that doesn't want to kill us?"

"Not that I know of," Athena said.

An hour after starting their journey, they found themselves approaching what had once been a solid stone door in the side of a crumbling tower.

"What happened here?" Athena whispered. "The place has been destroyed. Travel quietly, Sascha. We must find the Master, find out what happened."

Sascha climbed over the broken wall and followed Athena as she walked around the ruins, examining each of the rooms that remained. The area smelled of stale ash and bone and a faint, slightly metallic odor.

"What is his real name?" Sascha called out to Athena. "You wouldn't call him the Master all the time."

"His real name is Demipos," Athena said.

Sascha pointed to a skeleton in the middle of the destruction. Its arm had been crushed and part of it was missing. "Could that be him?"

"It can't be Demipos. He can't be killed, unless . . ." Athena shook her head. "Anyway, he would be wearing the armband I gave him."

"There's nothing else around here," Sascha said. "Is there any way you can know for sure who or what those bones belong to?"

Athena walked over to the skeleton and squatted next to it. She closed her eyes and waved her hand over the skeleton, as if she was searching for something. She pulled her hand back and opened her eyes.

"It is him. It's Demipos. There is still a hint of magic left from the armband, and the skeleton is covered with a dark magic . . ." Athena let out a slow, deep breath. "The missing armband is a real concern. And the fact he was killed by a dark magic I haven't seen for centuries. But who would have known about it, known how to use it?"

Athena stood and walked away from the ruins before turning to face what looked like massive golden pillars.

"What's over there?" Sascha asked as she clambered over the rubble to join Athena.

"That's Ares' castle. The magic used to kill Demipos was one that only Ares knows about. But he couldn't have entered these grounds. It's protected. So how did he kill him?"

"You're sure he did it?" Sascha asked. The mark on Sascha's hand started to tingle, then burn. Talons clicked on the ground behind her, and the air vibrated with the sound of sniffing and snorting.

"Look out," Athena called out. "Pit hounds."

"Great! They have pit hounds here, too?" Sascha twisted around, searching for the telltale shimmers, her heart pounding in her chest. "Where are they, Athena? I can't see anything."

Athena raised her arm and pointed straight ahead. "They're coming toward—no, wait. They've gone."

"What do you mean, gone?" Sascha snapped. "How can pit hounds appear and then disappear?"

A man's laughter roared around them. "Athena," the voice said, "the hounds were a warning. Don't sneak in here again."

"Ares," Athena called out, "show yourself."

"I don't think so. Not yet, anyway. I must go. See you next week when you present all your evidence against me to the council." He sniggered.

"Ares, you won't win this," Athena said, her voice loud and strong.

"You don't think so? Prepare for battle, Athena. The fun is only just starting."

"What the—," Sascha said.

"We can't talk here," Athena whispered. "Let's go somewhere safe—my cave."

∾

ERATUS – ATHENA'S HOME

"Wow," Sascha said as they stepped out of the portal and into Athena's cave. "This can hardly be called a cave."

Green balls of fire were captured in fine, glass ribbons that hung from the ceiling, their light reflected in the polished white marble walls and floors. The rear wall was glass, giving an undisturbed view of lush green fields edged with tall olive trees. Sitting on top of a chair under the nearest olive tree was the largest owl Sascha had ever seen.

Sascha moved closer to the glass wall to get a better view of the bird. "What a beautiful creature."

"Yes, it is," Athena replied. "But don't go near him. When he's in a bad mood, he bites."

"Not a bad strategy," Sascha said. "Is the fact that you can talk to an owl the reason you can talk to Soleil?"

Athena laughed. "I'm a God. I can talk to all creatures, including pyrans."

"That makes sense." Sascha stood in awe absorbing the beauty of the room around her. "Why do you call this place a cave? It's more like a mansion."

"The entrance is through a cave," Athena said.

"Where is this cave?"

"Thirty miles from your headquarters in Aynor's Stone." Athena walked to a writing desk, opened the middle drawer, and pulled out a piece of folded paper. "Take this. It's a map to this place so you know exactly where I am."

Sascha took the paper, unfolded it, and looked at the map before she placed it into her jacket pocket. "I'm surprised I don't remember this place. It's beautiful. And why didn't Soleil mention it?"

"Soleil never came here with you."

"Why? He seems to have been everywhere else with me."

"I have no answer for you, Sascha." Athena sighed. "Now that Ares knows we visited the valley, things are going to get a lot more complicated. I must find out how Demipos was killed. And I need to find someone else who can provide me with evidence showing how Ares is linked to all the tragedies that have been occurring on Eratus. I won't survive the council meeting if all I have is my gut feeling."

"What happens if the council doesn't agree with you, doesn't believe Ares was involved?"

"I have Zeus on my side . . . at the moment. He doesn't trust Ares. But because I accused Ares of being involved in the disasters on Eratus when I asked Zeus to agree for your memory to be returned, I need to provide the evidence to back up my claim. Otherwise there's every chance Ares could argue for Eratus to be given to him, and if that happened . . ." Athena walked to the glass wall and placed her right hand on the glass as she stared at the owl. "I had been hoping Demipos would help me, but now he's dead."

"Who was this Demipos?" Sascha asked. "How did you think he would help you?"

Athena turned away from the window and walked toward one of the long, comfortable-looking chairs in her sunken lounge. She waved a hand in Sascha's direction, indicating that she too should sit. Sascha glanced around and decided on an armchair not far from where Athena was sitting.

Athena stared at the pictures on the wall behind Sascha. "Centuries ago, High King Taolis created a design for a weapon he believed he could use to destroy his enemies. He then used that design to build several large batches of the weapon. He had a perverted idea that he would bring peace back to his land by destroying those who opposed him. Somehow the Ancients found out about Taolis's plans and sent an elite group of soldiers called the Masters to assassinate Taolis and retrieve the weapons. Once the High King was dead, they packed the batches of weapons into crates and hid them at various sites around Eratus. Two of the Masters were terrified of what releasing these weapons would do, so they came to me and told me what was going on. Demipos was one of them. The two of them helped me save Eratus. And since then Demipos has been gathering intelligence for me on what Ares has been up to."

"Then it's very convenient for Ares that Demipos is dead," Sascha said.

"Too convenient."

"Laela said Drakon was after weapons," Sascha said. "Are they the same ones?"

"Are you sure Drakon is after them?"

"It's what Laela said, but I don't know how true it is."

"Demipos wouldn't have let anyone get near the weapons. He would have stopped them." Athena furrowed her brow as she turned to face Sascha. "I wonder if there's a connection between Ares and Drakon. Drakon would have been able to enter the tower; the magic wouldn't have stopped him. And he might have taken the armband."

"Why wouldn't the magic have stopped him?" Sascha asked.

Athena opened her mouth to say something, and then stopped. "You'll find out soon enough. I think the more important conversation is about the weapons. If everything that has been happening is all about releasing the weapons . . ."

Sascha sat back in the armchair and crossed her arms.

What is Athena hiding? Why wouldn't the magic stop Drakon?

"Okay. So why weren't these weapons destroyed if they're so dangerous?" Sascha asked.

"Many have tried, but it's almost as if they're cursed, as if they can't be destroyed. The last attempt to destroy the weapons was a hundred and fifty years ago. High King Atticus released a wave of magical energy to destroy the weapons but the plan failed. And his brother betrayed him by sending a copy of the site map that detailed the locations of the weapons, along with the chronicle that showed how to use the weapons, to the Four Sisters." Athena shook her head. "I need to talk to Atticus, see if he can help us find out what happened to Demipos and see if there is a connection to the weapons."

"But if that was one hundred and fifty years ago, isn't Atticus dead?" Sascha asked.

"Before he died, he pleaded for time to make things right. I convinced Zeus to allow Atticus to stay with me until he completed his final task." Athena stood and paced along the glass wall. "If Ares is planning something with the weapons, I'm going to need your help, Sascha. Hopefully Atticus has some ideas that will help us but we must find a way to stop Ares. He must not get those weapons."

Help in a battle against Ares, against a god? Who is she kidding?

"Athena, I—"

Athena clicked her fingers. "Speaking of weapons, there's a couple of weapons I need to return to you. They were sent to me, but since then I've been given a vision, one that shows you will need them again."

Sascha's stomach dropped and her blood chilled as she stared at Athena. "What weapons?"

Athena pointed to a glass table in the corner of the sunken lounge. "Over there, on the table next to the sketches."

Sascha glanced at the sketches hanging on the wall and then forced herself to look at the table. In the middle was a bundle wrapped in golden silk. Her mouth went dry. "No, it can't be."

"What are you talking about?" Athena asked.

Sascha ignored her. She pushed herself out of the chair. Her legs felt heavy as she made her way toward the bundle, each step seeming to take more energy than she possessed. She stared down at the golden fabric as her heart pounded in her chest.

"Open it, Sascha," Athena said. "I don't have all day."

Sascha leaned over, picked up the bundle, and opened it. There, sitting in the bed of golden silk, were the Blades of

Light. Sascha felt the blood drain from her face. "No, I can't use these again," she whispered.

"Of course you can," Athena replied. "You must put what happened in the ceremony behind you. You'll need them one more time. Once your task is complete the blades will disappear and return to where they came from."

"But you don't understand," Sascha said.

"We can talk about it later," Athena replied. "We have to hurry and return you before Soleil comes looking for you. And I need to visit Atticus."

Sascha wrapped the blades up again as a wave of nausea flashed through her.

There's nothing to stop the dream from coming true now. If I find out Jenny does have a child, and the child has blue eyes . . .

She shook her head.

I won't be controlled by a nightmare. I have some say in what is to happen.

THE WEAPONS

ERATUS

*D*rakon walked down the stone staircase along the perimeter of the castle grounds. A cobbled pathway, edged by large white trees, led down the grassy slope to the large cave leading to Ocean's Mouth. A glowing barrier barred entrance to the cave. Drakon waved his arm in an arc and the barrier disappeared. As he stepped into the blackness, the barrier flicked up behind him and the glowing night creatures began to light up the space.

He walked around the waterfall at the cave's entrance, pushed his way past emerald-leafed vines, and followed the grassed path to where the maw of the cave led out to the ocean. He stood for a moment as he watched the suns rise on the horizon. The sunrise was getting later and later, which meant the season of the three moons was getting closer.

Drakon strode toward the circular pergola, which was covered with the same emerald-leafed vines that grew along the walls of the cave. Jugs of prumble ale rested in an ice mill on the table in the middle of the pergola. He was about to pour himself a drink when a burst of red light exploded in front of him, its pulsating glow filling the pergola.

Drakon stepped back and his hand dropped to the hilt of his dagger.

"Hello, Drakon," Ares said.

Drakon dipped his head in acknowledgment. He admired the strong, bearded warrior despite knowing he could never trust him. Dressed in his bronze armor and carrying a long sword, the pommel of which was shaped as a skull with a large ruby embedded in its mouth, Ares was a force to be reckoned with.

"Ares. I expected to see you days ago. I'm surprised Hades isn't with you."

Ares chuckled. "He tells me he's busy doing whatever Gods of the Underworld do. As if I don't know what he's really up to."

Drakon's hand gripped the hilt of the dagger tighter as anger flashed through him. Ares had betrayed him. He knew Ares had meant for him to die when Demipos had died, but he had survived thanks to the potion Chiane gave him. Only now he had to wear this . . . armband.

Ares is a god. Play it cool, Drakon. Revenge is best planned with a clear head.

"So you play games with each other, as well as with us mere mortals," Drakon said.

"Now, now," Ares said. "Everything is a game, you should know that. You need to learn the rules, that's all. I hope there's no bad blood between us after what happened with the Master. Everything worked out, as I knew it would."

"It nearly didn't," Drakon said.

"I had faith in you, Drakon." Ares smirked as he spied the armband Drakon was wearing. "And I see you're wearing Athena's armband now that poor Demipos is dead."

Drakon swallowed the fear that was rising in his throat.

Does Ares think I'm wearing the armband as a trophy? Or does he know what it does?

"Demipos? So that was his real name then?"

"Yes. I guess you wouldn't have known that." Ares nodded at the armband. "I wouldn't let Athena—or Sascha—see you wearing that, because then they will know who killed Demipos. And who would've thought that Athena had a soft spot for that brittle shell of a creature?"

"And how would they know Demipos is dead?" Drakon asked. "Apart from me, you're the only one who knows."

Ares bowed his head in mock submission. "Don't unsheathe your dagger yet. I happened to catch them searching the ruins that used to be Demipos's temple. She thinks I killed him. I won't tell her it was you."

Ares strode out of the pergola and stood staring at the ocean, the light of the rising suns reflected in his bronze armor. "Unless, of course, something happens to make me change my mind. . . ." He turned and peered at Drakon. "I mean, you don't need to wear that armband, do you?"

Drakon poured himself some ale and drank it down in one mouthful before putting the cup back on the table. "You don't have to worry about me, Ares. I'm not foolish enough to let her see me wearing her band." Drakon rubbed the band. "But give a man the chance to savor his victory."

Ares laughed as Drakon joined him on the beach. "I understand wanting to celebrate victories, but take care that arrogance isn't your downfall. Anyway, let's get down to business. It concerned me to see Sascha with Athena. I thought you would have Sascha under your control by now."

"My plans to capture Sascha are under way. Her support for Athena won't mean much when she's out of the way, will it?"

Ares tutted. "Plans are under way. . . . So you still have no control over her then? You'd better move a bit faster if you want your plans to succeed. You might be able to work out how to open the site where the weapons are hidden. But you don't have a way of unlocking the secret chamber, inside the site, where the weapons are stored. And you don't have a way to control them once you have them. You'll need Sascha's magic to do that. Unless . . ."

"Unless what?" Drakon asked.

"Unless I haven't been as honest with you as I perhaps should've been."

"Meaning?" Drakon snapped.

"Meaning I might know where you can find a clue so that you can at least unlock the secret chamber inside the site. Then when you *finally* capture Sascha, you will only need her help to control the weapons."

"You've always told me I needed Sascha to both unlock the secret chamber and control the weapons," Drakon said. "What's changed?"

"Now that you have your souvenir from your battle with Demipos I know you can unlock the secret chamber yourself." Ares coughed. "Hades knows I support you. He visited me the other day and told me that he can get the weapons faster than you can. And I have since found out that he has allied himself with Laela. I'm sure the idea of being beaten by Laela—and Hades—is as disturbing for you as it is for me. I'm proposing we join forces, which means whatever knowledge I have, I share with you."

Drakon's chest tightened.

So why is Hades bothering Ares about the weapons? Unless Ares is interested in them. But why would—

"I have a question, Ares. Why does Hades need Laela to get the weapons? Why can't he do it himself?"

"Ah, clever question, Drakon. One day I may share the answer with you, but for now you'll need to trust me."

"Like I did with Demipos, you mean?"

"It's not my dream to control those weapons, Drakon. It's yours. I'm here to help you, not the other way around."

He's lying. I'm sure of it.

Drakon ran his fingers through his hair. "So where can I find this clue?"

"Good to see you're being sensible about this. There was a book, a chronicle written by a consul back in the days of High King Atticus. This chronicle documents everything about the weapons, including how to unlock the secret chamber."

"If it documents everything about the weapons, then wouldn't it also say how to control them?"

Ares coughed again. "Well . . . those pages seem to have disappeared, but we have been given a cryptic message that says they can be controlled, once the way is revealed, by the powers hidden in magic's shadow. I have it on good authority that Sascha is the only one who will know what that means."

"Magic doesn't cast a shadow," Drakon said.

"Everything casts a shadow," Ares snarled. "And while I haven't got all the answers at least I know more than you do. And I'm offering my help. You can take it or leave it. Your choice."

"So where will I find the chronicle?"

"In the Four Sisters headquarters. It's locked away in the same room as the register of mages. I know you know where that is." Ares drew his sword from its scabbard and drew a design in the sand, a V symbol with a line underneath it. "One final thing, and this is important. After you have opened the chamber you will find a lot of crates." He used the sword to draw a circle around the design. "The crates with this design are the ones you need. Make sure you open one or two and double-check the contents. There are crates you don't want to take out of the cave—crates that contain items that have been cursed."

"Cursed?" Drakon spat. "What fool believes in curses?"

Ares' voice chilled. "Are you calling me a fool, Drakon? You may not believe in curses, but I suggest you do as I say. So you will remember this design?"

Drakon nodded.

Ares wiped the symbol away with his foot. "I must go now, so I'll leave the matter with you. Just remember you don't want Laela to beat you. If she obtains the power of the weapons, you'll be one of the first people she destroys with it." He put his sword back into its scabbard.

"Hades may be lying to you," Drakon said. "Is Laela really alive? No one has seen her since the healing ceremony."

"Oh, she's alive all right. Of that you can be certain. And she's a lot more powerful now than she was before she disappeared."

A loud clap of thunder forced Drakon to cover his ears. When he lowered his hands, Ares was gone.

DRAKON STRODE out of Ocean's Mouth cave and veered right toward the castle training grounds.

I need to see Chiane.

Chiane was leaning against the wall of the stables, feeding straw to one of the stallions as he talked to several of his men. He stopped talking the moment he noticed Drakon heading in his direction. He signaled to the men that he had to leave and walked over to join Drakon at the foot of the stairs that led up to the ramparts.

"My Prince," Chiane said. "You need me?"

"Yes. Ares has been to visit me. I need that armband, and soon."

"I'll speak to Archmage Pealack and tell him to speed it up."

"Good. Have you heard from Novo?"

"Yes," Chiane said. "He hasn't been able to open the site yet. He said the mages have not been able to interpret what the clues mean. Novo also mentioned he has one last idea he'd like to try. But he's concerned that the magic protecting the site is too strong now the Shield has been healed."

"Perhaps, but after my discussion with Ares, I'm wondering whether it's possible there are mages working for Novo that are being influenced by Laela. Maybe they're sabotaging Novo's attempts to open the site."

"Novo was particular about engaging mages that didn't belong to the Four Sisters," Chiane said. "He's paranoid that Laela may be looking for revenge for Reya's death. But it's worth following up. I'll send word to Novo immediately. I'll get him to see what he can find out."

"Make sure he keeps the investigation under wraps. I don't want Laela finding out what we're up to."

"She's definitely alive then?" Chiane asked.

"Yes. According to Ares, she's very much alive."

"I wonder where she's hiding out."

"I have no idea. You have apostates working for you at your camp in the mountains, don't you, Chiane?"

"Yes, I do."

"Are there any you trust, truly trust?"

"Yes, there are a few."

"Organize for them to join us when we leave for Earth. Given Novo's lack of success, you should start preparing for the trip to Earth immediately. We'll meet at the second portal before the second sun sets today."

"Yes, My Prince."

"And if this idea of Novo's doesn't work, tell him to travel to the site on Earth and join your men. Let's use all our efforts there."

"Yes, My Prince." Chiane brought his clenched fist to his chest in salute, turned on his heel, and strode away.

Drakon walked up the stairs to the ramparts and across the bridge to his chambers.

If the book had been hidden at the Four Sisters headquarters for all this time, Laela must have known about it. Which meant Reya had known about it as well. So how much did they know about how to access the weapons? Based on what Ares had said, Drakon was sure they didn't already have the weapons. And there had been no reports of them visiting either the Brun or Earth sites. He still had time, but he needed to make a move. And fast. First things first, he needed to keep Owain off his case. It was time to visit Connell.

Hang on a minute. If Laela is alive, is she still seeing Owain? Surely not, but if she is . . .

DRAKON KNOCKED on the door as he entered Connell's chambers. George and Rusty were absent, and the room was quiet. The peppermint scent of the ocean blew in through the open balcony doors, but it was mixed with the stronger mint smell of selecine and various herbal medicines that were ground on the table not far from where he was standing.

If he's being given selecine perhaps he's still in pain from the attack. But he never has been particularly brave.

It took Connell a couple of attempts to push himself up before he finally succeeded.

Drakon shook his head and rolled his eyes as he stared at the creature lying in the bed. This wasn't his adopted brother. It was a husk, a weak pathetic husk.

"You look awful, Connell. Or are you just trying to pull the sympathy vote?"

"Just trying to pull the sympathy vote, of course," Connell

answered. "Father asked me if you had visited. I told him you wouldn't."

Drakon smirked. "I wasn't going to, because I knew you would prefer me to stay away, but you know what Father is like. Sometimes it's better to let him win so he leaves you alone for a while."

Connell leaned across to pick up a glass of water and then took a sip. "Speaking of Father, he seems distant these days. As if there's something bothering him. And he keeps talking about dying."

Drakon found it hard to look at Connell, so he walked over to the healing table, picked up some herbs, and sniffed them. "Whose death are we talking about? Yours or his?"

"His," Connell snapped.

"I'd be worrying about my own health if I were you," Drakon said. "Father's got a lot of life left in him."

This is the perfect time to set the fire dragon among the hurlies.

"Anyway, Father has someone to look after him, keep him . . . healthy and happy." Drakon glanced at Connell from under lowered lids.

Connell's eyes opened wide with surprise. "Company? What do you mean? Who?"

"Laela. You knew about him and Laela, didn't you?"

"Laela? *Owain* and Laela? No, you've got it wrong, Drakon. You're just being spiteful, as usual. There's nothing between them. We would've noticed something."

"Are you surprised your spies let you down? I'm not. I don't think much of your spies. Or perhaps there's a reason they didn't tell you?"

"You shouldn't listen to gossip, Drakon. I expected more of you."

"I saw the two of them together, Connell. I know I'm right. If you don't believe me, ask Father about her. Tell him I told you. Anyway, I'd better go." Drakon ambled toward the door. As he reached for the handle, he turned back to face Connell. "Perhaps that's what's wrong with him. Having been in bed for so long, you might not realize that Laela has disappeared. Perhaps he's missing her."

Connell said nothing, but continued to stare at him. Drakon waved goodbye as he walked out of the room. He smiled to himself as he closed Connell's door behind him.

Now, let's see Owain explain himself out of this one. And I'll get to find out if the two of them are still together. What I wouldn't give to get my hands on Laela.

STAKEOUT

* EARTH

*E*mpty coffee cups and paper McDonalds bags littered the floor of Marco's car. He stretched and yawned. Spending all night cramped up in a sports car had taken its toll. He had thought Pat would do something more exciting than just hiding out in the motor inn all night. It felt like the stakeout had been a waste of time, but he still had a strong sense Pat would lead him to Eham and Jenny.

His stomach churned from the greasy burgers, and his eyes were heavy. It would be so easy to curl up and go to sleep. He was sure he'd be feeling better if he had eaten something from his coffee shop instead of takeout. Perhaps he needed to suggest to Mike they stay open later than eight o'clock at night.

It was time to get out of the car and wake himself up. The inn's receptionist had arrived earlier, so he decided to have a chat with her while he was stretching his legs. Maybe she could provide him with some useful information. He climbed out of his car and wandered into reception to speak to her.

"Excuse me. I know it's early, but I've got some friends who I'm expecting to come here, and I was wondering if they were here already. Eham and Jenny Morley. Are you able to tell me if they've arrived?"

"I can tell you if they're here, but I can't give you their room number." She pointed at the mobile in his shirt pocket. "Couldn't you call them?"

"I forgot to charge it before I left," Marco lied. "The battery is flat."

She looked at the computer screen and scanned down the list of names. "No, sorry, no one here by that name."

"That's okay. They might not have arrived yet."

I didn't think they would've booked a room under their own names, but it was worth a shot. I don't have anything else.

He clambered back into his car and checked his phone. Despite having sent several texts to the last number he had for Jenny, there had been no replies. He dialed his coffee shop, hoping Mike was an early starter. He breathed a sigh of relief when Mike answered the phone. "Hi, Mike. You work long days."

"I learned my work habits from you, Marco."

Marco laughed. "Just wondering, you said Pat gets takeout in the mornings. Does she come in at the same time?"

"She comes here for a double-shot latte after her morning jog."

"She jogs? She doesn't look like a runner."

"Well, she comes dressed in running gear, has a cap and a water bottle, and she talks about following the run along the creek."

"What time does she come in?"

"Usually around seven thirty—about an hour from now."

"Thanks, Mike." Marco ended the call.

It looks like I might have to go for a run, damn it.

He leaned over to the passenger's seat and picked up his jacket and sneakers. Despite smashing his elbow into the car door and knocking his leg against the gear stick, he managed to change into his running gear, ready for when Pat emerged. The next forty-five minutes dragged. At twenty-five past seven, Marco was beginning to worry that Pat had somehow given him the slip but then he saw her as she emerged from the inn. She was dressed in running gear, and she had a cap and a water bottle in her hand. But instead of heading toward the creek to go for a run, she crossed the road as if she was heading directly to the coffee shop.

Marco put on his cap and was about to climb out of his car when his passenger door opened and a body threw itself into his front seat with a thump.

Marco jumped and twisted around to see who it was. "Eham, what are you doing here?"

"I would've thought that was obvious considering you've been spying on Jenny and me all night. We thought you'd give up." He scrunched his nose. "Your car stinks."

"You saw me out here and you didn't come over?"

"We hoped you'd go away. But as it is, you're still here. Jenny told me I had to come and talk to you."

Marco positioned himself in his seat so that he didn't have to twist his neck around to talk to Eham. Even though it was early in the morning, Eham's gray hair and beard were neatly trimmed, and he was dressed in perfectly tailored pants and a shirt. "We expected you to return to Eratus, Eham. What happened?"

"Jenny is worried. She thinks we're safer here on Earth than on Eratus. I'm not sure I agree, but whoever was chasing her seems to have disappeared."

"Does she know who it was that was after her?"

"She says she doesn't, but I'm not convinced."

"I'm not sure she is safer here." Marco nodded in the direction of where Pat had just disappeared. "Have you seen a short, squat woman hanging around here?"

"That could describe a lot of women in this place, Marco. It wouldn't hurt for you to be a bit more specific than 'a short, squat woman.' "

"That woman who ran out in front of my car when we visited Sascha's. Sascha called her Pat."

"You mean the one you nearly ran over?"

Marco rolled his eyes. "Yes, her."

"I haven't noticed. Why are you asking about her?"

"I think Drakon sent Pat to follow Jenny, and I followed Pat here. I don't think it's a coincidence that you happen to be here too, so perhaps you need to reconsider."

"Well, you can talk to Jenny. See if you can convince her."

"What room are you in?"

Eham pointed at the first blue door on the left at the front of the inn. "The first room on the left facing this direction. A white Rolls is parked out the front."

"A white Rolls Royce? Not exactly acting inconspicuous then."

Eham snorted. "Says you, parked in front of a motor inn in a blue MG."

"I decided to blend in with the other flashy cars parked along the street."

Eham snorted again. "Sure. It's as good a lie as any."

"I'm glad I've found you both and you're safe," Marco said. "But before I talk to Jenny, let me see if I can work out if Pat is after you. I'd hate to have you chasing shadows. I won't be long."

"I'll tell Jenny to expect you." Eham opened the door and pulled himself out of the car with a grunt. "I really wish you'd get yourself a normal car."

Marco watched Eham amble back to the inn. Once he

was out of sight Marco climbed out of his car and walked toward the coffee shop.

Hopefully she's still there.

He retrieved his phone from his pocket and texted Mike.

On my way. Hoping Pat is still there.

Mike's response was instant.

Yes, she is, and she's with a woman I haven't seen before. They're sitting near the water fountain, not far from where you sat yesterday.

Marco arrived in the coffee shop, pulled his cap down lower on his forehead, and walked over to the same table he had sat at the day before. The woman with Pat had her back to Marco, so he couldn't see who it was. Her hair was pulled back into a short ponytail. Marco signaled the waiter and asked for coffee and toast. He plugged his earphones into his phone to make it look as if he was listening to music and inserted them loosely into his ears.

"She's healing well," the woman with the ponytail said.

"I hope someone makes him pay for what he did to her," Pat replied.

There was a chuckle, then the woman with the ponytail spoke again. "When she's well again, he'll definitely pay."

"And Miss Perfect should pay the price too," Pat said. "She'll regret ever getting her mem—"

"Shut up, you fool," the woman with the ponytail snapped. "You should know not to . . ."

The voices stopped and Marco glanced over to see what was going on. Both women were looking directly at him. He could see now who the ponytail belonged to.

"Well, well, well," Laela said. "Look who's here. It's Marco."

"Marco?" Pat asked. "But he's—"

Laela twisted back to Pat. "I told you to shut up."

Marco pushed himself up from the table. "Laela, I wouldn't have recognized you. You look so . . . different."

Laela stood and walked over to the counter to pay her account. "Say hello to Sascha for me. Give her my best, won't you? And do tell her to watch her back. She isn't exactly the most popular girl in town."

Laela turned and left the coffee shop with Pat skittering after her. Marco watched them turn left, away from the inn.

Sascha was right. Laela had been in hiding all this time. Was it possible that the woman of which they had spoken of, the one that was healing well, was Reya? He shook his head. No, she was dead.

Connell did say he saw her standing in the doorway. But he is still unwell. His mind must be playing tricks on him. The woman is dead!

Marco's stomach knotted.

It isn't possible. It can't be.

~

* EARTH

Marco strode past the white Rolls to the blue door. He knocked and waited. Hushed voices sounded from inside. There was a soft thud as if a door was being closed and moments later the blue door swung open.

Eham ushered Marco into the unit, his gaze bouncing up and down the street. "Jenny," he called out when he had closed the door. "Marco is here."

The room was clean and tidy and was filled with the scent of vanilla. Someone had been baking. There was a large timber dining table in the middle of the room, one end covered in books, pens, and pencils. Marco wandered over to the table and pulled out a chair. Before he had a chance to sit, the door to an adjoining room opened and Jenny walked in, her shoulder-length dark curly hair bouncing around her shoulders. She closed the door behind her, nodded in Marco's direction, and perched on the edge of a lounge chair facing him. She lifted her head to look at Marco. "So you're here to convince me to return to Eratus?"

Marco rubbed his forehead.

I hope I'm doing the right thing in telling her about Laela.

"To be honest, I'm not sure now." He glanced over at Eham. "Did Eham tell you about Pat?"

She nodded.

"I know Pat is linked to Drakon," Marco continued. "After we found Pat's . . . partner . . . dead, I found clues that made me think she was after you." He nodded in the direction of the coffee shop. "But I've just come from my coffee shop where I saw Pat talking to Laela. Now I'm not sure if Drakon is after you, or how Laela fits into all of this. Things could have changed."

"Laela?" The color drained out of Jenny's face as she stared at Marco. "Where—did you say your coffee shop?"

"Yes." He dropped into the chair he had pulled out earlier and sat facing Jenny. She fiddled with the edge of her teal-colored shirt and kept glancing nervously at the door to the other room. "Jenny, has Laela done something to you? I thought you were scared of Drakon but is it Laela you're afraid of?"

"I'm not afraid of her."

"You're as white as a ghost."

The door to the adjoining room opened a fraction. "Mummy," a child's voice whispered.

Jenny leaped from the lounge chair and raced toward the door. "I'll be back in a minute."

Marco's stomach dropped.

Was that a child?

Eham sat down opposite Marco. "There's something you need to know."

"Jenny has a—a child?" Marco stammered.

"Yes, a son," Eham replied. "And Laela is after the child."

"Why?"

"It's complicated, but it has something to do with who his father is."

"Who is his father?"

"Jenny will tell you when she's ready. But if Laela is here with Pat and you think Pat was following us, then Jenny and the child are in great danger if they stay here. We are safer on Eratus. At least there we have you and Connell to help us."

"How old is the child?" Marco asked.

"Nearly four years old."

"She had the child before she started working with Sascha?" Marco asked.

"Yes, she did," Eham replied.

"So why didn't she mention it to Sascha?"

"Jenny senses . . . things. She trusted the Sascha she worked for, but she sensed that a time would come when Sascha would return to Eratus. She was afraid of what Sascha would do to her child when she regained her memory."

Sascha's dream . . . At least she doesn't have the Blades of Light. There's still time to work out what is going on.

Marco found it hard to breathe as his chest tightened. "Do you have any water?"

Eham pointed to a jug and four glasses. "What's that in the middle of the table? Scotch mist?"

"Ah, thanks," Marco said as he poured himself a glass.

Eham studied Marco. "You think Sascha is a danger to Vonn too, don't you?"

"Vonn? Is that his name?"

Eham nodded.

"I know Sascha," Marco said. "She wouldn't hurt an innocent. But she had a dream and it terrified her. We all thought it was just a dream. We didn't really believe Jenny had a child."

Jenny came back into the room, leaving the door open this time.

Marco put his glass on the table. "Jenny, I need to know. Why are you afraid of Sascha?"

Jenny glanced at Eham and took a deep breath.

"Sascha and I need to talk."

"Mummy, I—"

The child stood in the doorway, his head tilted to the side, a smile upon his face. He had olive skin, dark hair, and sparkling, bright blue eyes.

"He's a beautiful child, Jenny," Marco said.

"Marco, we need your help. I'm scared to return to Eratus, but now that I know Laela is here, I'm terrified to stay. I think we will be safer on Eratus, but I need to keep my child a secret. I cannot let Sascha know, not until we've had a chance to talk. Please."

"What is it you're afraid of? Why do you think Sascha would harm him?"

"I can't tell you . . . yet. All I can do is beg you to keep him a secret. For Sascha's sake, as well as Vonn's."

"Does Laela know about Vonn?"

"Yes, she does. Connell, as well. It was Connell's idea for me to bring him here, to Earth, to keep him safe."

Vonn moved toward Jenny and wrapped his arms around her leg. Jenny rested her hand on his head. "But things have changed if Laela is here." Jenny shook her head. "I have to go. Vonn needs his breakfast." She glanced at Eham. "Please talk to Marco. Convince him to keep this a secret from Sascha; give us time to make this right."

She freed her leg from Vonn's grip and started toward the adjoining room. Before closing the door, she held it open for a second to allow a black weasel-like creature with red beady eyes to move through. Eham clicked his fingers and the creature raced toward him and twisted around his legs in much the same way a cat twists around the legs of its owner.

Marco stared at Eham. "You're bonded to a dread wisp?"

"Yes, unusual I know. But he's an excellent spy and understands any other creature's language, including ours. He came to me the day Jenny had her child. I didn't know about Vonn at the time, but the creature did. He's very protective of him."

"Does it worry you that Vonn is protected by a dread wisp, a creature of dark magic?"

"No. Each creature has a right to exist . . . until it proves otherwise. Are you going to honor Jenny's request? Are you going to keep her secret?"

"I'll give Jenny a chance to talk to Sascha. But there will come a time when Sascha will have to know."

"That's all Jenny is asking for. Time to talk to Sascha."

Marco nodded. "Okay. Do you want me to wait and go through the portal with you?"

"No. We will leave sometime tonight, when we feel it's safe. We'd prefer to travel on our own."

"It's not going to be easy keeping a child hidden when you're living in the castle," Marco said.

Eham nodded. "We know."

Marco stood and dug into a back pocket in his jeans. He pulled out the golden key, which he handed to Eham. "This might help. This will open a door to a secret room next to my chambers in the tavern. When you arrive, go straight to my chambers. There is a golden statue of a pyran with red eyes. Move it to the right and an opening will appear. Use the key I have given you to open the door."

Eham stared at the key in his hand. "Thank you, Marco."

"You will definitely return to Eratus, won't you, Eham?"

"Yes, we're tired of running. We need to make a stand sometime. I guess that time is now."

THE DRAGON HUNTERS

ERATUS

*C*onnell glared at the healer. "My spies have given me a way to help Father. I will do this with or without you. I would prefer to have your help, but it's your choice."

"My Prince, it's my responsibility to keep you alive."

"Your responsibility is to listen to me, to obey my orders."

The healer huffed. "Do you think I'm being difficult for my own amusement? If you go walking about, you will spread the venom, you will die."

"Which is why I need a carrier, Ciara, and the potion. I'll take George and one of my mages with me as well."

The healer paced around the room. "The potion will protect you from the venom for a short time only. Remember that my life is forfeit should the venom win the battle and you die."

"That is an ancient custom. Father will not follow it, not after everything you've done to help me. But I promise to behave, to stay in the carrier."

The healer nodded his head and sighed. "I guess I have no choice. I'll help you."

Connell grinned. "Thank you, Healer." He breathed a sigh of relief. "On a different note, how's it going with Rusty?"

"Rusty is a nightmare. She's always zipping around the laboratory, chasing things I can't see, crashing into everything. She never seems to run out of energy. I don't know if taking her on was such a good idea."

"It was hard for her to be cooped up in here with me all day."

"I know. I must admit she's amusing when we work outside in the garden. She loves it out there."

There was a knock on the door and Ciara strode into the room. Seconds later, George raced in and threw herself onto the floor next to Connell with a loud thud, panting as she smiled up at him. She was followed by Rusty, who stood in the center of the room, her head turning from side to side, her body vibrating with excitement, her long tongue lolling out of the side of her mouth. "You two look like you've been having fun," Connell said.

"Ciara," the healer said, "Connell has a job for you."

Ciara crossed her arms across her chest as she tilted her head to the side and studied Connell. "A job? What is it?"

"First," the healer said, "we need you to retrieve a carrier from the healing rooms, and then you will be going with him."

"Going where?" Ciara asked.

"To see my father," Connell said.

Five minutes later, Connell and the healer were watching the cone-shaped transporter in the corner of Connell's room as they waited for Ciara to return with the carrier.

"If it pleases you, My Prince," the healer said, "I've organized for my sister to join you instead of one of your mages. We can trust Raeshaan. I hope you'll understand. After all, my life is on the line as well as yours."

"Raeshaan is a master in air magic, isn't she?" Connell asked.

"Yes, she is."

"That's excellent then. She should find it easy to hide us under a cloaking spell."

A soft whir sounded in the corner of the room as the transporter came to life. Ciara stepped into Connell's room, guiding the carrier in front of her. Though the inside of it was lined with thick cushions, the terracotta-colored carrier looked like a large dragon egg. Ciara guided the carrier to a stand next to Connell's bed and locked it into the baseplate so that it didn't wobble. The healer and Ciara stood on either side of Connell and helped him climb out of bed and position himself inside the carrier.

"I brought a rug as well," Ciara said as she placed it across his lap. "We can't afford for you to get a chill."

"Come on, Rusty," the healer said, leaning down and grabbing Rusty by the collar. "Let's leave them to their adventure." The healer opened the door to find a tall, slim woman with long, curly, ebony-colored hair standing there, fist raised, ready to knock.

"Perfect timing, Raeshaan," the healer said. He turned back to Connell. "I've given Ciara another vial of the potion. If you start to struggle, take that vial and come straight back here. It'll be enough to get you through the trip but it won't last long. It would be dangerous to give you two full doses of the potion."

"If I need it, I'll take it."

Ciara guided the carrier to the transporter. George leaped to her feet and followed, Raeshaan not far behind her. As they stood in front of the cone, Connell twisted around to Raeshaan. "Did the healer tell you I need you to set up a cloaking shield around us?"

"Yes, he did."

"Would you set it up now, before we leave? I'm not sure if we'll have time once we arrive in the hall."

"Hall? What hall?" Ciara asked.

"It's a meeting place on the top of Kalurth's Peak. My spies found out that a group of dragon hunters meet there regularly. And it seems Father is on his way there as well. I'm hoping for some answers. Are we ready then?"

They nodded.

"Good." He took a breath, leaned forward, and touched the metal cone.

~

ERATUS: KALURTH'S PEAK

The stone hall was bitterly cold. Several burning torches set along the front of the hall provided enough lighting for people to see around them, but the flames emitted no warmth. An icy breeze blew in through the gaps around the barred windows and carried a stale, musty odor from the bodies covered in skins and furs that were seated on long wooden chairs. The chairs faced a stage area at the front of the hall, and on the side of the stage was a set of stairs that led down to a second transporter cone.

"I'm pleased we arrived through the cone at the back of the hall," Ciara whispered. "I'm not sure how we would have gone if we had arrived at the one in the front."

"I agree," Connell said. "But we'd better move away from it in case others arrive behind us. We don't want to be discovered."

Ciara grabbed Raeshaan's arm. "The cloaking spell is in place, isn't it? These people look like they'd skin us alive if they found us."

"Yes," Raeshaan said. "They can't see us. We're safe. Freezing, but safe."

Connell shivered. Raeshaan was right. It was freezing, and he was grateful for the rug Ciara had given him.

Raucous laughter reverberated around the room as the crowd sat waiting.

The cone at the front of the hall hummed, and the room fell silent as Owain, dressed in a long, thick woolen cloak, stepped into the hall and up onto the stage. He cleared his throat.

"Thank you for coming today. I thought it was time we got together and discussed what to do now that Laela is no longer a part of this group."

"We're glad she's gone," a short man in the back row screamed out. "She was evil. She should never have been a part of this group. Mages don't belong here."

There was a roar of approval. Owain took a step toward the front of the stage. "Mages are not our enemy. Dragons are, but after—"

"Of course you'd protect the mages," the man yelled back. "Your children are mages. You're trying to save them. You don't care about Eratus."

There was another roar of approval.

Standing at the back of the hall was a giant of a man who now pushed himself away from the wall. "King Owain, I think you should know that we met as a group outside of this meeting you organized for today. Following the events over recent weeks, we have agreed to broaden our attack. It is more than the dragons; it's all magic. Magic is the enemy and all those who wield it."

"Hear, hear," the crowd answered.

"And what was it that healed the Shield?" Owain asked. "Dragons and magic. You know how I feel about dragons. But dragons helped to save us. If you look out the windows of this hall you will see the site where the dragons and magic healed the Shield that protects our planet. If I can stand up here now and defend them, you must know that the reasons I have for doing so are good ones. We need to talk about this."

"The time for talk has gone," the giant said.

"Don't be a fool," Owain replied.

The giant drew his sword. "Are you calling me a fool?" He moved toward the stage, swinging his sword to and fro in front of him. "Perhaps the dragons have used blood magic to take over your mind. Which means we need to purge you, free you from the evil."

A low rumble vibrated in George's chest.

"Quiet, George," Connell whispered.

A man in the front row leaped to his feet. "We're not here to murder our King. How does that help our cause?"

"Sit down, Chambers," Owain said. "Don't put yourself at risk for me."

As the giant walked toward Owain, he nodded to a figure standing in the shadows at the side of the hall. The figure moved swiftly toward Chambers. Seconds later, Chambers was on the ground gurgling and twitching on the floor, his throat sliced open.

"No!" Owain called out.

The giant turned to the people. "Is there anyone else here who wishes to add something?" There was silence.

The giant walked up the stairs and held the tip of his sword at Owain's throat, giving the sword a little flick so that it nicked his throat and blood dribbled down and onto the collar of Owain's cloak. The giant studied the blood as if he was intrigued by the fact it was there. "King Owain, is there a reason I should let you live?"

"We must help him," Raeshaan whispered.

A soft growl echoed in George's chest as her tail swished in the air.

"Quiet, everyone. Wait. This is Father. But perhaps you

should prepare to use a storm spell, Raeshaan. Just to be on the safe side. Don't use it until I give the order."

Raeshaan nodded.

"If you have already met to discuss this, I'm sure you have a plan," Owain said.

The giant laughed as he glanced at the crowd. "Yes, we do. Your life and the lives of your children will be spared in return for your help. You will help us implement Laela's plan, help us retrieve the weapons."

"The weapons," Owain spat. "You don't even know how to use them. How do you think you can use these weapons to destroy magic?"

"If Laela wanted to use the weapons to destroy the dragons, they must destroy magic."

"You've no idea what it is you're playing with," Owain said, moving his feet apart to better balance himself. In the blink of an eye, Owain had clenched his fists and with his elbow bent, he lifted his left arm up and outward in a tight arc, catching the giant's arm and redirecting it safely off to the side. Taking advantage of the opportunity, he whipped out his dagger with his right hand and thrust it into the giant just below the rib cage. The giant collapsed, his sword dropping uselessly to the floor.

"Now!" Owain called out. Soldiers smashed their way into the hall. Within minutes, the people in the crowd were being dragged off for questioning.

The giant pressed his hand to his wound in an effort to stop the bleeding as he turned to face Owain.

"You'll pay for this, King. You'll pay for this betrayal. Laela did a good job in teaching us how to infiltrate even the most protected buildings, so we have spies everywhere. We'll get our revenge."

Owain stood on the edge of the platform and watched as

two soldiers chained the giant and dragged him out of the hall.

"Lower the cloak, Raeshaan. Let Father see us," Connell said.

"See us?" Ciara gulped. "He'll know we spied on him, on what happened here."

"I know. Lower it. Now."

Owain didn't notice them until Connell called out to him. "Hello, Father."

Owain's mouth dropped open. "Connell, what in Athena's name are you doing here?"

"I knew something was troubling you. You refused to tell me what it was, but now I know."

Owain scrubbed his face as he let out a huge breath. "Sweet souls and angels. We need to talk. I'll meet you in your chambers."

Connell gasped. He felt as if he was being stabbed in the chest with a knife. He massaged his chest to try and ease the acid burn, but instead the pain exploded and burned through his body. He was only dimly aware of the voices around him as he slumped forward into the darkness.

LEAVING FOR EARTH

ERATUS

*D*rakon strode into his chambers and called out to the guard. "Guard, send for my aide."

"Right away, My Prince."

A few minutes later, soft footsteps announced the arrival of Drakon's aide-de-camp.

"There is something I need to do," Drakon said. "It won't take me long, but when I return, I expect you to have a pyran loaded with everything I need for a visit to the site on Earth."

"Are you sure you don't want to fly Kalamar? It's supposed to be easier flying fire dragons than pyrans."

"Kalamar isn't a beast of burden. Pyrans do that work."

The aide nodded. "Is there anything in particular you need?"

"The usual supplies for site visits. Also, make sure Chiane has organized supplies for the camp and readied the group so we can take off the moment I return. And I'll need food for Kalamar. I'll be taking him with me." Drakon pursed his lips. "One more thing. Talk to the healer who is caring for Isabella. Isabella must be well when we return from Earth. There is something she needs to do for me."

"Yes, My Prince."

When the aide had left, Drakon changed into his black leathers and left his chambers using the door that led down to the dungeon. Fifteen minutes later, he had bypassed the group of workmen outside the Four Sisters headquarters and arrived at the underground entrance to the building. He sent himself into shadow. "So, Ares, let's see if what you said about the chronicle is correct," he whispered.

The place was quiet, but he stayed in shadow as he crossed the tiled floor of the reception area and headed for the stairs at the back of the building. He climbed the stairs and opened the panel that permitted him entrance into the room where the register of mages was hidden.

Now to find the chronicle.

He walked past the countless library shelves to the far back corner of the room. The register of mages still rested on the podium. He suddenly realized he had no idea what the chronicle looked like. But if they had hidden it, then perhaps

. . .

"There's a secret here I know, element of air, the secret show."

A glow appeared over a panel in the wall. He pressed it and the panel opened to reveal a small alcove. There was nothing inside.

He repeated the chant and another panel farther along the wall lit up. Again, he checked the alcove, and again, there was nothing.

He decided to try once more. The result was the same.

Why would the spell keep showing empty compartments? He walked back to the first alcove.

There's something I'm missing.

He ran his hand along the inside of the opening. He would have missed it if his fingers had been moving any faster. There was a long thin line, perhaps a crack, at the back. He pressed it. A soft click sounded beside the podium on which the register stood.

He went to the next alcove. There at the back was another thin line. He pressed it and was rewarded with another click.

He went to the third alcove, found the long thin line, and pressed it. A soft churning sound echoed from the podium holding the register, and a few seconds later, the podium had moved aside to reveal a glass-covered section of floor. He walked over to it and looked inside. The chronicle was resting on a bed of black fabric. He lifted the glass lid and took out the book.

Drakon ran his fingers over the chronicle's ornate golden cover. The delicately carved trim along the borders of the book was stained by a dark reddish-brown mark. It looked like blood, but whose blood had been spilled on this book? He rested the chronicle on top of the register of mages as he searched the text for any mention of the weapons. The book was well indexed and a lot easier to navigate than he had expected. He turned to the page he wanted, the clue to unlocking the secret chamber where the weapons were stored. There was a five-pointed star with various designs engraved into it. Underneath the design were instructions on how to use the star to open the chamber.

"Powers of Earth let it be, a sketching of this page for me to see."

Soon he was holding a copy of the star and the instructions. He decided to see if Ares had lied and the clue to controlling the weapons was also included in the book. It was then he realized that three pages had been expertly sliced out of the book—the pages with the information on how to control the weapons.

So who would have taken the pages?

Sounds came from the staircase. He had to go. He closed the book and placed it back in the box in the floor. As he was trying to work out how to close it, the panel in the floor slid over the opening and the podium slid back into place.

"That was handy," he whispered.

He slipped into shadow and hurried back down the stairs and outside. Excitement welled up inside him. Everything was becoming so much more real now.

As he arrived outside, the sound of a wolf howling reverberated around the forest. He glanced around him.

And Chiane's soldier thought that sound was an akhult. The man was a fool.

∼

ERATUS: THE CASTLE GROUNDS

Drakon changed into his golden chain armor, repositioned his bollock dagger, and arrived in the courtyard with Kalamar following him. He looked around at the group gathered there and grinned as a warmth spread through his body.

We're going to do this. We're actually going to do this.

"Chiane, report," Drakon called out.

"Yes, My Prince. I have heard from Novo. They had no luck in opening the site in Brun so they have left to join my men at the site on Earth."

"Novo has the coordinates for the Earth site?"

"Yes, My Prince."

"We'll succeed this time," Drakon said. "I feel it in my bones."

"Also," Chiane continued, "Pat reported in. It looks like Jenny and Eham are on their way back to Eratus. Pat is following them. She'll send a message as soon as they've gone through the portal. One of my men will deliver the message to us at the Earth site."

"Excellent," Drakon said. "Let's be on our way."

"Mount," Chiane called out.

Each of the men clambered up onto the back of his pyran.

"Check your transportation chips," he called out. The group raised their right hand and tapped it. Chiane glanced around as each person confirmed their chip was working.

Drakon closed the belts on his harness and tapped his hand. His transportation chip flashed. It was still working.

"Fly," Drakon yelled as he raised his right arm and waved it forward. The pyrans hunkered down, stretched their wings, and then leaped up into the air.

He glanced back at the castle grounds. Excitement flooded through him.

Enjoy life as you know it, little people. Your lives will never be the same after we return.

MISSING

ERATUS

*S*ascha opened the door to her chambers. As she walked to her bed she recognized Marco's writing on a note by the bed.

Hello, My Love.

I'll be back in a day or two. It seems Eham and Jenny have had a few difficulties. I've gone to help.

Love, Marco.

She looked at the date on the note. It had been written yesterday. Which meant he might even be back tonight . . . and with Eham and Jenny. She rubbed her stomach to ease the building tension.

It'll be all right. Even though I have the blades, Jenny would have to have a child. And there's no way she could have hidden a child for all the time she worked with us.

She placed the golden bundle containing the blades on the cupboard near Soleil's nest. She would have to work out what she was going to do with them.

And just because I have the weapons, I don't have to use them . . . unless . . .

She shook her head.

No, I don't murder children.

After a shower, she changed into a fitting black shirt, black pants, boots, and a teal-colored jacket. There was a sudden whoosh of air as Soleil crashed into the room and, breathing heavily, positioned himself on the exposed beams above Sascha's bed.

"You've returned," Soleil said.

"Yes. And I'm safe and sound, as you can see."

Soleil clicked his beak. "I guess you don't need me when you're with Athena?"

"I'll always need you, Soleil. You should know that. How is Fenix?"

Soleil leaped down to the floor and strutted over to Sascha. "Damn female is irritating to say the least. There's something eating away at her, but she won't tell me what it is. Please, Sascha, have a word with her."

"I will."

"Are you going to tell me what happened with Athena?" Soleil asked.

"Would you do me a favor and fly me to Ocean's Mouth? I wouldn't mind some time on the beach to collect my thoughts before I see Marco. I'll tell you on the way there."

Five minutes later, they landed on the beach at Ocean's Mouth. Sascha looked out at the pale green waves crashing against the shoreline. The colors in the sky were changing. Hints of purple, dark green, and tan showed the season of the three moons was nearing.

Sascha dropped onto the edge of a stone platform near the crashing waves. Soleil came up to her and rested his head on her hands as they sat in her lap. He felt warm and reassuring. Love for Soleil flooded through her as she freed one hand so she could stroke his warm feathers.

"Are you going to tell Marco about the blades?"

"Yes. We promised not to keep secrets from each other.

Speaking of secrets, why don't you bring Fenix here now? Why don't we see if she'll talk to me here?"

"Are you sure you're not too tired?"

"Not at all. Go and get her."

He leaped into the air. "We'll be back in a minute."

Sascha smiled to herself. Whatever it was that was bothering Fenix, she was sure they could work it out.

She caught a movement out of the corner of her eye. A shadow had arrived on the beach and it was limping toward her.

"Excuse me, Sascha," the voice said. "Marco sent me."

The voice sounded male. She raised her hands above her eyes to try and block out the light of the suns, see who the shadow was, but the angle of the sunlight made it impossible to see clearly.

"You know my name? Who are you?"

Sascha watched the shadow limp closer. A chill ran through her, and goose bumps dotted her skin.

Don't be silly, Sascha. There's nothing to fear. He's wounded.

"I work for the Fire of the Phoenix. I was with Marco on Earth. He told me to tell you that he found Pat. He was in a fight and he's been wounded."

"Is he okay?"

"He's going to have to stay in the hospital for a couple of days."

"The hospital at the headquarters?"

"Yes."

"Thank you. As soon as Soleil returns we'll leave for Earth."

"We need to go now," the figure said.

"Soleil won't be long," Sascha said as she stepped away from the figure. "I'll wait for Soleil."

A whirring sound started up behind her. She turned to

look. It was a portal. She turned back to the figure, but it had disappeared.

"Where have you gone?" she yelled.

Run, Sascha. Run, you fool.

"Look out, Sascha!" Soleil's voice screamed out at her.

Somebody crashed into her shoulder, sending her flying into the portal. She had time to see the face of the figure before the portal closed.

Laela! It was Laela.

TIME IS RUNNING OUT

ERATUS

*M*arco raced up the stairs, two at a time, and at the top of the stairs he turned left toward Connell's chambers.

Time to take Connell outside for some fresh air and to find out exactly what it is he knows about Eham and Jenny.

"Marco," a voice whispered.

"Healer, is that you?" Marco glanced up and down the corridor, searching for where the voice was coming from.

"I'm here. In the room with the door ajar."

Marco saw a figure step out of the doorway of the room next to Connell's. "Ah, there you are. What are you doing there?"

"We need to talk, Marco."

Marco walked over to join him. "What's going on?"

"It's Connell. Something has happened to him."

Marco's stomach churned as he studied the healer. "Don't be cryptic, man. Tell me, what's happened?"

"Ciara will fill you in on what happened in the hall, but when Connell returned . . . he's in a bad way. He keeps screaming out, remembering memories that aren't his. I did some reading after he was attacked by the pit hound. I hoped this wouldn't happen but it has."

"Healer, I said, stop being cryptic. What hall was he in and what the hell is going on?"

The healer took a deep breath. "Sorry, I'm rather stressed about this because it was I who let Connell go."

Marco gave a frustrated sigh and scrubbed his scalp with his fingertips. "Healer, slow down. Tell me what is wrong with Connell."

"The short version is that Connell was worried about Owain, so he sent his spies to follow him. They found out Owain was a member of the group that was trying to destroy the dragons."

"No, that's not possible," Marco said. "Owain wouldn't try to destroy them."

"That's what Connell thought, too. The spies said there was a meeting planned for the dragon hunters in a hall on Kalurth's Peak. He decided to go there."

"But isn't he supposed to be staying in bed?"

The healer wrung his hands. "Yes, but Connell was sure he could do it and I had to let him go."

"What happened?" Marco asked.

"The spies were right. Owain was a part of the group, but I believe the purpose of the meeting was to shut the group down. Ciara went with Connell, so she can tell you more."

"Or I could talk to Owain," Marco said.

"Yes." The healer nodded. "That would be a good idea."

"And what's this about him remembering memories that aren't his?"

"I did some research when I was trying to work out what I could give Connell to help him heal. He's been taking longer to recover than I expected."

"And . . . ," Marco snapped.

"The texts say that if a patient isn't improving as fast as is expected, it could be because there's still a link between the patient and the attacker—the one who created the pit hound that attacked them. One of the signs of this link is when they . . . remember . . . memories that aren't their own but are in fact their attacker's memories."

"But it was Reya who created the pit hound and she is dead," Marco said.

"Is she? Where's the body?"

"It . . . it disappeared."

The healer wrapped his arms tightly around his waist. "So she could still be alive. Which means she could be using the link to heal herself."

Marco shook his head. He felt light-headed. "It's impossible. Novo gutted her. She couldn't be alive. There must be some other explanation."

"There isn't another explanation. She is alive, and she's tapped into Connell's lifeblood to heal herself. I would bet my own life that's what's happening. Soon Reya will be healthy and Connell will be dead . . . well, worse than dead."

"How could she even do that, tap into his lifeblood?"

"I don't know for certain," the healer said, "but the only way you can save him is to break the connection before it's too late."

"How can I break the connection? I don't even know where she is. And even if I did and I tried to kill her, she would simply use more of Connell's lifeblood to heal herself."

"You must find a way to kill her and I would suggest you don't give her time to use the link. Destroy her body if you have to. If, as I suspect, their connection is growing stronger each day, Connell will soon cease to exist. His body may still live for a while longer, but the person you know as Connell won't."

"Can I see him?"

"He's unconscious, and Owain is sitting by his bed. Owain

has asked not to be disturbed. He is wracked with guilt over all of this. He thinks that if Connell hadn't followed him, he wouldn't be in the state he's in. I told him that's not true, but he won't listen."

"So I have to find Reya, kill her, and destroy her body."

"Yes, and soon."

"Marco, Marco!" Soleil screamed.

"Now what," Marco mumbled.

Soleil screeched into the room, nearly crashing into the healer.

"Soleil, calm down. What is it?" Marco said.

"It's Sascha. She disappeared through a portal. I don't know where she went, but she's gone. We have to find her."

Marco couldn't speak. He looked at the healer and Soleil. They were talking to him, but he couldn't hear what they were saying. He closed his eyes.

Focus, Marco. You're stronger than this.

"Sorry, Soleil, what did you say?"

Soleil gave a high-pitched shriek, forcing the healer and Marco to cover their ears.

"Stop that, Soleil," Marco yelled.

"You need to listen to me, Marco. I went to get Fenix and as we arrived back on the beach, we saw a figure push Sascha through a portal. I went racing after her to try and catch her, but the portal closed and disappeared. If we don't save her before the season of the three moons—"

"She could be stuck where—wherever she is," Marco stammered.

"If she's still alive," the healer said.

Soleil clicked his beak at the healer.

"Soleil, did you see who the figure was?" Marco asked. "Who created the portal?"

"It was so quick. I saw a figure, a shadow, but when the

portal disappeared, so did the shadow. We must find her, Marco. Save her."

"We will, Soleil. We will. But give me a minute. I need to think it through, work out what to do." He paced the floor as his mind worked through several possibilities. He stopped and turned to the healer. "Before we do anything else, Healer, find the most talented mages we have. Reya must be using magic to keep this link between her and Connell alive. We must find a way to track it, find the source of the magic. And also send one of the mages to meet me on the beach at Ocean's Mouth. A lot of magic is required to make a portal. I'm hoping we can track that too."

"But they won't be able to get through the cave to the beach," the healer said. "The magical barrier in front of the cave will stop them."

"I will sort that out. I will also talk to my Lieutenant Colonel—Zabir—and get him to help with a search. My men are already visiting each of the Kingdoms as they check on the progress of preparations for the storm season."

"Yes, right away," the healer said, racing out of the room.

Marco moved toward the stairs. "Soleil, show me where the portal was."

Athena protect Connell and Sascha, for I'm at a loss as to what to do if my idea doesn't work. And time is running out for the both of them.

PRISON

ERATUS

*S*ascha climbed to her feet and rubbed her knees. Apart from a few grazes she had survived the fall through the portal. A distant howling of wolves penetrated the walls.

Where am I?

She glanced around the room, searching for anything familiar. Her stomach dropped as she realized she'd landed in what looked to be a prison.

Pushing down the terror that threatened to overwhelm her, Sascha wiped the dirt off her stinging hands. Some of the few memories that had returned were from the time she had been kidnapped on the orders of her real father. That time was clear. Her father's grin as he watched his minions torture her had burned itself into her memory. Reya had told her he was dead. But he wasn't. He was alive, she was sure of it. And when she found him, he would pay for what he had done.

But this time it's different. This time you can defend yourself.

"Laela," she muttered, "I knew you were up to something. I bet you didn't expect Soleil to be there though."

But he doesn't know where the portal took you.

Sascha pushed the thought aside. Between Marco and Soleil, they would find her.

"Athena, please let Marco be okay."

It was a ruse. That was all it was. Marco will be fine.

Sascha wasn't sure if she was just trying to convince herself or if she really believed it, but there was nothing she could do for Marco while she was locked in here.

A door of thick metal bars sealed the only exit from her terracotta prison. A cool breeze drifted through a narrow window set high in the wall, carrying with it a faint wisp of sulfur. She rubbed her arms as she exhaled slowly. Everything here reminded her of Brun, but it was surely too cool for what was usually a hot and fiery land.

And if I was in Brun, they would have me strung up in chains. There would be priests chanting, promising to cleanse me, as they did to all those who practiced healing magic.

As a child, her father had forced her to watch the mages being driven off the edge of a cliff into a sulfur pit filled with the sort of creatures that liked to play with their food before they eventually devoured it. She still remembered the screams of those her father had called not worthy.

She walked to the door and looked out. Reddish-brown brick walls edged a pathway leading to a winding staircase. She could see half a dozen creatures in the corner of the room feasting on some sort of carcass. She twisted her head and squinted at the creatures, as she tried to work out what they were, but the darkness hid their shape. The one thing she could determine was that they were large. At least she was relatively safe on this side of the door. But seeing the creatures there put a stop to the idea of screaming for help. She had no interest in alerting them to her presence.

Sascha turned back to look at the room. A steel-framed bed with a lumpy, ripped mattress covered with various dark-colored stains sat next to a stone ledge on which a mug and a jug of water had been placed. The room was as silent as a tomb.

I only hope it won't be mine.

She went over to examine the bed with the vague idea of breaking it down and using part of it to dig a way out, but it was one solid piece of metal. There were no bolts, nothing she could pull off and use. She rolled her eyes as she glanced at the water jug.

Naturally the jug is made of plastic, not something useful like glass.

Sascha gave an exaggerated sigh. "There must be a way to free myself. All I need to do is find it." She felt a moment of regret that she hadn't brought the Blades of Light with her.

Sascha clicked her fingers as an idea came to her. If she had been able to sense a crack in a stone when she was healing Soleil, perhaps she could sense how to escape here. She sat cross-legged on the floor and closed her eyes. Sascha slowed her breathing and stilled her thoughts. For the first time, she noticed the slurping and cracking sounds as the beasts feasted on the carcass. She pushed the noise aside and instead focused on the wavering howls of the wolves. They were free, outside, where she wanted to be. She tried to visualize the prison. But nothing would come to her. All she could sense was darkness. Maybe the area was protected by magic.

Damn it.

Sascha opened her eyes as she tried to work out another way to escape. If the walls were protected, her options were limited. But there had to be a way. A rustling sound drew her attention to the mattress on the bed. It pulsated as if it were alive. She stood and walked over to look at it. Through the split on the top of the mattress she could see a mass of white maggots consuming something that seemed to still be alive. She shuddered.

"Gross!"

Thank Athena she hadn't sat on it. She stepped back, focused on her fingers, and created a small ball of fire which she threw at the bed. The mattress burst into flame, and the high-pitched screeches of the creatures that had been living in it reverberated around the prison.

What was in there?

The mattress was reduced to ash in a matter of moments, but the screeching noise continued.

"Where is that sound coming from?"

The sound was coming from outside her cell.

She walked over to the solid metal bars. It was then she realized her mistake.

The creatures feasting on the carcass were huens. They had all turned at the sound of the exploding mattress and moved forward, tilting their heads to the side as they tried to work out what was going on. She could see them properly now, and their full focus was on her.

"Huens," Sascha gasped. "Of all the things . . ." She took a step back from the door. At least they couldn't get her while she was in the cell.

One of the huens separated from the flock, the pitch of its call changing as it trotted toward her. The huen walked up and down the front of the door as it studied its next feast— Sascha. It let out another high-pitched screech, turned, and disappeared.

"What the—"

The next instant it appeared in the cell. She hadn't known that they possessed any type of magic.

The huen screeched again.

Sascha, her full attention on the creature, sensed the

change. The other huens were on their way to join their mate inside the cell.

Athena's voice echoed inside her head. "Don't look at it."

She knew her eyes would be the creature's first target, but she had to watch it. She had to know what the creature was doing so she could protect herself.

She noticed a shimmer around the huen. It was protected by a shield.

How strong is their magic?

Her first job was to destroy the shield that protected the huen. Only then could she kill it. She raised her hands and pictured fire. The mark on her hand warmed as fire came to life and flowed between the palms of her hands. She manipulated the fire, forming it into a ball.

The huen raised its wings, jumped in the air, and flew at speed toward her, its beak aiming for her face. Using all her strength, she threw the fireball at the creature and smashed it against the wall. Still alive, it staggered to its feet. Purple liquid oozed from its wounds. Now she had to finish it. Sascha raised her hands, but her fingers were stiff, as if she had somehow lost all ability to manipulate fire.

Concentrate! You need to create another, larger ball of fire.

She pushed aside the fear and concentrated on what she had been taught over her years in training as a fire mage. She felt the fire flow between her hands and, moving as fast as she could, created another fireball and threw it. It picked the creature up and smashed it against the wall again. This time it lay still. She took a huge breath and released it.

The air was shattered with the frustrated shrieks of the other huens as they sensed the death of one of their own. It would only be a matter of time before they, too, were in the cell.

Sascha felt ill. "I'm not going to die this way."

She pictured Soleil and Marco standing with her. "I have

to survive this for them. This next fireball is going to have to be the mother of all fireballs."

Sascha blocked out the sounds of the other huens and imagined herself back in Zeus's cave, sitting next to the bubbling creek. She pushed all other thoughts aside as she focused on building the fireball. The mark on her hand started to burn but she ignored the pain and focused on the fire.

The first fireball must do more than destroy their shields.

"Athena, help me, make it powerful enough to slow them down and give me time to renew my magic."

The silence in the cell was deafening.

She glanced around. The huens had disappeared. The battle would begin soon. She continued to build the fireball, ready for when they appeared. Adrenaline rushed through her as she stood and waited. Every sound was magnified. Her heart pounded, but her mind was clear. She knew what she had to do.

"Bibacr help?" a voice said as the huens materialized in front of her.

Sascha's heart skipped a beat. "Bibacr?" she cried out, not taking her eyes off the creatures for even a second. "Yes! Bibacr help Sascha."

A wave of soft blue air hummed as it shimmered over the creatures, dissolving their protective shields.

"Sascha use magic now," Bibacr said.

Sascha released the fireball and threw it at the creatures.

Their screams reverberated off the walls as the fire consumed them. A few managed to struggle toward her, but she destroyed them with a weaker fire spell. Soon, finally, there was silence. The stench of roasted fat hung in the air.

Sascha wanted to race over to Bibacr, pick him up, and hug him, but all her strength had disappeared. She shook her hand to ease the pain from her mark as she dropped onto the edge of the metal bed frame. She rested her head in her hands. The bitter taste of charcoal and roasted fat filled her mouth. In an effort to ease the building nausea, she swallowed.

"Sascha safe now," Bibacr said.

Sascha looked up at him. "You saved my life, Bibacr."

"Bibacr happy Sascha safe." He bounced up and down on one foot, then the other. "But Sascha never tell Soleil."

Sascha attempted a smirk. "Bibacr afraid of Soleil?"

"Bibacr not afraid," he said, sticking his chest out. "Bibacr want to be friends with Soleil. Soleil want to save Sascha. Soleil not like Bibacr helping Sascha."

"If Soleil knew you saved my life, he'd be happy. But honestly, Bibacr, at this moment I'll do whatever you ask. You saved me. But how did you find me?"

"Bibacr said he would follow Sascha. Bibacr jump into the portal."

Sascha glanced around her. "Do you know where we are?"

"Bibacr not know but Bibacr find out." He walked toward the door. "Sascha wait for Bibacr."

Sascha laughed. "Really, Bibacr? I'm in a cell. I don't think I'm going anywhere anytime soon."

He shuffled his feet as he focused on the ground. "Bibacr happy he found Sascha safe."

"Bibacr, I'll never forget what you did for me today."

He uttered a strange squeak as he pushed his way through the bars. "Bibacr return soon."

Sascha found the strength to stand and walk over to the door. She watched as Bibacr disappeared up the stairs. She glanced at the gap in the bars where Bibacr had squeezed through.

There isn't much of a gap here. How in Athena's name did he manage to climb through?

It was then she saw the black metal tracks.

Wait. Does this door slide open?

She squatted and ran her fingers over the floor. "It does slide open."

She studied the walls beyond the cell, but she couldn't see a button or a control panel.

There must be some way to open them. I'll get Bibacr to investigate when he returns.

Sascha stood and walked back to the bed. She saw the imprint in the dust from where she had sat moments before. She took her jacket off and used it to fan away what was left of the burned mattress, then wiped the back of her pants before sitting back down on the edge of the metal bed frame.

"Thank you, Bibacr," she whispered.

But his timing was . . . convenient. And if he jumped through the portal at the same time I fell through why did he take so long to let me know he was here?

Sascha shook her head.

That creature saved my life. Again. It's time I started trusting him.

~

ERATUS

Bibacr hadn't returned so Sascha sat on the ground in the corner of the room and waited. When the darkness descended it was impossible to see anything, so she pushed herself farther into the corner, covered herself with her jacket, and allowed herself to grab an hour or two of sleep. As the first rays of sunlight shone in through the narrow window, a heavy thump sounded from the top of the staircase. Footsteps stomped their way down. Before she could get a glimpse of who was coming, the footsteps stopped, turned, and raced away. A short while later, the footsteps returned, along with others.

She stood, flexed her wrists, and turned to face her visitors.

Sascha clenched her jaw. "Laela, it's you. I was wondering how long it would be before you showed yourself."

Laela stood next to two guards armed with staffs and protected by magical shields. One of them had white hair, the other was a redhead. Laela wore a neat, tailored burgundy tunic designed to show off her trim figure. Her polished ebony hair was styled to hide the mark on her face, the only indicator of her rank and race. She was carrying a tray laden with hot savory meats, fresh bread, and water. She stood at the bars and glanced over at the pile of burned flesh, her eyebrows raised.

"My dear, I'm so glad to see you're alive. My guards didn't expect you to survive the huens, but I knew you wouldn't be an easy kill. It seems fortune is on my side after all. I've brought you some food to celebrate."

Laela nodded at Whitehair. He walked over to a point on the wall twenty feet from the door and pressed his right palm to the wall's surface. The door glided open.

There's a control panel. But it seems to require a palm print. Bugger.

"Tell me, did I make you worry by telling you Marco was wounded?"

Sascha rested her hand on her stomach to ease the fluttering sensation. "I realized it was a ploy, Laela."

Laela giggled. "Yes, but it certainly distracted you and allowed me time to set up the portal. But you're right. It was a ploy. He's okay. At least, he was the last time I saw him."

Sascha's stomach clenched. "Where did you see Marco?"

"On Earth. I believe he was probably after Jenny and Eham."

Relief flooded through Sascha.

At least he's not in a prison cell, too.

Laela tutted. "Silly boy. There's more to those two than he can possibly imagine." She began to walk toward Sascha but stopped halfway into the cell. "But I sense you already know that."

"What are you talking about, Laela?"

Laela nodded at Redhead, who walked over to the stone ledge, picked up the water jug, and took it away.

"You don't want that old stuff," Laela said, "so I've brought you some fresh water. And lucky I did." She nodded in the direction of the dead huens. "Fighting monsters can be such thirsty work."

Laela walked over and placed the food and water on the stone ledge. She peeked at the ash on the floor. "You destroyed the mattress. Good idea. You never know what's been sleeping on it. I don't have anything else I can give you to take its place. But you won't be here too long, so I guess it's not a problem."

"How long do you plan on keeping me here?" Sascha asked.

Laela smirked. "Only until my plans are in place."

"What plans?"

"You'll find out soon enough. The true reason for my visit is to let you know where we are in case you are thinking of escaping. We're in Brun, and above us is the temple of the Fire Gods, which, as you know, is where people like you would start their journey to the sulfur pits."

"Why Brun?" Sascha said. "You're in as much danger here as I am."

"Oh, I'm not in danger. The High Priest is a good friend of mine. The two of us share certain . . . beliefs, and it seems he has some score to settle with you. I don't know what you did to him, but he hates you. All I would need to do is hint you're down here and you're as good as dead."

"What are you planning to do with me, Laela, if it's not to hand me over to the fanatics?"

Laela laughed. "Time will reveal all. You only need to be patient a little while longer."

She nodded at the food on the tray. "I've ordered my guards to stay for ten minutes. Whatever you haven't eaten by then will be taken away. It might be the last time you get to eat for a while, so I'd be making the most of this opportunity if I was you."

She picked up the jug of water. "But I'm taking the water with me. So, first . . ." Laela poured two glasses of water and handed one to Sascha. "Have a drink."

Black lyrium. Didn't Connell say the black lyrium was in the water he was given?

"I don't think so," Sascha said. "It's probably poisoned."

Laela laughed. "You seriously think I would poison you? No. You're worth more to me alive and healthy. You're safe . . . for now. But once he accepts you as my gift . . ." She shrugged her shoulders. "Whatever he chooses to do with you is up to him."

Sascha's blood turned to ice. "Who is he?"

"That would be telling. Now, drink. Oh, of course, you think it's poisoned. I'll drink mine first so you know the water is safe."

Laela gulped down the glass of water in a few mouthfuls. "There's nothing like the fresh water from the Silverkeep springs. Go on, drink. Bodies can survive without food for a long time, but not water. Anyway, seriously, what have you got to lose?"

Sascha studied the water and then drank it down. Laela wouldn't drink black lyrium. She needed her magic as much as Sascha needed hers.

"Good. Now, I have to rush." She flicked her fingers at Whitehair. "Ten minutes. Take anything she doesn't eat."

Sascha stared at the dead huens as Laela made her way toward the stairs. With Laela gone, it was only her and the guards. This was her opportunity to make her move, to escape.

But how?

Ten minutes later, as the guards were walking out with the untouched tray of food, Sascha spotted her opportunity.

ARRIVING ON EARTH

* EARTH

*D*rakon pressed his right heel into the side of his pyran as he guided it to a patch of grass in the middle of an ice-covered field in the Forgotten Land on Earth. He unfastened the harness and slid down to the wet grass. As he rubbed his gloved hands briskly together to warm them, Chiane clumped through the snow toward him.

"The men say the camp is on the other side of that copse of trees, only a short walk from here."

"Can't we fly there?" Drakon asked.

"The trackers say the route is safer to travel on foot than by air," Chiane replied. "The last group who tried to fly there didn't make it."

"What happened to them?" Drakon asked.

"The trackers said they disappeared halfway across. No one saw what happened."

"I'll change my boots and then we'll go." Drakon leaned against the pyran as he took off his shoes and pulled on long boots with thick soles. He retrieved his long black woolen coat from a bag that hung across the pyran's shoulders.

"Major," Chiane called out, "your group is responsible for

protecting Prince Drakon. Captain, your group will protect the rear. We don't want to be caught in a surprise attack, so we all need to stay on the alert."

"Yes, sir," they replied in unison.

"I thought the danger was flying over the trees, not walking through them," Drakon said.

"One can never be too careful, My Prince."

"Kalamar," Drakon called, "stay close."

Kalamar answered with a soft chatter as he soared into the air and circled the group.

Drakon and Chiane marched into the woodlands, the major and his group following closely. Progress soon slowed when the cover of fresh snow deepened. As Drakon trudged through the snow he couldn't help but think of Sascha.

Sascha should be here. We should be discovering the weapons together. She belongs to me, not Marco.

"Halt," Chiane called out.

"What is it?" Drakon snapped.

"It's those dark patches twenty feet ahead, My Prince. Everywhere is covered by fresh snow except there. They look like . . . scorch marks."

"Well, send one of your men to investigate but move along. We'll freeze if we stay in this weather for too long."

"Major, you heard the Prince."

"Yes, sir," the major replied.

The woodlands had fallen quiet, the only sounds those of the men shuffling to keep warm and the flapping of Kalamar's wings as he flew overhead. Drakon watched the two men as they made their way toward the area Chiane had pointed to. When they reached the spot, they squatted to examine the marks. They exchanged some words that Drakon couldn't hear and then stood. "Sir, there's nothing here."

"Return to your positions then," Chiane barked.

They started to make their way back, but stopped. "What's—"

Their guttural screams pulsated through the forest, triggering several flocks of squawking birds to leap skyward.

"We have to help them," Chiane said, pulling his sword from its sheath.

Drakon reached out and grabbed Chiane's arm. "Don't be a fool, Chiane." He swallowed hard as he stared at what was left of the two men. "They're dead now anyway."

Kalamar, flying overhead, dived toward the dead men and blasted the area with fire. Loud screeches vibrated through the woodlands as a pair of creatures burst into flame, their flesh melting from their frames. Their dark glistening carcasses dropped onto the snow.

"What is that stench?" one of the mages complained. The rest of the group stood in silence as they stared at the bloody, burned mass on the ground and the glistening black bones.

"The dark shadows have gone," Chiane said.

"Pit hounds," Drakon muttered. "Where the hell did they come from?" Drakon turned to Chiane. "Was this a trap? Were those trackers sending us on foot in the hope that the pit hounds would finish us off?"

"I'll send a couple of our soldiers back to find out," Chiane said. "It certainly seems like it."

Drakon shook his head as he pulled out his sword. "If this was a trap . . ." He turned to the men. "Arm yourselves. Keep an eye out for any more of those scorch marks."

The journey became even slower, each of them treading more carefully and examining the ground ahead of them for any signs of the hounds. Finally, they saw a wispy trail of smoke in the distance.

"We're nearly there," Chiane called out.

The pace picked up when the aroma of roasted meat told them they weren't far away from their camp.

Drakon pushed past the edge of the woodlands and stepped out into a clearing on which tents of all shapes, sizes, and colors had been arranged. Fires had been lit in the middle of the campsite, and the air was filled with the aroma of frying meat and crushed berries.

"There's no one here," Chiane whispered.

The group muttered quiet prayers to Athena as they moved closer to the fire.

Chiane took a step back as he stared at the campsite. "Where could they have all gone? There were over a hundred men in my camp alone and then there were Novo's men. Novo and his group would have arrived here by now. They left Eratus before we did."

"Come with me, Chiane," Drakon said, walking toward the closest tent. They walked through the campsite, flicking open the tent flaps as they searched for any signs of life. As they stepped out of the kitchen tent, Chiane stopped for a moment and glanced back at the stove and the benches covered with plates and bowls. "It looks like they had begun to prepare breakfast, but left partway through preparations."

Drakon nodded. "Something is not right here."

They came to the last tent, the largest one on the site. Chunks of charcoal were still glowing in the fire, and pieces of fresh fruit sat on a table next to a water jug and a half-filled glass of water. But no one was there. Drakon and Chiane sheathed their swords.

"Where do you think they could have gone?" Chiane asked.

Several texts and handwritten notes lay on the table. Drakon walked over and picked up one of the notes as heavy metal boots ground to a stop outside the tent.

"My Prince," a voice called out. "May we have a word with you?"

Drakon stared at the closed tent flap. "Do you recognize the voice, Chiane?"

"It sounds familiar, but I don't know who it is."

Drakon raised his eyebrows at Chiane and waited a moment before twisting on his heel and flicking the tent flap aside. He left the tent, Chiane close behind him, and came face-to-face with three soldiers standing in a line.

"And you are?" Drakon asked.

One of the soldiers glanced at his companions and took a step forward. He brought his fist to his chest in salute. "My Prince, we're glad to see you. I'm Captain Lewin. These are Corporals Jabit and Togun." He glanced nervously around the campsite. "We were attacked this morning. We fear we're the only ones who survived."

"Attacked by who?"

"It wasn't a person." He looked back at the two corporals. "They were creatures. We awoke this morning to find the ground covered with what looked like burn marks."

"Burn marks?" Chiane asked.

"Yes, sir."

"And did you see what it was that attacked the camp?" Drakon asked.

"The creatures were invisible, My Prince. We weren't equipped to fight them. It was a massacre."

"Pit hounds?" Drakon gripped the hilt of his sword as he stared at the men. "This camp is in good order. It doesn't look like there's been a massacre here. Tell me, how did you three manage to survive?"

"We were sent to gather berries for breakfast."

Drakon's voice chilled. "A captain and two corporals were sent to gather berries?"

"We didn't agree either, but we were ordered to. We heard the screams and saw the creatures attack the last few men when we returned. We were too late."

Drakon glanced around the campsite as his hand dropped to the hilt of his dagger. "And yet there are no bodies here."

"The corporals and I have just returned from burying the remains of all the victims. That's why we weren't here when you arrived."

Drakon withdrew his bollock dagger and tapped the bottom of the pommel three times. The pommel extended as the blade glowed and changed to the color of ice.

"A staff," Corporal Togun whispered. "The dagger is a staff. But that's not—"

"Tell me . . . men, if you've just carried all those bodies—how many men did you say were here, Lieutenant General Chiane?"

"Well over a hundred, My Prince."

"Well over a hundred," Drakon repeated as he studied the captain. "If you carried well over a hundred bodies and buried them, how come you're not covered in blood from head to toe. And how come there are no pit hound bones? Or did you bury them too?"

"We . . ." The captain stepped back and glanced at the other two men, who took several steps back and drew their swords. "You're right," the captain sneered. "That isn't what happened. But do you even care to know the truth? You knew there was an evil that lived at this site, an evil that goes back centuries, yet you warned none of us. All you care about are the weapons. The blame for everything that has happened here lies with you." He drew his sword. "In the name of the Ancients, we offer our bodies as a sacrifice."

Drakon raised his staff and sliced it through the air toward the ground. Brilliant white jagged flashes of lightning shot up from the ground and three lifeless bodies crumpled before him.

Drakon lowered his staff. "What the hell is going on here, Chiane? Assemble your mages. I want a defensive shield around this campsite as soon as the mages have purged the area. And where is this site that everyone has supposedly been working on? I want answers. And now!"

"Yes, My Prince," Chiane said.

Drakon turned back to the tent. "And Chiane, find Novo and the other men. They must be around here somewhere. Even if they're not alive, their bodies must be here." He swiveled around and pointed his staff at the three dead men. "There's no way those fools buried all the bodies."

Drakon flipped open the tent flap. "Kalamar, in here with me."

The fire dragon flew through the flap and landed neatly on the floor in the center of the tent.

"And Chiane, I want you to pair up the mages with the soldiers. Make sure there are four pairs on duty at all times, facing all four points of the compass."

"Yes, My Prince."

The echo of a wolf's howl shuddered through the camp.

"Let's move, everyone," Chiane barked. "Now. We don't have much time."

WAITING FOR NEWS

ERATUS

*M*arco examined the beach sands of Ocean's Mouth as Soleil flew ahead. "I haven't found any clues here of who the figure was. Let's hope Raeshaan can sense something."

He heard the soft whistle sound of footsteps on dry beach sand behind him and turned to see Raeshaan stepping out of the cave leading to the beach at Ocean's Mouth.

"You're waiting for me?" Raeshaan said.

"Yes, did the healer tell you what has happened?"

She nodded. "Yes, I'll see what I can find. You'd think there would be some magic left behind. It takes a considerable amount of magic to make a portal." She glanced around the beach. "Where did Soleil say he saw it?"

Marco pointed to the stone ledge. "Over there, not far from the ledge. Did the healer talk to you about sending someone to trace the source of the magic draining Connell's health?"

"He did. It's a dark magic I haven't come across before. I've spoken to the grandmaster who trained me, asked him if he would see if he can trace the source. That's what he's doing now. I'll meet with him after I've finished here."

"I don't believe it's a coincidence that Sascha has been taken now," Marco said. "Right when Connell has taken a turn for the worse."

"Neither do I, and neither does the grandmaster. We believe there's a connection." Raeshaan walked over to the ledge. She held out her hands, in which rested a lead crystal ball, and closed her eyes. She murmured a prayer and then opened her eyes and stared into the ball.

A mournful whistle, long and low, filled the air.

"Soleil, we will find her," Marco called out. "Come down here. You need some rest."

Soleil continued to fly low across the beach, all the while studying Raeshaan.

Marco walked to the pergola and sat, then stood and walked down to the water. He put his hands in his pockets, closed his eyes, then returned to the pergola. He wanted to give Raeshaan time. He needed to give her time. But she remained silent, her gaze never moving from the crystal ball.

I can't stand this waiting.

He walked back to the ledge. "Raeshaan, are there any signs of magic? Have you found anything?"

Raeshaan sighed and shook her head. "Not much, I'm afraid. There's a very faint trace of magic that I may be able to use to follow her. It would have been easy to miss if we hadn't known exactly where to look. Whoever created the portal was highly skilled. But it's a bit hard to do this with you watching my every move."

"Do you think you'll be able to find her?"

"I need time to answer that question. Go back to the castle. As soon as the grandmaster and I have finished, we will find you and tell you what we have found." She glanced up at Soleil. "And take Soleil with you. He's stressing out and disturbing my focus."

"Pyrans are bonded to their masters in ways beyond our ken," Marco said. "I can't even imagine how he's feeling. But I'll have a word with him. Please find her, Raeshaan. We can't lose her again."

"I know," Raeshaan said. "And the sooner you both leave, the better. I promise to come and find you when the grand-master and I have finished."

"Soleil," Marco called. "We have to leave Raeshaan to complete her search in peace. Let's go and see Owain while we're waiting."

I have no idea what I'll do if he refuses to leave. Only Sascha seems to be able to control him.

Soleil swooped once more across the beach and then changed direction and flew toward the castle.

"Thank you, Soleil," Marco whispered.

Marco left Raeshaan and made his way back to the castle. When Soleil had told him of Sascha's disappearance, a heaviness had settled in his chest and limbs. Every movement seemed so difficult. It would be easy to give into the dark cloud of despair that was following him around, but he had to keep a clear mind. He needed to find her. To think of her trapped somewhere for the season of the three moons was too hard to bear. And when he found her, he would never let her out of his sight. Ever again.

Marco had no idea how he made it to the castle. He couldn't remember walking up the stairs to Owain's chambers, walking out onto the balcony, and pouring himself a mug of silkar. But he must have. The only thing he did remember was ordering the guards to summon Drakon. They were going to have to work together if they wanted to save Connell and rescue Sascha. He pulled a chair closer to where Soleil was sitting quietly, his head hanging low. Unshed tears stung Marco's eyes.

Pull yourself together, man. You can't greet Owain crying like a baby.

He needed to focus on something other than Soleil. He stared over at the several large circular mats that covered the stone. Each of the mats was embroidered with the kingdom's crest—a winged manticore sitting underneath a canopy of gray fangs.

"Poor George. I bet she's struggling to deal with Connell's illness."

"She is," Soleil said. "But she won't leave him. I understand that. If Sascha was ill, I wouldn't leave her. But then again I left her when she needed me most."

"What are you talking about, Soleil?"

"Sascha wanted to help Fenix. She was already tired from her trip to Earth. I should have said no, but instead I left to find Fenix."

"If Sascha couldn't save herself, you couldn't have saved her either. The only difference is that you'd both have disappeared and we would have no clues, no way of knowing where to start looking. Raeshaan will come through. Wait and see."

"I can't lose her again, Marco."

"I know. Neither can I. But don't give up. It will all work out. You'll see."

"If Fenix had just told us what was wrong," Soleil said, "this might not have happened."

"That's not fair, Soleil. The only one at fault here is the one who took Sascha. You didn't tell Fenix this was her fault, did you?"

"I haven't seen her since Sascha disappeared."

Slow, heavy steps climbed the stairs. Owain was here, and by the sound of it, he was in a bad way, too. Owain walked out onto the balcony and poured himself a silkar. "What has Raeshaan found?"

"She said there was only a faint trace of magic on the beach, but she and the grandmaster believe there must be a link between the two incidents. They don't believe it's a coincidence that Sascha has gone missing at the same time Connell has taken a turn for the worse."

"I agree." Owain drank the mug of silkar in a couple of mouthfuls. "Did the healer tell you what Connell was doing when this attack happened?"

"He told me what he could. But I haven't spoken to Ciara or Raeshaan about the specific details. Is what the healer said true? Are you connected to the dragon hunters?"

"Yes, I am. Or rather, I was."

"But why? Why would you want the dragons killed?"

"It's a long story."

"I need a distraction," Marco said. "Waiting for Raeshaan and the grandmaster to find something is killing me."

Owain sighed. "Did Kira tell you about the enchantress who the dragons sent to the sulfur pits?"

"Yes. She was being punished for trying to kill the dragons. The dragons hoped it would deter other mages from becoming dragon hunters."

"What if I told you they didn't send only one enchantress there? That they sent others."

"But there's no record of that," Marco said.

"Well, they did, and one of the women they sent was an old woman, my grandmother. They sent her and the other women to the sulfur pits to die horrendous deaths and struck their names from all records, including the register of mages."

"How did you find out?" Marco asked.

"Laela found the records when she was hunting for the

chronicle that documents the history of the ancient weapons."

"So Laela told you this story?"

"No, Laela gave me the documents. I read them. Grandma disappeared when I was young. I was devastated. She was a beautiful woman, the only one who showed me any compassion when I was a child. I loved her as if she were my own mother. When I found out what happened and how many had been sent to the pits, I knew I had to do something about it. The dragons have too much power. No one reigns them in, tells them enough is enough. And when we learned about the weapons, we realized we could change things."

"Owain, did you know the dragons believe it was dragon hunters who killed Sascha's mother? And perhaps Kira's mother, too?"

Owain slumped forward and rested his head in his hands. "Marco, there's a lot more to this story. There's too much to tell in one sitting."

"So you do know."

Owain shoved his chair back and jumped to his feet. "That's enough, Marco. Do you hear me? You need to focus on saving Connell and finding Sascha. Leave the dragon hunters to me. Do you hear me? Leave them to me."

"Sire, Sire," a voice called out from the stairs that led to Owain's chambers.

"What is it?" Owain growled.

A guard entered the room and brought his clenched fist to his chest in salute. "Sire, the dragon hunters . . . they've . . ."

"Out with it, man," Owain said.

"They've escaped, Sire. The soldiers guarding them have been killed, and there's no sign of the dragon hunters anywhere. But they left a note." The guard strode over and handed a folded sheet of paper to Owain.

Owain opened it and read it. The color drained from his

face as he dropped into his chair. "Sweet souls and angels." Owain handed the note over to Marco. "Read this."

Marco glanced at Owain before he looked down at the note and read it.

We have a new leader, someone we can trust. We no longer need your help to locate the weapons. Our leader has a copy of the map you and Laela protected so carefully. He will help us finally retrieve the weapons. And then we will release them. That will mean the end of magic on Eratus. You may live through this Owain, High King of Eratus, but none of your family will. The war has just begun, and the weapons are just a sample of what is in store for you and your people.

"Could this—could this be true?" Marco stammered. "Who would this leader be? Who would know the location of the weapons?"

Owain shook his head as he stared at the note. "I have no idea. But we have to find out. They cannot release these weapons. Drakon needs to know about this." He stood and walked to the top of the stairs. "Guard, bring Drakon to me. Now!"

The guard glanced at Marco. "He's gone, along with some of his men, including Lieutenant Generals Chiane and Novo."

"Gone? Gone where?"

"His aide wouldn't say."

"When did you speak to his aide?"

"I asked the guard to bring Drakon here," Marco said. "I thought we could use his help with Sascha and Connell."

"Did the aide say when Drakon would return?" Owain asked.

"He said Drakon wouldn't be back for a couple of days," the guard replied.

"A couple of days." Owain shook his head. "That could be

too late. I want him sent here the moment he returns. You go and tell his aide that."

"Yes, Sire," the guard said, turning and racing back down the stairs.

"Owain," Marco said, "there's something else you and I might need to discuss, something that makes finding Sascha even more urgent. It's about the season of the three moons."

ESCAPE

ERATUS

This is it. The guards are leaving; I have to move now, before they close the gate. I have no idea if this will work, but it's worth a try.

While the guards had their backs to her, Sascha moved closer to the dead huens and picked up a couple of the small blackened bones. She ambled toward the bars.

Redhead whipped around when he heard her behind him. She was only steps away from the door.

"Stay where you are," he yelled. He nodded at Whitehair, who walked over to the control panel and put his hand on it.

The door started to close.

"I'm hardly going to escape. Where would I go?"

Redhead mumbled something she couldn't understand.

I have to time this perfectly.

She turned as if she was going to walk away, then stumbled and fell against the strike plate that the door touched when it closed.

"I told you to get back," Redhead snapped.

As she pushed herself away from the wall, Sascha wedged the bones into the groove in the plate.

She raised her hands in mock surrender and backed away. "Okay, okay. I tripped."

Sascha's heart pounded as she watched the door close. The bones would probably crack under the pressure. Or maybe the door would fail to close and the guards would realize what she had tried to do.

Seconds later, the door closed. Redhead stood and stared at her for a moment before turning to his partner and nodding his head in the direction of the stairs. The two of them climbed the stairs and disappeared.

I'll give them time, make sure they've gone before I look.

ERATUS

She sat quietly in her prison. Finally, she built up enough courage to go and have a look at the door, see if her idea had worked. As she walked over to the plate, she saw that the lock hadn't engaged. Excited, she pushed the door, expecting it to slide open. It didn't.

Damn it. What now?

She examined the door. The lock definitely hadn't engaged. She grabbed the bars with both hands and used all her strength to pull the door toward her.

Nothing happened.

She flexed her fingers, adjusted her grip, and focused all her strength on pushing the door. She was rewarded with the tiniest of movements.

It's working.

Ten minutes later, covered in perspiration, she had managed to open the door wide enough to slip through. She walked over to the bed, retrieved her jacket, put it on, and stepped out of the cell. She glanced back into the cell.

Bibacr had asked me to wait.

She exhaled a heavy sigh as her mind tried to work out if this was a dumb move. Perhaps waiting in the cell for Bibacr to return was the right thing to do. She shook her head.

No, I can't do it. I'm sorry Bibacr but I can't wait any longer.

Feeling a twinge of guilt, she took off her shoes and shoved them in her jacket pocket so her footsteps would fall silently on the ground, then snuck up the stairs, her senses on full alert for any danger.

At the top of the stairs was a large trapdoor. Her shoulders slumped. "It's probably locked," she muttered. She pushed it and it opened.

What do you know! The Gods must be on my side.

She levered herself up and into a narrow corridor, taking care to close the door behind her. The air smelled of stale sweat and urine and the only lighting was provided by a couple of burning torches set in sconces on the wall. She followed the corridor along to where it finished at a T-junction.

"Which way leads out of here?"

She decided to go left. She was beginning to think she had made the wrong choice when she heard voices.

Shit.

She scanned the corridor for somewhere to hide. A short distance ahead, a door lay slightly ajar. She raced toward the door and dove into a dark room, closing the door behind her. The voices stopped outside the room she was hiding in.

"They're coming in here," she whispered.

She blinked several times to help her eyes adjust to the darkness. She needed to find somewhere else to hide. Her heart pounded. It seemed so loud that she was terrified the people on the other side of the door would hear it.

"Where is that damn medicine?" a voice yelled. "How long does it take to walk a hundred feet?"

There was a scampering of feet and a high-pitched squeak replied, "I have it here, Enchantress. I'm coming."

Silence fell again. Sascha's eyes finally started to adjust to the darkness. There was a glimmer of light coming from a glow around the edge of a door on the other side of the room. The room was large and cool with a tiled floor. Glass cupboards, metal tables, and tall white fridges were dotted around the perimeter. She could smell anesthetic. It looked like the medical supply room at the Fire of the Phoenix head-quarters.

She tiptoed closer to the door on the other side of the room and stood for a moment as she listened.

Laela. She was sure one of the voices had been Laela.

Sascha rested her hand on the doorknob and turned it inch by inch, hoping the people on the other side of the door wouldn't notice the movement. The door opened easily. She pushed it open a couple of inches and peered into the room. A figure covered in a purple silk sheet lay on a bed. Laela was sitting on a silver stool next to the bed, her left hand holding the hand of the bed's occupant.

"You're healing."

There was a low mumble in response.

Laela held her right hand up and the figure on the bed stopped talking. Laela glanced around the room.

Sascha held her breath.

She must have heard me.

Laela turned back to the patient. "It's okay. I thought I heard something. Why did you push it? Novo could have waited a little while longer."

Novo? Who is Laela talking to about Novo?

The person was speaking too softly for Sascha to hear what they said.

I must move closer. I need to know what's going on.

Sascha looked around the room. A tall cupboard that

stood near the door would make the perfect hiding spot. She held her breath as she pushed the door open a little farther and slid into the room and behind the cupboard. She half-expected Laela to see her and call out to the guards. But she didn't.

Laela sighed and repositioned herself on the stool, giving Sascha a glimpse of the figure in the bed.

Sascha covered her mouth with her hand to muffle the gasp of surprise. The pale, slim woman lying in the bed, her raven-colored hair gleaming in the light of the room . . . was Reya.

Reya is alive. But that's impossible.

Reya squeezed Laela's hand. "It was so rewarding. To see the shock on his face when he realized I was alive. He paid for what he did to me, he truly paid. And it was all thanks to you, Laela."

Laela leaned over and adjusted a blue bracelet that glowed on Reya's arm. "And thanks to Connell, of course." She chuckled.

Sascha frowned as she studied the bracelet. A thin cord hung from it and linked up to what looked like an IV drip.

Connell? What did Connell have to do with Reya healing?

"Have you had any luck with finding Jenny?"

"Shush, my love," Laela said as she gripped Reya's arm. She glanced around the room and then leaned toward Reya and whispered something. She sat back. "Now, sleep, my love. I have work to do and must leave you alone for a short while, but I'll be back soon. And with some more good news, I hope."

A loud clang came from the room behind Sascha. It was then she realized she had left the door slightly open. Sascha cringed and pulled back farther behind the cupboard.

Laela got up and started toward the door.

"Laela," Reya said. "Please don't trust her. She may be

family, but she's head over heels in love with Drakon. She may be loyal to him rather than us."

Laela walked back to the bed. "Don't worry, Reya. I've already thought about that."

As Laela leaned over to kiss Reya on the forehead, Sascha saw her opportunity to slip away. She retraced her steps back through the room and into the corridor. Sascha glanced to her left and right. She took one step to the left, hoping that way would lead to an exit, then stopped a minute and glanced back in the direction she had come from.

Not now. It's too dangerous to escape now. I'll wait until it's night. With any luck, everyone will be asleep then and my escape will be much easier.

"Athena, let this not be the worst idea I've ever had," Sascha whispered.

She turned and raced back to the trapdoor. Relieved to find it still unlocked she clambered through the door and headed down the stairs to her cell. She'd been hoping Bibacr might be there waiting for her, but he wasn't. It was just as difficult to close the door as it had been to open, but she finally managed to get it closed.

Footsteps sounded from the stairs. Someone was coming. She was panting. She would have to slow her breathing so that it looked as if she had been in the cell all along. She gulped, took a deep breath, and moved into the corner of the cell where it would be hard for them to see her clearly. She spread her jacket on the ground and sat cross-legged with her hands resting on her knees. She flexed the muscles in her shoulders and back, and closed her eyes. With any luck, her visitor would think she'd been meditating. Isn't that what all mages were supposed to do?

The footsteps stopped. She kept her eyes closed but her stomach twisted. What would happen if her visitor decided to come into the cell and realized the door had been tampered with?

The next few seconds were excruciating. She wanted to open her eyes, to see who her visitor was and what they were doing. But she didn't.

There was a crunch of gravel as the feet turned and walked away, telling her that her visitor was leaving. She took a peek in time to see that it was Laela walking away.

"Rest as much as you can, Sascha," Laela called out. "You will need all your strength for what is to come." Laela's laughter reverberated around the dungeon as she climbed back up the stairs.

THE ANCIENT WEAPONS

*D*rakon's stomach rumbled and he rubbed it to ease the building hunger. He grabbed one of the red apples out of the fruit bowl and took a few bites before he put it back down on the table and pushed himself out of his chair.

It must be lunchtime and Chiane still hasn't returned.

Drakon started to pace inside the tent. "How long can it possibly take for Chiane to find me something—anything—about the weapons site, or the men?"

"My Prince?" Chiane called out.

Drakon swiveled to face the tent flap. "Enter."

Chiane pushed the tent flap aside and stood in the opening. "We've found the entrance to the site."

"The site where the weapons are hidden?"

"Yes," Chiane replied.

"About time."

"There's more." Chiane flashed a look behind him and then rested his hand on the hilt of his sword, flexing his fingers as he did so.

"Well? What is it?"

"We saw blood trails and drag marks that stopped at a large stone door. The door itself was also covered in blood."

"Did you find any of our soldiers there?"

Chiane shook his head. "No. Only the blood and the drag marks. And it looked like vines had once hidden the entrance. They'd been cut back."

Excitement welled up inside Drakon.

This is it. After all this time.

Drakon walked over to where he had placed his pouch and retrieved the copy of the sketch from the chronicle and the cryptic message Novo had found. He shoved them into the pocket of his coat before he turned to Chiane. "Show me."

Drakon held the tent flap open to allow Kalamar to fly out. "Kalamar, come."

Chiane led the way. They crossed over a wooden bridge and under a narrow archway covered in brilliant purple flowers to a hollow carved into the side of a mountain. The ground was covered in what looked like sand, but as Drakon moved closer he realized it was not sand but finely crushed bone. He was barely aware of the stench of battle as his gaze followed the trail of blood leading to the doors.

"Maybe the men found a way inside?"

"I don't know if they did get in." Chiane walked to the edge of the stone door and pushed back the vines. "But if they did perhaps they worked out how to use these."

Drakon stepped closer to examine what Chiane was showing him. Set into the stone were five orbs. There was one red orb and one white. There were two blue ones, one of which had a faded symbol engraved into the stone surface below it. The final orb was black. He cleaned each of the orbs with the cuff of his jacket.

It looks like we need to press these orbs in the right order.

"There's a secret here I know, element of air, the secret show."

Nothing happened.

He repeated the spell, but again nothing happened.

"That spell should have worked." Drakon ran his fingers through his hair. "I haven't come all this way to be beaten by a simple bloody puzzle."

Drakon reached into his pocket and retrieved Novo's clue and read it.

Your faith will reveal the next steps you must take. Do you destroy the dark, or allow the light to awaken? The circles will slow and the protection will rise. The future will then be yours to decide.

"What would represent faith?" Drakon asked.

"Blood sacrifices are often given to gods, so perhaps it's red," Chiane said. "And dark would have to be black."

"And light would be the white orb," Drakon said. "So why do you think there are two blue orbs?"

"I don't know," Chiane answered. "Press them and see what happens. If it doesn't work, we'll just try again until we get it right."

"If the verse is the clue I'll use it as a guide as to which color to press," Drakon said. "Firstly, red for faith." Drakon pressed the red orb. "Now, the black orb for the dark." Drakon pressed the black orb. "The white orb for the light." Drakon pressed the white orb. "We must press something for the remaining two lines of the verse."

"I'll press one of the blue ones," Chiane said. "There are the only two left."

Drakon saw a shadow pass over the orbs. It was a warning. "No," Drakon cried out as Chiane pressed it.

The world exploded around them as pit hounds sprang into life. Kalamar screeched, leaped into the air, and flew over the top of the creatures, spraying them with fire as Drakon and Chiane finished off the ones that tried to escape.

Breathing heavily after the battle with the hounds, Chiane

glanced over at Drakon. "I won't do that again. I'll get the mages and soldiers to join us. The mages can protect us with a shield while the soldiers help Kalamar fight off any other creatures that may appear."

An hour later, they were still trying to work out the combination. The men and Kalamar were exhausted after a series of battles with pit hounds. The mages were busy healing the wounded.

"How hard can it be?" Drakon said. "There are only so many combinations."

Chiane rubbed the back of his neck. "We must be missing something."

"Search the area," Drakon ordered. "Perhaps there's something around here that can help us."

Chiane turned to stride away.

"Chiane," Drakon called out. "No one is going home to Eratus until we get this open. And need I remind you that if we don't leave here before the season of the three moons starts . . ."

"We'll find it, Prince Drakon. I promise you, we will."

While Chiane and his men were searching, Drakon sat on a boulder away from the putrid gas oozing from the dark glistening pit hound carcasses. He studied the card the clue was on.

"Blue could be faith, but why are there two blue orbs?"

He gave an exaggerated sigh as he leaned forward and formed his hands into a steeple.

Think, Drakon. Think!

"The symbols of fire, earth, water, and air at the top of the card," he muttered. "Do they mean something? Could they be more than just symbols stamped on the top of the card?"

But there had been no sign of those symbols around the door. If there had been, he would have realized that they had meant something.

But the door was covered in blood. Perhaps the blood is hiding something.

He looked around him. Chiane and his men hadn't returned yet. He knew it was probably foolish, but it was at least worth trying. He walked back to the campsite, grabbed a scrubbing cloth and a bucket of water from the kitchen tent, and returned to the hollow.

"Kalamar," he said, striding toward the stone door. "Stay with me. I may need your help."

Drakon stood back and examined the door. He moved forward, covered the stone with water, and proceeded to scrub the blood off the stone surface. Then he stood back and looked at the door. He couldn't see anything but he could sense something was there.

"There's a secret here I know, element of air, the secret show."

In the center of the door four symbols shimmered, the symbols of the four elements—fire, earth, water, and air.

He chuckled. "This is it. This is what's missing."

Drakon examined the symbols and could see what he needed to do. He pressed each of them in the same order as the magic had shown him. As each one was pressed, it glowed, and Drakon heard a soft click. Soon all four elements were glowing.

Now to do the same for the orbs.

He chanted the spell. One of the blue orbs began to glow. He pressed it. He said the spell again and the second blue orb, the one with the symbol engraved below it, lit up, and he pressed it.

"My Prince," Chiane said, striding toward Drakon. "We searched everywhere, but found very little. We did find—"

"Quiet," Drakon ordered. "I may have worked it out."

He repeated the spell, pressing each of the orbs as the magic showed what to press, until it came down to the last two orbs—the black and the white. Instead of only one lighting up, they both did.

"How could both light up at the same time?" Chiane said. "That makes no sense."

"Novo's clue explains it all. Destroy the darkness or allow the light to awaken." Drakon scratched his chin as he studied the door. Suddenly the glowing symbols stopped glowing. He was back to square one. "Damn it."

"It must be timed," Chiane said. "You must have to do it within a certain time or it resets."

"You think so? So glad you told me that, Chiane. I wouldn't have worked that one out on my own." He shook his head. "At least I remember the order. Tell me, Chiane, if it were up to you, which orb do you think I should press—the black or the white?"

"Well, it was Athena who put the magical barrier in place with light magic—the white orb—so perhaps you need black magic—the black orb—to undo it."

"Unless there's a trick to it. Unless . . ."

I know what to do.

Drakon pressed the elements and then the orbs in the same order as last time. When the black and white orbs glowed, his hand hovered over the black orb. At the last moment, he pressed the white one.

Everything fell silent. The wind held its breath and the forest around them seemed unnaturally quiet.

"Did it work?" Chiane whispered. "There are no pit hounds."

A grinding sound reverberated below them. Moments later, the large stone door started to move. Drakon held his breath as he watched the stone roll away. A wave of musty stale air wafted out of the cave.

"You did it, My Prince," Chiane said. "You did it. The cave is open."

* EARTH

Drakon stood at the entrance to the cave. "Before we go in there, Chiane, what did you find?"

"We found Novo's body."

"What about the other men?"

"We couldn't find any sign of them." Chiane glanced at his men. "What happened to Novo has left the men shaken." Chiane blinked slowly and took a deep breath.

"Chiane, what happened? Are you going to tell me, or do you plan on keeping it a secret?"

"He had been tortured. Parts of him had been removed and there was blood everywhere. In the end, he'd been gutted. I pray to Athena the poor man passed out while he was being tortured. Someone took great pleasure in inflicting as much pain as they could."

"So he finally met his end," Drakon said.

"The mages detected hints of magic," Chiane continued, "as if a portal had been used to bring someone here. But it must have been a master in the craft because the magic was only faint."

"He could have been killed some time ago," Drakon said. "It may not have been a master."

"The wounds were fresh, still bleeding, and the body was warm."

"Still warm?" Drakon asked. "But that would mean . . ."

"Yes, he was still alive while we were trying to open the door."

"Do you think they could have seen what we were doing?" Drakon asked.

"I'm not s-sure," Chiane stammered. "But I wish we had known so we could have helped him."

Drakon shrugged his shoulders. "There was nothing we

could have done for him. If we stopped them this time, they would have found another way to kill him."

"The mages suggested he may have been attacked out of revenge for killing Reya."

"They're very possibly right."

"I've asked a couple of the mages to work with my soldiers and see if they can track down who attacked him."

"Why?"

"He . . . he was one of our own."

"He was a drunken lout, a fool. Yes, he was good at his job, but he had an attitude and that's what got him killed. We have more important things to do than sorting out some sort of vendetta. If we don't want to be stuck on this side of the portals when they close, we have a lot of work to do in very little time."

"But—"

"You heard me, Chiane. Now, let's have a look at what's inside this cave. Tell the men to be on their guard."

THE ANCIENTS

ERATUS

*S*ascha had stayed in the corner of the room well after Laela had left. As she rested against the wall she dozed off and woke when the room had started to darken. It was time to move. But Bibacr still hadn't returned.

Damn it. Bibacr, where are you?

She knew she had to make a move soon. She didn't know how long it would be before Laela returned, but she knew it wouldn't be long before someone discovered the door wasn't locked.

It's time to go.

As she pushed the door open, voices sounded above her. She stood frozen to the spot as she tried to work out if they were coming closer. It was then she realized they were singing the same song over and over again. They were chanting. She tried to work out the words, but the voices were muffled.

It sounds like they're preparing for a sacrifice.

She shivered.

If it's mine, they're going to be disappointed. I'm not going to be here.

Sascha put her jacket back on, placed her shoes in her jacket pocket as before, and snuck out of the cell. She hoped the fact that it would be dark soon would make her escape easier. She snuck up the stairs, pushed the trapdoor open, and levered herself up and into the narrow corridor, closing the door behind her. She jogged to the end of the corridor. When she reached the T-junction, she saw glowing torches to her right and heard the repeated hum of the chants echoing around her.

If that way leads to the sacrifice, then I'm going left.

She ran as fast as she could. It wasn't long before she saw that the corridor led into a large cave. A couple of groups of brown-cloaked figures were several feet ahead of her, and they were walking in the same direction—into the cave. Sascha glanced behind her. She couldn't go back. She swallowed hard.

I have to keep going. There's no choice.

She took a deep breath and followed the figures. The cavern's onyx walls shone like glass. Sascha's jacket seemed overly bright in the darkness, so she whipped it off and bundled it up under her arm. She hoped the black clothes she was wearing would help her blend into the shadows. At the back of the cave was a large stone stage on which stood a long, thin black table. Half a dozen skulls of various sizes had been placed on the table along with a selection of various implements that were glistening in the torchlight. Sascha shivered as goose bumps prickled along her skin.

Perhaps I should turn back. But where would I go?

She moved closer, keeping to the shadows.

Whimpering sounds were coming from below the stage. Sascha rubbed her eyes as she tried to see what was making the noise. A long pole ran along the front of the stage. Chained to the pole was a group of young girls and they were being guarded by several hooded figures. They looked to be about the same age as Kira, but one of them, the one with fiery red hair, looked like she was half their age.

Sascha's eyes widened as she shook her head.

I thought I was escaping the sacrifice, but instead I've walked right into it. But young girls. Surely they weren't going to sacrifice them.

A door set into the wall at the back of the stage opened and a young girl was dragged out, crying, pleading for help. She couldn't have been more than eight years old. The girls chained to the pole alternated between calling out calming words to her and pleading with the hooded figures for the young girl's release.

An icy breeze whipped around the room and the girls fell silent, their full attention on the door. A scrawny frame three times Sascha's height and dressed in a long, flowing, red silk cloak moved out of the doorway. She couldn't see its face under the cloak's hood, but its scrawny form swayed with every movement. Seconds later, claws skittered across the floor as semitransparent insects the size of large dogs followed the red-cloaked creature into the room. The insects skittered away from the creature and circled the young girl, poking and prodding her with their spindly legs.

The being in the red cloak studied the insects and the girl they were now circling, and then turned its focus to the young girls chained to the long pole. It swayed from side to side on its way down the steps and toward the girls. As it walked past them, it prodded each one in turn. The whimpers of the girls as they tried to pull away from the creature echoed around the cave.

Another figure, also dressed in a red cloak, left the shadows and walked to the creature. It bowed, then stood and flicked back its hood.

"Lae—Laela," Sascha stammered.

"Esteemed Leader of the Ancients, she has been

prepared," Laela said as she turned and waved her hand in the direction of the terrified young girl.

Sascha's eyes bulged as she realized who the thing was. The sound of her heartbeat thrashed in her ears.

This creature is the Leader of the Ancients? That man I fought in the healing ceremony . . . he didn't look like that.

The Ancient burped and a green-colored liquid dribbled down its chin. He studied the terrified girls once more before walking back to the stage and jiggling over to the young girl, who was still surrounded by the insects. He made an odd clicking noise with his mouth and the insects shot long strands of silver thread at the girl. Within seconds, the girl's hands and feet were tied together. The insects bowed before the Ancient and moved backward, giving the creature easy access to the girl.

"Yes, My Leader," Laela said, responding to a voice Sascha couldn't hear. "All of these girls have recently activated their powers, but this one has the mark of dark magic. I'm sure you heard the hum in each of the girls, but this one is the youngest. And this mark tells us that she is the most potent." Laela nodded at one of the brown-cloaked figures. "Thea, show the leader the mark."

Thea edged her way in between the insects, careful to avoid any contact with them. She leaned over and pulled back the young girl's hair, revealing a charcoal-colored crescent moon on the side of her neck.

The creature tilted its head to the side as it studied the mark. It pointed a gangly finger at the table.

Laela flicked her fingers. "Thea, the dagger."

Thea raced to the table, picked up a long, thin, ceremonial dagger, and then handed it over to Laela.

Laela took the dagger, walked over to the creature, and placed it in the creature's claws. It expertly flicked the blade so that it was positioned in between two of its claws. The blade glistened in the torchlight as the creature raised it to the young girl's throat.

"No . . . please . . . ," the little girl shrieked as she struggled against the thread that held her.

It was instinct that forced Sascha forward. "Stop this," she screamed.

The insects screeched and retreated to the rear of the stage as the gangly creature glanced around, irritated at the interruption.

Sascha raced out of the shadows toward the creature. She raised her hands as she tried to summon a fireball spell. Nothing happened. She glanced at her mark; it hadn't changed. She couldn't feel a thing. Confused, Sascha stood staring at her hands. She raised her hands again, but again there was no magic.

Laela's laughter splintered through Sascha's bones. Laela signaled to Thea. "Take the girl away," Laela said. "Let her live another week." She turned to Sascha. "This one will take her place."

Laela turned to Sascha. "I was hoping you'd had enough black lyrium. I wasn't sure, but you never can be sure, can you . . . until, of course, you test it out."

"But you drank it, too," Sascha said, "which means your magic isn't working either."

Laela shot a bolt of electricity at Sascha, sizzling the earth beside her. Sascha twisted away and dropped into a crouching position as a group of cloaked figures armed with staffs surrounded her.

Laela cackled. "The lyrium wasn't in the water. Your glass was coated with the stuff." She rubbed her hands together and turned to the leader. "This is Sascha—the one I was telling you about. The one Hades is after."

"Sascha?" he repeated. "What is she doing here? I thought you had imprisoned her."

"I knew it would only be a matter of time before she escaped," Laela gloated. "In fact, I rigged the door to make her . . . escape a little easier."

"You didn't rig the door," Sascha said. "I found a way to stop it from shutting."

"What? With a few dead huen bones? Really? You think that would stop a motorized door?" She laughed. "But ten points for trying."

"Enough of this," the Ancient said. "Is this the one Hades said was working with Athena to destroy the weapons?"

"What?" Sascha snorted. "I'm not doing any such—"

Laela smirked. "Yes, this is the one. And Hades said it was a waste to kill her when you could have her instead."

"And she has the mark?"

"Yes."

"Show it to me."

Circles of yellow light shimmered around Sascha. She tried to move, but every muscle in her body was frozen. She was paralyzed.

One of the cloaked figures moved forward and raised Sascha's hand for the creature to examine.

"She has one of the most powerful marks I've ever seen," Laela said. "It's the same as the marks engraved into the Blades of Light."

The creature grumbled. "The mark may be as you say, but she's too old. She's over twenty-one. Her magic would be stale."

"Sascha lost her powers when she was at the height of her magic," Laela said. "She has only recently been through the ceremony to restore her magic. Her powers are fresh, and because of all her training, she is much more potent than the young girl."

The Ancient nodded. "If she is as good as you say, you will get your reward, but if I am to consume her she needs to be prepared in the same way you have done the other girls. In the meantime, I'll take the youngest one as an appetizer—the one with hair the color of fire." He turned and pointed his finger at the girls chained to the pole. "The one at the end there."

"No," the girl screamed.

Sascha tried to yell, tried to move, but she could only stand there and watch.

As if sensing Sascha's struggle, the creature moved closer and sniffed at her. "You don't want me to take this young one? At least this one will no longer have to suffer while she waits for her time to come. She will have peace, knowing she has been used to serve a greater purpose." He sniffed at Sascha and tutted. "I'm looking forward to my time with you. If you're as good as Laela says, you will give me the blood infusion I need to help me build my strength so I'm ready for when Ares frees me."

He pointed at the young girl. "Take her," he snapped. "Send her to my rooms."

"Yes, My Leader," Laela said.

The girl's screams broke Sascha's heart.

Athena, please help them.

Laela nodded at the white-haired guard Sascha had seen earlier. He picked Sascha up, threw her over his shoulder, and followed Laela out of the cavern and into the corridor.

"The girls are sacrificing their lives for the greater good," Laela said as she led the way out. "They know that. But you . . . your sacrifice will give me what I've been dreaming of for so many years." She cackled as she stepped to the side and allowed the guard to pass. "Take her to the cleansing rooms. It's time for her to be readied for our Esteemed Leader."

The guard kicked open a door, walked over to the corner of the room, and dropped Sascha into a chair. He snuck a glance at her as he made his way out of the room. She heard the click of a lock and then she was alone. Sascha tried to move her fingers, then her head. She couldn't move at all. Her mind started to imagine what was going to happen, what that creature was going to do to her. She could feel the panic start to build.

No, I'm stronger than this.

She forced herself to think of Marco, of Soleil, and Rusty. They would be looking for her.

They will find me. I need to be strong until they do.

The magic would wear off. And when it did she would be ready. She had her own magic.

THE WEAPONS

* EARTH: IN THE CAVE

*T*he golden glow of the setting sun cast long shadows on the ground as Drakon rubbed his hands and stepped into the cave.

After all these years, I'm so close to finally possessing the ancient weapons.

Drakon peered into the darkness. "Chiane, have your men take the lead. But be on alert. There will probably be more traps."

"Yes, My Prince."

"Kalamar, stay with me," Drakon ordered.

The mages created lanterns that floated along in the air and provided the only light in the dank, dark cave. They pushed their way past thick cobwebs. Every so often there was a scuffle as someone battled the horrific-looking spiders and oversized rats that inhabited the cave.

"Look," one of the soldiers called out.

A number of dead bodies were piled together along the cave walls.

Drakon walked over to the nearest pile, covering his mouth to block out the stench. "It's impossible to tell if they're our men or not. But it certainly isn't all of them. There aren't over a hundred bodies here."

"We will need to see if we can find anything to identify these poor souls," Chiane said. "We need to let their families know they're dead."

"Not until we have retrieved the weapons," Drakon said. "I'm not going to be stuck here when the portal closes."

"Yes, My Prince." Chiane moved closer to the bloody pile. "How did they get in here? They couldn't have come through the stone door. They would have left it open."

"Unless they closed it thinking they were protecting themselves from something outside the cave," Drakon said.

Chiane shivered as he glanced around the cave. "That's worrying. I'll organize some soldiers and mages to scout ahead. We can't be caught unprepared like these . . . men were. If these are our men, where are the rest of them?"

"I guess we'll find out soon enough," Drakon said. "Tell your men to keep a lookout."

They pushed ahead and came to what looked to be a large stone auditorium. The seats formed a semicircle around a long, narrow platform that was probably used as a stage. A set of stairs led up to the platform, and a roof of ornately carved wooden beams covered the area.

Drakon walked over to the stairs and climbed onto the stage. He looked down at the seats as Kalamar landed on the beam nearest to where he stood.

"What type of ceremony would have been held here?" Chiane asked.

Drakon studied the area. "I have no idea. Take some of the men and make sure the rest of the cave is clear. And get the mages to light the torches around this auditorium."

"Yes, My Prince."

As the light of the torches banished the surrounding darkness, Drakon studied the area. It was then he noticed the design carved into the floor in the middle of the room. It was an exact copy of the design he had reproduced from the chronicle—a five-pointed star. Carved above the star's upper point was a shape that looked like a human skull with a horizontal line dividing the shape in half.

"The symbol for death," Drakon muttered.

At each of the star's other points was a pyramid representing one of the four elements of air, water, fire, and earth. At the very center of the design was a silver star-shaped tile.

Drakon glanced at the page he had copied from the chronicle. "We found it."

He reread the instructions. The silver tile at the center of the design was what they had to focus on, to hit with the magic. The warning marked beneath the design made him rethink the idea of being a part of the first attempt to unlock the magical barrier. If it went wrong, they could afford to lose a couple of mages. It was stupid for him to put himself at unnecessary risk.

When the men returned Drakon summoned Chiane.

"Chiane, I want six of your best mages. One must be a master in death magic and must take their place at the top of the star. Four of them must be masters in elemental magic, and they should take their place next to the symbol that reflects the magic they will be using. The sixth mage will stand in the middle of the star and blend the magic of the five mages together into a single beam of white light, which they will direct toward the silver tile in the center of the design."

"Yes, My Prince."

Six mages arrived a few minutes later and took their places in and around the design.

"You, there, in the middle," Drakon called out. The tall, skinny man with long white hair turned to face him. "It's your job to hold your staff high. When everyone's magic is touching the top of your staff, blend the magic into a single white light and bring your staff down in one quick movement onto the tile."

"I could do this with both hands tied behind my back, My Prince. You do not need to fear."

"It is not me who is in danger, mage. Remember, you're unlocking a trap. If you don't do it right, the magical protections will kill you." Drakon turned back to Chiane. "Chiane, have everyone but the six mages move onto the stage and have one of the mages cast a protective shield over our group."

"Yes, right away."

Drakon felt the hairs on his arms stand on end as a sizzle of electricity filled the area and a blue barrier formed around the group. He moved forward to watch the mages prepare for the ceremony, making sure that he stayed within the shield's protective barrier.

The mages drank their vials of dragon blood, tilted their heads back, and lifted their staffs toward the roof of the cave, chanting as they did so. Colored lights spilled into the air above them, forming luminous arcs of red, green, gold, orange, and blue. The mages guided the arcs until they touched the top of the staff held by the sixth mage.

The sixth mage moved his staff in circles, blending each of the lights until he had a single white beam of light. The mage raised his staff and closed his eyes . . . a moment too soon. As he brought the staff down toward the silver tile, the color changed and when his staff hit the silver plate, the light was no longer white.

"It's the wrong color," Drakon yelled. But his warning came too late. Plates of fire burst into life below the mages, and within a matter of seconds, they had been consumed by the fireball racing across the floor.

"Idiots," Drakon yelled. "All they had to do was create a spell. Isn't that what mages are supposed to do?"

Drakon turned to Chiane. "Have your men clear the place and we'll do it again. Choose another six mages."

Chiane dragged his gaze away from the disaster. "Yes, My Prince."

After the mages had cooled the walls and floor down and the soldiers had disposed of the dead mages, they prepared for a second attempt. Drakon stood on the edge of the stage area, protected by the shield.

"Mages, you've seen the price of failure. Concentrate on what you're doing."

The mages glanced at each other. "Yes, My Prince," they answered.

When their second attempt also failed, Drakon twisted around to Chiane. "I thought you said your mages were good."

"The mages were focused," Chiane said. "Everything was going perfectly until that last second. It's almost as if something is missing."

Drakon's voice chilled. "Are you telling me I'm wrong?"

"No, My Prince. Not at all. I was looking for an explanation as to why it wasn't working."

"It's rather simple," Drakon said. "They refuse to follow instructions." He turned away from Chiane and strode down to the five-pointed star. He stood over the silver tile and stared at it as he tried to work out what he was going to do next.

Maybe Ares was lying again.

Drakon shook his head. That didn't make sense.

He was about to walk back onto the stage when he noticed the fine engraving in the middle of the silver star—an olive tree and an owl. The design was the same as the design on the armband he was wearing. Ares' words came back to him.

"Now that you have your souvenir from Demipos, I know you can do it yourself."

The magic needs the armband to work. I need to be the one blending the lights.

"Chiane," he called out.

Chiane stepped in front of him and bowed.

"I can't afford for this to be another wasted opportunity. Seeing as the mages are unable to follow even the simplest of instructions, I've decided I have to do this myself. Find me five more mages."

"You can't, My Prince. What if it fails? We can't afford to lose you."

"Well, tell them that unless they want to be known as the killers of princes and kings, they had better do exactly as I tell them, when I tell them. If they do that, we will survive."

"Yes, My Prince."

Drakon glanced up at Kalamar. "Be ready," he whispered.

Kalamar emitted a soft warble and flew down to perch on the back of a seat not far from where the ceremony would begin.

The mages huddled together in whispered conversation as they stood at the edge of the stairs to the stage.

"Sokentash," Drakon growled. "Come here and take your position or I will—"

A young woman stepped forward and curtseyed. "My Prince, we're worried we will fail. The ones who died were better at magic than us."

"We don't want to die," a young man from the back of the group said as he stepped forward to join the young woman.

"Either you—"

"My Prince," Chiane said, as he moved toward the mages.

"Allow me to handle this. I can help them. All they need is reassurance."

"Hurry up, man," Drakon snapped. "We don't have long."

Several minutes passed and finally the group dispersed. The mages stepped up hesitantly to take their positions around the engraving. Drakon sensed their fear, but the dragon's blood would take that away. He took his place near the silver star. He retrieved his bollock dagger and tapped the bottom of the pommel three times. The blade glowed and the pommel extended as the blade changed to the color of ice.

"They were right. It's a staff," one of the mages whispered. "That's the most—"

Drakon glared at the mage. "Focus on what you're doing, not on me. Do you want to live through this?"

The mage's head bobbed up and down. "Yes, My Prince."

Drakon waited until the room was silent. "Drink your vials and focus your powers. When I say so, direct your powers to the top of my staff."

"Yes, My Prince," they answered in unison.

They retrieved their vials, drank them down, and placed the empty vials in their cloak pockets. The mages lifted their staffs toward the roof of the cave as they chanted. Colored lights spilled into the air above them, once again forming luminous arcs of red, green, gold, orange, and blue.

Standing with his feet planted firmly apart, Drakon drank the contents of his vial, closed his eyes, and raised his staff.

He opened his eyes and concentrated on the lights. "Now," he called out. When the lights were touching the top of his staff, he twirled it, bringing the colors together until they formed a perfect white light. His arm warmed and he sensed the powers in the armband coming to life. He waited a few heartbeats and then, in one quick movement, lowered the staff with a sharp thump onto the tile below his feet.

The magic flashed and the tile rumbled as it moved aside. The ground beneath them shook as a set of stairs leading down into the bowels of the cave appeared in the newly formed opening.

"It worked," Chiane muttered. "It actually worked."

Drakon strode to the top of the stairs. He couldn't see a thing in the darkness. "Light," he demanded.

Several soldiers arrived at his side with lit torches in their hands.

"You go first. Light the path for me," Drakon said. The room was freezing and the stairs were icy. He took each step slowly, taking care to place one foot before lifting the other. When they arrived at the bottom of the stairs, they stared around in awe. They were surrounded by a small, perfectly preserved but uninhabited city.

"This is amazing," Chiane said as he strode around and surveyed the buildings on the edge of the city. "People must have lived here. But how long ago?"

Drakon's focus, however, was not on the city. His focus was the stacks of crates that covered a large paved area on the outskirts of the city.

"The weapons," he muttered. "We've found the weapons." Excitement welled up in him. After all this time, he finally had what he had wanted for so long.

So much for the Ancients or whatever is buried here. There's nothing here now but the crates.

Whispers echoed from somewhere in the distance. The whispers grew louder, the pitch becoming higher and higher as the voices grew more excited and turned into piercing screeches. An icy wind whipped around them, consuming the lights and leaving them in darkness. Men scrambled in panic as they desperately tried to relight the torches. There was an intense silence before the torches burst into flame.

"What in Athena's name was that?" Chiane asked.

Drakon shuddered.

Perhaps I spoke too soon. But if there are any Ancients here, they're Earth's problem now.

Drakon stared at the crates. Ares had told him to open them before moving them out of the cave but that instruction didn't rest easy with him. There had been a couple of incidences lately where he had trusted Ares and his life had been threatened. And Ares' response was that everything was a game. But what would be the risk of opening these crates now?

He moved forward to study them as he tried to decide what he would do. He ran his hands around the edges and tested the lids on the crates. Everything was well sealed. It made no sense to unseal these, look at them, and then seal them again for transportation to Eratus.

My gut feeling says I should stick with my plan so that's what I'll do. The boxes will remain sealed until I can get my test subjects in the laboratories to open them.

A silver box rested on the top of the first stack of crates. Drakon walked over to it. Inscribed upon its lid was the picture of a small vial with a cross through it, and another picture of a larger vial, but there was no cross on the larger one. Next to it was the circled V symbol that Ares had drawn in the beach sands.

How strange. What is the meaning of the vials?

Drakon pocketed the silver box before anyone else saw it. Moments later Chiane joined him. Drakon withdrew his dagger, squatted, and carved the circled V symbol into the ground. "Organize for all of the crates marked with this symbol to be taken to the laboratory underneath the Awakening headquarters on Eratus. Leave the others here. But no one is to open any of the crates . . . or damage them. Is that clear?"

"Yes, perfectly clear, My Prince."

"The portals will close soon, so tell everyone to get moving."

Chiane nodded. "As you command."

"Come, Kalamar," Drakon said as he strode back up the stairs. "Time for us to return home."

*T*he sweat poured off Marco as he practiced his footwork with a double-weighted sword in his hand. The early evenings were the best time to practice because routine training had finished for the day. He stopped long enough to wipe his forehead with the back of his hand before starting his lunges.

"Colonel," a voice called out.

He stopped, pulled the towel out of the belt of his training leathers, and turned to the voice.

"Lieutenant Colonel Zabir. You're back. Do you have news?"

"Yes, Colonel. We searched everywhere for the castle's telepath as you requested but it seems he has disappeared."

"Disappeared? Is there any question of foul play?"

"It's hard to know. His room has been emptied, all of his belongings have gone. It's like he decided to up and leave."

Marco glanced around the training grounds. "I'm sure somehow Drakon is behind this, in which case you will never find the body. It's too much of a coincidence that he wanted the destruction of the portal kept a secret and the one person who could confirm how the portal was destroyed has suddenly decided to leave."

"We have organized for another telepath to be appointed," Zabir said. "Prince Drakon won't be happy but we have asked him to tell the other telepaths there has been an unexplained closure of the portal in Tasuna. We didn't give any detail on what happened, not until you tell us we can. Do you have any idea when that might be?"

"The High King now knows what happened to that soldier," Marco said. "I told him. He was furious with me for not telling him sooner. It's time to start telling our people the storm season isn't far away."

"That is good news. When we checked in on the regions, some of them didn't see the need to focus on preparing for the storm season. Now that we can tell them what happened in Tasuna, I'm sure that will change."

"Be careful not to cause panic," Marco said. "And I'm assuming you haven't seen any sign of the akhult?"

Zabir shook his head. "Nothing has been confirmed yet, Colonel, but the weather is certainly turning cooler a lot quicker than we expected."

Marco strode to the edge of the training area, Zabir in tow, and picked up a water flask. He wet the towel in his hand and placed the flask back down. "The King wanted me to organize for the portals to be shut down, as per our usual practice, but with Sascha missing, he's unsure what to do. And it seems that Drakon has disappeared, too."

"Prince Drakon's disappeared?"

"Yes, it's rumored that he's gone to Earth, but his men are being tight-lipped about what he's actually doing there."

"He's probably after the weapons," Zabir said.

Marco gave Zabir a sideways glance and then wiped his face with the cool towel. "How do you know about the weapons?"

"All of the men know about them," Zabir said. "They thought it was a joke, thought Prince Drakon was losing it. But it seems there's something to it and he wasn't just barking at the moon."

So the weapons aren't such a well-kept secret after all.

"Zabir, I need you to do something else for me."

"Yes, Colonel."

"It seems the dragon hunters we were investigating have disappeared, gone underground. The King had organized their capture, but it seems they somehow overwhelmed the High King's soldiers and escaped. And they left a note, threatening the King's life."

"The King's life?" Zabir repeated.

"Yes, so we need to find them. Can you also organize some backups for the High King's guards? They were . . . overwhelmed once, and I don't want it to happen again."

"You don't believe the story, Colonel?"

"It seems to be too convenient for my liking," Marco said.

"I'll get onto it right away." He turned and strode off toward the barracks.

Marco needed to keep his mind clear, so he tucked the damp towel back into his belt and continued with his training until the second sun was setting. He walked back to his flask, picked it up, and took a swig of water.

"Marco," a voice called out.

Marco glanced around him to see where the voice was coming from.

"Bibacr need to talk to Marco," the voice said.

"Where are you, Bibacr?" Marco called out.

Bibacr stepped out of the long shadows beside the stairs leading to the ramparts so that Marco could see him and then disappeared back into the darkness.

Marco took another swig of water, glanced around, and

then walked over to join Bibacr. "Bibacr, what're you doing here?"

"Bibacr found Sascha."

"What? You found her? Where?"

"Sascha in prison in Brun."

"Brun? What the—we have to get her out of there. How did she end up in Brun?"

"Bibacr see Laela."

"Laela? But why would Laela capture her? We must work out how to rescue her. I should tell Raeshaan, but—"

"Marco," a voice screeched from the roof of the castle, "there's a gibleree standing next to you." Soleil leaped off the roof and dived toward Bibacr, all claws and beak. Bibacr squealed in fright and threw himself even farther back into the shadows. Soleil missed him by inches.

"Stop, Soleil," Marco ordered. "Come down here now."

"It's a gibleree," Soleil protested.

"It's Bibacr, and he's found Sascha."

"Found Sascha? But how?"

"In my chambers, both of you. Now! And, Soleil, ask Fenix to join us."

"She's probably not talking to me," Soleil said. "I haven't seen her since Sascha's disappearance."

"Find her and make friends," Marco growled. "We will need her, too. And then join me in my chambers."

Soleil clicked his beak at Marco and then launched himself into the air.

FENIX

ERATUS: CASTLE GROUNDS

*D*rakon flexed his neck and shoulders as he walked toward his war room. The night was cool, but it was warmer than the weather on Earth. He was pleased to be back on Eratus. Once Chiane had reported in to say the weapons were safely stored in their new home, he would go and see Owain. It was time to talk about the signs of the akhult and to suggest the portals be closed. He didn't want anyone to escape Eratus once the weapons had been delivered. But there were a few things he had to do first. He glanced at the guard standing in front of his war room.

"Guard, summon my aide."

"Yes, My Prince."

He entered the room, the silver box concealed underneath his jacket. He had enough time to hide the box in a cupboard behind where the fire dragons slept when he heard the soft footsteps of his aide-de-camp.

"My Prince," the aide said.

"What's been happening while I've been away?" Drakon asked.

"Prince Connell has taken a turn for the worse. A number

of mages are working with the healer to see if they can help him."

Drakon walked to the balcony and poured himself a glass of prumble ale. "You've got to give it to him. The way he looked before I left . . ." Drakon shook his head. "I half-expected him to be dead. He's got more tenacity than I thought."

"And the High King was searching for you. It was probably something to do with Connell."

"I'll talk to Father when I leave here. Anything else?"

"Sascha has disappeared. No one seems to know where she's gone, and Marco is frantically searching for her."

Drakon felt a weight lift off his shoulders. He finished his ale and put the cup back on the table. It looked like Fenix had come through. Sascha was finally where she should be— away from Marco and that damned Soleil, and under his control.

"So you haven't seen Fenix then?" Drakon asked.

"Now that you mention it, I don't think I have." He stood in silence as he stroked his chin. "No, I haven't seen her in the castle since Sascha disappeared. As for the timing of Sascha's disappearance and Connell's illness, there has been a lot of speculation. The nobles are convinced the two are connected."

Drakon smirked. "Nobles have too much time on their hands. I'm assuming there's nothing else."

The aide tucked his hands into the pockets of his long yellow cloak. "No, that's it."

Drakon nodded. "Go now."

"Yes, My Prince."

A chained fist knocked on the door. Chiane entered the room, then stood back to allow the aide to walk past.

"My Prince."

"Chiane. Are the weapons locked away now?"

"It all went smoothly. I'm pleased to report everything is ready for your visit to the laboratory tomorrow."

"Good. Tell the soldiers guarding the test subjects to have a group of subjects waiting in the laboratory before the first sun rises. I want five subjects from each of the groups. And organize for Isabella to be there, too. I'll have need of her services."

"Um . . . yes, My Prince."

"Is there something wrong, Chiane?"

"No, not wrong exactly. Isabella has been unwell and—"

"Unwell?" Drakon asked.

"Yes, she won't say much about it, but I know she's been holed up in her chambers for days now."

"I'm sure she'll be fine. Changing the subject, I need you to follow up with your contacts in Cirrone. It looks like Fenix has come through. I've been told Sascha is missing. I'm going to stir up a bit of trouble here, so I want to make sure she's protected. No one must find her."

"Yes. One more thing, My Prince. If it please you, I would like to send a few men to Earth to see if they can identify those bodies we found in the cave and to search for any signs of the rest of our men."

"Those bodies might not even be our men," Drakon said.

Chiane glanced at the ground and then lifted his chin to face Drakon. "They might not be. Which means instead of searching for a few missing men we need to find all of them."

"I don't know how long we have before the portals close, Chiane."

"I know my men are prepared to keep looking even if that means they are to be stuck on Earth for the season of the three moons."

It would be good to know what happened. Find out who's behind it all.

"You have my permission to send a small group to Earth, Chiane."

"Thank you, My Prince." Chiane turned on his heel and walked out the door.

Today has been a good day. I'd better go and see Father.

As he walked out of the war room, he caught sight of Soleil hunkering on the edge of the ramparts, his head moving backward and forward as if he was searching the castle grounds.

The gods must be on my side. And now to give the finishing touches to a perfect day.

"Soleil," he called out, "I'm so sorry to hear about Sascha. But don't believe the rumors. I don't believe for a second it was Fenix who organized Sascha's capture. Of course, if it's true that she had to choose between you or her children . . ."

Soleil ruffled his feathers. "What?"

"Oh, I'm sorry. You haven't heard the rumors. I doubt they're true. Try not to worry."

Drakon turned away quickly to hide his smirk from Soleil and headed off toward Owain's chambers.

*M*arco stormed up the tavern stairs toward his chambers.

"The ones I find the most difficult to manage are the creatures of this damn world," he muttered. "I'd rather be responsible for a whole army of rebellious soldiers than these creatures who seem determined to kill each other."

He opened the door and saw Bibacr standing in the corner of the room.

"How did you beat me here?" Marco asked.

"Bibacr don't like being outside. Bibacr don't like men with swords."

Marco chuckled. "I guess I can understand that. I'm sure Soleil won't be long. This should be a relatively easy rescue, especially if you know where she is."

Bibacr shook his head. "Sascha not easy to rescue. Sascha captured in dungeons below temple of Fire Gods in Brun. Sascha in great danger."

"In the temple? But they'll kill her."

Bibacr's head bobbed up and down. "Bibacr know how to save Sascha."

The window crashed open as Soleil smashed into Marco's room.

"Soleil, stop. Leave Bibacr alone. For Sascha's sake, put your issues with Bibacr aside."

"I'm not worried about Bibacr," Soleil hissed. "Have you seen Fenix since Sascha disappeared?"

"Not that I can remember. Why? Is something wrong?"

"I was searching the castle gardens one final time on my way here when Drakon spoke to me."

"Drakon?" Marco asked. "He's back?"

"Yes, and he told me that Fenix was behind Sascha's disappearance."

"Surely you don't believe Drakon."

"Well, where is she then? And don't you think it's strange she disappeared the same day Sascha did?"

"Yes, it is strange," Marco acknowledged. "But this must wait. We need to save Sascha."

Soleil clicked his beak. "Yes, you're right. But after this is over—"

"Bibacr speak. Laela captured Sascha. Not Fenix."

"Fenix was told to organize it," Soleil said. "I had assumed it was Drakon who told her to do it, but she must have been working with Laela. She saved us from Laela once, so why would she do this now?"

"Fenix will turn up," Marco said. "And when she does, we will give her a chance to defend herself. You of all creatures, Soleil, know how Drakon lies."

Bibacr hopped up and down on his feet. "Bibacr need to save Sascha."

"So, Bibacr, what can we do to help you rescue her?" Marco asked.

"Bibacr found way out of temple, but temple surrounded by guardians, lots of guardians. Bibacr saw priests give guardians orders."

Marco gasped. "Guardians can be trained to follow orders?"

Bibacr nodded.

"What exactly is your plan, Bibacr?"

"Bibacr get Sascha out of the temple, but Bibacr need Soleil to carry her home. Bibacr escape like last time."

Marco strode around the room, scratching his head. "I am the Lord of Kilmarnock. I could get an army there to rescue her."

"They would kill her before you got there," Soleil said. "I can't believe I'm going to say this, but Bibacr's idea is a good one. If he can sneak her out of the temple, I can carry her over the guardians."

Marco sighed. "You're right. But I'm going with you."

"Marco be careful," Bibacr said. "Guardians see Marco, guardians warn priests, and priests kill Sascha."

"I'll be waiting for you on the top of the cliffs that overlook the southern section of the temple, but if you get into trouble . . ." Marco gave his head one final scratch. "We should leave now, while it's dark. Soleil, are you ready to go?"

Soleil and Bibacr glanced at each other. "We're ready."

HADES

ERATUS: TEMPLE OF THE FIRE GODS, BRUN

A red band of light appeared in front of Sascha, its pulsating glow filling the room. As the glow receded, a dark-bearded man holding a bird-tipped scepter appeared in front of her.

"Hello, Sascha, I was hoping I would find a chance to meet with you again." He looked around the room. "But not like this." He glanced at her. "You're not talking?"

Sascha stood and stared at him, unable to move.

He tilted his head to the side as he looked at her. "It's unusual for you to be this quiet." He moved closer. "Ah, I know the problem." He touched her on the shoulder with the scepter.

An uncomfortable tingling and prickling sensation raced through her body. She flexed her neck and shoulders and shook her arms. "I can move again. What did you do?"

"Simple spell to break with dark magic. No big deal."

"And who are you?" Sascha asked.

"Oh, how rude of me. Of course, you had that thing where your memory was taken away."

"That . . . thing?" Sascha mocked.

"You know what I mean." He bowed before her. "Let me introduce myself. Hades, King of the Underworld and God of the Dead." He studied her face. "You know, since you've been away, you've grown into your beauty. You're very similar to my beautiful Persephone. Ares was right."

"Hades?" Sascha glared at him. "You're the one who said I was working with Athena to destroy the weapons?"

He wiped some invisible dirt off the top of his scepter. "It's the truth, isn't it?"

Sascha studied Hades as he stood there before her. "I hadn't made any decisions. But after Laela telling that *creature* in the cave you said it was a waste to kill me when I could be sacrificed to him instead—I know which God I want to support. Unless, of course, Laela lied and you didn't say that."

Hades sniggered. "You certainly have spunk. She didn't lie. I did say that. Laela wanted to kill you, but to me, it seemed such a waste when the Ancient could use your powers." He tutted, "But I understand why you're a wee tad upset at me."

"Upset? That's an understatement. So why are you here? To gloat over what's going to happen to me?"

"No, not at all. I'm here to free you. I possess a helmet that renders the wearer invisible, meaning you can simply walk out of here and no one will stop you."

"And, of course, there's a catch," Sascha said.

He chuckled. "Of course."

"And what is it?"

"You take Laela's place and help me find the weapons and instead of destroying them, do what you were born to do and help me release them." He glanced at her.

Sascha snorted. "I'll never work with you to release them, but I'm sure you already know that."

"So instead you'd prefer to work with Athena to destroy

weapons you don't even understand? These weapons can bring peace to Eratus. Isn't that what you want?"

"So how do they work?" Sascha asked.

Hades tutted. "Not until you say you'll work with me."

Sascha shook her head. "No way."

"Don't be so quick to make up your mind. You're not exactly in a position to say no to someone who wants to help you. And in return for your help, you can have everything I've promised Laela and more."

"You'd betray one of your own soldiers to help me?" Sascha said. "I don't think so."

"I didn't choose her. It's a long story, but the short version is I have never been keen on Laela. But I like you. You show promise."

Sascha studied Hades as he wandered around the room, touching what little furniture there was. "And what have you promised Laela?"

"The power over all magic on Eratus." He glanced sideways at Sascha, "And Jenny's child."

"Jenny's chi—child?" Sascha stammered. "You mean when she has one?"

Hades roared with laughter. "Jenny never told you then. She has had a child for—now how old would it be? I guess it would be over three years old, nearly four."

"That can't be true. She would have been too young, only fifteen. And she would've told me."

"It's true all right. And if my information is correct—and it usually is—Jenny and child are back on Eratus, living in your castle."

"Why have you promised this child to Laela? What does she want with it?"

"That child will be far more powerful than any mortal has ever been. But then again, I guess it isn't exactly mortal."

"Isn't exactly mortal? What does that mean?"

Hades tilted his head to the side. "I don't know if it's that you can't remember these things or if Laela has kept everything from you. You were the leader of the Four Sisters. I'd be very surprised if you had known nothing about this."

Hades rubbed his chin, then continued. "I found out when the Ancients came to visit me one day. Laela had struck a deal with them. If they gave a girl of her choosing a child, then she would give them blood offerings that would sustain them until Ares finally released them."

Hades stepped up close to Sascha and whispered, "They seem to think Ares will give them Eratus." He stepped away and continued to stride around the room. "But plans always change. Jenny was meant to be impregnated by an Ancient, not a Master, yet it was a Master who bedded her. So Laela refused to honor their deal and give them the blood offerings and the Ancients were not happy. But a child is a child. I told Laela that unless she wanted to join me in hell sooner than she planned, she would honor the deal with the Ancients. She was a fool to think I wouldn't side with the Ancients, especially considering their connection to Ares."

"Are those young girls the blood offerings?" Sascha spat.

Hades turned and looked in the direction of the cavern. "Yes, it's a tad unfortunate. They're all so young and pretty." He shrugged his shoulders. "But it is what it is. If I could convince Ares to move his butt and finally release the Ancients, then we could stop with the offerings. I believe the Ancients have since lived up to their side of the deal. A couple of girls here have been impregnated now, so everything seems to be moving smoothly."

"But how can no one notice so many young mages going missing?" Sascha asked.

"Why do you think the headquarters are in Brun? No one here cares. It's your choice, but if you take over from Laela, you could try and refuse the Ancients. I mean, the deal was with Laela, not you. Anyway, this is a one-time offer. If you agree to work with me, you can leave here now with your power restored. The alternative is to let Laela sacrifice you to the Ancients, giving your power to the very creatures you want to kill."

Sascha shook her head. "A deal with the devil has never appealed to me. You never know the true cost until it's too late."

"That's unfortunate. I had thought you would be more sensible than this. Such a shame. Think back on this moment when the creatures consume you. I believe it's a very painful process." He bowed before her, giving a flourishing sweep with one hand. "It's been a pleasure, Sascha. Good luck in your next life . . . if you believe in such things."

With a flash of red light, he was gone.

Sascha considered what Hades had said. She had to save the girls. None of them deserved this. And Laela would pay for her part in all this. She was sworn to protect those with magic, not . . . sacrifice them.

She had to tell Athena what Hades said about Ares' connection to the Ancients. Why would two gods work with Laela and the Ancients to get their hands on these weapons? What is it that these weapons do?

Sascha flexed her fingers as she started to practice her magic. She had no idea how long it would be before the black lyrium wore off, but when it did, she would be ready.

THE DOOR SWUNG open as Thea, dressed in a polished red silk robe, walked in, followed by Redhead and Whitehair.

"Time to begin your preparations," Thea said. She turned to the guards. "Bring her."

Sascha was taken to a room filled with the aroma of

minty citrus and mixed berries and lit by a number of tall red candles. A large bath filled with a bright red liquid stood in the center of the room.

"Everything you need is here, Sascha." She pointed at the bath. "You must bathe yourself. There are some cloths for you to use. I have placed the robe you are to wear on the seat over there. When you are dressed, sit and wait."

Sascha walked over to the bath. "Is that water? It looks like—" She cupped her hand and scooped up a handful of water. She sniffed it. It was scented with mixed berries.

"It looks like blood, doesn't it?" Thea said as a smile crossed her face. "But we would hardly make you bathe in blood. That's a barbaric practice."

Sascha's mouth dropped open. "And sacrificing those young girls to the Ancients isn't?"

"You don't have long, Sascha. I'll be back, and when I do come back, you will be ready. If you're not . . . well, I doubt you would want these two guards bathing you."

Thea followed the guards outside. As she was about to close the door, a misty figure whipped past her and hid in the darkness in the corner of the room.

Bibacr.

As SOON AS the footsteps faded, Sascha raced over to Bibacr. "I've never been so glad to see you, Bibacr."

Bibacr squeaked. "Sascha to follow Bibacr. Soleil waiting outside to take Sascha home."

"Wait. You and Soleil are working together to save me?"

Bibacr gave a vigorous nod. "Soleil still not like Bibacr, but Soleil more worried about Sascha than Bibacr's darkness. Sascha follow Bibacr."

"Hang on. There are young girls here who are about to be

sacrificed to the Ancients. We must save them. I can't leave them for these"—she shuddered—"creatures to consume."

"Bibacr only have Soleil. Soleil only carry one. Sascha rescue the girls after Sascha safe."

"We must save them now. There is one young girl who will die tonight if we don't save her. The creature has had her taken to his room. She looks like she's only eight or nine. I can't leave her, or the others."

"Sascha's life more important. Bibacr knows."

Sascha shook her head. "I won't leave without them. And when my magic returns, I'll be rescuing them. It would be good to know there are others willing to help me."

"Sascha not have her power?"

"No. Laela gave me black lyrium."

Bibacr gasped. "Sascha in danger. Bibacr beg Sascha to come."

"If you want to get me out of here, rescue the girl locked in the creature's chambers and then help me rescue the other girls."

Bibacr stomped his foot. "Bibacr—"

Sascha squatted in front of him. "I know you want to help me. But what sort of person would I be if I left these young girls to their fates? Is your family close by?"

"Bibacr's family always close."

"Please, Bibacr, rescue the girl. You and your family can get into places I can't. And then bring your family to me so that we can rescue the other girls. We cannot leave them here."

Bibacr stomped his foot again. "Bibacr protect Sascha."

"I'll come with you, once we have rescued the girls. I will not leave without them."

Bibacr's head hung low as he shuffled to the door.

"Bibacr." Sascha walked over to him. "Sascha loves Bibacr. Thank you for doing this."

Bibacr shuffled his feet. "Bibacr sad to leave Sascha. Soleil be very angry with Bibacr."

"Take the young girl to Soleil. Get him to fly her to safety and she will help us rescue the others. I know it."

He nodded. "Bibacr do as Sascha ask."

"And find out where the other girls are being held, so we know where to go."

He sighed and stared up at her. His big eyes made Sascha feel so sad. He looked like a puppy being booted out of his home.

"Please, Bibacr, try to understand. You need to go now, before anyone discovers you here. It's time for you to get out of here."

Sascha walked over and tested the door. It was unlocked. She glanced over at Bibacr. "Are you ready to leave?"

He nodded.

She opened the door and the two guards whipped around to face her. They crossed their chest with their arms and stood facing her. "You can't blame a girl for trying to escape," she said, winking at the guards. By the time she closed the door, Bibacr had gone.

Fifteen minutes later, Sascha had bathed, changed into the robe that had been left for her, and was sitting in the chair. The door opened and Thea walked in. "I'm surprised to see you sitting."

"Isn't that what you told me to do?"

"Oh, yes. It's just that people usually pass out when they bathe in the berries—something to do with the toxicity. But your skin must be treated before the Ancients consume you. I'm impressed that you didn't pass out."

What was in the berries?

Thea tilted her head to the side. "You did bathe, didn't you? Guards, bring her to me."

The two men dragged Sascha over to Thea. She grabbed

Sascha's arm and sniffed. "Yes, you did. Good girl." Thea glanced at the guards. "Bring her."

Thea turned right into the corridor and headed down a set of stairs. She opened a door and stood back to let Sascha and the guards pass her.

Sascha's heart sunk. The room was full of cages.

How do I get out of here? Will Bibacr find me?

Thea flicked her fingers at a cage nearest the door. "Lock her in there."

Whitehair grabbed her and threw her in, banging her arms against the metal walls of the cage.

"Careful," Sascha said, rubbing her arms. "I'm not sure the leader would appreciate you damaging the goods."

Redhead brought in a bottle of wine and a glass on a tray. "Laela wanted you to have this," he said. "Sort of like your last meal. It's a special edition of your favorite wine. She said she guarantees it will make what is to come a lot less . . . painful." Redhead smirked as he followed Thea to the door of the room.

Thea stopped quickly, causing Redhead to crash into her. "Out of the way, you idiot" she snapped. She faced Sascha, "By the way, the ceremony is planned for tomorrow when the second moon is at its peak. Our Esteemed Leader should have renewed his energy after consuming his . . . appetizer. Sleep well. See you tomorrow."

PLANS TO RESCUE SASCHA

ERATUS

*M*arco paced up and down the gravel pathway that ran along the top of the cliffs overlooking the southern section of the temple. The two moons were bright, and the sky was clear, so it was easy to see the temple from where he stood. His war pyran was watching him, waiting for instruction. Marco checked and rechecked the time.

"They should be here by now," he muttered. "Where the hell are they?"

"Marco?"

"Bibacr, is that you?"

"Bibacr here. Sascha stayed in temple."

"Sascha what? What in Athena's name is—?" A crash in the trees to the left of where they were standing caused Marco to stop midstride. Broken branches and scattered leaves dropped onto the bushes at the base of the trees as a bird screeched.

"Soleil, get down here."

Soleil dropped from the branch and glided over the bushes, landing on the ground next to Marco.

"What is it with females?" Soleil growled. "Sascha won't leave until she's saved some girls she doesn't even know. Bibacr should have forced her to leave. I would have."

"Soleil, hold on," Marco said. "You know that Sascha cannot be forced to do anything. Bibacr, tell me what happened."

"Sascha tell Bibacr girls are being sacrificed to Ancients. Sascha refuse to leave without them."

Marco gave an exaggerated sigh. "This was supposed to be an easy rescue. Who are these girls? How many are there?"

"Bibacr not know. Bibacr sent Father to save young girl Sascha wanted rescued and look for other girls Sascha ask Bibacr to find. Bibacr come talk to Marco." He glanced at Soleil. "Bibacr sorry."

Marco scrubbed his face. "It's not your fault, Bibacr. What young girl did Sascha want rescued?"

"Sascha told Bibacr to save young girl locked in room with Ancient Master."

"Okay. We need to move. We don't know how long she will be safe there."

"Sascha locked in cave. Bibacr follow to make sure she safe. Bibacr hear they sacrifice Sascha tomorrow when the second moon is at its peak."

"Sacrifice her? To the Ancients?"

Bibacr gave a vigorous nod.

"We have to save her." Marco paced along the gravel path. "I can't send my men up against a hoard of guardians. The death toll would be too high. And even if they survived the fight, there's the guardians' poison to consider. Are there any creatures that you know of that are immune to their poison, creatures that might help us?"

"Bibacr know fire dragons immune."

Soleil spat at him. "Fire dragons can't be immune. They're not better than pyrans and pyrans are not immune."

"Bibacr seen guardians hurt fire dragons. Fire dragons not die if claws hurt them. Dragons quick and breathe fire. Dragons kill guardians."

"Where can we find these creatures?" Marco asked.

"Drakon has fire dragons," a voice whispered from the darkness surrounding them.

"Fe—Fenix?" Soleil stammered. "Is that you?"

The bushes parted as Fenix pushed her way through the trees to join them. They all stood in silence as they studied Fenix.

"You're here, in Brun," Soleil whispered. "So Drakon was right. You did organize this." He stared at her, fluffing his feathers so he appeared twice his usual size. "You're a traitor, Fenix. You deserve to die a traitor's death."

Marco moved in front of Fenix so his body protected her. "No, Soleil. Stay. If you care for Sascha at all, you will not do this."

"Fenix betrayed us . . ."

"I didn't betray you. Drakon wanted me to, threatened my children. But I didn't betray you or Sascha. I promise you, Soleil. I didn't."

"Soleil," Marco said, "we need to focus. We don't have time for this. We can sort this out after we save Sascha."

Soleil nodded, but didn't take his eyes off Fenix. "Yes, Sascha comes first, and then Fenix dies."

Marco turned to face Fenix. "I know Drakon has fire dragons but that doesn't help. They won't work with us."

"They will if Drakon tells them to."

"And why would he do that?"

"He loves Sascha. If he found out what Laela has done, he would send his dragons to seek revenge and to save Sascha."

"Connell was right," Marco muttered. "But that is just wrong. Sascha is his sister, unless—I thought his interest was in her powers, but I was wrong, wasn't I?"

Fenix said nothing as she studied Marco.

Bibacr nodded at a hill that stood behind them. "Bibacr seen fire dragon cave. Lots of dragons."

Marco rubbed his temple with his fingertips.

Connell was right. Drakon is in love with Sascha. I need his help to save her but if he so much as looks at her in the wrong way, I'll—

"Marco talk to Bibacr," Bibacr said hopping from one foot to the other.

"Sorry, Bibacr," Marco said. "I was thinking of something else. If we can somehow use Drakon's fire dragons to coordinate the wild dragons that live in that cave and they work together to distract the guardians . . ." He nodded. "I need someone to talk to Drakon, tell him what's happened."

"I'll speak to Drakon," Fenix said.

"But if he asked you to capture Sascha, and you didn't—," Marco said.

"He won't punish me until after Sascha is safe," Fenix said. "Sascha must come first."

"I'll go with Fenix," Soleil said. "I'll make sure she does what she says she will."

"Before you do that, Soleil, go and see Eham. Eham and Jenny should be back on Eratus by now. I've set them up in the room below my chambers. Take Eham with you when you go to see Drakon. Eham has a dread wisp. If his dread wisp can talk to Drakon's dragons, ask them to help us, we might have some hope."

Marco turned to Bibacr. "You and your father get us numbers, so we know exactly what we're up against. I'll get my father to help us. There must be benefits to your father being a duke. And kidnapping a princess is a crime punishable by death. Father will help us, I know he will."

Marco glanced at Fenix, Soleil, and Bibacr. "We will all meet back here before the first moon rises tomorrow.

Assuming everything goes to plan, at that time we will send the fire dragons to begin their attack."

ERATUS—THE DUKE OF KILMARNOCK'S HOME IN BRUN

Marco's war pyran carried him over the town of Kilmarnock and landed in the center of his father's castle grounds. Marco climbed off the shoulders of his pyran and walked into the stables. The familiar smell of leather, honey-wood, and pine greeted him as he arrived at the stable doors. A young woman raced toward him and curtseyed.

"Can I take your pyran, My Lord?"

"Yes, thank you, Nori. You've grown up a lot since I was here last time."

A flush crept across her cheeks. "Yes, My Lord." She turned away from him. "I'll take good care of your pyran, My Lord," she said before she skittered away, the pyran in tow.

"Thank you, Nori," he called after her. The stables were still in perfect condition and the other pyrans that were housed there looked fit and healthy. His father always liked the green pyrans, so he was surprised to see a golden-red pyran in the last stall at the back of the stables.

I wonder who owns that creature.

He took a deep breath to release the stress from the time on the cliff.

Father will help.

He felt a twinge of guilt because he hadn't been back to see his father for quite a few years. He strode out of the stables, past the armory, and up the stairs to the main entrance to his father's castle. He pushed open the two solid doors and walked into the large entry hall with its twelve-foot ceiling and wide polished floorboards. A tall, slim maid with a thin face, large glasses, and no smile greeted him at the door.

"My Lord," she said, curtseying.

"Where's Rosetta?" Marco asked.

"Her mother has joined Athena. Rosetta will be back in a couple of days."

"What is your name?" he asked.

She peered at him over her glasses. "Fran." She dug into the pocket of her skirt. "We received a missive for you, My Lord. I was going to forward it to you at the High King's castle. I didn't realize you were coming here."

"Thanks, Fran." He took the slip of paper from her and put it into his jacket pocket. "Where's Father?"

She glanced toward the polished moonstone staircase. "In the library."

"Excellent. Thanks."

He made his way up the staircase two stairs at a time and then strode into a massive paneled library with built-in shelves and an overly large chandelier.

"Father," he called out.

The fire had been lit, which was an unusual sight in Brun, even in winter. He rubbed his arms.

But it is cool today.

"Hello, son," a husky voice said.

Marco turned around. His father looked well, his tanned skin evidence of a life spent outside. A head shorter than Marco, his thick dark hair showed streaks of gray. "Father, it's good to see you." He took a couple of steps forward, reached over, and pulled his father into a hug. He breathed in that familiar smell of spiced berry shaving lotion and tobacco.

He's so thin.

"Father, you've lost weight."

"Humph," his father mumbled. "That's the way you greet your father after . . . now, how many years is it?"

Marco cleared his throat. "I guess it's been over five years."

"You guess. You don't even know. In five years a man could nearly forget he had a son."

"I'm sorry, Father."

His father tutted. "It's not a bad thing. Being away from Brun is not a bad thing."

"But you got the invite to our wedding?" Marco asked.

"Yes. Next month. The invite was to Geraud plus one. Can I bring someone with me?"

Marco laughed. "Of course you can. I know the invite says next month, but it would be good if you could come to the castle before then. I know Owain would love to see you."

"Don't talk to me about him."

"Father," Marco warned. "It was my choice to stay there and join the Fire of the Phoenix. He had nothing to do with it."

"I don't want to hang around his castle for too long. Why do I need to be there earlier?"

"Have you noticed how much cooler it has been lately?" Marco asked.

"Yes. Your men visited me. Preparations are well under way."

"Well, I think it's possible the season may be here sooner than we think. Should the worst happen, it would be good if you were in the castle with us rather than here on your own. And it would be good to spend some time with you."

"I'll think about it, but I don't like to travel so much these days."

"I thought you loved flying on your pyrans," Marco said.

"I stopped flying a while ago. I prefer to use the portals."

"Father, I'm not sure how safe the portals are, and they could be shut down very soon."

"Pfft. Son, after all these years, I think I know how to look after myself. I'll pour us a mead and then we can sit down and you can tell me why you're here."

Fifteen minutes later, Marco put his empty glass on the table in front of him and sat back in his chair. "So, can I take some of your men, Father?"

"Yes, we'll only take what we need. I need men to keep the peace here when I'm gone."

"When you say 'we'll' . . ."

"I'm coming with you, Marco. These men have broken the law of my land. It's only right I am there to make sure they pay the price."

"Thank you, Father. It will be good to have you there. But what is this about the peace? Are you having problems here?"

"There have been strange happenings around here lately and my people are afraid. When they see the soldiers wandering around the castle grounds, they feel . . . protected."

"What sort of strange happenings?" Marco asked.

We'll talk about it later. Perhaps when we catch up for your wedding. There's nothing to be done about it. The soldiers keep the calm, and everything keeps operating."

"Speaking of strange . . . it was unusual to see a golden-red pyran in the stables. Who owns it?"

Geraud glanced away from Marco and picked up his empty glass. "I think we need another mead. I'll be back in a—"

Marco snapped upright and dug his hand into his jacket pocket. "Damn it. The missive. I forgot to read it."

"What missive?" Geraud asked.

"Fran gave it to me when I arrived." Marco opened the note and read it. "Shit." He pushed himself out of the chair and walked to the window as he slowed the panicked thoughts that were whirling around in his head. "How the hell am I going to manage this?"

"What's wrong, son?"

"It's Owain. Zabir uncovered a plot to assassinate Owain before the first moon rises tomorrow. But I've organized for the others to meet me to rescue Sascha at that same time."

Geraud joined him at the window and placed his hand on Marco's shoulder. "Don't worry, son. I'll lead the attack on the temple. Give me all the details and I'll organize the men you need."

"This is Sascha we're talking about. I need to be there. I can't lose her, not now, not after everything we've been through. But it would be good to discuss the plan with you and if I'm delayed, would you be my backup, keep everything going until I get there?"

"Of course. I understand how you feel about Sascha. I felt that way about your mother."

Marco nodded. "Thank you, Father. There is one other thing. I believe Laela is connected to all of this and I've got a gut feeling that Reya won't be too far away from wherever Laela is."

"You mean Drakon's Reya? Isn't she dead?"

"I thought so, but a couple of things have happened lately that have made me think she may be alive. And Reya has pit hounds."

Geraud visibly gulped. "Pit hounds."

"Yes, but I have something that will help you fight them. They're magically crafted weapons called the Vengeance of Hephaestus. They're designed to kill any creatures of darkness. You only need to touch the pit hounds with the blade of one of the weapons to kill them. I have daggers and swords."

"Can I have the daggers?" Geraud asked.

"The swords are safer."

"They may be, but I prefer the daggers."

"Okay," Marco agreed. "They're in my chambers so in case I'm late, I'll give them to Eham. He can give them to you when he sees you. Promise me that you'll use them."

"I will, son. Stop worrying. Come and meet my captain, and let's discuss the attack. It will feel good to finally have a chance to punish those creatures that call themselves priests."

THE ANCIENT WEAPONS

ERATUS: THE AWAKENING HEADQUARTERS

*T*he skies were still dark when they opened the heavy metal doors that led down to the dungeons of the Awakening headquarters. Laboratory One had been set up in the lowest level of the dungeons, a secure spot, away from prying eyes. Drakon rested his hand on his bollock dagger as he made his way down a stone corridor filled with the stench of rotten leaves and large puddles of brackish water. Set in sconces along the wall were several burning torches, their weak flames struggling to permeate the oppressive darkness. Drakon grumbled as he did his best to dodge the screeching rats that skittered across the floor. He flicked a glance at Chiane and saw him shiver.

"Chiane, you haven't said a word since we left."

"Doing my best to navigate this foul place," Chiane replied.

They arrived at the bottom of a set of stairs and walked toward a pair of solid metal doors.

Drakon rubbed his nose. "You'd think they'd have made this place a bit more habitable."

"The odor is truly putrid," Chiane replied.

Drakon knocked twice. A grill slid open and a pair of eyes in a black metal helmet glared out at them.

"My Prince," the guard spluttered. Metal locks clanged as they were pushed aside. The door opened, allowing Chiane and Drakon to enter.

"Guard," Chiane said, "Mage Isabella will be joining us soon, so please allow her to pass through the gates when she arrives."

"Yes, sir," the guard replied.

They continued to the end of the corridor where they found a glass door. Drakon pressed a button and the glass door slid silently open. They stepped into a narrow chamber. The ceiling flickered into life as the door closed behind them and a purple glow flooded the room.

"This decontamination system wouldn't be needed if they did something about the rest of this place," Drakon muttered.

"I agree," Chiane said. "But the scientists said it was a waste of time to try and neutralize the entire cave. They said this was all that was needed."

Drakon grunted.

Fifteen seconds later, the glow disappeared and the door to the antechamber opened.

Drakon nodded in approval as he surveyed the room. "This is more like it. Even the air is fresh."

In the right-hand corner of the room was a set of stairs that led down to the laboratory. A glass wall allowed those in the antechamber to observe the experiments being conducted below. Two armed guards stood at the top of the stairs. They snapped to attention as Drakon moved toward the glass wall.

"My Prince," the taller of the two guards said. "Everything has been prepared as per your orders."

"And the subjects have been selected from each of the groups?" Drakon asked.

"Yes, My Prince. Five from each group."

Inside the laboratory stood several groups of people—the test subjects. Each of the subjects wore a colored neckband that had been marked with their race and their position within their society. The color of the band differed depending on the subject's temperament, indicating how closely they needed to be watched. Those with white and yellow bands were considered to be more compliant, while those with black bands required closer supervision due to their tendency to take control. Those with red bands showed a tendency for defiance and aggression.

"When is Isabella arriving?" Drakon snapped. "She should be here by now."

"She'll be here any minute, My Prince."

Chiane walked over to join Drakon at the window. Set along the far wall of the laboratory were several of the crates that had been taken from the cave. A long silver table stood against the wall closest to them.

"I want her to deal with the troublemakers," Drakon said as he turned to the guard. "Guard, have all subjects been tagged?"

"Yes, My Prince."

Chiane shivered. "Tagging seems an extreme form of control, especially when many of them are too scared to do anything."

Drakon glanced over at Chiane. "It was Reya's idea, and I liked it. She also told me that some of the men were tagging the subjects so that they were only maimed when the tags were detonated."

"Yes," Chiane grimaced. "They'd detonate the tags and then release the wounded subjects into the park so they could hunt them for sport."

"I told Reya to sort it out," Drakon said. "It was her job."

"She did stop it. She tagged a couple of the main culprits

in the same way they tagged the subjects and then released them in the hunting park. They didn't last long."

"They were lucky no one else ever realized what was happening here," Drakon said, "otherwise I would have hunted those men myself."

A muffled squabble between a few of the subjects caught Drakon's attention. A couple of the men wearing red bands were having a disagreement.

Drakon stepped forward and placed his hand on a microphone. "If Isabella isn't here in the next few minutes . . ." He switched the microphone on. "That's enough of your squabbling." His voice boomed across the room.

The men stopped what they were doing and glared up at the glass wall.

"Good. Now I have your attention, let me tell you why you're all here. You're here to help me carry out an experiment." There were a few muffled gasps before an eerie silence filled the room. "The good news is that you can all go home when the experiment is over. I need you to be patient just a little longer."

He turned the microphone off. There were nods of approval as those who weren't wearing red or black bands accepted the lie.

Look at the hope in their faces. The fools. They won't be alive at the end of this, let alone going home.

Drakon caught a glimpse of the expression on Chiane's face. He had that same look of hope. Before Drakon could say anything to him, the door swished open and Isabella walked into the antechamber.

"About time," Drakon growled. "I need you to use your magic to control any of the subjects who cause trouble, particularly those with red and black bands."

"Yes, My Prince."

Drakon smothered a smirk as Isabella edged along the far

wall in an effort to keep as much distance between the two of them as she could. When she reached the glass wall, Isabella glanced at the people in the laboratory below and then gasped. She slapped her palms on the glass.

"Mama! Papa!" She took her hands from the glass wall and turned to Drakon. "My family is in there. I'll give you whatever you want if you please, please release them."

Drakon tutted. "I don't think that's fair, Isabella. What about everyone else? Why should your parents be given preferential treatment?"

"They're royalty," Isabella said. "They're not commoners."

"Then that makes them even more perfect for this experiment." Drakon shook his head. "No, they stay."

"They have access to money, to armies. They would pledge everything to you if you let them go."

"No," Drakon said. "In the name of fairness, they stay."

Isabella turned back to face her parents, tears flowing down her cheeks.

"Isabella, you have a job to do," Drakon said. "Keep the troublemakers under control. You don't want them starting a brawl and hurting your parents."

Isabella nodded.

Chiane walked over to her and put his hand on her shoulder. "It will be all right, Isabella. Prince Drakon will be releasing everyone when the experiment is over."

Drakon slowly shook his head.

Is Chiane really that naive? Surely not.

Drakon turned the microphone back on. He decided to pick one of the older subjects wearing a white band. "You with the orange jacket."

The short thin man turned to face the glass wall.

"Yes, you." Drakon pointed at the far wall. "I want you to collect one of those boxes and carry it over to the silver table next to this wall. You can get some help to carry it if you need it. Then I want you to open it. The nails have been removed, so it should be easy to do."

The man gulped and then nodded. "Yes, okay."

An older woman with a red band spat on the floor in front of the thin man. "Don't be so gutless. Say no." She turned to face the glass wall. "Who do you think you are? Standing up there, telling us what to do."

The guards drew their swords and moved toward the door to the laboratory.

"Stand down," Drakon ordered. "This is Isabella's job."

Isabella glanced at Drakon and then raised her hands. Yellow bands of light circled the woman.

Drakon chuckled. "You have spunk, woman, but you will find that my mage here has paralyzed you. You can try to move if you like, but the truth is that you can't escape the magic. You are vulnerable to whatever whim overcomes me. You'd better pray to whichever god you serve that I don't want to teach you a lesson."

The man with the orange jacket nodded to one of the men standing next to him, and together, they carried the box over to the long silver table. A young female moved closer to the table as the man took off the lid. The inside of the box was lined with a fine silver mesh.

"There's nothing here," the man said.

Drakon leaned against the glass and looked into the box. The man was right—there was nothing in the box but dust. Disappointment flashed through him. The weapons must have been destroyed or stolen. They would have to open another box.

The lining inside the box began to emit a soft hum and then turned a vibrant blue.

"Wait," the man called out. "The dust is changing color. It's pulsating."

The female put her hand in the box and allowed the dust

to filter through her fingers. Color drained from her face as she stared at her hand. She squealed and tried to flick the dust away. "My hand . . . it tingles. Really tingles."

When she opened her mouth to scream, her body sparkled and then disappeared. Nothing remained of her, not even the neckband.

As everyone stared at the empty space in shocked silence, the dust in the box exploded into the air. High-pitched screams reverberated around the room as the subjects fell over each other, trying to escape an enemy they had no idea how to fight. The battle was over in seconds.

Chiane gulped. "The weapons—is *dust* the weapon? But that's . . ."

Drakon stood frozen to the spot. How could dust be a weapon? And didn't Ares say it needed to be activated somehow. But how do you activate dust?

Ares told me to open the crates before I moved them. Is it possible he knew this would happen when the crates were opened? And all this talk about 'activating' the weapon was a lie?

Isabella made a high-pitched squeaking noise. Her family had vanished. "No," she cried, shaking her head. "Please, no."

It took Drakon a few seconds to realize that a few of the subjects were huddled together in the corner of the room. He studied them. Each of them was wearing either a white or yellow band. He glanced around the room. There were no red or black bands anywhere. What did that mean?

His focus shifted back to Isabella as she gave a gargled scream. She was pointing at the glass wall. The dust had glued itself to the glass. The glass seemed to be vibrating, as if the dust was trying to free itself.

"We need to get out of here, My Prince," Chiane said. "Guards, you come, too. Move!"

Drakon nodded and headed for the exit. Chiane and Isabella followed.

"Isabella, help me with a barrier spell," Drakon said when they were standing on the other side of the glass door. "We must seal the door and the gates. No one must ever get in there."

"But there were survivors," Chiane said. "We can't leave them like that."

"Fine," Drakon snapped. "You're welcome to go back in there."

Chiane stared at him, but made no move to go back in.

"As I thought," Drakon growled.

After putting the first barrier in place, they moved beyond the steel gates and locked them. Within a couple of minutes, the second barrier was in place. The laboratory was secure.

Drakon took a step back from the barrier as he tried to digest what had just happened. Isabella dropped to her knees and sobbed.

"Time to get back," Drakon said. "Chiane, when Isabella has collected herself, return to the castle with her. I have a couple of things to do."

Chiane walked over to Isabella, crouched down next to her, and put his hand on her shoulder.

"Guard, come with me," Drakon said. When they were out of Isabella's earshot, Drakon turned to the guard. "I haven't seen many of the guards down here but you look surprisingly familiar."

"I have one of those faces, My Prince," the guard replied. "I've been down here for years and you haven't been down here for a long time, so we couldn't have met."

"Okay. Anyway, all of those people were definitely tagged before they were brought in here?"

"Yes, My Prince," the guard replied. "We have their names and their tag numbers."

"Who can detonate the tags?"

"Security on the top level, My Prince."

"Good. Go directly there. Tell them to detonate the tags of all the subjects that were in that laboratory."

"All of them, My Prince?"

"Are you questioning my orders?"

He shook his head. "Not at all, My Prince. I apologize."

"If any of them are still alive in there," Drakon said, "they will wish they weren't. It's a kindness to end their lives, not a cruelty. Go."

Drakon left Chiane behind with the still-sobbing Isabella and made his way back to his chambers. He needed time to think, time to work out what had just happened.

ERATUS—BACK IN THE CASTLE

Drakon was sitting back on his balcony as the second sun appeared on the horizon. On the table beside him lay a flask of vimberry, a jug of prumble ale resting in an ice mill, and plates of fresh fruits and baked sweets. He swallowed down a couple of mugs of ale before allowing himself to think about what had happened.

How did some of those people survive the attack?

He should have stayed there a bit longer to see if those still alive had some sort of immunity to the dust or if it simply took longer to work on them. Those with white and yellow bands were supposed to be the most compliant ones, pose the least threat. They should have been the first ones to die. Was it possible that the dust killed only the strong? But that didn't make sense. Why would any ruler kill off their strongest subjects? They would have no armies, no one who could defend them.

No one who would defy them either.

"Sokentash. If only I knew what this dust is meant to do."

And the silver mesh . . . what was it? Had it been treated with some sort of magic? Ares' words flashed into his mind: "We have been given a cryptic message that says they can be controlled with the powers hidden in magic's shadow."

What does that even mean? Was the mesh treated with a type of magic?

Drakon closed his eyes and exhaled slowly. And what was in the silver box? Perhaps the vials engraved on the lid meant that the box contained samples of this dust. But why would someone go to all the trouble of creating samples? He poured himself a third ale and swigged it down. He needed to examine the map he had of the weapons site in Brun. Perhaps that site held some answers.

I need to find a few more answers before I do anything else.

DRAKON STRODE into his war room, clapped his hands to turn on the lights, and walked past his fire dragons to the table in the middle of the room.

"Mirror, show me the weapons site in Brun."

"Yes, My Prince."

A soft blue glow surrounded the carved marble table. Drakon rubbed his chin as he studied the map.

I have to go to Cirrone and talk to Sascha. If Ares insisted on her being a part of this, she must know what powers are hidden in magic's shadow.

He sighed. He was probably clutching at straws. It might be something that was still locked away in those memories she hadn't recovered.

Claws clicked on the balcony rim of his war room.

Is that Fenix? But I told her to stay with Sascha.

Fenix trotted into Drakon's chambers. Her onyx eyes watched Drakon's every move.

"Fenix, didn't I tell you to stay in Cirrone with Sascha?"

"She's not in Cirrone. I never took her there."

"What do you mean?" Drakon took a deep breath as he stared down at his hands, which were gripping the edge of the table so tightly that his knuckles were white. An intense burning rage, a need to destroy Fenix, roared through him. He closed his eyes, took another deep breath, and then released his grip on the table. "Kalamar, it looks like I have a job for you. But before I offer you her children, I offer you Fenix."

"No, give me a moment to explain," Fenix said. "Laela has captured Sascha."

"Laela? You're lying. Why would Laela capture Sascha?"

His gut twisted.

Is it possible that Laela wants to see if Sascha knows what powers can be used to control the dust? No, that can't be right. Ares wanted to beat Laela—and Hades. He'd hardly help them.

Kalamar stood, shook himself, stretched his wings, and prowled toward Fenix.

"You must believe me," Fenix pleaded. "Laela has captured her. I'm here to ask for your help to rescue her."

"Where is Laela holding her?"

"In Brun, in a cage below the temple of the Fire Gods."

"I find that hard to believe," Drakon said. "Laela's sense of self-preservation is too strong for her to be working with those uneducated . . . morons. The people in Brun would kill Laela just as quickly as they would kill Sascha."

Kalamar stopped midstride and glanced at the door that opened onto the ramparts. He turned to face the doorway.

"What is it, Kalamar?" Drakon asked.

Eham stepped into the room. A weasel-like creature, its beady eyes focused on Kalamar, rested on Eham's shoulder.

"What Fenix says is the truth," Eham said as he moved aside to allow Soleil to enter the room.

"Well, look who it is. Eham. So you and Jenny have finally decided to return to Eratus."

So much for Pat letting me know of their return. I need to have a word with her.

Drakon nodded at the creature on Eham's shoulder. "You do walk with the dark side of magic if you're bonded to a dread wisp."

"We need your help, Drakon. Well, to be more specific, we need your fire dragons' help. Laela is sacrificing Sascha to the Ancients when the second moon reaches its peak tonight."

"What are you talking about, Eham? Why would she do that?"

"We don't know, but what we do know is that we must save her."

"It's easy . . . if you're serious," Drakon said. "Get an army and attack the place."

"If it was that easy, we would have done it by now," Eham spat. "The priests have surrounded the temple with trained guardians."

Drakon folded his arms across his chest and rested his body against the edge of the table. "Can guardians be trained?"

"It seems so. And the only creatures that can defeat them are fire dragons."

"My couple of fire dragons can hardly be expected to fight off a hoard of guardians."

Eham moved closer to Drakon, his gaze drawn to the map in the middle of the table. "There is a fire dragon cave not far from the temple. We were hoping that your fire dragons might persuade the wild dragons to help clear a pathway through the guardians so that our army can get into the temple."

"And once a pathway has been cleared?"

"Marco will lead his father's army into the temple. After all, Laela and the priests kidnapped the daughter of the High King. That is a crime of the land, punishable by death. And as Marco is the son of the Duke he has the right to bring the criminals to justice on his father's behalf."

Heavy boots sounded from the ramparts. Eham turned as Marco strode into the war room.

"Marco, what are you doing here?" Eham asked.

"The plan has changed slightly. There's a plot to kill the High King. They're planning to attack before the second moon rises."

"That's only hours away," Drakon said.

"I know. We need to save Owain." He turned to Eham. "But you need to continue to prepare for the attack. I will join you after we have killed those who want to attack the King. Father will take the lead in the attack if I am late."

"But can this lot be trusted to help save Sascha?" Drakon asked.

"This lot can answer for themselves," Eham said as Soleil snorted. "And you'd better hope we *can* be trusted."

Drakon sighed. "Okay. Show me how you plan to rescue Sascha. If I'm satisfied, I'll ask my fire dragons to help out. Then, Marco, you can tell me how we're going to save Father."

THE GOLDEN TOOTH

ERATUS

*M*arco walked into his chambers and over to his weapons locker where he had stored the daggers he wanted to give to his father. After he retrieved them, he bolted the locker door and walked over to the golden statue of a pyran that was positioned on the shelf near the window. He moved the statue to the right and a portion of the side wall slid back to reveal a door. He knocked twice on the door and then once.

The door opened and Jenny stood there, a smile on her face. "Hi, Marco. Come in," she said, stepping back to allow him into the room beyond. It was a large room with floor-to-ceiling windows. The windows had been treated so that the occupants could see out, but people couldn't see in. A soft peppermint-scented breeze wafted through the room, ruffling Vonn's hair as he concentrated on the text he was reading.

"Thanks, Jenny, but I won't disturb you. I know it's Vonn's study time. I was hoping you could do me a favor. Would you give this package to Eham before he leaves for

Brun and ask him to give it to my father? It's a pair of daggers I promised him."

"Of course. Are you sure you don't want to come inside for a minute?"

"No, but thanks anyway. I'd better go."

"Hey, Marco. I wanted to thank you for allowing us to stay here. It's very generous of you."

"Just keep yourselves safe," Marco said.

"We will."

Marco stepped back from the door as Jenny closed it. He turned and walked over to the ladder that led up to the tavern's roof. It was an easy climb, and when he reached the roof, he sat down on the clay tiles and stared down at the people in the courtyard. He loved being up here, away from the milling crowds. It was a good place for a man to think.

Drakon was a tactical thinker, and together, they had put in place various levels of security to protect Owain. They had tried to brief Owain on their plans, but Owain refused to be a part of the discussions saying they were making a big deal of nothing. Now, all they could do was watch and wait. He breathed in the savory aroma of roasted meats and listened to the laughter echoing from the tavern as diners enjoyed a couple of silkars over lunch. A couple wandered out of the tavern and strolled toward the memorial bell set up in the tavern gardens. The memorial was a way to remember those lost in battle at the Fire of the Phoenix headquarters on Earth. All those poor souls that never had a chance to return to their homeland. He never did understand the point of the bell. He had thought a plaque and a torch would have been more appropriate.

A tall, slim woman with long, curly, ebony-colored hair and wearing a bright tangerine-colored tunic caught his attention. She was having an animated conversation with a gaunt, gray-haired man dressed in a white robe. He was about a foot shorter than her. She stopped talking, stood up straight, and looked directly at Marco. It was Raeshaan. He flinched. He hadn't spoken to her since Bibacr's visit. She nodded in acknowledgment, tapped the man she had been talking to on the shoulder, and pointed at Marco. Then they both turned and headed toward the tavern.

"Damn," Marco said. "I should have talked to her before now."

He climbed off the roof and then strode down the stairs into the tavern. He sat at a table in the corner, away from the noise of the crowds, and waited for Raeshaan and the old man to enter. When they did a few seconds later, Marco waved his hand at them.

"We've been looking for you," Raeshaan said, taking the seat beside Marco. "We have some things to tell you. But firstly, this is Grandmaster Huwein. He is the one I was talking to you about, the one who trained me."

"Yes, I remember," Marco said. "It's good to meet you, Grandmaster. Please take a seat. I have something to tell you, too. We found Sascha. We're preparing to rescue her."

"That is good news." Raeshaan breathed a sigh of relief. "I assume she is in Brun?"

"Yes," Marco said. "You were able to trace the magic then?"

"Yes. We were leaving Ocean's Mouth to come and find you when the High King found us."

"You saw Owain?"

"Yes." Raeshaan glanced around the room before moving her chair closer to Marco's. She moved her fingers as she muttered a soft chant. A hum whispered around the table.

Marco cleared his throat. "What are you doing, Raeshaan?"

"I wanted to ensure our privacy, so I've put a shield

around this table. What I have to tell you is for your ears alone."

"Is it about Connell?"

"That's one of the things."

"One?"

"Yes." Raeshaan studied her hands, which were resting on the tabletop. "The High King asked us to help him. Tonight, it will appear to those around him as if he dies."

Marco stared openmouthed at Raeshaan. "Like he dies? Of all the harebrained schemes. I'm going to—"

Marco was pushing himself up from the table when Raeshaan's hand gripped his wrist. "Please sit, Marco. Hear us out."

"Why in Athena's name would he want people to think that he's dead?"

"He said the dragon hunters are only a distraction. There's a more powerful enemy behind them, one that is connected to the Ancients. He told us he had discovered a clue. The catch is that the only one who can follow up on this clue is someone who knows how the more elite levels of the dragon hunters work, knows how to infiltrate their defenses without putting the hunters on alert. And there isn't any weak link in that elite circle that Owain can exploit. They're all loyal to their leader. So Owain has to do this himself."

Marco's stomach churned. This discussion was all so surreal. He had sworn to protect the King and now he was going to stand by and let this happen? A thought struck him.

"That doesn't make sense," Marco said as he studied Raeshaan and the grandmaster. "If he is dead, he is approaching them as someone new—so wouldn't he have to start at the lowest level of the hunters and work his way up?"

"No," Raeshaan said. "Everyone, including the dragon hunters, respects money and position. That is what he will have when he approaches them. He has been working to create a false identity that will give him what he needs to reach a high status—and quickly."

"Then give that identity to someone else. Let them do the work."

The grandmaster sat forward in his chair. "It's not that simple, Marco. If it was, he would have done that. Owain is not a fool. The politics in the dragon hunters is complex and an outsider would do the wrong things and could unwittingly trigger the very situation we're trying to prevent."

"A High King has to die so that he can become a spy? Is that what you're telling me?"

"Marco, he isn't really dying. It is appearing as if he dies so that we can flush out the enemy. Let them think he's dead. Once the attention is off him, he will follow up on the clue and with Athena's help they will discover what the plans are and work out how we can stop it."

"Does Athena actually know about this?"

"Yes," Raeshaan said as she put her hand into the pocket of her tunic.

Marco shook his head. "And she has agreed to help him?"

"Yes, she has. But Owain needs you to look after Connell and destroy the ancient weapons."

"We don't even know how to open the sites that have the weapons," Marco said. "Or what they do, let alone how we can destroy them."

Raeshaan and the grandmaster sat quietly for a minute. Raeshaan withdrew her hand from the pocket in her tunic and rested it in her lap. "Sascha knows where the map is, knows how to find them. Once you have rescued her, get her to talk to Athena, find out how to destroy the weapons. You read the note left by the dragon hunters. Their first plan of attack is to release the weapons. That cannot happen. Those weapons must be destroyed."

Marco sat at the table in silence as he tried to digest what he was being told. He only knew a little about both Raeshaan and the grandmaster. Why should he trust them? Surely, in all of Eratus, there must be someone who could follow up on the clue, instead of Owain.

"No disrespect to you two, but I need to talk to him. I need to hear this directly from Owain. He could have told Drakon and me all about this when we were trying to brief him on the security we were putting in place."

"He couldn't tell you then, Marco. There are . . . complications in Drakon knowing about what Owain is planning."

"Complications?" Marco repeated. "Drakon is his son."

Raeshaan placed a golden dragon's tooth and an envelope on the table in front of Marco. "Owain expected you to react like this, so he asked us to give this to you. He said you would know the meaning of the tooth."

Marco's eyes stung. The last time he had seen this tooth was when Owain had helped him stop his father from killing himself following his mother's death. Though he had only been a child, Marco had made a promise to Owain. If he could ever repay the debt, Owain only needed to return the tooth. Marco pushed down the sadness that flooded over him. That had been such a long time ago. So much had changed. It had never occurred to him that Owain might have kept it. "Yes, I understand its meaning."

He picked up the envelope. On the back was the royal seal of the Grayfang realm—a winged manticore sitting underneath a canopy of gray fangs. He broke the seal and took out the note.

Marco,

I'm sorry I didn't tell you this in person when you tried to brief me today on the security you were putting in place to protect me. It's just that at the moment I have to be careful about who knows of my plan.

I know my request is highly unusual and that you must be

struggling to understand my motives. There is a lot at stake, but I know I am the only one who can help us finally work out what's happening. I need your support, which is why I have returned the tooth to you. You read the note I was given when the dragon hunters escaped. You know how real the threat is.

Please listen to what Raeshaan and the grandmaster tell you. I trust them as I trust you.

While I am gone, I need you to look after Connell and keep an eye on Drakon. Use your influence in whatever way you can to stop them from doing anything stupid. Leaving Connell at this time worries me immensely, but I know you will protect him.

And one final thing. Once you find Sascha, you must tell her about all of this. I need the both of you to ensure these ancient weapons are destroyed. Ask Sascha to meet with Athena. Athena has promised to help in giving you whatever information you need to destroy the weapons.

I'm sorry to leave you with such a burden, but you can always count on Raeshaan and the grandmaster if things begin to turn sour.

Owain.

Marco sat staring at the note in his hand.

"Owain wanted to talk to you personally," Raeshaan said, "but there can be no connection between you and what is about to happen. When he dies, every person he spoke to in the days leading up to his death will be suspected."

"What about the ones who will be blamed for his death? They will be tortured, their people hunted."

"The attempt will be real, so the punishment will be well-deserved."

"What about you two? You met with him. He isn't worried if the blame falls on you?"

"No," the grandmaster said. "No one will remember the meeting we had with the High King."

"What do you mean?"

"Magic can change many things," Raeshaan said.

"You used magic to make it seem as if the meeting never happened?" Marco asked.

Raeshaan nodded.

"What is the point of having your own private forces," Marco muttered, "if you can't rely on them when you need them? Instead Owain organizes these secret, totally unsatisfying meetings."

"He *is* relying on them. You and us."

"That's not what I mean. He would rather trust you—strangers—with all of this, but not his own family or me?"

"We're not strangers, Marco," Raeshaan said. "The High—Owain, the grandmaster, and I have been friends for many years now."

"I've served Owain for many years myself," Marco said. "And I haven't seen any sign of your friendship."

"There are many reasons for that. One day we'll tell you the story, but for now we need you to trust us."

"This plan is so dangerous. So many things could go wrong." Marco scrubbed his face with his hands, then took a deep breath and released it slowly. "What are we supposed to do now? Can we tell Drakon anything about Owain's plan?"

"No!" Raeshaan and the grandmaster said at the same time.

"Why not?"

"Owain doesn't believe Drakon's reactions will be believable if he realizes his father is still alive."

"Believable?" Marco snapped.

"Drakon can't help himself. His ego influences his reactions. Someone will work it out if Drakon doesn't react in the way Owain is expecting him to. And Owain isn't sure that Drakon isn't involved in all of this."

"Fake or not, Owain's death will make Drakon the new

ruler of Eratus. And I believe it's possible that Drakon might not even be Owain's—"

"He knows everything," Raeshaan said. "And yet he still believes this is necessary. Doesn't that tell you something?"

Marco shook his head. "You know he might not even be Owain's son?"

"Yes, I do, and so does Owain."

Marco's mind raced as it searched for another option, but nothing would come. He exhaled heavily. "What is the plan then?"

"Owain has everything worked out," Raeshaan said. "It must look like the dragon hunters killed him."

"What will happen at the funeral? You need a body for a funeral."

"We have taken care of that, Marco. We will be using illusion magic. Everyone will believe the body they see is Owain's."

The grandmaster leaned over and pointed at the note. "Marco, have you finished with that note now? We had better destroy it in case someone finds it."

"Fine," Marco said as he pulled a match from his pocket. He lit the match and then held it up to one corner of the paper. They all sat in silence as they watched the paper burn.

The grandmaster pushed himself away from the table. "It's time to go. Raeshaan, tell Marco about Reya."

"Reya?" Marco echoed.

"Yes. We've had it confirmed that Reya is still alive. My brother is correct. And she is using the connection she has with Connell to heal herself. You must save Connell, kill her and destroy any chance of her ever using that link again."

"But I don't know where she is," Marco said.

"She's in Brun with Laela. The sooner you kill her, the better." Raeshaan stood and followed the grandmaster out of the tavern.

Marco sat staring at the tavern's closed door. He glanced down at the tooth in his palm. Reya was still alive. But he wouldn't deal with her until after he had rescued Sascha.

ERATUS

The first sun was resting on the horizon. It was time to meet Owain. Marco strode up the stairs and greeted Chiane and Zabir, who were standing in the corner of Owain's chambers, keeping an eye on everything that was happening. On the far wall were four glass doors that opened onto a balcony. Tall decanters of prumble ale and silkar and plates of appetizers were laid out on a glass ebony-colored table.

Marco studied the balcony. The only way someone could sneak up there would be by climbing the slippery stone walls, but the walls had been protected with a series of magical traps. So the balcony was secure. Marco's soldiers were guarding the entrance to the castle, while Drakon's soldiers were guarding the stairs. As the dragon hunters no longer allowed mages into their ranks, they didn't need to protect against magical attacks. Owain was the safest he had ever been, yet somehow he was going to die.

Athena, give me the wisdom to deal with whatever happens tonight. I cannot leave Owain alone, so I have to be here. But please keep Sascha safe until I get there.

Marco wandered to the balcony and watched as the tavern keeper lit the torches set alongside the pathway leading to the tavern's front door. It wasn't long before the scent of beeswax and warm honey was wafting through the air. Marco turned his back on the scene and leaned against the balcony rim. Footsteps raced up the stairs, and Drakon, dressed in black, his dagger tucked into the belt at his waist, stepped into the room.

"Everything seems to be in place," Drakon said.

"Now, we wait," Marco replied.

Owain, dressed in golden chain mail, paced up and down the room.

"Father, take a seat," Drakon snapped. "Have a few drinks. Calm yourself. Nobody is going to kill you while we're here. Why aren't you wearing your plate armor?"

"I will not be forced to wear plate armor in my own chambers. And with all these men here, how in Athena's name would anyone get to me anyway?"

Marco watched as the first sun dipped out of sight and the second sun began to melt into the horizon.

"It won't be long before the first moon rises," Drakon said. "The attack can't be too far away."

Marco's stomach started to churn.

I should talk to Owain, convince him not to do this. But what would I say?

Marco flexed his neck and shoulders to ease the building tension in his muscles. His mind kept wondering what was happening with Sascha's rescue but he had to concentrate on what he was doing here. He struggled with the irony that he was here to save someone who was determined to die, and not with the group that was trying to save someone who wanted to live.

It seemed to take an eternity for the second sun to set and for the first moon to begin climbing into the sky.

Drakon strode over and joined Marco on the balcony. "Are you sure the intelligence you were given is correct? No one has turned up and the second moon isn't far away. The attackers are several hours late. And we need to go to Brun to make sure nothing goes wrong with Sascha's rescue. I tell you, when I get my hands on Laela . . ."

"The intel came from a reliable source," Marco said. "I'm sure it's correct. But you're right, we need to get to Sascha."

Owain rested his back against the wall, several feet from Chiane and Zabir. "I'll give you another fifteen minutes. If nothing has happened by then, everyone can leave. And what's all this about Sascha?"

"Laela is planning to sacrifice her to the Ancients," Drakon said.

"How come you're only telling me this now?" Owain snapped. "When is she doing this?"

"When the second moon is at its peak," Marco answered.

"I couldn't be any safer here," Owain said. "You two don't need to be here. Go."

"Father is there, along with Bibacr and Soleil," Marco said, pushing down the fear that was eating away at him. "They won't let Laela win. Eham is there, too."

"I don't care," Owain said. "Consider it an order."

"Well, nothing is happening here," Drakon said. "We may as well go. I'll leave Chiane in charge; Father and the soldiers will stay here during the night. Once we have Sascha we will return."

"Go," Owain snapped. "Now!"

Marco felt guilty as relief flooded through him.

Drakon turned to Chiane. "Stay here with Zabir and keep the High King safe. Is that clear?"

"Yes, My Prince."

Marco nodded at Zabir, who saluted and glanced at Chiane.

"Well, then," Drakon said, "that's that. Time for us to take our leave."

As Drakon started to turn toward the stairs, a blazing white light exploded close to where Owain stood. Its thunderous boom reverberated off the walls.

"What the hell. . . ." Marco pulled his sword out of its scabbard as several figures burst out of the light and raced toward Owain.

Zabir and Chiane grabbed two of the figures moments before they reached Owain. Marco leaped forward and felt the satisfying thud and heard the scream as his sword sliced through the back of the third figure, killing him, but only after the figure's sword had hacked through the air in front of Owain.

Marco's stomach lurched.

Owain, no!

As Marco looked over at Owain, everything seemed to slow. He heard Owain's rapid breathing slow, he smelled the strong stench of copper. Owain's eyes widened and his hand dropped to his stomach. Owain and Marco stared at Owain's hand as he turned the palm upward. It was covered in blood.

"So sorry, Drakon, Marco. It looks like they got me."

"No," Marco whispered.

Owain's knees buckled as he collapsed onto the floor.

"The future belongs to the dragon hunters," one of the men screamed as he threw himself onto Chiane's sword.

Zabir whacked the other man across the side of the head, knocking him unconscious. "We need you alive," he muttered.

Marco raced over to Owain and pressed his hand against the wound to try and stop the flow of blood. "Remember your promise, Marco," Owain whispered.

"Healer!" Drakon yelled. "Chiane, get the healer."

"He's on his way," Chiane said as footsteps sounded on the stairs.

The master healer arrived and raced over to Owain. He took Marco's hand away from the wound and assessed the damage. The healer picked up a jar of green liquid and smothered the liquid over the wound. "I've given you some selecine, Sire. That will help with the pain."

"How did this happen?" Drakon said. "Marco, I thought

you said the dragon hunters didn't believe in magic. What happened in here was definitely the result of magic."

"I—I didn't—," Marco stammered.

"I . . . I told him that," Owain grunted.

"Father," Drakon said. "We'll get revenge for what happened here tonight."

"We must get the King to my rooms so we can treat him," the healer said.

"Drakon," Owain said, "if I don't make it, I'm trusting that, as the next High King, you will rule wisely and that you will make . . ." Owain fell silent.

The healer put his fingers to his throat. He looked up at Drakon and Marco. "He is dead."

For a moment, Drakon gaped wordlessly at his father, but then, recovering his composure, turned to Chiane. "Find out where the rest of the dragon hunters are. Find them and make them pay, truly pay. They are to be an example of what happens to anyone who attacks the High King."

"Yes, My Prince," Chiane replied.

"And I want a list of everyone who has spoken to the High King since the first sun rose yesterday. Someone helped those hunters with the timing and with magic. I want them found."

"As you command." Chiane saluted, turned on his heel, and left the King's chambers.

Marco gulped. Owain was right. If he and Owain had met . . .

"Marco," Drakon said, "I need to stay here and take control of this, but you must save Sascha. Take Raeshaan with you. You might need a healer."

RESCUE

ERATUS: BRUN

*S*ascha yawned. Her eyes were dry and gritty from too little sleep and her back ached from resting against the bars of her cage. The room appeared to be darker, but with the torches lit and no windows in the room, it was hard to get a sense of the time. She looked over at the jug of wine. She was tempted. She knew that it would contain green lyrium, and if she really believed this was her last meal, she would probably have drunk it down. But it was important to keep her wits about her. She had to be ready for when Bibacr returned.

The door to the room swung open and Laela strolled in. "You're awake. That's good. I need to have a word with you."

Laela stood in front of the cage, smoothed down the white robe she was wearing, and, folding her arms across her chest, studied Sascha. "So tell me. Although you tried to hide it from me, I do remember you having dealings with giblerees when you were on Eratus. Now I can't help but wonder exactly how friendly you were with those creatures."

Sascha felt the warmth creep up her neck and into her face. In an effort to hide the blush, she turned her back on

Laela and slowly clambered to her feet, grunting with each movement, as if standing required all of her energy. She took a deep breath and faced Laela. "What are you talking about? Everyone knows giblerees are creatures of darkness, and from what I've seen, you're more likely to be friends with those sorts of creatures than I am."

Laela chuckled. "I don't know whether I should believe you or not. But it doesn't matter now. The creature is dead."

Sascha felt light-headed. Her hand reached out for the wall as she steadied herself and tried to breathe.

Bibacr. He can't be dead.

"What do you mean?" Sascha sputtered.

Laela raised her eyebrows. "For someone who claims to have no connection to the giblerees, you certainly seem to be struggling to comprehend the death of one."

"I'm weak," Sascha lied. "I haven't eaten or drunk anything since yesterday, so what do you expect? Anyway, what creature are you talking about, Laela?"

"A gibleree snuck into our Esteemed Leader's chamber several hours ago. It tried to steal the girl but the leader killed it before it had a chance." Laela laughed. "That'll teach the dumb creature not to steal something from our leader."

Sascha shook her head as she tried to gather her thoughts. "The gibleree was trying to save a child from being consumed by a monster. And yet that doesn't seem to bother you. Were you always this evil, Laela?"

"That monster is a means to an end. And as for that child, everything has a purpose. The child's purpose is to serve the darkness." Laela tilted her head to the side and looked at Sascha. "And how do you know the creature wanted to save the girl unless you'd sent it to do exactly that? So I'd be careful about finding fault in me. If you're friends with creatures of the darkness, you, too, serve the darkness. You might pretend you have nothing to do with them, but I know better. We've never seen giblerees here. But now that you're here, this gibleree just happens to show up and attempts to steal away the very same girl our leader said you wanted to save. Don't you think that is all too much of a coincidence?"

"You believe what you want to, Laela," Sascha said. "What happened to the girl?"

Redhead strode into the room, carrying the young girl on his shoulder.

"Excellent timing," Laela said. She smiled at the guard before turning back to face Sascha. "Terrible thing, really. Before it died, the gibleree touched the girl, which means she has to go through the final purification ceremony again. I wouldn't want to go through that ceremony once, let alone twice. But because of you, that's what has to happen."

"Laela, how can you do this? Have you no compassion at all?"

Laela cackled. "Of course I don't. I would have thought that was rather obvious." She took a step closer to Sascha and lowered her voice. "All you've done, Sascha, is delay the inevitable. And to punish you, I am going to allow the girl to watch our Esteemed Leader consume you. She will hear your screams, see your pain, knowing all the while that she is next. You have made what would have been a quick death for this young girl a brutal and torturous experience."

Hatred flashed through Sascha like a burning acid. Somehow she had to make this woman pay for all of this. But with Bibacr dead, how would that be possible? Her hopes now rested with Marco and Soleil.

Redhead opened the cage door and threw the young girl in.

"Take that wine out of Sascha's cage. She is not to be given any chance of easing the pain of what is to come." Laela turned to the door. "Thea will be back soon, and then you begin the final part of your journey. Trust me when I say that what your father's men did to you is nothing compared to what you are about to face. And if I had my way, that gibleree would be facing the same fate as you. It's such a shame it's dead."

She cackled again as she walked out the door. Redhead picked up the wine and mug, shut the cage door, and followed Laela out of the room, slamming the door shut behind him.

Sascha turned around to the young girl, who was sitting in the corner of the cage. "I'm so sorry for—" Sascha hiccupped as she tried to smother the desperate need to sob, to grieve the loss of one so special as Bibacr.

He's dead, and this girl . . . I should have gone with him when he came for me. And then he would be alive. But the girl would be dead.

Sascha hadn't realized she was sitting cross-legged on the floor until she felt a small hand resting on her shoulder.

"It will be okay," a young voice whispered. "He's not dead. He's coming back to help us."

Sascha reached out to touch the girl's hand. "Bibacr . . . Bibacr isn't dead? Are you sure?"

The girl nodded.

Sascha shook her head and closed her eyes. "Thank Athena."

"Laela thinks he died, because that's what the leader told her. But he escaped." The girl frowned. "He spoke funny and made me laugh, but he said he was Bibacr's father, not Bibacr."

Sascha exhaled slowly before twisting around to face the girl. "You're sure he said he was Bibacr's father?"

The girl nodded again.

So Bibacr had managed to escape and was now putting their plans in place. Sascha hoped Bibacr's father was okay, but she was relieved that Bibacr was still working to release her and the girls.

"What is your name?"

"Nadiya."

"How old are you, Nadiya?"

"I turn eight next week," Nadiya replied.

"Well, Nadiya, I think you are the bravest young girl I have ever met."

"I was scared," she said. "I cried so much. But then your friend found me. He told me not to be afraid. He told me to be brave, because you were sent by the gods to save us. And you were going to kill the creatures that tortured us." Nadiya looked up at Sascha and grinned, her brown eyes shining in the torchlight. "And he said giblerees never lie."

Sascha pulled the girl into a hug. "We will get through this together," she said as her stomach clenched.

Athena, we have to save these girls. We cannot let this continue.

ERATUS

Sascha moved Nadiya's fiery red hair off her face as she studied the pretty child's fine features.

"What is your story, little one?" she whispered. "How did you end up here?"

The door swung open and Thea, dressed in fitted leather pants and top, walked in. "Time to begin the final part of your jour—" She stopped midstride and stared at the girl asleep in Sascha's arms. "Nadiya," Thea whispered.

Sascha thought she saw tears in Thea's eyes. Was it possible that Thea cared about what happened to Nadiya? "Thea, I need to know. Was Laela lying when she talked about how painful the next part of the journey is?"

Thea shook her head, still staring at the girl.

"If that is true, is there anything we can do to at least ease Nadiya's pain in all this?"

Thea started to nod and then stopped. She glared at Sascha. "Is this a trick? Are you going to tell Laela I tried to help Nadiya?"

"No, I promise it's not a trick," Sascha said. "With Athena as my witness, all I care about is making this next part easier for Nadiya."

Thea stared at Sascha, her cheeks wet with tears. "There is a tablet we can give her. It will render her unconscious so she won't feel a thing."

"Can you get her one of those tablets?"

Thea flinched at the sound of heavy metal boots striding along the corridor toward the room. The pulse in her neck beat visibly faster.

Thea is afraid.

"I promise I won't tell anyone you helped Nadiya. Please. Let's not make her suffer through this ceremony a second time."

Thea wiped her cheek with the back of her hand, nodded, and left the room.

Sascha's heart pounded as she waited for Thea to return.

Athena, please let Thea return. If we can help Nadiya, buy her some time . . .

Though it felt like hours had passed, Sascha knew it could have only been minutes when the door opened again and Thea slipped back into the room. She was carrying a glass of water.

"Thank Athena," Sascha muttered.

Thea frowned as she dug into the pocket of her cloak and retrieved something. She opened the cage door and held out a pink tablet and a glass of water. "You didn't think I'd return?"

"I wasn't sure. But I'm grateful you did."

"Give this to her, and hurry," Thea said. "The guards could return at any time."

Sascha took the tablet from Thea. "And you're sure this is safe? It isn't going to hurt Nadiya?"

Thea shook her head. "It won't hurt her. It will help her sleep through it all." She moved away from Sascha and stood in the corner of the room.

"Nadiya," Sascha called gently to the girl. "Wake up."

The young girl opened her eyes.

"I want you to take this tablet. And take a sip of this water."

Nadiya pushed herself up. She glanced at Sascha before taking the tablet and popping it in her mouth. She took the glass of water and drank down several mouthfuls. As she wiped her mouth with the back of her hand, she handed the glass back to Sascha.

"You can go back to sleep now," Sascha said.

Nadiya snuggled back down and closed her eyes.

Sascha stroked the girl's cheek and smoothed the over-sized rose-colored robe she was wearing. "May Athena protect you."

"I'll come back in a few minutes and get you," Thea said. "The tablet should have taken effect by then."

"Thea," Sascha called, "why are you being kind to Nadiya?"

Thea swallowed. "She's . . . she's my sister's daughter."

Sascha stared at Thea. "How could you leave her here to go through this if—"

"Don't judge me. You don't know anything about what is happening here."

"I didn't mean to offend you, but . . ." Sascha took a deep breath.

Thea could be useful. Alienating her won't help.

"She's only a child. Can't we save her?"

"It was my sister who gave her up, not me. And if I tried to help Nadiya escape this place, Laela would take one of my girls to replace her." She shook her head. "I can't do that." She closed the cage door again and walked out of the room.

"Laela," Sascha spat, "you will pay for this. Somehow you will pay."

Heavy footsteps were making their way down the corridor, moving closer and closer. Sascha gulped and pushed down the fear that was building inside her. She would face whatever she needed to so she could get through this. She had to. At least Nadiya wouldn't know a thing about any of it.

TO THE TEMPLE

ERATUS

*M*arco raced down the stairs of Owain's chambers.

Owain was dead.

He shook his head.

It isn't real. None of this is real. It's all planned.

He struggled with a wave of sadness, even though somewhere down deep his mind was telling him not to worry.

He raced toward Sascha's chambers and waved at the mage who was waiting for him there. "Go to the roof and prepare the portal. Do you have the exact coordinates of the clifftop in Brun?"

"Yes, Colonel. Eham gave them to me before he left."

"Good. I only need a minute to pick up a couple of things."

Marco had stored his blades in Sascha's chambers to save time. Her chambers were the closest to the roof. He strode to the cupboard next to Soleil's nest and unlocked it. He was about to retrieve his blades when he noticed a golden bundle sitting on top of the cupboard. He reached over and opened it. He gasped. Inside the parcel were the Blades of Light.

The blades, Jenny's child. Everything is just as Sascha dreamed it would be.

He had to get rid of them, hide them. The moonlight glinted off the blades, highlighting the symbol etched into each of them—a sun with a blade of jagged lightning across its face. Marco shuddered. It wasn't a coincidence that Sascha had been born with an identical mark on her hand.

Sascha saw these blades destroy Jenny and Eham in her dream. Could they be used to destroy Reya? Jenny and the child won't be at the battle, so it should be safe to take them to Brun.

He rewrapped the blades in the golden material and shoved them into his belt. He retrieved his own weapon from the cupboard and raced to the roof. The portal was whirring loudly, and the mage was tapping his foot impatiently.

"I'm here. Let's go."

They stepped into the portal.

≈

ERATUS—SASCHA'S RESCUE

The first moon was high in the night sky when Marco and the mage stepped out of the portal and onto the cliff overlooking the fire temple in Brun. Marco searched the sky for any sign of the second moon. It hadn't started to rise. Marco breathed a sigh of relief.

We still have time.

The fire dragons' cave was to the right of where they stood. It looked dark and empty. He choked as he breathed in a whiff of the sharp, acrid smell of smoke and sulfur. The high-pitched shrieks of fire dragons and the gargled screams of guardians and priests shattered the air as the battle raged along the walls of the temple. Marco strode over to Eham and Soleil. They were perched on the edge of the clifftop, watching the spectacle below them. Several of the larger fire dragons were pelting the guardians with showers of molten fire.

"Where's my father, Eham?"

"I'm up here."

It took Marco a few moments to realize his father was sitting on the shoulders of a green pyran. "Father, I thought you said you didn't want to fly anymore."

The ground shook as the guardians along the temple walls lumbered around, trying to destroy the creatures that were attacking them.

"I didn't want to, but Eham told me this was the only way."

Marco nodded. "Eham is right. It is." He glanced around the clifftop. "Where are the men?"

"Over there, under the shelter of the trees," Geraud replied. "The men and their pyrans are hidden, just in case the priests down there can see what is happening up here."

"Good call," Marco said. He moved toward the tree line. It was no wonder he hadn't seen them. They were all dressed in black armor, which blended in with the darkness of the forest.

"Your men are with them, covering the rear," Eham called out.

"That's good." Marco moved to Eham's side. "Have we heard from Bibacr yet?"

"Yes," Eham replied, still watching the battle below. "Bibacr and his family will be waiting for us in the temple's courtyard. Bibacr will take you to Sascha. His family will take your father and a few of his men to the girls. Then they will help us take back control of the temple."

"What does Father think of being led into the temple by giblerees?" Marco whispered.

Eham shook his head and smiled. "He accepted it but didn't like it much. When he met my dread wisp, he crossed himself and said that you and he would be having a talk when this was over."

Marco smiled. "I'm sure we will." He glanced at the horizon and saw that the edge of the second moon was beginning to rise. "How soon before we can go? We don't have long."

"We're waiting for the signal from the fire dragons," Eham said. "They're still clearing a path for us."

"We can't wait too much longer." Marco stepped between Eham and Soleil. "Are you okay, Soleil?"

Soleil clicked his beak. "I would be better if Fenix wasn't here."

"Where is she?"

"Over near the soldiers."

"We'll sort this out when Sascha is safe. Okay?"

Soleil eyed Marco silently.

"And we will give Fenix a chance to talk," Marco said. "Won't we?"

Soleil snorted and moved away from Marco.

"Fine," Marco said, "act like a child if that's what makes you happy."

Soleil clicked his beak at Marco, then ruffled his feathers and hunkered down on the edge of the clifftop.

A chilly air whipped around Marco's legs as the dread wisp raced over to Eham and leaped into his arms. Eham deposited the wisp onto his shoulder, where it moved in closer and nuzzled into his neck. Eham nodded, acknowledging whatever the creature had whispered in his ear.

Eham glanced at Geraud and then at Marco. "A path has been cleared. My creature will show us the way."

Fenix moved toward Eham and lowered her neck so that he could climb onto her shoulders. Marco climbed onto Soleil.

Geraud raised his right arm and waved it forward. "Let's fly. Eham, you take the lead."

"Yes, Your Grace."

THEY GLANCED down at the battlegrounds as they flew toward the temple's entrance. The dead bodies of the guardians and priests were scattered across the ground, but there were no signs of any dead fire dragons. Marco could see Bibacr and his family waiting for them in the corner of the temple's courtyard. He breathed a sigh of relief. He knew Bibacr wouldn't let him down, especially where Sascha was concerned. He glanced over at his father, who crossed himself again when he caught sight of the giblerees.

"Eham," Geraud called out, "ask your creature to remind the fire dragons to join us in the temple's courtyard when they've finished with the guardians."

"Yes, Your Grace," Eham replied.

"Everyone, be on your guard," Geraud said. "It looks quiet down there and that worries me. These priests are fanatics. They won't go quietly, which means they must have something planned."

THE PREPARATIONS

ERATUS

The door swung open, and Thea and the guards stood in the doorway to Sascha's prison. Redhead walked up to the cage and opened it.

"Time to go," Thea barked. "Let's get a move on. Wake that child up."

Sascha glanced at Thea. "Nadiya is exhausted. Let her sleep a little while longer. I'll carry her."

Thea turned to the redheaded guard. "You carry the girl." She waved a finger in Sascha's direction. "I don't want this one tripping and damaging herself and the child before she is taken to the leader."

Redhead leaned down, picked up the child, and swung her over his shoulder. He stood behind Sascha and pointed to the open doorway. Sascha stood. Her legs trembled as she followed Thea out of the room. They walked in silence down corridors and up flights of stairs until they finally arrived at the entrance to a small room. In the center of the room was a silver table and several tall machines from which hung clear plastic bags filled with liquids of different colors. On one side of the room was a bench covered with various sharp implements.

Sascha clenched her teeth and breathed the nausea away.

A woman wearing thick glasses and dressed in a white tunic and long pants walked toward them. Her hair had been pulled into a tight bun, which was positioned on the top of her head.

"Lie on the table," she said to Sascha, pointing to the silver table. She turned to Thea. "Get your guards to put the child in the chair. I'll take it from here. And make sure you close the door behind you."

Redhead pointed at Sascha. "This one will escape if you give her half a chance."

The woman clicked her fingers and an armed soldier appeared in each corner of the room.

"Don't tell me how to do my job, sonny," the woman growled. "I've been doing this more years than you've been alive."

Sascha's stomach churned as she watched Thea and Redhead leave. She dragged herself to the table, her heart pounding as if it were going to explode from her chest. If she was this terrified, how would a young thing like Nadiya have felt when forced to do this? She levered herself onto the table and sat on the edge.

"Here, drink this," the woman said. "It will make the drugs I give you easier to bear."

Sascha shook her head, unable to speak.

"Are you sure?" She glanced around her. "These walls still echo with the screams of those who refused to drink. Do you think you're so much stronger than them?"

Again, Sascha shook her head.

"Very well. If that's what you choose, so be it."

Sascha looked around the room. The soldiers had disappeared from view, but she knew they were still there, hiding in the shadows. She glanced over at Nadiya, who was still asleep in the chair.

Now is not the time to try and escape. Those soldiers would get to Nadiya before me, and I'm not leaving without her.

The woman straightened Sascha's arm and examined it before placing a cuff on it. She tapped Sascha's arm until she found a suitable vein and then inserted a needle.

"Now the fun begins." She grinned. "I love my job so—"

Sascha heard a soft thud and watched as a garish red mark spread over the front of the woman's white tunic. The woman stared wide-eyed at Sascha before crumpling to the ground, dead.

"Marco make good shot," Bibacr squealed as he raced toward her.

Sascha finally found her voice as the woman's soldiers suddenly appeared several yards from the child. "Bibacr, Marco! The child. Look after the child." She glanced at the needle and pulled it out of her arm, throwing it at the dead woman's body. She pressed on the spot with her fingers to stop the bleeding.

"It's okay, Sascha," Marco replied. "We've got her. She's safe."

Sascha looked over to see the woman's soldiers lying on the ground, dead, and the child being carried away in the arms of Marco's men. Tears rolled down her cheeks. She removed her fingers from her arm and wiped away the tears with her knuckles. But the tears kept coming. "Marco, you're here, you're actually here. Bibacr, you were true to your word, you came back."

"Bibacr scared woman hurt Sascha," he said, hopping from one foot to the other.

"I'm safe, thanks to you two. Bibacr, is your father okay? Laela said the Ancient killed him."

Bibacr snorted. "Bibacr's father is good. Bibacr's father fooled the Ancient."

Sascha smiled. "That is so good to hear."

When Marco had finished giving his men their new directions, he turned to Sascha and took several large strides toward her. He swept her off the table and pulled her close. They stayed wrapped in each other's arms for several moments. "We're going home soon."

Sascha snuggled into Marco and breathed in his familiar scent. She felt her muscles relax. "Thank you, Marco."

The girls!

Sascha reluctantly placed her hands on Marco's chest and pushed herself away. "Marco, we have to find out where Laela has taken the girls."

"Bibacr's father is helping," Bibacr said. "Bibacr's father taking the duke to rescue them."

"What would we have done without you, Bibacr? Marco, if you could see what Laela has been doing . . ." She shivered. "That woman is evil, truly evil. These sacrifices were going on while I was leader of the Four Sisters. How did I not realize? At least I hope I never realized." Sascha shook her head. "I failed my people in so many ways."

"Sascha, you have to put everything in context. Life wasn't easy for you then, and the green lyrium you were addicted to made every day an ordeal."

"Then I shouldn't have been the leader. I should have been removed."

Marco rubbed Sascha's arm. "If you feel so strongly about it, make this time different. You have a chance to do those things you wish you had done before."

"You're right." Sascha took a step toward Bibacr when she stumbled. Marco caught her around the waist and helped her to regain her balance. She turned back to Bibacr. "Bibacr, thank you." She leaned over and kissed him on the cheek. "I owe you and your family for everything you have done for the girls and me."

Bibacr turned a bright pink. He coughed into his arm and then began to splutter. Marco patted him on the back.

Sascha glanced around her. "Where are Soleil and Fenix?" She stepped away from Marco to get a better view of the room, but everything started to spin, faster and faster. She heard Marco's voice answer her, but his words were slurring together. She heard Marco call for a healer as he supported her and guided her back to the silver table.

Another woman arrived and stood next to Marco. This one had no bun or glasses.

"Sascha, my name is Raeshaan. Drink this potion. We will have you back to normal in no time."

After several mouthfuls, Sascha felt her energy returning. As she finished the potion, she watched Raeshaan wander around the cave.

"What are all these liquids? Do you know, Sascha?"

"They're supposed to make offerings suitable for the Ancients to consume," Sascha said. "I've no idea what's in them, but the process is supposed to be a painful one, so I don't suppose there's anything good in them."

Raeshaan stopped walking and turned to face Sascha. "You might have given us our first real clue in the fight against the Ancients. If the offerings must be treated before consumption, then they have a weakness." She fingered one of the bags of liquid. "And these liquids will tell us what that is." Raeshaan walked over to join Sascha. "Now, lie down on the table and rest," she said as she lifted Sascha's legs onto the table. "Soon you will be as good as new."

"Raeshaan, I need you to do something for me."

"What is it, Sascha?"

"When we rescue the girls, I believe a couple of them may

be pregnant. I need you to separate those two girls from the others and keep a close eye on them for me."

"I will, but who did they—"

"We'll talk about that when we get out of here. Is that okay?"

Sascha watched as Marco told his men what to take from the room. He glanced around to see her watching him. When he smiled at her, she couldn't stop the fluttering sensation in her stomach or the warm glow that filled her heart.

I must have done something right to end up with someone like Marco.

"Close your eyes for a few moments," Raeshaan whispered. "Let the magic do its work."

Sascha gave a huge sigh, yawned, and closed her eyes.

Only for a moment . . .

≈

ERATUS

"Sasch." Marco touched her shoulder. "Father has imprisoned Reya. We need to go."

Sascha rubbed her eyes as she sat and swung her legs off the silver table. She felt wonderful. Energy shimmered in her blood and the mark on her hand tingled. "Have I been asleep long?"

"I would have preferred to have given you longer," Marco said.

"I don't need longer. The potion has done its work and I feel totally refreshed. Did you say your father has imprisoned Reya?"

Marco nodded. "Yes."

"If your father has Reya, does that mean he has Laela, too?"

"No. It seems that Laela has disappeared, along with the

Ancient." Marco shook his head. "After everything that has happened Laela was prepared to leave Reya behind. I thought their connection was a lot stronger than that."

"We can't afford to underestimate Laela. She must be up to something. Have they located the girls?"

"The girls are safe," Marco said. "Raeshaan is treating them. And Soleil, Fenix, and Bibacr are working with Father and his soldiers to secure the rest of the temple. Our job is to save Connell, which means we must deal with Reya."

"How will dealing with Reya help save Connell?"

"I forgot," Marco said. "You wouldn't know. When Connell was attacked by the pit hound Reya had created, a dark magical link was established between the two of them. Reya is using that link to heal herself . . . at the cost of Connell's life."

"So that's what Laela meant when she made a comment about Reya healing well, thanks to Connell?" Sascha said.

"I suppose so. Come on, let's get moving." He hesitated and glanced at Sascha. "But before we do—" With one quick movement, he pulled out a bundle from his belt.

Sascha froze. The sparkle of the golden fabric . . . Marco had the blades. "Why did you bring those things here?"

"I found them on the cupboard in your chambers. Did you know they were there?"

"Yes, I put them there after Athena gave them to me."

"Athena found them?"

"She said they were given to her. She also said I would need them one more time."

"Perhaps that one more time is to kill Reya, not Jenny and the child," Marco said.

"Reya? You want me to kill my sister with these blades?"

Marco reached out and rested his hand on Sascha's arm. "It's a better option than killing Jenny and the child. Reya is using dark magic to drain Connell's life. If we allow Reya to live, Connell will die."

"There must be another way."

"There isn't, Sasch. And if these blades killed the Ancients and the darkness in the Shield, then they could kill Reya."

Sascha's stomach dropped. "It suddenly makes sense," she whispered.

"What does?" Marco asked.

Sascha stared at the bundle in his hand. "The purpose of those blades is to destroy the darkness. We know that. They follow the darkness to where it begins and destroy anything that has been tainted by it. If we use them to kill Reya, will they follow the link between Reya and Connell . . . and destroy Connell?"

"Why would they destroy Connell?" Marco asked.

"Perhaps that's what my dream was telling me. These blades follow the darkness no matter where it leads, no matter what form the darkness takes. They don't pick and choose according to our sensitivities. The dream was warning me of the dangers of using the blades."

"But Connell isn't darkness, the link is. It would kill the link."

"I would never have said Jenny is darkness either, but in my dream, the blades killed her, because she is the mother of the child and the blades considered the child to be darkness."

"Then why did they kill Eham?" Marco asked.

"Eham is Jenny's grandfather and he is a dark mage."

"So the blades kill the dark magic, along with those that create it?"

"It seems so."

"Do you still think that the child is evil?" Marco asked. "He certainly doesn't look—"

Sascha tilted her head to the side. "You've seen Jenny's child?"

"Um . . . yes." Marco studied the ground, as if the answer to Sascha's question were written there. After a moment, he lifted his head and looked Sascha in the eyes. "Yes, I met the child when I went to Earth to find Jenny and Eham. They were supposed to have returned, so I was worried something had happened."

"And had it?"

"They made a choice not to return. Jenny was worried about how you would react when you saw the child. She had some sort of vision, a warning. Because of that, she decided to stay on Earth. Until Laela turned up, that is."

"Laela?"

"It seems Jenny was more terrified of Laela than you. She asked me to keep the child a secret until she could meet with you, explain what happened." Marco took his hand off Sascha's arm and studied her face. "You don't seem surprised to hear the child exists."

"A lot has happened while I've been here. I just can't believe Jenny never let anything slip."

"I asked Jenny why she kept her son a secret."

"A son," Sascha spluttered. "So it is a boy?"

"Yes," Marco replied. "Jenny said she knew you would return to Eratus one day and when you did, the child would be in great danger. That was the reason she never mentioned him."

Sascha nodded. "With everything that was happening in this temple while I was the leader of the Four Sisters, I'm not really surprised Jenny was scared of me. But there's still one thing that worries me, and that is how much the child in my dream looked like the Ancient I faced at the healing ceremony. That connection is terrifying."

Don't ask, Sascha. Don't ask.

"Marco, I need to know. What does Jenny's child look like?"

"His name is Vonn, and he has dark hair, olive skin, and bright blue eyes. He is a beautiful child."

Sascha's heart sank. Marco's description of the child seemed to match the child in her dream. She looked at the blades resting in Marco's hand.

And now I have the weapon to kill it.

"What are you going to do about the boy?" Marco asked.

Sascha shrugged her shoulders. "I honestly have no idea."

"Should I put these blades away?" Marco asked.

"Where are Jenny and the child?"

"They're back at the castle."

"I'll take them then, but I don't know if I can use them on Reya. Especially if there's a chance it could also kill Connell."

"If it follows the darkness and kills the darkness that is attacking Connell, surely that's a good thing," Marco said. "Anyway, if we don't kill Reya, he will die."

"But if I killed my own brother and sister . . ."

Marco put his hand on her shoulder. "We'll take one step at a time." He handed the blades to Sascha.

She pocketed them and pushed herself off the table. "Let's get this over and done with."

Sascha and Marco made their way out of the room together. "Marco, why do you think the connection was still there for Connell, but not for me? I was attacked by that pit hound's mate and yet Reya has no control over me."

Marco shook his head. "I don't know."

∽

ERATUS

A tall man with tanned skin and thick, dark hair stood outside the room.

This must be Marco's father, the Duke of Kilmarnock.

He looked familiar but Sascha couldn't remember ever having met him.

"Father," Marco said, "we've come for Reya."

"She's locked up in the next room, son." He nodded at Sascha. "Enchantress, I apologize for what has happened to you here."

"It's not me I'm worried about, Your Grace, it's the children who have been sacrificed here. And as the leader of the Four Sisters, it is something I should have known about. The shame is with me."

"It's something neither of us will ever let happen again. And I'd prefer it if you call me Geraud. 'Your Grace' makes me sound so old and officious."

Marco chuckled.

"And that's enough out of you, son," Geraud said.

Sascha glanced down the corridor. "Where are the others?"

"They're clearing out the last section of the temple," the duke replied.

Sascha's palms were sweating and her stomach was churning. "Okay. Shall we do this?"

The duke nodded at one of the guards, who leaned over and opened the door. He stood back and allowed Sascha and Marco to pass. Sascha glanced around the room. The door to the next room was closed. Reya sat on the edge of the bed. The cord attached to the bracelet she was wearing had been detached from the drip and was now secured to a hook set into the wall next to the bed.

"Hey, sis." Reya laughed. "Nice to see you out in the open and not skulking behind that cupboard over there."

"You knew I was here?" Sascha asked.

"Of course we did. We were playing with you."

Sascha's cheeks warmed.

I should have realized that they knew.

"I have to ask, Reya. How did you escape after Novo attacked you in the cave?"

"Laela rescued me. You were all so focused on the archers that you didn't notice Laela."

"Well, she's not here to save you this time," Marco said.

Sascha looked at the satisfied expression on Reya's face. "Laela hasn't abandoned Reya. They've been waiting for us to arrive."

"Clever girl, Sascha," Reya said.

The ting of metal against metal sounded next to Sascha as Marco drew his sword and moved closer, ready to protect her.

"Now!" Reya yelled.

The door to the corridor slammed shut. The door to the next room burst open as four priests, armed with staffs, crashed into the room. Two of the priests raced over to the door that led out to the corridor and erected a magical barrier. The door shook under the weight of the duke's soldiers as they tried to force the door open, but Sascha knew they wouldn't get through.

"Marco! Sascha!" Geraud yelled. "Magic is barring the entrance to the room. I'm getting help."

The other two priests took up their positions in front of the door that led to the room Sascha had hidden in just a day or so ago. Laela strode past the priests and headed toward Reya. "Reya, my dear. I hope these horrible people haven't been lying about me."

Reya smirked. "They were saying all sorts of terrible things, Laela. They were saying that you had abandoned me, left me all alone."

Laela laughed as she rested her hand on Reya's shoulder. "Everything has been prepared. How about we get you out of here, give you a chance to finish your recovery."

"What an excellent idea," Reya said.

Laela leaned down, wrapped her arm around Reya's waist, and helped her to her feet. "Hopefully, Connell has enough life left in him to allow you to make a full recovery."

They both laughed. "Let's hope so," Reya said.

"So it's true," Sascha said. "You're using the link to Connell to heal yourself."

"I would rather it be your lifeblood, sis," Reya said, "but Connell's will do."

"Why, Reya? Why do this to your own family?"

"Family?" Reya spat. "You're not my family. My only family is Laela."

Laela rubbed Reya's arm.

A loud whirring sound reverberated around the room as a large circle of spinning air opened up behind the priests.

"They're escaping," Marco whispered. "We can't let Reya escape. We won't find her a second time. Not in time to save Connell anyway."

Sascha's heart pounded.

She's my sister. If I had been there when she needed me . . .

Laela was close to the portal, which was building in strength.

"Sascha, please," Marco whispered. "Do it now."

"And when we're gone," Laela called out to the priests, "kill them. You may kill them however you choose. Her father tires of her being alive."

"My father? I knew it. He's alive. What Novo said about Drakon killing him was a lie."

Laela cackled. "Novo was a fool that believes any story Drakon tells him." She glanced at Reya who was leaning heavily against her, "He had no idea who your father is. Nor do you for that matter."

"Was . . . So you killed him?" Sascha asked.

"You always were too clever for your own good," Laela said. She stopped, turned, and grinned at Sascha. "Who do you think the High Priest is? It's your father. He is loyal to the Ancients and he has allowed me to sacrifice the mages to our Esteemed Leader of the Ancients for years. And even though you and your friends think you're stopping him, you're not. Because of his loyalty to the Ancients my friends will help him rebuild the empire you and your friends have tried to destroy. But I guess you won't care because you will be dead. And believe it or not, you should be grateful. Your father is far more powerful now than he ever was when you knew him, so the ways he could make you suffer now . . ." Laela chuckled as she tightened her grip on Reya and they continued toward the portal. They were only a few feet away from making their escape.

"Sascha," Marco called out. "Please."

Marco is right. I cannot let Connell die this way.

Sascha put her hand into the pocket of her robe. The mark on her hand started to tingle, then burn. She looked down to see the blades in her pocket glowing. She retrieved the blades and glanced up at Laela and Reya, who were moments away from disappearing forever.

She grasped the tips of the blades between her thumb and fingers, bent her wrist back toward her forearm, swung her arm forward, and released the blades.

The blades spun in circles, becoming brighter and brighter the faster they spun.

Laela glanced at the moving blades. "We have to move quickly, Reya."

Reya's eyes took on a glazed look. She shook her head as she tried to work out what was happening. She put her hand up to protect her eyes from the light of the spinning blades. As she moved her hand, the blades touched her. She gave a bloodcurdling scream. "Laela, help me!"

The color drained from Laela's face as she watched Reya's hand disappear, then her arm.

"No," Laela screamed. "Stop it, Sascha." Tears streamed down her face as she watched Reya's body disappear. When she realized there was nothing she could do for Reya, Laela dived into the portal and shut it behind her.

A heavy silence fell after the portal had disappeared. The blades whirred in the air and then, deciding on a direction, headed for the priests. The priests panicked and clambered over each other as they tried to escape the blades. One by one, they fell and then disappeared. When all of the priests had fallen, the blades dropped to the ground with a soft thud and the glow disappeared.

"The blades dropped," Sascha muttered. "They're not still searching, they're not wanting to go after Connell."

"Which means he should be okay," Marco asked.

"I hope so."

Seconds later, the magical barriers on the doors disappeared and Geraud and his men crashed into the room. Geraud raced over to Marco and hugged him.

"We thought the screams were yours. We thought you were dead. Thank Athena you're both alive."

As Sascha retrieved the blades, Bibacr and Soleil raced into the room. Bibacr bounced up and down on one foot, uttering a strange squeak. Soleil twirled around the room, emitting a sweet harmonious song that brought a smile to Sascha's face. "You're alive, you're alive."

"Yes, I'm alive. And safe, thanks to you all." She turned to Marco. "We need to check on Connell. I need to know he is okay and that I didn't . . . kill him."

"I will take you, Sascha," Soleil said.

"Bibacr come too?"

Sascha braced herself, ready to intervene in the argument that she was sure would erupt between them.

"We can find somewhere for Bibacr and his family to rest and recover, can't we, Sascha?" Soleil asked.

Sascha stood and stared at the two of them. "What happened? You two are being nice to each other."

"Bibacr and Soleil friends," Bibacr said.

"I never believed this day would come," Sascha said. "Perhaps I should get kidnapped more often."

"No," they both screamed.

Sascha laughed.

"Sascha making joke?" Bibacr asked.

"Yes," Soleil replied. "She is only joking, though sometimes I find her sense of humor concerning."

"Sascha," Marco said, "there is something we need to talk about on the way to the castle. It's about Owain."

THE NEW HIGH KING

ERATUS

*D*rakon stood on the ramparts, eating a handful of berries as he studied the training routines of Chiane's men. The first sun was just peeking above the horizon, giving little warmth. The icy winds that whistled through the grounds were an ominous sign that the season of the three moons was arriving weeks ahead of time. As soon as Sascha returned, he would issue an order for all portals to be shut down until the storm season had ended.

A thrill of excitement sparked in him. He could issue these orders now that he was High King. He had to keep up the pretense that he was sad at Owain's passing; after all it had only been a few hours since he was killed. But he couldn't stop the buzz that sizzled in his blood. He was finally doing what he had been born to do. And Sascha would be standing at his side at the coronation ceremony that was to take place next month. He would make sure of it.

Drakon admitted to himself that while he wasn't sad at Owain's passing, there was a twinge of regret. And the least he owed Owain was to find out whoever was behind the attack. After all, no one should get away with attacking a

High King. Drakon glanced at the door on the far side of the training grounds that led down to the dungeons. The interrogations of the dragon hunter had not provided him with any useful information, but the hunt for the remainder of the group had begun. He would get his answers one way or the other. Someone would pay.

Heavy footsteps headed up the stairs as Chiane made his way up to join Drakon.

Chiane better have good news.

"Sire," Chiane said, bringing his clenched fist to his chest in salute. "You will be pleased to know that Sascha is on her way back to the castle."

"That is good news. And what news have you had of my fire dragons?"

A squeal of delight sounded above them. Drakon looked up as a whoosh of wings and warm air whipped around him. The fire dragons twirled in the air before landing neatly on the balcony rim.

"Your dragons led an exceptionally successful attack against the guardians and opened a path for the duke to enter the temple. It was because of them that the duke and his men were able to rescue Sascha. Reports say that terrible atrocities had been happening in that temple for years. But it's been shut down now."

"What sort of atrocities?" Drakon asked.

"I don't have many of the details, but Marco will report in as soon as they return. He will update you on everything that happened at Brun."

"Good."

Kalamar sidled up to Drakon and puffed his chest out. Drakon reached out and stroked his neck. "You and your family did me proud. Chiane, organize a special reward for my fine creatures. And I want the kingdom's crest to be changed in honor of my dragons. Fire dragons are a better representation of our realm's power than manticores. Make it happen."

"Yes, Sire."

Drakon glanced at Kalamar. "What do you think of my new title, Kalamar? I'm the new High King." Drakon was rewarded with a soft, deep purring sound. "Go, my creatures. Rest and recover."

As Kalamar leaped up into the air, Drakon noticed the package Chiane was carrying. "What is that parcel, Chiane?"

"Your new armband. It was ready yesterday evening, but as you were . . . interrogating the dragon hunter, I thought I would wait until you had finished."

"We will change the bands now," Drakon said. "Follow me."

"As you command."

Several minutes later, Drakon entered his chambers with Chiane in tow. He strode over to the table on the balcony and poured himself a mug of ale, which he swigged down in a couple of mouthfuls. He placed the empty mug down on the table and turned to Chiane. "Now, Chiane, show me the band."

Chiane placed the red felt parcel on the table and unwrapped it. The armband was made of three types of braided gold, which had been woven together in the shape of a fire dragon. The gold glinted in the sunlight, and the eyes of the fire dragon glowed.

Drakon couldn't hide his grin. "Chiane, you and the Arch-mage have done well. That is exquisite workmanship."

"Thank you, Sire. But there was something the Archmage wanted me to make sure you understood."

"What is it?"

"With the armband on, your powers are limited to what you can perform. Without the band you would have the power of the Ancients, which would make you a formidable opponent. The Archmage said if you want to meet with him he will show you what is possible."

Drakon snorted. "The man has no tongue. There's no point in him meeting with me."

"He writes—"

"The Archmage has no idea what he's talking about, Chiane. And I have no intention of meeting with him. I certainly hope his work is better than his advice." Drakon ran his finger along the design of the band.

What if this isn't successful?

He took a deep breath. "Right then. Put it on my arm. It's time to see if it works. Once I'm sure of the fit, I'll take Athena's band off. If I find that the voices start to return . . ."

"The Archmage is talented, Sire. This will work."

"I hope so, for his sake . . . and yours."

Chiane took the armband from the table, leaned over, and clipped it onto Drakon's arm. He took a step back. Drakon swallowed hard as he clenched and unclenched his fists in an effort to calm his nerves. He took a deep breath and exhaled slowly.

This is it.

He took Athena's band off his arm and held it in his palm while he listened for the voices. Nothing. He glanced over at Chiane and saw a fine sheen of sweat on his forehead. "Nervous, Chiane?"

"No, not at all, Sire."

Drakon smirked. "Let's hope your mage doesn't disappoint."

He rested the band on the table and slowly took his hand off it, all the while listening for the voices. Again, nothing. He stepped back from the table. Still nothing. The voices hadn't returned. The new band was working. He grinned, then he laughed. He walked over to Chiane and slapped him on the arm. "You did it. Good work, Chiane."

They turned and stared at Athena's band.

"Do you want me to get rid of it, Sire?"

"No, I'll do that myself. But I think this new band deserves a toast." He picked up the jug and poured two glasses of ale. They raised their mugs. "A toast to new beginnings."

"New beginnings," Chiane echoed.

They stood in silence on Drakon's balcony as they finished their ale and watched the construction teams prepare the courtyard for the wake that would follow Owain's funeral in three days' time. Men and women were setting up the stalls that would sell foods and beverages from each of the four kingdoms in Eratus. Members of the nobility would be arriving tomorrow morning, so everything had to be ready for when they arrived. The aroma of fresh fruits and roasted meats wafted in the air, reminding Drakon he was hungry.

Chiane put his mug down and turned to Drakon. "If it pleases you, Sire, I need to follow up on a couple of leads we have been given on the location of the dragon hunters."

Drakon waved his hand, dismissing Chiane. "Yes, go. I want that group destroyed. And make sure you thank the Archmage. You have both done well."

"Yes, Sire."

Minutes later, Drakon watched Chiane striding across the grounds.

Firstly, I need to know what's in the silver box. But this time I won't involve Chiane.

As he made his way out of his chambers, he picked up Athena's armband and put it in his pocket. It was time to retrieve the silver box from where he had locked it away behind the cupboard in his war room. And hide the armband.

∼

ERATUS—THE AWAKENING HEADQUARTERS

The corridor below the Awakening headquarters was well lit. Each of the torches set into the corridor's stone walls burned strong and true. Drakon sniffed the air. It didn't seem to smell as much on this level as it did on the lower levels. He made his way down the corridor toward a pair of solid metal doors. Drakon knocked twice. A grill slid open and a pair of eyes looked out at him.

"Si—Sire," the guard stammered, "we've been expecting you." The heavy metal locks clanged as they were pushed aside to allow the door to be opened.

Drakon walked past the guard. "Is Laboratory Two ready?"

"Yes, Sire."

He continued down the corridor to a glass door. Once he had passed through the protective screening process, he strode into the antechamber.

As in Laboratory One, a set of stairs that led down to the laboratory below was located in the right-hand corner of the room. Also, as in Laboratory One, one wall was made entirely of glass, allowing those in the antechamber to view the experiments being conducted below. Two armed guards stood at the top of the stairs.

Drakon strode over to one of the guards and handed him the silver box he was carrying. "This is the box I want opened. If the subjects do anything other than what I ask them to do, kill them. Is that clear?"

"Yes, Sire."

"And there are two female subjects?" Drakon asked.

"Yes, Sire. One wearing a yellow band and the other a red one."

"Good. And be prepared to seal up these chambers if we need to."

"As you command."

Drakon moved to the glass and watched as the guard walked into the laboratory. He placed the silver box on the table next to the wall closest to Drakon and left.

Drakon studied the subjects. They kept glancing at the silver box, no doubt wondering what it was, but neither of them moved closer for a better look. He decided to use the woman wearing the yellow band for the task. Drakon lifted the microphone that was placed on the ledge of the glass wall and turned it on. "You, in the green dress. I want you to go to the table and open the silver box that has been placed there."

The women glanced at each other. The one in the green dress walked to the table, leaned forward, and opened the silver box. Drakon held his breath as he waited for the hum or the screams. But there was nothing.

"What can you see?" he asked. "Push the lid back properly so I can see inside, too."

The woman pushed the lid back and looked up at Drakon. "There are a dozen large glass tubes covered with silver mesh. They are filled with what looks like fine sand."

Fine sand. That would be the dust.

"Lift one up and show me," he said.

As she did so, Drakon studied it. The mesh was the same color as the mesh in the boxes they had opened in Laboratory One.

These are bigger than just samples.

Excitement flashed through him.

I have containers of the weapons that I could easily hide, easily carry with me when I choose to use them. They are the perfect weapons. And a lot easier to hide than those massive crates.

He wondered if he should get the woman in the yellow band to break one, so he could see how long she survived.

But he didn't know if the dust would attach itself to the glass wall in the same way it had last time. If it did, he wouldn't be able to stay and watch her. Not knowing how long the dust remained active was limiting his options for testing it.

I need to see if I can find out more information about these weapons.

"Put the vial back in the box, close the lid, and then step back against the far wall." He turned to the guard. "Go down to the laboratory, check that the lid of the box is firmly shut, and then bring it back to me."

"Yes, Sire. And what do you want us to do with the two women?"

"Put them back in with the others."

"As you command."

A couple of minutes later, Drakon was walking out of the laboratory with the silver box clasped in his hands. He had a dozen tubes of a weapon that he could use in whatever way he chose. He needed to protect the hiding space where he would stash this dust until he needed it. There was no way he wanted someone to accidentally find it. For a moment, he wondered if the dust would kill a god, but then decided he needed to know more before attempting anything so ambitious.

~

ERATUS—THE VISITOR

Drakon sprinted up the stairs to Owain's chambers. Soon these rooms would be his. He ambled around the rooms, deciding what changes he would make. The first thing would be to replace everything marked with the kingdom's crest, especially those revolting large circular mats. He didn't mind the glass doors that led out onto the balcony, but he wanted pictures of his fire dragons etched into the glass, rather than scenes of the cave leading to Ocean's Mouth. He would get an artist in to do that. He thought about ignoring the law and starting construction before the funeral, but he had other things he needed to do first.

If I had my way, the funeral would be tomorrow. What is the point in waiting three days?

He wandered onto the balcony. The high-pitched whining of drills and the bang of hammers drew his attention to the clifftop, where an elaborate platform was being built for Owain's funeral pyre. The pyre would be placed on top of the platform and the whole thing would be set alight once the funeral proceedings were over. A dozen women were busy decorating the area with flower arrangements and intricately designed incense burners.

So what happens when you die? Do you get to see any of these celebrations, or is it all a waste of time?

When he turned to walk back into Owain's chambers, he saw a figure standing in the middle of the room.

"And what the hell are you doing in here?" he yelled.

The figure turned to face him. It was a woman with olive skin, flowing dark brown hair, and sparkling gray eyes. She was dressed in a gown of white and gold.

"Hello, Drakon. Now that you are about to become High King, I thought you and I should talk."

"Athena! Do all gods ignore an individual's right to privacy? You might want to talk to me, but I don't want to talk to you."

"All gods?" Athena asked.

"Yes, you and Ares."

"Ares," Athena repeated, shaking her head and rolling her eyes. "Ares has been in contact with you. I knew it."

Drakon stretched himself to his full height and rested his hand on the bollock dagger tucked into his belt. "Then why are you talking to me? I could be his servant. And you and he are hardly on good terms."

"You're right, we're not. But, Drakon, you are about to become the High King of Eratus, and the High King serves me, not Ares."

"I'm already High King. Owain is dead and I am his successor. But where does it say anywhere that I have to serve you? I don't serve any gods. I choose my own destiny."

Athena wandered onto the balcony and looked over at the work being done on the clifftop. "You really think so?" Athena said. "Every ruler needs a god sooner or later. Or should I say, every ruler calls out to a god when they find themselves in trouble. The question is, who would you call out to?"

"Ares is dangerous, but I know him. I don't know you."

Athena tutted as she turned back to face him. "It looks to me like Ares is trying to destroy you, yet you think you can call on him when you're in trouble?"

"He sees everything as a game. I need to learn the rules, that's all."

"Surely you have realized that he sees you and Sascha as the biggest threats to his plan to rule Eratus. Or, to be more specific, the biggest threats to his plan to put his own people in power so *they* can rule Eratus."

"And who are his people?"

Athena frowned. "Do you really not know? The Ancients, of course."

Drakon's stomach dropped. What she said made a strange sort of sense. It could explain the close calls. But he couldn't trust Athena any more than he could trust Ares.

"You're lying, Athena," Drakon snapped. "Ares doesn't want to rule Eratus."

"So he didn't tell you to open the crates containing the weapons when you found them?"

"How did you . . ."

"I have my ways," Athena said.

Drakon snorted. "And so, out of the goodness of your heart, you want to save me? Is that it?"

Athena strolled back into the room. "The truth is, Drakon, that the only reason I care about what you do and who you are connected to is that you are going to be the High King. And because I care, I cannot allow Ares to destroy you. I will help you with the weapons."

"I already have them," Drakon said.

"I know. But now that you have them, you must have a lot of questions about how to control them, how they work."

"I don't need your help. I know where the chronicle is. The answers I need will be in there."

Athena smiled. "I'm sure Ares has told you that there are pages missing from the chronicle, pages that have been hidden so well that even he won't find them. I know where they are. But if you don't want my help, don't want to know exactly what it is you have discovered . . ."

"What is it you want me to do?" Drakon asked.

Athena fingered the pictures engraved on the glass doors. "I want you and Sascha to visit someone. His name is High King Atticus."

"Atticus? He died centuries ago."

"A while ago, yes, but not centuries. He has the answers you seek and he knows how to help you. He has a vested interest in saving Eratus. Until he does that, he can't pass over to the other side."

Saving Eratus? What does that mean?

"So why does Sascha need to see him?"

"She has her own questions about these weapons. So it makes sense for the two of you to go together. And as you're in love with Sascha I doubt that will be a hardship for you."

Drakon tilted his head as he studied Athena. "She has questions? Now that is interesting. Where is he?"

"Not so fast, Drakon. Sascha will be told how to get there. She will also be under strict instructions to keep that information to herself. I trust her. She doesn't work with Ares."

Drakon chuckled. "And neither do I, but that is a matter for another day. I'll go with her but on one condition: she doesn't take Marco or Soleil with her."

"You are hardly in a position to make demands, Drakon. Believe it or not, at the moment I hold all the cards."

Drakon tapped his foot. "So is it a deal?"

"I can make no promises on her behalf. She will come and tell you what she has decided after I have spoken to her."

"When do we leave?"

"It's up to her to decide on when. It's time for me to go now, but before I do, who gave you the armband?"

"What?" Drakon spluttered, grateful he wasn't still wearing Athena's band.

She can't know I killed Demipos.

"I recognize the aura of magic around you. That band protects you from the voices of the Ancients, doesn't it?"

Drakon felt the color drain from his face.

She knows what the armband does. It must have done the same thing for Demipos. That's the only way she could know.

"Not everything is about the Ancients, Athena," he said, desperate to keep his voice sounding even and controlled.

"Your problem, Drakon, is that you underestimate the situation you are in. There will come a time when you will need the band you have gone to so much effort to replace with this . . . substitute. If you wish to keep Ares at bay, there is only one band that will protect you."

"Like it protected Demipos?"

The words slipped out before he had a chance to stop them. Athena raised one eyebrow and was staring at him.

"You mean, your father? So it was you who killed him."

Drakon unfolded his arms and rested his hand back on his bollock dagger. He flexed his fingers as his mind raced from one idea to the next, trying to work out the best way to deal with his mistake.

Idiot. Of all the gods you tell that story to, you tell Athena!

He forced himself to smirk. "That took you a long time to work out. I thought gods were supposed to be all knowing."

"I was almost positive it was you. A special type of magic protected Demipos and the only one who could bypass that magic and kill him would be a child of his own blood. Ares knew that. And when you said you talked to Ares I connected the dots." She took a step toward Drakon. "At the moment, you have a choice about what direction you take, what decisions you make. But there may come a time when the consequences of your decisions leave you without the power you need to save yourself from a living death. I would suggest you step carefully, Drakon."

CONNELL

ERATUS

*S*oleil landed on the balcony of Connell's chambers. The curtains were closed, but the balcony doors were open.

"This place is quiet. Too quiet."

"Connell will be okay, Sascha," Soleil said.

Sascha released herself from the harness, detached the satchel containing the Blades of Light, and slid down from Soleil's shoulders.

She checked the straps on the satchel were secure. If the blades were only meant to be used once, they should have disappeared.

Unless the blades have some sort of . . . destiny? But that seems crazy.

The powerful thumping of wings sounded above her. Fenix landed on the balcony and twirled around to face her.

"Fenix," Sascha said. "Thank you for carrying Marco."

"I'm glad to help," Fenix replied, flicking a glance at Soleil.

"Don't trust her," Soleil snapped. "I'll meet you in your chambers, Sascha. We have a lot to talk about."

"Would you take this satchel with you? I don't want to take it inside, not while I'm visiting Connell."

Soleil nodded, then took the bag in his beak and launched himself into the sky in a burst of feathers and warm air.

As Marco undid his harness and clambered down to the balcony, Sascha studied Fenix. "What's happened, Fenix?"

"Soleil is angry with me. I don't blame him, but he doesn't understand. I . . ." Fenix stared at her intently for a few seconds, emitted a low protracted warble, and then flew off.

However much Sascha wanted to know what was going on, she knew Connell had to be her focus.

Marco touched her shoulder. "Are you ready?"

Sascha flexed the muscles in her neck as she looked at the silk curtains. She was surprised George hadn't come out to greet them. That didn't bode well, but she would know the truth soon.

She pushed the curtains open and took a step forward. The room was cool and the soft peppermint scent of the ocean wafted in the air. Connell lay on his bed, a single sheet covering most of his body. All that showed of him was his head. George rested alongside him, her wings pulled in close to her body. Her massive head rested on the bed next to his hand and her large, warm brown eyes focused on him.

Sascha walked over to Connell and sat on the edge of his bed. He was so pale, and she could have sworn that his skin had a slight tint of blue. She held her breath as she placed a couple of fingers on the side of his neck. There was a pulse— a faint one, but it was a pulse. Connell was alive. She breathed a sigh of relief.

Thank Athena.

Sascha leaned over and patted George. "Hello, beautiful. You're doing a brilliant job of looking after Connell."

George swished her tail in the air in response.

The door to Connell's chambers swung open. In the

doorway stood a tall, lanky man with twinkling blue eyes and polished pink cheeks.

"Healer," Sascha said. "It's good to see you."

As he stepped into the room, Rusty pushed her way past him and bounded up to Sascha. Sascha bent down to say hello and was rewarded with a long, wet lick on the face. The greeting felt so familiar, so heartwarming, that she laughed. "Hello, Rusty."

"I should have known you two would sneak in the back way," the healer muttered as he ambled over to Connell. He put his hand on Connell's forehead and turned back to Sascha. "You killed her, didn't you?"

"Do you mean Reya?" Sascha's throat ached. "Yes, we did. Is he . . ."

"You saved his life. I've given him some medication to help him sleep. That's all he needs now. The venom has disappeared, and his strength is returning."

"I didn't kill him," she whispered.

"He's alive, thanks to you," the healer said, walking over and resting his arm around Sascha's shoulders. "What made you think you had killed Connell?"

"It's a long story," Marco said. "But Sascha was worried that when she destroyed the darkness in Reya, the result would impact Connell."

"It did impact him, but in a good way. Look, he's even got color."

"That is him with—with color?" Sascha stammered. "What did he look like before?"

"He was whiter than the fresh snow on the ice-covered mountains in Tasuna," the healer said.

"Does he know Owain is dead?" Marco asked.

The healer mumbled something to himself before crossing his arms. "Yes, one of the servants told him. I was worried that the news would set his recovery back, but it's done the opposite. He seems even more determined to get better. And now that the connection with Reya has gone, he will heal."

"Does he know Drakon is to be the next High King?" Sascha asked.

The healer nodded. "Yes, he does." He walked over to the door. "I have to prepare his next treatment, but now that you have seen him, I would recommend that you let him sleep."

"What about George?" Sascha asked. "Should we take her outside for some fresh air?"

"George is fine. Ciara takes her out regularly, but she never wants to stay out long. I have never seen anything like it. That creature adores him."

"Would you let us know when Connell is awake?" Sascha asked. "It would be good to talk to him."

"Of course. I'll send someone for you." He turned to Rusty. "Come, Rusty. We need to get out of here, too."

Rusty backed away from the healer, tilted her head to the side, and gave a soft whine as she backed onto Sascha's lap.

The healer smiled. "I think Rusty wants to spend some time with you, Sascha. I think she's missed you."

"It'd be good to have her around. Soleil would love it, too. It's been a while since the three of us were together." Sascha patted Rusty before pushing her off her lap. She stood and stretched. "I guess we should go then."

"You don't have to worry, Sascha," the healer said when Sascha was at the door. "Connell has turned the corner. You have done a good thing."

"Thanks, Healer. It's reassuring to know that he's in your care."

Sascha took Marco's hand as they followed Rusty out of the room. "On the way back to my chambers, Marco, would you tell me what's going on with Fenix and Soleil?"

"Are you sure you don't want to have some rest before

you start trying to sort out everyone else's issues?"
Marco said.

Sascha pulled his face down to hers and kissed him. Her
lips lingered for a moment as she savored the taste of him.
Then she put her hands on his chest and gently pushed him
away. "After everything that has happened, I know how
important it is for us to make time for those we love. And
Soleil loves Fenix, despite his actions. I need to help them
finally get together."

"In that case," Marco said, "I'll tell you."

~

ERATUS

The familiar scent of honey-wood, pine, and cinnamon
greeted Sascha as she strode into her chambers. Soleil was
in his nest in the corner of the room. Rusty trotted over to
the nest, climbed in, and curled herself up into a tight ball
next to Soleil's chest. She gave a huge sigh and went
to sleep.

What Marco had said about Fenix kept churning away in
her mind. "Do you think Fenix did betray me, Marco?"

"No, I don't. But I'm not sure if she didn't betray you
because she wasn't going to or because Laela captured you
first. I do think that Drakon was behind it all though. I know
what that man is capable of."

"But why would he want to capture me? He sees me here
all the time. It doesn't make sense."

"Of course it makes sense," Marco said. "The man is in
love with you. He thinks that if he can get you away from us,
you will fall in love with him."

"He's my brother, Marco."

"No, he's not. He's not even your adopted brother.
Connell said he told you. Drakon's father was marked in the

register of mages as unlisted. There is no family connection between you two at all."

"Do you think Owain had any idea?"

"Raeshaan said he did. And he and Laela were good friends for a long time, and I know that Laela knew. She must have told him."

Sascha nodded. "And you're sure Owain is still alive and that this isn't some sort of plot to disguise the murder of a High King?"

"To be honest, Sasch, I wasn't sure." Marco reached into his pocket and pulled out the gold tooth. "But Owain returned this tooth to me. The only person who knows what this tooth means is Owain. He was asking for my help. So that is what I will give him."

"But there is still the funeral. The people will want to see his body."

"Raeshaan said they will use illusion magic. Everyone will believe the body they see is Owain's." Marco glanced over at Soleil and Rusty. "Those two creatures are asleep, so why don't we go for a walk along the ocean? Switch off for half an hour."

"That's a good idea. But first I need a couple of minutes to have a shower and change."

Marco leaned down and kissed her. "I can wait, Sasch. It's so good to have you back home."

Sascha walked to her wardrobe, collected a change of clothes, and then pressed a button mounted on the wall. When the door in the wall opened, she strode into the bathroom and closed the door behind her.

"Welcome back, Sascha," Crystal said. "I'll run a warm bath for you."

"No, thank you, Crystal. I'll just have a quick shower."

"Very well, Sascha."

Ten minutes later, Sascha was dressed and ready to face

whatever was next. She frowned when she heard the sound of muffled voices coming from her chambers.

Who is here?

She opened the door and looked out. Chiane and Isabella were standing in the middle of the room. Marco looked at Sascha and then nodded in the direction of the balcony.

"Can you two give me a moment to talk to Sascha?" Marco said.

Chiane put his arm around Isabella's shoulders. "Yes, of course."

"Thanks." Marco followed Sascha out onto the balcony.

"So . . . ," Sascha said, "what's going on?"

"Chiane and Isabella are asking for our help to defeat Drakon. They said they have evidence to show what Drakon is really up to, and once we see it, we will know why Drakon must never be crowned High King."

"But, Marco, Owain has organized it so that he becomes High King for a reason. And hasn't he asked that we focus on the weapons, not on whether Drakon should be High King?"

"We will search for the weapons as well," Marco said. "We've always thought Drakon was up to something. This could be our chance to find out."

"But at what cost? I didn't trust Owain. And when I challenged him, I was sent to Earth. How much worse would it be if it was Drakon who was challenged? We both know that man doesn't know the meaning of mercy."

"I still think we should at least see this evidence."

"But we're talking about Chiane." Sascha rubbed the back of her neck. "Chiane is one of Drakon's favorites. This could be a trap."

"It could be, but my gut tells me it isn't. Isabella seems to have really suffered at Drakon's hands." Marco shook his head. "But I don't know, I really don't know. I do think they're both petrified of Drakon if that counts for anything."

"Yet they're both willing to testify against him?" Sascha said. "Doesn't that seem particularly strange to you?"

Marco nodded. "What do you want to do, Sascha?"

"Why the hell didn't they give us this evidence before now?" Sascha asked.

"They say they've only just found out what Drakon is up to."

"Convenient," Sascha growled. "Do you believe them?"

"Yes, I do," Marco said.

"Make a time and place to meet them so that they can show us this evidence," Sascha said. "But make it clear to them that we're not committing to anything. What they are proposing is treason. And before we go down that road, because it's Drakon we're talking about, we'd better be totally convinced we're right."

"You wait here," Marco replied. "I'll talk to them."

"I pray this isn't a trap," Sascha said.

Sascha remained on the balcony while Marco went inside to give Chiane and Isabella their answer. She watched the hurlies' antics in the bushes along the edge of the garden. In the wild, the cute, fury little creatures would only come out to play when they felt completely safe. At the first sign of trouble they disappeared in a puff of white magic. But here on the castle grounds the creatures had nothing to fear. How much easier life would be if the only things you had to worry about were food and sleep. She sighed and leaned against the balcony rim.

A movement from down below caught her eye. She looked closer. Sitting cross-legged in the middle of the lawn was Jenny. Sascha was about to raise her arm to call out to Jenny when a young boy raced out of the bushes and dived into the young woman's arms. His infectious laughter filled the air. He stopped laughing and looked up at Sascha. Her blood chilled. The child's face was the same face she'd seen in her nightmares. A wave of dizziness swept over her. She gripped the balcony rim to balance herself.

The one who bedded Jenny . . . was he the creature she had killed? Was he the father of this child? But that would mean . . .

A spine-tingling howl echoed through the forest that surrounded the castle.

The child leaped to his feet and cast an arcane protective shield around Jenny and himself. Sascha gaped at him.

What sort of child has the capability to create that sort of magic —at that age? And why would he feel the need to protect Jenny from a wolf?

VISITING ATHENA

ERATUS

*C*iara stood in the doorway to Sascha's chambers, George by her side. The late afternoon suns warmed the air as a soft peppermint sea breeze wafted into the room.

"I'm sorry I have to ask to borrow Rusty so soon," Ciara said. "I went to see Connell after you and Marco visited earlier this morning and walked into a . . . disagreement between George and the healers. George needs to take a break before the healers say something and cause trouble for her. And Rusty seems to be the only creature who is strong willed enough, and brave enough, to force George into having fun."

Sascha chuckled as she stroked the top of George's head. "That's fine, Ciara. I'm finding it hard to switch off anyway." She turned toward the garden balcony. "Rusty, look who's here."

Rusty was sprawled across the floor of the balcony watching Soleil. She lifted her head, stood, and stretched before she padded toward Sascha. As Rusty caught sight of Ciara and George she changed direction and raced toward them, barking and wagging her tail so hard her whole body wiggled. "Arf, arf."

"One day we'll have to go with Ciara," Marco said. "I'd love to see someone take George on and win."

Sascha smiled. "It must be lovely to see the two of them together, especially when George is feeling grumpy."

Ciara laughed. "It certainly is entertaining." She clapped her hands. "Rusty, are you ready?"

"Ar-ruff."

"Good. Let's go then."

Sascha couldn't help but feel disappointed. After what had happened in Brun she had desperately wanted to spend some time with Marco, Soleil, and Rusty. She had wanted them to do something normal together. But things hadn't worked out that way. Soleil wasn't himself. Although he refused to admit it, he was missing Fenix. Learning that she may have betrayed them had taken a toll on him. And Chiane and Isabella's morning visit had left a sour taste in Sascha's mouth. She couldn't push past the idea that going to see this evidence Chiane and Isabella had spoken about would impact their lives a lot more than they were expecting.

Athena, I pray we aren't walking into a trap.

As Ciara led George and Rusty down the corridor, Zabir marched toward them.

"I'm sorry, Colonel, but we have a situation. The villagers of Unidern, who are protecting the second portal in the Kingdom of Breyth, have ignored our repeated warnings to prepare for the storm season. Now we've received reports of a hoard of akhult heading their way."

Marco shook his head. "How could the akhult have moved that far east so soon? Are you sure the intel is correct?"

"I had hoped the report was wrong," Zabir said, "so I had it triple-checked. But it's accurate."

Sascha studied Zabir before she turned to Marco. "You need to help them, Marco."

"Unless we leave them to their own fate," Zabir said. "We did warn them time and again."

"Zabir!" Marco snapped. "Our duty is to protect our people."

Zabir lifted his chin and squared his shoulders. "One day we may be forced to consider whether it is worth sacrificing good men and women to save the lives of the ignorant and the stupid."

Sascha moved to position herself between Marco and Zabir so that Marco couldn't act on the thoughts that were etched upon his face. "Zabir does have a point," Sascha said. "But it is also your duty to protect. Go and see what you can do. I'm going to meet with Athena. I need to find out more about the blades and these ancient weapons. Hades is right. I don't know anything about them. All Athena and Owain have told us is that we must destroy them."

"Owain is trusting us to do the right thing," Marco whispered.

"I know. But it won't hurt to understand what it is we're destroying." Sascha leaned up and gave him a quick kiss. "When will you brief Drakon on what happened at Brun?"

"I'll do it before I leave for Unidern," he replied.

"Good. Go now before I change my mind and keep you here all to myself."

"Promises, promises," Marco mocked.

"You're hardly by yourself, Sascha," Soleil called out from the balcony. "What am I? Chopped sweet meat?"

"I don't like chopped sweet meat," Sascha replied, "so I hope that's not what you are."

Zabir coughed. "I can come back—"

"No, it's fine, Zabir," Marco said.

Marco cupped the back of Sascha's neck with one hand

and pulled her to him. He brushed his lips against hers and a flash of pleasure sizzled through her blood. She sighed as she put her hand on his chest and pushed him away. "Go," she whispered.

"Only if you promise to keep safe."

"And you must promise to do the same, Marco. If you hear from Chiane—"

"I'll let you know the details," he said.

Sascha waved her hands in the direction of the door, ushering him out of the room. "See you when you return."

She closed the door behind him and walked past the teal-colored silk curtains to join Soleil on the balcony. He was hunched on the balcony rim searching for signs of Fenix. There was a lot of activity around the castle grounds as nobility had started to arrive before the funeral for Owain. Angry voices drifted on the breeze as the more arrogant groups of nobles demanded extra considerations because of who they were. Sascha shook her head. It all seemed so surreal. So much had happened in such a short time.

A flock of pyrans flew overhead and circled the court's gardens, their soft musical calls floating on the breeze. Sascha leaned against the balcony wall, next to Soleil. "You haven't seen any sign of her return yet?"

"No," Soleil said. "She's probably too ashamed to face us."

Sascha pulled her jacket closed to block out the cool winds. "Soleil, we need to give her the benefit of the doubt."

"Don't you start that. I've already hard Marco harping on about the same thing."

"Soleil, I need you to take me—"

A quick knock sounded on the door.

Soleil clicked his beak as he narrowed his eyes. "More visitors?"

Sascha lowered her voice. "Be nice, Soleil." She turned so

her back rested against the balcony wall. "Come in," she called out.

Raeshaan rushed into the chambers. "Sascha—" She stopped for a moment as she covered her mouth with her hand while she yawned. Then she continued. "I only have a minute before I have to catch up with the grandmaster, but I thought I should let you know my findings from our assessment of those girls we rescued."

"What did you find?"

"They're all very fragile and not really up to answering many questions, but they're healthy enough, particularly when you consider what they've been through. But none of them are pregnant."

"None of them?"

"No. Even though I couldn't ask the questions I wanted to, I can confirm that none of them are expecting."

"Do you think Laela hid some more girls somewhere else then?" Sascha asked.

"I thought about that too, and because of the importance of the matter, I decided to ask them that question. The girls were adamant that there weren't any other captives. It was interesting to note that the girls do display a strange sort of protectiveness toward two of the girls."

"So perhaps they could be the ones I heard about?" Sascha said.

"They could be. But if they were pregnant, they're not anymore. What made you think they were?"

"That's what I was told," Sascha said. "But it could have been a lie so let's wait until the girls are ready to talk."

Raeshaan yawned again and rubbed her eyes. "We'll need to give them some more time to recover before we ask them anything."

"I agree," Sascha said. "We weren't there to protect them

when they needed us so giving them time is the least we can do."

"But we did rescue them," Raeshaan replied. "That's a good thing. Anyway, I do have to rush off but I wanted you to know."

"Thanks, Raeshaan," Sascha said. "And it looks like you should do yourself a favor and get an early night. You look tired."

When Raeshaan had left, Sascha flexed her neck and shoulders and concentrated on loosening the tightness in her muscles. She would make sure no other child suffered the way those girls did.

"Soleil, can you take me to Athena's cave?"

"You want *me* to take you?"

She frowned. "Yes, of course. Who else would I ask?"

"You've never asked me to take you there before."

"That's right. Athena told me that, too." She shrugged her shoulders. "That was then. I plan on doing a lot of things differently this time."

"I don't know how to get there," Soleil said. "Do you?"

"Athena gave me a map." Sascha clambered up onto Soleil's shoulders and strapped herself into the harness. "Let's get going. Head west."

Soleil hunkered down, stretched his wings, and leaped up into the air heading in the direction of Athena's cave.

∿

ERATUS

The suns were hanging heavy in the sky when they arrived at the spot marked on Athena's map. Soleil flew in under a canopy of jade vines, glided past a small pool at the bottom of a waterfall filled with flying fish that glittered in the filtered sunlight, and landed neatly on a stone platform in front of a large vine-covered entrance to a cave. In the center of the entrance was a gate marked with petite white flowers that formed the shape of a large owl. A warm gentle breeze filled with a sweet citrus-and-honey aroma drifted across the platform.

"It's beautiful," Sascha said as she undid the harness and slid down from Soleil's shoulders. Moving closer to the vine wall she ran her hand along what appeared to be the edge of the gate. She searched for a latch or a lever, some way to open it. But there was nothing.

"There must be a way to open this thing," Sascha said.

"Do you think there could be another entrance?" Soleil asked.

A soft rustling of leaves whispered in the air.

"The gate," Soleil said. "Look at the gate."

Sascha watched wide-eyed as the vines rolled back revealing a panel of green light along one edge of the gate. The panel pulsed and the gate moved silently aside to reveal a large grassed pathway through a neat lush forest. The same fine, glass ribbons she had seen hanging inside Athena's cave hung from the branches of the trees that edged the pathway. Green balls of fire set into the ground flicked into life, lighting their way. As they stepped onto the pathway the same sweet, warm breeze that they had first smelled on the platform wrapped itself around them like a soft woolen cloak. Bird whistles and the soft hoots of owls echoed around them as white shadows with glowing blue-gray eyes darted in and out of the trees.

"It's like we've stepped into a different world," Sascha whispered.

"I don't like it," Soleil muttered. "Keep an eye out for traps. Something isn't right."

They trod warily along the pathway, examining the ground ahead of them for traps. Several minutes later they arrived at a solid wooden door. Glass panels etched with intricate designs of olive trees were set into the wall on either side of the door. Sascha peered in through one of the panels and could see the light of green firelight reflected in the polished white marble walls and floors.

"This is it," Sascha said.

"I'll wait for you here," Soleil replied.

Sascha glanced back at Soleil. "You hurly."

Soleil clicked his beak at her and hunkered down at the entrance as he prepared to wait.

Sascha pushed the door open and strode into the cave. "Athena, are you here?"

"Who do you think let you in?" a singsong voice answered.

Sascha walked toward the sound and found Athena sitting at a writing desk in the corner of the room.

"I had planned to come and visit you," Athena said as she put some papers into the top drawer of her desk. "But I thought I would give you a day to recover from Brun. I'm surprised you're not spending the day with Marco."

"He had to go away to visit one of the villages. There was some sort of emergency."

"Oh, I see. How are you after your horrible experience in Brun?"

"That's what I'm here about."

Athena swiveled in her chair to face Sascha. "I thought it might be."

"I need to discuss the blades with you," Sascha said. "I also had an interesting conversation about the weapons with Hades."

"Hades! " Athena gestured for Sascha to sit. "I hadn't heard about that. I'll get us a drink and then we can talk. I can only offer a sweet nectar. Will that be acceptable?"

"Yes, thank you," Sascha replied.

Athena returned with a couple of glasses of nectar and offered one to Sascha. Then she walked to the long chair next to where Sascha was sitting and plopped herself down. "I have heard some of what happened in Brun via the grapevine."

"The grapevine?" Sascha asked. "I didn't know gods had a . . . grapevine."

"It's not that exactly, but it's as good a word as any to describe how we find things out. So, you said Hades spoke to you about the weapons?"

"Yes. He promised to help me escape if I'd join him in his search for the weapons and then help him to release them."

Athena sighed. "I should have known that if Ares was involved, Hades would be too. But why don't you start at the beginning and tell me everything."

Sascha drank a mouthful of the nectar, expecting it to be too sweet, but instead finding it fresh and flavorsome. It tasted like a rich fruit drink, but there was something else she couldn't place, something that left her feeling relaxed. By the time Sascha swallowed the last mouthful of her drink and placed her empty glass on the coffee table in front of her, she had told Athena everything. She relaxed back into her chair as she watched Athena fiddle with the empty glass in her hand.

"So it is true," Athena said. "The temple has been sacrificing young ones for all this time?"

"Yes, and I allowed it to happen. I only hope that when all of my memories return I don't find out that I knew about it and chose to do nothing."

"You didn't know. You would have told me if you had. Many things would have escaped your notice because of your addiction to green lyrium."

Sascha shook her head. "Why was I allowed to continue

as leader? Surely there was someone who could have taken over from me?"

"You mean like Laela?"

Sascha sighed. "It devastates me to know that we weren't there to protect those young girls."

"And you say Hades knew about this?" Athena asked.

"Yes. In fact, it was him who told Laela to continue with the sacrifices, and all because of the connection between the Ancients and Ares."

Athena stared through the glass window at her owl as it sat on top of a chair under the nearest olive tree. The owl had its head tilted to the side as it looked at Athena. It was almost as if the two of them were having their own private conversation.

"Gods are not supposed to interfere in the lives of mortals," Athena said finally.

"Tell that to Hades then," Sascha said. "And Ares for that matter."

"I shall," Athena said. "But back to your first question. You want to understand why the blades returned to you, if I saw you only needing them once more."

Sascha nodded. "I thought they would have disappeared."

Athena put her glass on the coffee table and sat forward in her chair. "I think you already know the answer. The blades have a sort of . . . destiny, or purpose, and until that destiny is fulfilled they will remain with you."

"Destiny?" Sascha repeated. "It's odd to hear of blades having a destiny."

"I know. But it is why they returned to you. You will be able to use them until their destiny is fulfilled." Athena tapped her fingers on the arm of the chair. "Perhaps I should have told you this sooner. Atticus is the one who found the blades, and he is the one who gave them to me. He told me to give them to you because you would need them one more time."

"Atticus, as in the High King Atticus?"

"Yes," Athena replied.

"Did he say what I would need them for?"

"He refused to say because he couldn't be sure what the fates had in store for you."

Sascha frowned. "What are you saying? Are you saying this might all play out differently from the way I have seen it in my dreams?"

Athena stood and picked up the two empty glasses. She pointed one of the glasses at a sketch on her wall. "I'll top up our drinks while you have a look at that drawing over there."

Sascha glanced in the direction Athena was pointing, pushed herself out of the chair, and moved closer to study the drawing. It was an excellent one of Athena. She was sitting in a chair, behind which stood three men. Two of the men looked similar enough to be twins. Blood drained from Sascha's face as she studied the two identical men.

"Don't you think the artist did a brilliant job?" Athena asked.

Sascha leaped at the sound of Athena's voice behind her, her blood pounding in her ears. "Don't sneak up like that, Athena."

"Guilty conscience?" Athena stopped and stared at the drawing. "That's obviously me sitting in the chair. On the right is Demipos. It was his remains that we found at the temple in the Peaceful Valley. On the left are the twins. They're the ones you were studying so closely. Do they appear familiar?"

"Yes, Sascha said. They almost look like—"

"The Ancient you killed?"

"Yes." A chill raced down Sascha's spine.

"That's because one of them is."

UNIDERN

ERATUS

*T*he suns were low in the sky as Marco and Zabir flew over the Valtros and headed toward the village of Unidern. The village was positioned next to the second portal, which, for safety reasons, had been established on one of the largest platforms in Eratus. Three sides of the village edged the Hills of Silent Death, so named because they were teeming with clay traps that quietly and efficiently dragged unwary travelers down to the black desert serpents that lived beneath the surface. On the other side of the hills lay a swampland that was said to be home to Necromancers. The northern end of the village backed onto the edge of a large chasm.

"Can you see any signs of activity?" Marco called out to Zabir.

"The place is deserted," Zabir answered as he rubbed his arms to warm them against the icy winds. "But the reports I received this morning stated the village was still fully occupied. I can see the portal is still working but the guardians are no longer guarding it. I've been told the creatures go underground when they hear the storm season is close. I just don't understand why the guardians on the first portal haven't hibernated underground as well."

"It's really strange, that's for sure." Marco squeezed the side of his war pyran with his knees as he pushed his feet downward, signaling for the pyran to land. But the pyran's neck and shoulders pulled against the movement and instead of going down it pulled up higher into the sky. Marco pushed his heels gently into the creature's sides, but it still refused to obey his instructions.

"What's the matter?" Marco said stroking the creature's neck.

"Bad people down there," the pyran replied. "And bad magic."

"We've been here before," Marco replied.

"It's different now," the pyran said. "The people . . . the magic . . . they're different."

Zabir twisted in his harness so that he could speak to Marco. "I'm trying to fly lower to get a closer look. But my pyran won't obey my commands. He keeps pulling away."

"Mine is the same," Marco said. "He keeps saying there's bad magic and bad people down there. This doesn't bode well. Let's choose somewhere safe to land on those hills to the south of the village. We'll walk down to the village on foot."

"Land on th—*those* hills?" Zabir stammered. "But what about the clay traps?"

"If we land on the edge of the hill closest to the village we should be safe."

"The traps and the monsters beneath them are probably frozen anyway," Zabir muttered. "Even at the peak of the storm season I haven't known it to be this cold."

"So when do I get my apology for forcing you to wear your winter gear?" Marco asked.

"Okay, okay," Zabir answered. "I have to admit I thought

you were a wuss, but you were right. I would have frozen to death in my chain mail."

Marco chuckled. "Lieutenant Colonel, I don't think it's respectful to call your Colonel a wuss."

They circled the top of the hill nearest the village to check it was clear. Moments later they landed on a bare patch of land. After Marco climbed down from his pyran he opened the pouch attached to the harness and retrieved his blades. He had thought that bringing the Vengeance of Hephaestus might be overkill but now he wasn't so sure. He took one of the blades and handed it over to Zabir. "If I tell you to use this, do it. But only if I tell you."

"Yes, Colonel."

A gust of wind blew across the village and up to the hills carrying with it a foul stench of blood and bone. The pyrans squealed and shook their heads furiously in an attempt to escape the odor. Marco patted his pyran's neck. "Rest easy. We won't be long."

Marco walked to the edge of one of the hills and stared down at the village and the swamp that circled it. Wisps of smoke were floating up from the chimneys. Marco pointed at the smoke. "Somebody is there. It looks like the fires are burning."

"Maybe everyone is indoors," Zabir said. "But it's bad form to leave the place un—"

Marco held up his hand, stopping conversation. "Zabir, listen. Tell me what you can hear."

Zabir stood for a moment as he listened to the silence. "I can't hear anything."

"Exactly," Marco said. "Have you ever known this place to be this quiet? Be prepared. We may be too late."

As they slogged their way down the muddy road toward the village, the intensity of the stench increased.

"What do you think that smell is?" Zabir asked. "It's

getting worse. It's like we've landed in the middle of a field covered by dead bodies that have been left out in the sun to rot."

Marco's stomach clenched. Zabir was right. That was what the odor reminded him of, too. "I guess we're about to find out what it is."

Several minutes later they trudged into the village. Goose bumps prickled over Marco's skin. The village was far too quiet.

"Where is everyone?" Zabir whispered.

The doors to the huts lay open. They walked into one hut after another and found fires still burning and pots of food sat in various states of readiness. The people had been preparing their meals, probably their dinner. Children's toys were scattered on the floors; pet bowls lay filled next to the door to the huts.

"This is very strange," Marco said. "It's like the village was in the middle of preparing for their evening meal and everyone . . . vanished."

"Perhaps they were attacked and flew off to the nearest protected village," Zabir said.

"But there are no bodies," Marco said. "Could they have all escaped?"

"I don't know," Zabir answered, "but there must be some explanation."

Marco walked into the largest hut. It was neat and tidy, and there was an abundance of food and drink laid out on the dining table. Zabir leaned over to pick up a piece of fruit.

"Don't!" Marco snapped. "Until we know what happened here, don't consume anything."

Marco noticed a bundle of papers and a small wooden box at the head of the table. He picked up the papers and flicked through them. There were several handwritten notes on the activities that had been going on in the village. Marco pocketed the papers and the box. "I'll take these with us. There might be something in it, some clue as to what happened here."

They left the hut and stood outside as they scanned the area for any sign of where the people had gone. "Look." Zabir pointed to a hut in the far corner of the village. It was the only hut where the door was closed. Marco shivered. He glanced over at Zabir. Together they turned and strode toward the hut.

Marco pushed the door open and they stepped in. Their eyes were still adjusting to the darkness when the smell hit them. They grunted and covered their noses and mouths with their hands. "This is where the stench is coming from," Marco said. "It's a killing hut."

Zabir's face turned white. "And look what they've been killing. Pyrans. No wonder our creatures didn't want to land here. They could smell the blood of their own kin."

"But why would anyone kill pyrans when they live in such an isolated area?" Marco said. "Pyrans would have been their only way to get out of here, and they knew about the coming storm season. It doesn't make sense."

A piercing wail echoed through the village, penetrating the hut's thick timber walls. Seconds later other cries joined in, harmonizing with the first, and forming a single heart-chilling howl. As suddenly as it started, the sounds stopped.

Zabir glanced over at Marco as he drew his sword. "I'm not sure which is more terrifying—the howling or the silence."

"Definitely the silence," Marco said.

As if in response to Marco's words, a high-pitched shriek split the silence.

"The pyrans," Zabir yelled. "Something is attacking our pyrans. If we lose them we're trapped here."

They opened the door and raced out of the hut. Standing

before them were a horde of giant wolves, each one larger than a great bear. Their eyes glowed yellow and their claws were the color of blood. They stood in a line, their lips pulled back in silent snarls, revealing their perfect white fangs—and their full focus was on Marco and Zabir.

"Athena's ghost," Zabir whispered. "Those creatures are wearing armor. Since when do wolves wear armor?"

Marco's hand dropped to the hilt of his blade. "They're not wolves, and that's not armor. These creatures are akhult."

As they scanned the village desperately searching for a way of escape, they realized the creatures weren't moving. They were standing and watching, their heavy breathing thundering around them.

"Why aren't they attacking?" Zabir said as he readjusted his grip on his sword.

"It's like they are waiting for ord—" A soft breath warmed the back of Marco's neck.

Shit.

The heat in his blood chilled. Something was behind them. Marco gripped the hilt of his sword and slowly withdrew it from its scabbard. The blade glowed with the colors of fire.

These blades only react to dark magic. What is the connection between magic and the akhult?

Marco glanced over at Zabir who was still focused on the akhult blocking the road in front of them. He hadn't noticed there was at least one more behind them. "Zabir," Marco whispered, "when I count to three withdraw the blade I gave you and twist away to your left."

"But—"

"Do as I say," Marco growled.

"Yes, Colonel."

The creature behind him moved closer as the sound of its breathing grew louder. "One," Marco counted out. "Two . . .

THREE!" Marco twisted to his right, and pushed himself into a crouching position, his blade flaming in front of him. The creature that had been behind them was two heads taller than the others.

It's the leader. But how did we not hear him come up behind us?

The creature snarled, his brilliant white teeth glistening in the light of the setting suns. His snarls were echoed by the others as they lowered their heads, bared their teeth, and crouched down ready to lunge. A piercing blast of a horn vibrated across the village. The creatures twisted their heads to the side as they listened. The horn sounded again and the pack's attention turned to their leader. The leader sniffed the air and turned toward the hills. He lunged into the air, shimmered, and disappeared. The others followed his lead.

"What in Athena's name just happened?" Zabir said as he stared ahead at the cleared roadway.

"I have no idea," Marco said. "But let's get the hell out of here."

"The pyrans," Zabir said. "Do you think they're still alive?"

"We're not going to find out standing here," Marco said as he sheathed his sword. "Let's go."

They raced out of the village. They were halfway up the hill when a whoosh of wings sounded above them. The pyrans twirled in the air before landing neatly on the ground several feet in front of Marco and Zabir.

"You're both alive," Marco spluttered. "Thank Athena."

They clambered onto the shoulders of their pyrans, strapped themselves into their harnesses and launched into the air.

"Wait a minute . . ." Zabir pointed toward the chasm at the northern end of the village. "What's that over there? It looks like hordes of akhult but there's another type of creature too."

Marco squinted and leaned forward as they flew closer to

the gathering. His eyes widened and he snapped back into his harness. "You're right. They are akhult, and those other creatures, they're ice ghouls."

"But the ghouls are wearing plated armor and carrying spears," Zabir said. "Since when do they wear that sort of armor or fight with weapons? I thought they were supposed to use ice magic."

"These ones appear to be more skilled," Marco answered. "There are hundreds of them. Someone . . . or something . . . is planning a war."

"But who?" Zabir asked.

"I don't know. We need to get back to the castle. When we return I want you to check in with all the kingdoms one last time. Ensure they have briefed their telepath network on what is required of them. All shields must be activated the moment the leaders receive a message from their telepath to say their portal has been shut down."

"Yes, Colonel."

"And the only ones who are allowed to send or receive messages are those who have mastered the skill of remote telepathy. The message will have to be sent over long distances and we can't afford mistakes due to inexperience. People could die if we don't get this right."

"Colonel, what are we doing about Unidern's portal?"

"I'll talk to Drakon and let him know what we found. I want it closed immediately. We'll ask the telepaths to spread the word. I don't want anyone coming here until we know what's going on."

"And we still have to sort out the first portal," Zabir said. "The guardians are still at that portal and the telepaths are scared to get too close."

"Tell the telepaths to watch from a distance. The bright explosion of lights when the portal is shut down will make it easy to see from far away. There's no need for them to be close."

"As you command, Colonel. All we need now is for the shields to survive the attacks," Zabir said. "I've never seen these creatures in such large numbers before."

"The akhult and ice ghouls have never worked together before, either," Marco said. "They have always been enemies . . . until now."

As they turned away from the chasm and headed across the Hills of Silent Death toward home, the air around them was shattered by a high-pitched scream.

Marco's heart pounded as he twisted to the right and left trying to work out what was going on. "Zabir, can you see where the sound is coming from?"

"No, there's nothing. I can't . . . wait a minute." Zabir pointed at a clay trap to his right. "Someone's caught in a clay trap."

"Where?" Marco snapped as he tried to see what it was Zabir was pointing at. Then he saw her. A woman with long blond hair was caught in one of the clay traps. She clawed at the ground as she tried to save herself from being dragged down beneath the surface. A dead golden pyran lay next to her, its lifeless body already half swallowed by the ground.

"Faster," Marco screamed out to his pyran as they hurtled toward the woman.

The screams stopped and were replaced with silence. They were too late.

As they flew over the spot where the woman had disappeared, they saw that the surface of the clay pit was still. There was no sign of the horror they had just witnessed.

Marco and Zabir circled in the air above the pit in stunned silence.

Marco whispered a prayer for the soul of the dead woman. "The poor woman . . . and that poor creature.

There's nothing we can do for them now. We had better head back home."

"I wonder who she was," Zabir said. "She had a pyran. How did she end up in a clay pit?"

"The pyran was dead," Marco said. "Perhaps it was killed in the air?"

Zabir scanned the horizon. "But what could have killed it? I can't see anything close by and killing a pyran in the air is no easy feat. They're exceptionally fast when they need to be."

Marco remembered what had happened with Soleil and how he had flown Sascha to safety despite his own wounds. "It must have been a quick death. I've known wounded pyrans to fly for miles just to save the one they were carrying."

It suddenly felt so important to get home to Sascha, to reassure himself that she was safe.

A woman with blonde hair and a golden pyran. It can't have been Sascha. Please, let it not have been Sascha.

ATHENA'S CAVE

ERATUS

*S*ascha was finding it hard to tear her gaze away from the drawing on Athena's wall.

"Come and take a seat while I explain why I asked you to look at that particular picture," Athena said.

Sascha walked back to her chair and sat.

Athena offered her a glass of nectar before taking a seat in the lounge next to Sascha. She rested her glass on the arm of the lounge. "You were asking if things might all play out differently from the way you've seen it happen in your dream. Do you remember how I told you that there were two Masters who warned me of a planned attack on Eratus?"

"Yes."

"One of the men who helped me was Demipos. The other one was one of the twins—Wiskari. He's the one on the far left of that sketch. I believe you killed Wiskari's brother during the healing ceremony."

"That creature had a twin brother?" Sascha asked.

"Yes, but I wouldn't describe Wiskari as a creature."

Sascha turned and stared at the drawing. "Do you really think I killed him?"

"Yes, he is dead all right. If you hadn't killed him with the blades I couldn't be so sure, but you did."

But everything about the child . . . after what I heard in Brun that child could still be his.

Sascha took a sip of her nectar. "If Wiskari helped to save Eratus, why would his brother seek to destroy it?"

"Wiskari's brother was an Ancient," Athena said. "And the Ancients want to rule Eratus, at any cost."

"What does all of this have to do with my dream?"

"If the child in your dream looks like the one you killed in the ceremony, perhaps Wiskari is the father. Didn't you say Jenny was meant to be bedded by an Ancient but ended up with a Master instead?"

"That is what Hades told me."

"It would make sense that Wiskari tried to save Jenny from an Ancient."

"Whether Jenny was forced to sleep with a Master or an Ancient is irrelevant," Sascha said. "Whichever way you look at it, it was a crime."

"If the father is Wiskari, there will be more to the story. Wiskari protected children. He didn't abuse them."

Sascha sat quietly for a moment as she digested what Athena had said. "In which case I need to ask Jenny what happened?"

"Yes," Athena said. "Which means you're going to have to talk to Jenny, not avoid her like you have been doing."

"I haven't been avoiding her," Sascha said.

Athena raised one eyebrow and looked at Sascha.

"Well, I guess it's possible." Sascha put her glass down on the coffee table. "But what does it mean if Wiskari is the boy's father?"

"I believe your dreams are being influenced by the power behind the dragon hunters."

"And that's not creepy at all," Sascha said.

Athena smiled. "Everyone has strange things happen in their dreams but as an enchantress you are a lot more susceptible to influence from other forces. I think the power understands your hatred for Wiskari's brother and is trying to convince you to destroy the child. It might be that this child is a threat to the ones who are plotting against Eratus, the ones behind the dragon hunters."

"But the child does look exactly like the creature I destroyed. He's the spitting image of him."

"Or the spitting image of Wiskari, the one who helped me save Eratus."

Sascha shook her head. "Is that even possible?"

"I can't tell you for certain. But Atticus may be able to give you some more ideas on how it all fits together, especially considering he was the one who said you needed the blades."

"I need to meet with him," Sascha said.

"I'm glad you said that. I want you *and* Drakon to meet with him."

"Drakon? Why do you want *him* to meet with Atticus?"

"Because Drakon is soon to be crowned as High King, and I need Atticus to assess Drakon's reaction to a task I need him to carry out."

Sascha pinched the bridge of her nose. "I don't understand. Why is that important?"

Athena pushed herself up from her chair and walked over to the window. She looked out at the gardens. "The position of High King of Eratus serves me, and so I now have a responsibility to see what sort of ruler Drakon will be." She turned to face Sascha. "You see, Drakon has the ancient weapons."

Sascha gasped. "He what? Hades can't have known or he would have said something."

"Ares has probably told him by now. I have a strong sense

that Ares helped Drakon work out a way to retrieve the weapons."

"Why would Ares help Drakon to retrieve them?"

"I believe Ares wants the weapons for himself, or should I say, for the ones he wants to rule over Eratus."

"You're talking about the Ancients?"

"Yes."

Sascha studied Athena. "Ares is helping the Ancients to free themselves from their prison and destroy Eratus. Does he really hate Eratus that much?"

Athena glanced at her owl again. "No, he hates *me* that much."

"You're referring to this war between the two of you?"

"Yes," Athena said. "And now that Drakon has the weapons, I need to know if he is willingly helping Ares or if he will listen to reasoned argument and help us destroy them."

"Is this the task you want Atticus to assess Drakon's reaction to?"

Athena nodded. "Yes, it is."

"Drakon has wanted those weapons all his life. He's not going to want to destroy them."

Athena fiddled with the empty glass in her hands. "I would have agreed with you but now that he has the weapons, he has realized he needs to know more about them. I'm hoping that once Atticus explains how they work he will understand why we need to destroy them."

"Hades said I was being naive in wanting to destroy the weapons."

"I'm sure he did. When you hear what Atticus has to say I'm hoping you . . . and Drakon . . . will understand the dangers they present."

Sascha yawned and stretched. It was getting late and she was tired. "This is going to be an interesting visit."

"There is one other matter," Athena said. "Atticus has the evidence I need to show Ares is behind a lot of the troubles that Eratus has been struggling with. He has promised to give it to you. Please don't let Drakon know about it, at least until we know more about how much he and Ares are working together."

"This is the evidence for the council meeting?" Sascha asked.

"Yes."

"If you take that evidence to the meeting will that mean the other gods will help us defeat this power behind the dragon hunters?"

"It is what I hope but I cannot promise anything. The least I can promise is that with this evidence the other gods won't interfere, they won't help Ares—or Hades."

Sascha shook her head. "And that's all? We still have to battle the creatures the gods have helped to create?"

"Yes, I'm afraid that is more than likely what will be agreed. Atticus will show the both of you how the weapons work, and how to destroy them. Atticus will be assessing Drakon's reaction to that information. He will advise me if Drakon is still determined to save the weapons and if he is . . . I can't allow him to take on the role of High King."

"Drakon believes the role of High King is his already," Sascha said.

"I know. But it isn't."

Sascha stared at her hands as they rested in her lap. "Do you think Owain had any idea Drakon has the weapons?"

"No, I don't."

Sascha exhaled as she looked out the window at the gardens and for a brief moment wished she was back on Earth in her veterinary clinic. "How are we going to tell Drakon all of this?"

"He already knows," Athena said. "He's waiting for you to tell him you're prepared to go with him."

Sascha's eyes widened. "You've spoken to him?"

"Yes. He wasn't happy with me dropping in for a surprise visit but he does want to meet with Atticus."

"Where is Atticus?"

Athena put her glass on the table next to Sascha's. "I had planned on giving you the instructions but since you managed to overwhelm the odds and escape the temple in Brun, Ares has become . . . interested in you. He may try and follow you, see where you go. To be on the safe side, the both of you need to go to Zinnath and Kalurth's cave on Earth. Zeus protects that area so you will be safe. The dragons will transport the both of you to Atticus."

"Marco and Soleil are going to be furious when they find out I'm going somewhere with Drakon."

"That can't be helped. They can go with you to the dragons' cave and there's nothing to stop either of them from staying there until you return. While the dragons can travel under a cloaking spell, keeping themselves, and whoever they're carrying, invisible, they can't cloak others traveling with them. And I can't afford for Ares to find Atticus."

Sascha, Marco is looking for you. Soleil's voice echoed in her mind. *We need to go. He's stressing out.*

Sascha pushed herself out of her chair. "I need to go, Athena. Marco is getting worried because I haven't returned yet."

"I guess that's to be expected considering everything that has happened over the last few days. I bet the girls didn't react well to your disappearance."

"Marco didn't tell them. Kira has already lost one mother. He couldn't bear to make her think there could be a possibility of losing another."

Athena stared at Sascha. "They would have had to know

what was going on, Sascha. Marco's soldiers have been looking everywhere for you."

Sascha pushed away the feeling of betrayal. They couldn't have known. She turned toward the doorway, avoiding looking in Athena's direction. "If they had heard they would have been at the castle, waiting."

"Well, if they don't know, they're going to be angry when they do find out," Athena said. "I would suggest you tell them."

Sascha could feel the pink warmth creep up her neck and into her face. She wasn't sure why she felt guilty, felt as if she was in trouble. "I had planned on telling them when I go to see them tomorrow."

Athena gave a quick tap to her forehead with her fingers. "I forgot I hadn't told you."

"Told me what?"

"Zeus wants to meet with you and the girls in his cave tomorrow, at dusk. Lee's and Ella's parents are making their own way there. They were supposed to have told the girls but can you do me a favor and make sure they do know? I don't want any complications."

"I had been thinking about that," Sascha said. "I was wondering if it could be postponed until we deal with Laela."

"Why?" Athena asked.

"Even though I'm older than the usual offerings that were sacrificed to the Ancients, I was considered a perfect sacrifice because my powers had recently been renewed. But I escaped, and I killed Reya. Laela might look for revenge by hurting the girls."

"And if the girls had their powers renewed . . . ?" Athena asked.

"They would make perfect sacrifices too. Without their full powers the Ancients won't be interested in them.

Renewing their powers now, while Laela is still free would just be putting targets on their backs."

Athena sighed. "Sascha, the only one you can make the decision for is Kira. The other families have rights to make up their minds on this matter."

"For the first time," Sascha said, "I almost agree they should be sent away. Except for the fact that sending them to Earth without their powers would be like sending hurlies to defeat fire dragons. They would be killed; it would only be a matter of time."

"We can talk about this when we have everyone together tomorrow," Athena said. "But whichever case you plead, it will ultimately be Zeus's decision to make."

After saying goodbye to Athena Sascha walked out of the cave with a heavy heart. She hadn't heard a word from the girls since before she had disappeared. Ella's behavior had been odd the last time she had seen them, and she should have followed up. Athena was right. If Marco's soldiers had been everywhere looking for her, then the girls must have known what happened to her—well, at the very least they must have known she had disappeared. So why weren't they at the castle waiting for her to return?

Maybe something has happened to them.

"Sascha," Soleil called out, "we need to leave, get you back to Marco."

I'm sure there is a perfectly simple explanation. I'm worrying over nothing.

ERATUS

Howls echoed throughout the forests as Soleil landed on Sascha's balcony at the castle. "It's freezing," Sascha said as she clambered off Soleil. "I would swear it's a lot colder than it was when we left here a couple of hours ago."

"I'm not talking to you, Sascha. And you can fly yourself to the dragons' cave. If you're going to do something as stupid as trusting Drakon—"

"I'm not trusting Drakon. I'm trusting the dragons and Athena. I will be safe."

A piteous cry echoed from deep within Soleil's chest, sending an icy chill up Sascha's spine. Soleil twisted his head to the side and glared at Sascha before letting his gaze drift downward. "You can't keep doing this to us, Sascha."

"Doing what to you, Soleil? I have a job to do. I thought you were going to help me with that. If I've got that wrong —" Sascha instantly regretted her tone and her words. Soleil had done so much for her. "I'm sorry, Soleil. The truth is I need you. Please don't give up on me yet."

Soleil hung his head and emitted a soft warble. "I'll always be here for you, Sascha, but sometimes it's hard to sit back and wait while you do these things. If anything happens . . ."

Sascha reached over and stroked his neck. "Soleil, Athena and the dragons will protect me. Drakon won't be able to do a thing. And you will never lose me. I promise to be around to make your life a misery for a long time yet."

Soleil clicked his beak at her. "I'll wait here to take you to see the girls. I don't envy you having to give Marco this news. He's going to flip."

Sascha grimaced. Soleil was right. Marco wasn't going to like the news at all. She raised her hand to open the balcony doors when the handle disappeared and the door whipped open.

Marco pulled her into a strong embrace. "You're okay. I knew you were safe, you just had to be."

"You knew where I was, Marco. And Soleil would hardly let something happen to me."

"I've just come from Unidern. On the way back, I saw a woman and a golden pyran being dragged down into the clay traps on the hills that edge the village. I tried to convince myself it wasn't you, but when you were late I thought . . . all I could think of was making sure you were safe."

Sascha looked at Marco. "I'm sorry I scared you, Marco. I'm fine. Sit. Tell me what happened at Unidern, and then I'll tell you what happened when I visited Athena."

Fifteen minutes later Sascha was sitting in the chair in the corner of her chambers, staring out at the golden afterglow as the second sun drifted below the horizon. Marco was pacing the floor in front of her.

"So are you going to see this High King Atticus with Drakon?" Marco snapped.

"It's important, Marco. You know it is."

"Well I'm coming with you. There's no way I'm going to leave you alone with that man. Athena knows how many times he tried to capture you."

"You can come with us to the dragons' cave, but no further. It's for Atticus's safety. We can't risk revealing his location to Ares."

"Damn Atticus, and Athena for that matter," Marco snapped.

"Marco!" She breathed in and out slowly in an effort to keep herself calm. She picked up the cushion sitting next to her on the chair and ran her finger over the design of a pyran that had been embroidered onto one side of it. She rested it on her lap as she lifted her head and studied Marco. He had dropped onto the edge of her bed and his shoulders had slumped forward.

Marco is finding this hard to deal with. He needs time. I can't blame him for his reaction.

"Marco, you're going to have to trust me—and the dragons."

"It's not that I don't trust you . . . it's just . . ." Marco shook his head.

"It's just—you don't trust me," Sascha said. "But let's face it. Drakon is High King now. He no longer needs to resort to kidnapping."

"Assuming he becomes High King," Marco said. "Remember, Owain isn't dead. He may make a surprise appearance before the ceremony. Even if he doesn't make an appearance, didn't you say Atticus is supposed to be assessing him?"

"Okay. *If* he becomes High King. Has Chiane spoken to you yet?"

"We're meeting this evening. He had to wait until he felt it was safe to talk."

Sascha's stomach knotted. This was a big move. She hoped they weren't going to regret it. "There's one other thing," Sascha said. "I need to go and talk to the girls. I must convince them to hold off on restoring their powers and memories until we destroy Laela."

"I'll go with you tomorrow morning," Marco replied.

"I want to see Atticus tomorrow morning, so I want to visit the girls tonight. Besides, this is too important to put off. And Athena said something that worried me. I need to put my mind at rest."

"No." He shook his head. "You're not going out there at night. That's not up for discussion."

Sascha stood up straight, the cushion dropping from her lap. She squared her shoulders. "I beg your pardon, Marco. What did you say?"

"I've just told you what we saw at Unidern and what I saw happen at the clay pit. We have no idea what happened to that pyran, how it was killed. How do I know the same thing won't happen to you and Soleil?"

"That's Unidern, and I'm not flying over any clay pits. Not

to mention there have been no reports of akhult here, not yet anyway."

"Be realistic, Sascha. We're heading into the season of the three moons. Of course they're around. And it's time you wake up to the fact that Laela is going to be as angry as hell with you. She will be after your blood."

Sascha glared at him. "You might talk to your men like that, but I don't work for you, Marco. Don't you ever speak to me like that again."

"Perhaps if you did work for me," Marco spat, "you wouldn't have made so many bad decisions and I wouldn't have had to rescue you all the time."

She turned away from him and balled her fists. She closed her eyes and took a deep breath before stalking to the balcony. "That was a low blow, Marco." She climbed onto Soleil and strapped herself into the harness. "Let's go, Soleil."

Soleil ruffled his feathers. "Do you think you should—"

"Soleil," Sascha snapped. "Now!"

Soleil launched himself into the air. Sascha refused to look back, refused to see if he was watching her leave, to see if he regretted his words to her. Hot, angry tears stung her eyes.

"Don't expect me to be waiting for you when you return," Marco yelled after her. "This waiting around for you to do something else stupid, something that might kill you this time, is too much. No more. Do you hear me, Sascha?"

Don't look at him. Don't look at him.

Sascha swiveled in the harness. Marco was standing on the balcony staring after her. Her heart broke. "I'd prefer it if you weren't here when I return, Marco. I can't do this guilt thing anymore."

Sascha turned back in her harness and let the winds dry away the tears.

"Are you okay, Sascha?" Soleil whispered.

Sascha gulped as she tried to swallow the tears. "I don't want to talk right now. Okay, Soleil?"

"Okay."

It seemed as if they had just left the castle when Soleil spoke again. "We're here, Sascha. And it looks like they have already put up their defensive shield."

Sascha studied the scene below them. The whole area was enclosed by a vibrant blue shield. The hairs on her arms and the back of her neck bristled as they moved closer to the electrical field. She looked beneath the shield and saw that work on the buildings had been completed. The place was ablaze with light and looked like a child's idea of a fairyland. It was beautiful.

"We can't get in tonight," Soleil said as they circled above the shield.

"Yes, we can," Sascha replied. She pointed to a fork in the river below them. "Fly down to the Ohork River. There's a way we can get in from there."

"If you can get in, then what's to stop the monsters from getting in that way, too?"

"There's a magical gateway that the girls set up so that I always had access if I needed it. The gateway only responds to my magic—or Kira's."

When they landed on the river's edge Sascha undid the harness and dismounted. "Follow me," she said heading toward the blue shield. Just beyond the shield was a solid brick wall covered by thick green vines. Sascha closed her eyes and pushed aside the burning pain she still felt following her fight with Marco.

"Let us see behind magic's shadow
As all magical protections forgo
The powers of green ice, red fire, and dark magic
As I order, let it be so."

The blue shield, the wall, and the vines dissolved. In their place stood the entrance to a tunnel. As they stepped into the tunnel, fire flickered at the top of narrow carved wooden poles set into the walls and then burst into life lighting up the path ahead of them. Sascha turned back to face the shield.

"With the powers of green ice, red fire, and dark magic
Cover this entrance with a magical fabric
And using the powers of magic's shadow
Replace the protections over this grotto."

There was a sizzle of electricity as the shield flickered back into place and the vines and walls consumed the vacant space.

"Now," Sascha said. "Let's find the girls."

ERATUS—FOUR SISTERS HEADQUARTERS

The headquarters of the Four Sisters was quiet, and the reception area was filled with the aroma of warm peppermint and vanilla. Someone was baking. "Lee might be in the kitchen, Soleil. Let's go and find out."

Sascha crossed the tiled floor of the reception area. The only lighting came from several magical balls of white light that floated in the air several inches beneath the ceiling. She turned to her right. The kitchen door was at the end of the corridor. A little way down, next to a glass staircase, the door to the sitting room stood slightly ajar. Sascha could hear two women arguing in whispered voices. She moved closer.

"Time is running out. You have to make up your mind. Do you really want to be beholden to *her* all your life? Come with me. Let's see if what Laela is offering is real."

"Nothing Laela has to offer is good, Ella. She lies."

"Lee, please. Choosing between Sascha and Laela is a no-brainer for me. Sascha let me down when I needed her the most. Laela didn't."

"That's not fair, Ella. In all the years she looked after us, she never let us down. Are you really able to forget all of that so easily? And what's more, you haven't even spoken to Sascha about it."

"Things change, Lee. Laela made me realize that. We were Sascha's family back then. We're not now. When I go, it would be good to have you with me."

"Don't be stupid, Ella. Don't listen to Laela. Of course we're still Sascha's family. And what about Kira? We can't leave her here by herself."

"She isn't by herself. She has Alex and the teachers. Anyway, she's always studying. She probably won't even notice we're gone."

"Why don't we wait until after we talk to Zeus and Sascha tomorrow?"

"Tomorrow will be too late. And I'm not going to meet with Zeus. Laela lied to my parents for me, told them I had already left for Earth. I don't want them to realize that I'm still here."

Sascha had heard enough. Her stomach churned.

What the hell is Laela doing talking to the girls?

She breathed out her tension as she strode into the sitting room. Lee and Ella were standing in front of a blazing fire that provided warmth and light to the room. "Hello, girls."

The two girls pivoted around and stared at Sascha as she stood in the doorway. A pink flush crept up Lee's neck. "So the two of you were going to disappear, without letting anyone know."

Sascha sensed the movement as Soleil trotted to the doorway and stood next to her.

"And you care because . . . ," Ella snapped.

"I care about the three of you," Sascha said.

Ella snorted. "You have a funny way of showing it."

"What do you mean, Ella?"

Ella narrowed her eyes and lifted her chin. "You wrote us off the day you bundled us off to our families. You forgot about us so that you could spend time in the castle with your real family."

"What are you talking about Ella? I came to see you the day you and Lee returned home from visiting your families."

"I'm not talking about since we returned, Sascha. I'm talking about those six weeks we were supposed to be with our families."

"Supposed to be . . . Ella, you have to help me. I'm confused. What happened during those six weeks? If you needed me all you had to do was come and see me."

"That's not true, Sascha." Ella gulped, closed her eyes for a brief moment, and then continued. "I was only with my family for one day before I realized they wanted me gone. My own parents were talking to some stranger about the best way to make me disappear . . . permanently."

Lee walked over to Ella and put her arm around her. Ella gave Lee a brief smile before continuing. "I ran away that night. I stole one of their pyrans and went searching for you. Everywhere. It was only by accident I bumped into Connell. He said you were spending time with Owain and Marco and couldn't be disturbed."

Guilt sliced at Sascha like a hot knife. She tried to remember what she was doing with Marco and Owain, but nothing would come to her. "Ella, I'm so sorry. I—I didn't know. I promise, I didn't know." And then it clicked. "Wait a minute, did you say you bumped into Connell?"

"Yes. He was heading back into the castle from the gardens."

A cold chill prickled across Sascha's skin. She frowned as she studied Ella. "And this was about six weeks ago?"

Ella stared at her. "Yes. Why are you looking at me like that?"

"Whoever it was that bumped into you that day, it wasn't Connell. For those six weeks Connell was bedridden. He was seriously ill after being attacked by the pit hound. We thought he was going to die."

Ella shook her head. "But that's not possible. He said he had healed, he was better."

Sascha glanced at Lee. "Before I came in here I overheard you and Lee. You said Laela helped you. How did you find her?"

"I didn't. She found me after my second visit with Connell."

Laela found her? But how could she have been there at the exact moment Ella was meeting with this fake Connell? Unless . . .

Sascha's heart sank. Laela had used illusion magic to make herself look like Connell.

I didn't know Laela was trained in illusion magic. And now I have to convince Ella that Laela has been lying to her.

How could she do that without sounding as if she was defending herself. And then an idea came to her. She knew what to do.

Laela, you bitch. You won't get your hands on these girls.

"Ella, I want to tell you something and then talk about your plans to go with Laela. Will you give me a couple of minutes?"

"There's no point in trying to stop me from leaving, Sascha?" Ella said.

Sascha clenched her jaw to stop herself from saying the wrong thing.

Oh hell yeah it does. After what I've seen I'll be stopping you all right. I just pray that it doesn't come down to that.

Sascha knew that if she voiced her thoughts it would only make Ella want to go even more. "If, once I've had my say, you still want to go, then I won't stop you."

Ella glanced over at Lee. "This is a waste of—"

"Ella, after everything Sascha has done for us, you owe her this," Lee said.

"Ella exhaled, pulled away from Lee, and walked over to the chair in the corner of the room. She dropped into the seat. "So say what you want to say."

"Before I do I have one quick question," Sascha said. "When did you girls decide to activate your defensive shield?"

"Our shield?" Ella repeated.

"It's just that I was surprised to see it activated because you are so much earlier than everywhere else. Did Laela come and see you about three days ago and tell you it was time to activate it?"

Ella stared at Sascha. "How did—"

"I thought so. It was about that time Laela captured me and locked me in a prison in Brun."

"She was worried about us," Ella snapped. "It had nothing to do with what happened between you and her. Our shields were ready and so Laela told us to activate them. She said the castle didn't realize how close the season of the three moons was and she wanted to protect us."

"She wasn't protecting you, Ella," Sascha muttered. "She was isolating you so that you never found out the truth of what it was she was doing."

"I don't—"

"Stop it, Ella," Lee grumbled. "Sascha, how did Laela capture you?"

"Three days ago I was on the beach at Ocean's Mouth. I should have realized then that Laela knew illusion magic, but I didn't. A figure distracted me, pretending to be a friend of Marco's. By the time I realized it was Laela it was too late. She had pushed me through a portal which transported me to a prison in the temple of the Fire Gods. Her plan was to sacrifice me to the Leader of the Ancients. It was there I found out that Laela had been sacrificing powerful mages to the Ancients for years. She preferred to sacrifice teenagers because they were at the peak of their power."

"No," Lee gasped. "Surely she wouldn't do that."

"It's not true, Lee," Ella said. "Why would Laela bother with Sascha if she wanted teenagers?"

"I may not be a teenager but because I recently had my powers renewed, and I had all the training that comes with being a part of the Four Sisters, I was a perfect sacrifice." Sascha took a step toward Ella. "If you had seen the brutal things that were done to those girls, you wouldn't have anything to do with her."

Lee and Ella looked at each other.

"You're lying," Ella spat. "Laela wouldn't do that. She abhors cruelty."

"Ella, there's a child I want you to meet. Her name is Nadiya. She is only eight years old but because she is a powerful mage Laela was going to sacrifice her to an Ancient —a brutal death by any standards."

"Laela was going to sac—sacrifice an eight-year-old?" Lee stammered.

"She would sacrifice any powerful mage. This young girl will tell you what happened to her, what Laela is like. It's horrifying." Sascha shuddered. "The pain she and the other young girls have gone through is beyond my comprehension. Once you have talked to her, you will see what Laela is truly capable of. If the other girls we rescued are willing to speak to you about what happened to them, it would be worth spending time with them as well. The healer, Marco, and all the staff in the castle will tell you where Connell was for those six weeks. I'm convinced the person you thought was Connell was in fact Laela. She used illusion magic to make you think she was Connell."

"But Laela helped me. She told my family that I'd left for Earth so they'd stop searching for me. She helped me."

"Laela wants powerful mages to sacrifice to the Ancients. And you are about to go through a ceremony to activate your powers, which makes you the perfect sacrifice."

Ella shook her head. "No. No, that can't be right."

"Face the truth, Ella," Lee said. "Before it's too late."

Ella put her head in her hands. "Sascha, I need to know you're not lying."

"I'm not lying, Ella. When I leave here to return to the castle, come with me. Talk to the girls, talk to the staff. They will leave you in no doubt that what I am saying is the truth. Ella, you may not realize it, but you, Lee, and Kira are my *real* family."

Tears rolled down Ella's cheeks. "I thought you had—" She half-choked, half-sobbed. "I thought you didn't need us anymore."

"I will always need you. I need all three of you. We have been through a lot together and I love you, very much."

Ella stood and took a step toward Sascha. "Sascha, I will go and see the girls. But if you are lying . . . "

"If you go to the castle," Sascha said. "You will see that what I say is the truth."

"I'll go with you Ella," Lee said. "Let's both hear what these girls have to say."

Ella walked to Sascha and hugged her. "Thank you for listening to me and giving me a chance to make up my own mind. Laela said you would explode at me the moment I said I was going with her, but you didn't."

"Maybe Laela doesn't know me, or you, as well as she thinks?" Sascha said.

"Maybe," Ella replied.

"You will wait until you've spoken with Nadiya and the

girls before you make your decision about Laela," Sascha asked.

"Yes. And I won't do anything until I've spoken to you again."

"I can't ask for more than that," Sascha said.

"Sascha," Lee said, "If Laela can make herself look like Connell, then what's to stop her from pretending she's one of us?"

"It's worrying," Sascha said. "We're all going to have to be on our guard. It might be worth visiting our reserves and retrieving a few dispel magic scrolls. We can use them, at least until we can find a better way to expose her. But if you go to meet with Zeus—"

"Sascha, I don't want to meet Zeus," Ella said. "My parents think I'm already on Earth and I don't want them realizing I'm still here."

"The truth is," Sascha said, "I came here tonight with the hope of persuading all of you to postpone going through the ceremony until after we've stopped L—" Sascha flicked a quick glance at Ella. "Until we know it's safe for you to do so."

"You were going to say Laela, weren't you?" Ella asked.

"Yes. Laela will be looking for revenge because when I was rescued, I ended up killing Reya."

"But Reya was killed in the dragons' cave," a voice called out from behind them.

Sascha spun around to see Kira standing in the middle of the staircase. "Kira. I wanted to come and find you, but you're here. Excellent." Soleil gave a happy whistle as he trotted over to greet her.

Kira stroked Soleil's head. "I've been buried in my studies. I heard voices so I thought I would investigate. So did she live through what Novo did to her?"

"Yes, she did. But only by using a dark magic to drain Connell's life so that she could use it to heal herself."

"How could she create a link to Connell?" Ella asked.

"When Connell was attacked by the pit hound Reya had created, a dark magical link was established between the two of them. Reya was using that link to heal herself . . . at the cost of Connell's life. I killed Reya because it came down to a choice: Reya or Connell."

The room fell silent.

"And you want us to wait until after you've dealt with Laela before we go through the ceremony?" Lee asked. "What about the Ancients?"

"After I'm sure you're safe from Laela," Sascha said, "we could meet together and discuss the next steps then. I'll plan on dealing with the Ancients when the time is right. As for the meeting with Zeus, none of you have to go. Your parents can't force you to do what you don't want to do."

Lee stood up and wandered over to the window on the far wall, leaned against the window sill and pushed the window open. "You don't know our parents, Sascha," Lee said. "We're terrified that they will convince Zeus to do what they want. And if Zeus says we have to go . . ."

"I will do whatever I need to do to protect you. And I'm sure Athena will help us." Sascha turned to Kira who was sitting on a step caressing Soleil. "And what do *you* want to do, Kira?"

"I've waited this long so I guess I can wait a little longer. The only thing that worries me is if Zeus says we can go through the ceremony and we don't do it now, will he give us another chance?"

"I don't know how it will work out, Kira. He might not. But I will see what Zeus says when I ask him to give us time. Athena knows what has been happening. Once I explain everything to Zeus I'm sure he will see sense."

"If our parents don't interfere," Ella muttered.

"Girls, the decision about whether you or not you go to meet Zeus is a personal one for each of you to make. Whatever you decide, I will support you. But it's time for me to return to the castle. I have a few things to organize before I call it a night. Ella and Lee, did you want to come with me tonight? You can meet Nadiya and we can see if the other girls are ready to talk about what happened to them?"

"We will leave it until tomorrow morning, if that is okay," Ella replied.

"Of course it's okay. I'll be away in the morning, but I'll be back briefly in the afternoon before I leave to meet with Zeus."

"I wanted to talk to you about the wedding?" Kira said. "Would you mind if we had it here, rather than at the castle?"

After our fight the wedding may not even happen.

Sascha's stomach knotted at the thought of losing him, but he had to realize she wasn't going to change. Her job was a dangerous one and he had to accept that. It wasn't any easier for her when he went off on some of *his* missions.

"I think that's a lovely idea, Kira," Sascha said.

Kira clapped her hands. "I was hoping you'd say that. At the back of these headquarters, on the edge of the village in Aynor's Stone, we found the most beautiful little cove. It has the feel of magic, a warm magic that will touch the hearts of all those who come to the wedding. You will love it, Sascha. I promise you."

"That sounds perfect, Kira. Thank you so much for all you're doing, and you too, girls." She walked over to each of the girls and hugged them goodbye. It felt good to feel the strength of Ella's embrace. She didn't pull away like she did last time. "C'mon Soleil, let's go." They walked out to the landing pad outside the front of the headquarters.

"We'll take the shields down and give you enough time to get away before we activate them again," Lee said.

"Don't take too long," Sascha said. "I have to admit I feel better knowing you are all safe here."

Sascha climbed on Soleil's shoulders and strapped herself in. "Soleil, before we go back to my chambers I need to see Drakon and tee up our visit to Atticus tomorrow."

"I have a bad feeling about this, Sascha," Soleil said as he launched himself into the air.

"You have to trust me, Soleil. I need to do this."

*D*rakon arrived on the roof of the castle's western tower. The suns hadn't started to rise yet and the breeze was still chilly. Flickering torches lit up the rooftop, their echoes reflecting on the dark clouds that hid the stars and the moons.

He gave his outfit—tailored black leather jacket, white shirt, black pants, and boots—a final check. It was important that he make a good impression on Sascha. He had to admit he was surprised when he received her message to say she would go with him to see Atticus.

He turned as footsteps sounded on the staircase to the rooftop. As Sascha arrived at the top of the stairs, Drakon took a rare moment to breathe in the sight of her. Sascha looked gorgeous dressed in a dark jade fitted leather jacket, blue jeans, and long black riding boots. Her long blond hair hung down her back in a plait.

"Hello, Drak—I mean, Sire." Sascha pushed a stray piece of blond hair behind her ear. "I thought I would beat you here."

"I will always be Drakon to you, Sascha. There is no need

for you to call me Sire, especially when we're alone." Drakon's welcoming smile disappeared when he heard another set of footsteps racing up the stairs and moments later Marco appeared. He clenched his fists to control the anger that flared within him.

Drakon. Relax. Of course Marco would want to say goodbye. Imagine the pleasure when you take off and leave him behind.

"Marco, what are you doing here?" Sascha growled.

"I'm coming with the both of you to the dragons' cave," Marco replied.

"But you can't come to see Atticus. We discussed this."

"I know," Marco said irritably. "But I'll wait for you at the cave."

Sascha sighed. "If you must."

So there's trouble in paradise. Perfect.

Drakon busied himself checking his transportation chip so that Sascha didn't notice his grin.

I can suffer Marco's presence as far as the dragons' cave. Then I can turn their difficulties to my advantage.

The whoosh of wings sounded above them as Soleil and two other pyrans arrived.

"What is Soleil doing here?" Drakon snapped.

"He's taking me to the dragons," Sascha said. "Who else would I get to fly me there?"

"But he's not coming with us to see Atticus?"

"No. Athena said both Soleil and Marco could come as far as the cave. Only you and I will go with the dragons to see Atticus."

Drakon felt his tension disappear. He would be the only one making the journey with her. Marco and that creature were staying behind.

"Not that I'm happy with that arrangement," Marco grumbled.

"I promise to look after her for you, Marco. She will have

my personal, undivided attention." Drakon turned to Sascha, bowed, and gave a flourishing sweep with one hand. "I am but your humble servant, My Lady."

Sascha smiled at him. "Thank you, Sire."

Drakon was rewarded when he glanced back at Marco and saw him glaring at him. Drakon clambered up onto his pyran and strapped himself into the harness. "Sascha, what did I say about calling me Sire?"

Sascha smiled. "Yes, Drakon."

"Is everyone ready?" Drakon asked. "It's time to go."

"Why didn't you ask Fenix to come with us?" Sascha asked.

"She's disappeared," Drakon said. "We can't seem to find her anywhere. I thought you might know where she is—or more specifically Soleil might know."

"We haven't seen her either," Sascha said. "Hopefully she returns soon."

"Let's fly," Drakon called out.

The pyrans hunkered down and launched themselves up into the air, heading for the portal to Earth.

The flight to the first portal went a lot quicker than Drakon had expected it to, and soon they had flown over the sleeping guardians and through the portal and were heading for the dragons' cave.

As they neared the cave Drakon was surprised to see how well hidden it was. The bushes and shrubs that surrounded the cave did an excellent job of hiding the entrance from view and unless you knew exactly where the cave was, you would never find it. After they landed in the glossy-walled cavern, Drakon slid down from his pyran and looked around him. It was an excellent spot. The cave looked like a fortress.

He strode over to join Sascha as she stood in the middle of the cave. He glanced around again. "So where did Novo knife Reya?"

Sascha pointed to where there was a dark stain on the floor. "Over there."

Drakon wandered over to have a look. The woman certainly had lost a lot of blood. Marco had said Reya was with Laela in the temple in Brun. How anyone survived that amount of blood loss was beyond him. But she always was tough. "So where are these dragons?" Drakon asked.

"Hopefully, they won't be long," Sascha answered glancing toward the mouth of the cave.

Moments later a large majestic dragon of gold and bronze, twice the size of Kalamar, flew into the cave on a breeze of pine and honey. "Hello, Drakon. I'm Zinnath." He was closely followed by another dragon. This dragon was smaller than the first and the color of emerald and diamonds. "And I'm Kalurth," the smaller one said.

"They're spectacular," Drakon muttered.

The dragons pirouetted in the air and then landed with grace at the side of the cave. They stretched their wings and then tucked them in by their sides. The clicking of their sharp talons echoed in the cave as they settled themselves down on the polished stone floor. Zinnath turned to a semi-circle of candles, gave a short burst of fire, and grunted approvingly when the candles popped into life.

"We believe we're to take you to see Atticus," Zinnath said.

"I really don't understand the need for all this secrecy," Drakon said.

"You would if you realized how keen Ares is to stop this meeting."

"Ares wants to stop it?" Drakon repeated.

"Yes. We know you two are friends. I'm surprised he didn't tell you."

"Friends? We're not friends. He's a god and visits me sometimes, but neither of us trust each other."

Zinnath glanced over at Kalurth. "Time will tell," he said. "The last thing Ares wants is for you to meet Atticus but he has no influence over what happens in areas under Zeus's control. And we will never let him find out where Atticus is."

"My heart," Kalurth said, "we had better move. Atticus is expecting us."

"You are right of course, Kalurth," Zinnath said. "Sascha, you are flying on Kalurth. Drakon, you're with me. And Marco and Soleil, don't be tempted to follow us. You will sign Atticus's death warrant if you do."

"I thought Atticus was already dead," Marco mumbled.

Drakon watched Sascha as she climbed up onto Kalurth's folded front leg, and then pulled herself onto Kalurth's back. The harness she strapped herself into was larger and had a different design to the ones that were on the pyrans. Drakon watched Sascha tie her harness so that he would know what to do when it was his turn to climb onto Zinnath. When she was strapped in, Sascha rested her hands on Kalurth's back and gripped the sides of the dragon using her knees and ankles.

Zinnath leaned down and provided his folded front leg for Drakon. It didn't take Drakon long to climb up and secure his harness, positioning himself on Zinnath's back in the same way Sascha had. They were ready to fly.

∽

TO A SECRET LOCATION:

The dragons leaped out of the cave and Drakon's stomach dropped. He should be used to it but riding a dragon was different. Even though he had flown pyrans for years, in some ways it was like he was learning how to ride all over again. After flying through a portal the dragons turned north and climbed higher in the sky. The flight was much smoother than he expected, and the creature's strong muscles moved constantly beneath him, its strength a reminder of the power of the dragons. They flew across forested lands and seas. Drakon hadn't meant to fall asleep but he did, and when Zinnath's voice boomed he leaped in fright.

"We have arrived," Zinnath said. "Get ready."

They flew across the rubble remains of a castle toward a stone building surrounded by a small picturesque garden. Neither the building nor the garden showed any sign of damage. It seemed incongruous to see a building in perfect condition among such ruin.

"What is this place?" Drakon asked.

"This is where Atticus lives."

Drakon glanced at the rubble on the grounds surrounding the building. "And the rest?"

"That is what remains of his castle, after the battle against the ancient weapons."

Zinnath twirled around in the air and landed on a paved patio that circled the building. A rocking chair sat on the outside patio.

Zinnath nodded toward an intricately carved door. "Atticus is in there. When you're ready to leave stand outside that door and we'll come and pick you up."

Once Drakon climbed down from Zinnath he stood for a moment and watched as the powerful creature leaped back into the air. He walked to a set of stairs that had been carved out of white polished stone. On the side of the staircase was the remnants of a small construction. The blackened stones made him think it had probably been a furnace. Drakon turned away from the furnace and walked over to the door to the building. The design had been expertly carved but he struggled to understand the fascination with manticores? He zipped up his jacket before he sat on the rocking chair and waited for Sascha to arrive.

Even here it's cold.

He surveyed the destruction that surrounded them. There were hints of what would have once been a spectacular castle and gardens. All now in ruin, apart from the small picturesque garden that edged the stone building.

Kalurth landed on the patio and hunkered down to allow Sascha to climb down from her shoulders.

When Kalurth had flown off, Drakon pushed himself out of the chair and walked over to Sascha. "Are you ready, Sascha?"

"Yes, ready. Let's go in."

The door was stuck in place and Drakon had to use his shoulder to force the door open. The first thing Drakon noticed when he stepped into the room was the ticking sound of a clock. The clock was mounted on the far wall and still ticking away time as if it was unaware time was no longer an issue here. Drakon and Sascha stood and gazed around the immaculately maintained workshop. The tools that lined the workbenches gleamed and bundles of wood and handcrafted items in various stages of completion lined the walls.

In the middle of the room was a fireplace in which a fire had been recently lit. The smell and warmth of the fresh wood fire had started to fill the room.

"Look at this beautiful place," Sascha said. "I don't get it. How is it that the rest of the castle and the grounds have been turned to rubble but this is in perfect order?"

Drakon snorted. "Maybe Atticus was too busy doing work in his workshop to realize what was happening to his own kingdom."

"Or maybe it could be that I have been rebuilding my

workshop to kill time until I was needed," a voice said from a doorway behind them.

They twisted around to see an aged man with curly gray hair, leaning on a cane. He was dressed in black pants and a blue tunic and was a head shorter than Drakon. Drakon stretched himself to his full height, and let his hand drop to the bollock dagger tucked into his belt.

This one should be easy to intimidate, but there's something about the man that puts me on edge.

He noticed Sascha shake her head.

Sascha must have noticed something about the old man, too.

Sascha sniffed the air. "I hope you don't think I'm being rude but I love your aftershave. The scent of watermelon and ginger brings back some happy memories for me."

"It was my queen's favorite," Atticus said.

"This is a beautiful place," Sascha said. "You've done an incredible job in rebuilding. But why didn't you rebuild your castle? Why only the workshop?"

Atticus was silent for a moment. "The castle reminds me of everything I've lost. This workshop allows me to believe that I can repair the damage that occurred that fateful day we released the energy to destroy the ancient weapons." Atticus shook his head. "Anyway, follow me. You haven't come all this way to talk about why I live in a workshop. Let's have some ale and discuss the weapons."

Atticus led them down a carved wooden corridor to a large room with golden timber walls. Glass ribbons from which hung floating balls of fire were suspended from the ceilings and rugs covered the floor. In the corner of the room was the largest manticore Drakon had ever seen. And it was sitting, studying them as its deadly tail swished in the air. A deep rumble echoed from the creature's chest as its gaze focused on Drakon.

"Kan, these are friends," Atticus said. "Rest easy."

Atticus poured each of them an ale and asked them to take a seat in one of the plush tan lounges set up around a glass-topped coffee table.

"As time is of the essence, let's get down to business. What do you want to know first about these weapons?"

Drakon took a sip of his ale. "What exactly are they?"

Atticus nodded. "Good question. They're computer-created organisms, the size of dust, that seek out living organisms with a specific genetic makeup and then destroy them. It was believed that this genetic makeup, or what some inaccurately call the warrior gene, is what makes living organisms brutal and aggressive. The inventors of this weapon believed that if they destroyed all living things with this specific genetic makeup they would restore peace to the land of Eratus."

"Does that mean it attacks anyone who demonstrates brutality or aggression?" Drakon asked.

"No. That's what it was supposed to do. There are many individuals who may have that genetic makeup but show no sign of aggressive behavior. But the weapon is a computer organism that has one instruction, and one only—to destroy any living organisms with that specific genetic balance whether they be adult or child, human or animal."

"What sort of individuals would have that makeup?"

"At least thirty percent of our male population would carry that specific balance. Some of them, however, are protectors, not destroyers. But the weapons, or dust, doesn't make any distinction. It is an efficient and effective killing machine, the likes of which I have never seen before."

"Who created it?" Sascha asked.

Atticus finished his ale and placed his glass on the coffee table as Kan wandered up to him and sat by his side. "Have you heard of High King Taolis?"

Drakon nodded.

"Yes," Sascha said. "Athena told me about him."

"The High King heard of a plot against him and his family. He'd heard many tales about these criminals and knew he couldn't defeat them. Taolis sent out a call to all of his people offering a reward for the person who came up with a way of destroying his enemies. A scientist from one of the lands on Eratus came up with the blueprint for the weapon and the High King was hooked. It wasn't long before Ares found out what the High King was trying to build and so he convinced Hephaestus, God of Fire and the Forge, to help Taolis with its creation. Once they tested a prototype of the weapon and found out how powerful it was they mass produced it and stored it in crates. Once they had a large supply of weapon crates Ares decided to steal it from Taolis and deliver it to the people he wanted in power—a group of Necromancers known as the Ancients."

Sascha glanced at Drakon. "So the gods were involved in the creation of these weapons?"

"Yes," Atticus said. "I'm afraid so."

"Based on what you've told us," Drakon said, "Necromancers couldn't use the weapons. It would destroy them."

"You're right," Atticus said. "To get around that they built underground cities. They planned on living underground once the weapons were released and then after sufficient time, apply a treatment so they could take over leadership of Eratus."

Sascha placed her half-empty glass on the table. "What treatment? How does it work?"

"In simple terms, it changes the orders of these computer organisms so that they see themselves as the enemy and they destroy themselves."

"And the only ones that would have survived the attack of these weapons would be the weak or the more compliant?" Drakon asked.

"Yes," Atticus replied.

"But surely even the weak individuals in a society would one day rebel against their oppressors?" Sascha said.

"Perhaps. But unfortunately for Ares, Athena found out what he was up to and stopped it. Zeus ordered that the Ancients be buried in the cities they had built, along with the weapons. Athena told me she was worried about the weapons being released, or falling into the wrong hands. I was supposed to destroy the weapons along with a chronicle, which contained a lot of detail on the weapons or the dust, and a map that showed the locations . . . but I failed."

Drakon considered everything Atticus had told them as he swallowed the last couple of mouthfuls of his ale. The Necromancers' plan gave him an idea. Drakon glanced at the band on his arm.

I wonder what would happen if I used the weapons to destroy the Ancients who torment me? I could free myself from ever having to wear the band again. And what was it that the Archmage said to Chiane . . . without the band I could have the power of the Ancients. I need to find out exactly what that means. And I bet the weapons would destroy Marco, and Soleil.

The room had fallen silent. Drakon looked over at Atticus and Sascha. They both appeared to be lost in their own worlds. He wondered what Sascha thought of what Atticus had told them.

Atticus leaned over and stroked Kan's back. "I have gone over what happened on that final day so many times, and I keep thinking of ways I could have done things differently. But we have another chance to get it right. We can't fail this time."

"What is it you want us to do?" Sascha asked.

"There is only one way to keep Eratus safe. You need to do what I couldn't. Destroy the weapons. And then destroy the map and the chronicle."

Drakon placed his empty glass on the table before pushing himself up from his chair. He wandered over to a wall covered with pictures of a castle surrounded by gardens. There were also a number of pictures of a slim woman with long onyx-colored hair wearing a fitted navy gown, and a skinny man dressed in what appeared to be a uniform of black pants, white shirt, and white gloves.

The woman must have been his wife. I wonder if the skinny figure next to her was their aide.

"We could learn so much from these weapons," Drakon said.

"My brother thought the same thing," Atticus replied. "He decided future generations had a right to learn from our mistakes so he saved the map and the chronicle. And now look where we are. We're right back where we were when my world was destroyed."

Drakon glanced back at the wall. There were no pictures of any other men, no pictures of his brother.

Maybe Atticus hasn't forgiven him for what he did?

"From what I know," Drakon said, "it isn't people who are responsible for this but the gods."

"Everyone is at fault here, Drakon, including me. I had thought the energy field would neutralize the weapons, but I should have tested it first. But even if I didn't do that, if I had at least destroyed the map and the chronicles you would never have found them. And the gods wouldn't have known where they were buried."

Sascha pushed a strand of blond hair off her face. "I see the value in keeping a record of what happened. Apart from helping us to understand the weapons, there might be some information recorded in the chronicle that will help in the battle against the Ancients."

"The chronicle might have helped us to understand the weapons," Drakon said staring at Atticus, "if certain pages hadn't gone missing. Athena said she knew where those pages were."

Atticus coughed. "Did she? I don't know about that. But I will share the information that was on those pages with you. Drakon, what happened when you opened the site on Earth? Did you find a city?"

"How did you know about the Earth site?"

Atticus stroked Kan before answering. "I use my time here wisely, Drakon. I have kept a close eye on what's happened with the weapons. After all, I have a vested interest in them. Did you find the city? Or see any sign of the Ancients who may have been buried there?"

There's no way I'm telling him about the voices we heard when we opened the cave. Anyway, it's Earth's problem now.

Drakon walked back to his chair and plopped himself on the seat. "How would I know? All I saw were crates and an abandoned city. There were no strange beings living there if that's what you're asking."

"Perhaps none of the Ancients were buried at the Earth site. But you clearly found the weapons. Have you seen what it is these weapons do?"

Drakon exhaled slowly to give himself time to work out the best way to answer the question.

Is it possible Atticus knows what happened and is trying to expose me? Surely not. He's stuck here away from everything.

Drakon rubbed his chin. "A few of my subjects disobeyed my orders and opened one of the crates. What happened next was unfortunate."

"Did they all die?" Atticus asked.

"Yes, but not all because of the weapons. There was a massive explosion in that area and it killed those who had happened to survive the devastation caused by the dust. I secured the place when I realized what the dust was capable of doing."

"What sort of explosion?"

"I haven't got the exact details but suffice it to say everyone in that area of the cave was killed. There were no survivors."

"Have the rest of the weapons been locked away in a secure location?"

"Yes, for now."

Atticus studied the ground and then nodded his head as if he had decided on something. "I need to know. Are you both prepared to help me destroy these weapons?"

"Of course," Sascha said.

"Drakon?" Atticus asked. "What about you?"

Drakon sighed as he tapped his fingers on the arm of the chair, giving himself time to think.

I have the vials. Does it worry me if they destroy the crates of weapons? I don't need more than the vials to do what I need to do. But I need more time to think. This old man is a fool so I'll just tell him what he wants to hear and make up my mind later.

"To be honest, Atticus," Drakon said, "before I came here I had every intention of preserving the weapons. But after everything you've told us I see the need to destroy them."

"Re—really?" Atticus stammered. "I'm surprised. That is sensible thinking, Drakon. Perhaps you will make a good High King."

The fool bought it. No wonder his kingdom was destroyed.

"In that case, I have a treatment that the two of you can use on the weapons. But you are going to have to fully secure each of the sites. Destroying the weapons is a two-step process. Firstly, a minor explosion opens the crates and exposes the weapons. Then a second explosion to release the treatment follows seven seconds after that. Everything must be timed or it won't work. I have gathered all the materials you need to destroy the weapons at all the sites. Everything can be done remotely, using codes and a beacon. You place the explosives, the treatments, and the beacon." Atticus pushed his hand into a pocket on the front of his tunic and retrieved an item the size of a cell phone and handed it over to Sascha. "This might look like a phone but it's a powerful computer. Once you are in a safe location, type the crate and treatment codes into the SAWA40 application on that computer you have in your hand. Then you'll need to click the green light for the initial explosion to open the crates holding the weapons, and seven seconds later click the blue light to release the treatments. I have it all written down so that you have something to follow."

"SAWA40," Sascha repeated. "I assume that's an acronym? What does it stand for?"

Atticus giggled. "Smash Ancient Weapons Application. I thought the name suited its purpose. Forty is the version number."

Sascha laughed. "What if some of the weapons escape?"

"You can't let it escape. You will need to erect a magical barrier around the sites in the same way Drakon did when his men released the weapons. But I've been thinking about this, and I know the season of the three moons is nearly upon Eratus. So only detonate the explosives once every region has their defensive shields in place. That way, should anything go wrong when you set off the explosives, all the people are protected."

Sascha studied the item in her hand. It was thin and the color of ebony. It was hard to believe it was a powerful computer. "How do you open it?"

"There's button on the side," Atticus said. "Press it."

Sascha pressed the button. In the middle of the black screen was a flashing red application called SAWA40. She double-clicked on it and a screen came up asking her to enter the codes. At the bottom of the screen were two buttons. One said, *Enter Code*. The other said *Submit*. "So how does it know if I'm entering a weapons code or a treatment code?"

"You will be given the choice. When you have all codes entered you click on the Submit button. That's when you will be given the option to press either the blue or green button. But as I said, I have written everything out. All you need to do is follow the instructions."

"Where did you get this computer and this application from?" Sascha asked.

Atticus sat tall in his seat and stuck his chest out. "I built it."

"Wow," Sascha said. "Very clever."

"I would never have figured you as clever enough to do that," Drakon said.

"You can't judge the strength of your vimberry by the color of the mug." Atticus relaxed back into his chair. "Drakon, did you get all the weapons from the site on Earth?"

"Yes, everything."

"Good. We don't need to worry about the Earth site then."

"What about the site in Brun?" Drakon asked. "We haven't been able to open it."

"The magic on Eratus is strong since the healing of the Shield," Atticus said, "and the entrance to the site has been hidden in magic's shadow. Sascha can undo that magic." He turned to Sascha. "You know how to undo the magic when a place is hidden in magic's shadow, don't you? I know you've done it before."

"Yes, I have. I know what to do."

"We will also need a few mages," Drakon said. "There's a trick to opening the door to the underground city."

"How many?" Sascha asked.

"Five."

"Five?" Sascha said. "That's a lot."

"It is, but we do need them," Drakon said.

"You two don't have much time," Atticus said. "You'll need to work fast. Ares is planning on releasing the Ancients soon and these weapons must be destroyed before that happens. The battle against them will be hard enough without there being a chance of the Ancients securing the weapons." Atticus nodded in the direction of a silver door on the left side of the room. "I have boxes of explosives, and the treatments, along with the beacons in that room. They're small but don't judge them by their size. The power in just one of the explosives could flatten your castle." He held out a key to Drakon. "Take this. The containers are on the far side, near the wall. There are satchels you can use to pack them in. That should make it easier to carry the supplies with you on the dragons. There's a sheet of paper sitting on one of the boxes in there. It gives you the instructions I was telling you about. Take everything."

Sascha placed her hands on the arm of the chair as she readied to push herself up.

I want to do this alone, without Sascha. I don't want her to know exactly how many supplies we are given. I need to keep some, just in case . . . .

"I'll get them Sascha," Drakon said as he pushed himself up and took the key from Atticus. "You rest and keep Atticus company."

"Thank you, Drakon," Sascha said dropping back into the seat. "That's very gracious of you."

Drakon grinned to himself. He still had the knack.

SECRETS

ATTICUS'S CAVE

*S*ascha watched Drakon walk toward the room with the silver door. He fumbled with the key before finally opening it.

Atticus turned to Kan. "Kan. Watch."

Kan jumped to his feet and wandered over to the silver door where he sat on his haunches to watch Drakon's every move.

"Now, Sascha, while Kan helps us grab a few moments alone, I want to tell you a couple of things." He dug into a pocket on the inside of his tunic and pulled out a thin red box. He pushed himself up from his chair and walked over to Sascha. He handed the box to her. "Take this now, before Drakon returns. He must not know about it."

Kan was still keeping a close eye on Drakon, so she popped the box into a pocket in her jacket.

"Why do we have to hide this from Drakon?" Sascha asked.

"It seems like we can at least trust him to help us destroy the weapons but I don't know how far we can stretch that trust. There are three things in the box. The first is an antidote. If anyone is exposed to the weapons, you must give them this antidote. Even though they may survive the attack, they will be infected, and should they ever try to have children, there is a risk that the pregnancy will be terminated if the infection considers the child to be the wrong genetic makeup. The antidote works in much the same way as the treatment. It causes the virus to see itself as the enemy."

"And destroy itself," Sascha said.

"Yes, exactly."

"Can you use it to protect someone against the weapons?"

Atticus glanced over at Kan, who was yawning. "I can't answer that. It's never been tested."

"And the second thing?" Sascha asked.

"It also contains all the evidence Athena needs to take with her to the council meeting. Athena won't have any trouble convincing Zeus and most of the council that what I've told you is the truth. The evidence includes the missing pages from the chronicle, which supports your argument that the information contained in the chronicle may be worthwhile."

"Athena didn't have those pages," Sascha said. "You did."

"I couldn't let Drakon know that. Not yet, anyway."

"What's on those pages?"

"Evidence of how Ares has been involved in all of this from the beginning."

Sascha nodded as she watched Kan flex his wings. "You said most of the council?"

"There are those on the council who fully support Ares and Hades. It will be interesting to see how the council meeting goes. The third and final thing will make sense when I give you and Drakon a map—which I will do when he returns. The map includes all the details you'll need to find the hidden caches of ancient weapons. I have given you four little autobots. Once you've made your way into the site where the weapons are stored, hold one of the bots in your hand and it will locate the cache of weapons for you. All you need to do then is set up the explosives and the treatment."

Sascha picked up her glass of ale from the coffee table and finished it. "How will we know everything has worked as we wanted it to, other than physically visiting the site?"

"SAWA40 will give you a listing of successful and unsuccessful attempts. The beacons you will place at each site will transmit the messages to say whether the treatments worked or not. If you do visit the sites, then the beacons should be showing a green light. But if any of the treatments are unsuccessful, come and see me so that we can reassess. But I'm hoping that doesn't happen."

"If we receive a message to say the treatment was successful and the beacon is showing a green light, will the area definitely be clear?"

"Yes. The beacon cannot turn green if any of the weapons are left. And the beacon cannot send a successful message unless it is green."

"You have thought of everything, Atticus," Sascha said.

"You might not think so when you arrive at the weapons sites. The sites are protected by creatures, some more deadly than others. You may need to fight them to clear a pathway to the weapons. And, again, I must emphasize the importance of setting up a protective shield around the entrance to the sites after you have set everything up. You don't want anyone or anything wandering in afterward and interfering with the work you have done. But can I ask that you don't tell Drakon about these bots until you arrive there? He may use the bots to find the weapons before you."

"You don't trust him, Atticus?"

"I can't answer that question honestly. There's a dark side to him, one I can't see into."

Sascha put her empty glass on the table, next to Drakon's.

"Athena said you were going to assess Drakon, determine if he is suitable to be High King."

"That is true," Atticus said. "He seems keen to help, but I can't help feeling that he has another agenda. Tell her you met with me. If she needs an answer before she goes to the council meeting, ask her to come and see me. Otherwise I will take a little more time to find out more about him."

"I'll do as you ask, Atticus. But can I ask a question?"

Atticus rested his elbows on the arms of his chair. He formed his hands into a steeple and looked directly at Sascha. "I'm listening."

"The blades you gave to Athena and said I needed one more time."

"Ah, yes. The Blades of Light."

"Can you tell me what it was you thought I would need them for?"

"I'm sorry, Sascha, but I can't. These blades were your mother's. She told me that as long as they exist you would need them. I was given a vision of a single battle in which you used them but it appears you have used them already and they returned to you."

"Yes. Did Athena tell you what happened?"

"She did. I'm afraid I don't have any more answers for you. All I can tell you is that I know you will need them for something specific, but it appears you can use them for other battles as well."

Sascha rubbed the mark on her hand. "I've been having this nightmare where I see myself using the blades to kill a child that looks like the Ancient I destroyed in the healing ceremony."

"Wiskari's child. Yes, I've read some interesting things in the stars about this child."

"You said it's Wiskari's child. Do you know that for certain?"

"I'm as certain about that as I am that Kan and I will be together to the end. It is worth talking to Jenny about him. You might find it enlightening."

"I will do that, Atticus. Thank you."

"The child may not be an Ancient, Sascha, he may even need your protection, but nothing is ever what it seems. You'll have to trust yourself to make the right decision when the time comes."

"Atticus," Drakon yelled. "Would you move this beast of yours out of the doorway?"

"My humble apologies, Drakon. Kan is curious. He hasn't seen many visitors—for obvious reasons." Atticus winked at Sascha. "Kan. Come?"

Kan stood up, shook himself, and strutted back to Atticus.

"You were right," Drakon said. "The sizes of the packages are deceiving. I hope you aren't lying to us. I will be after blood if we have been conned."

"Have no fear, Drakon. They work as I said." He dug his hand into his pants pocket. "And I do have one more thing for you. Drakon, this map is the one the Sisters were given a hundred and fifty years ago, not the one that you found. This one details information that isn't recorded on the other map you have. It shows all the weapons sites."

"So where did my map come from?" Drakon asked.

"It is one of the earlier versions. Luckily my brother copied the wrong one."

"So how can we use this map?" Sascha asked.

"You will need to make sure you visit every site on the map. Look for a circled V symbol, the sign of the weapons storage area, and destroy those weapons. Let's make sure Eratus never has to face this danger again. Sascha, I have a copy for you, too."

Sascha pushed herself up from her chair, took the map from Atticus, and gave it a quick glance before folding it and placing it in the pocket of her jeans. "Thank you for everything, Atticus."

"It's been a pleasure to meet you both. And I wish you all of Athena's blessings in the battle ahead of you."

Sascha leaned over and hugged him. "I guess we won't be seeing you again."

"We will meet again," Atticus said. "In the final battle, the one against the Ancients. What you do now will determine our chances of success in that battle. I'll be forever grateful if you can manage what I could not. Destroy those weapons. It would mean Kan and I are one step closer to returning home. I will finally get to see my queen again and Kan will get to see his family. I often dream of them waiting for us to return. We both miss our families . . . a lot."

Sascha swallowed the lump in her throat, then turned to follow Drakon back up the corridor to the patio at the front of the workshop, where they would wait for the dragons. She glanced behind her in time to see Atticus wipe his cheek with the back of his hand before he put his arm around Kan's neck. They watched her and Drakon leave. Sascha's heart grieved for them. She could feel the weight of their losses.

"We won't fail you," she whispered.

～

* EARTH: THE DRAGONS' CAVE

Sascha wasn't sure how she felt when she saw Marco standing in the dragons' cave, waiting for them to return. She loved him but what he had said to her had really hurt. If he meant what he had said, truly meant it, how could they possibly last? She was sure she would make many more mistakes in the future. What she wanted was someone who loved her despite that, not someone who loved her in the hope she would change.

"That didn't take long," Marco called out as they flew in on the dragons. "It only took you a couple of hours. Soleil and I had settled in for the day."

"If you're complaining," Zinnath said, "we can go away again."

"I was surprised, that was all," Marco said. "How did it all go?"

"Enlightening," Drakon answered. "Sascha makes a very good traveling companion. Thank you, Sascha, for all your . . . support."

Sascha knew Drakon was baiting Marco but she couldn't resist the chance to make Marco suffer. "Anytime you want to do that again, Drakon, let me know. I enjoyed your company."

She climbed off Kalurth and walked past Marco to Soleil. She stroked Soleil's neck. "Did you miss me, Soleil?"

Sascha smirked at Soleil's quick glance at Marco. The two of them had been talking. "I always miss you, Sascha. *We* always miss you."

"Okay. Enough with the games," Zinnath said. "What happened?"

Drakon opened one of the supply satchels and retrieved the package he had wrapped up for himself before he placed the satchels on the cave floor. "You explain it to them, Sascha. I have a few tasks to complete. When I return to the castle I'll study the map Atticus gave us and work out exactly what it is we're up against." He walked over to his pyran as it stood and stretched, climbed onto its shoulders and strapped himself in. "Sascha," he said as he pointed to where he had left the satchels, "I've left the supplies from Atticus over there, near the wall. I thought Marco could bring them for us."

"And why can't you take them?" Marco asked.

"I'm the High King, Marco, or have you forgotten?"

Drakon grinned as Marco glared at him and flexed his fingers.

I love his anger.

"Sascha, come and see me early tomorrow morning so that we can plan how to tackle the destruction of the weapon caches. Oh, and you can come too, Marco. After all, as leader of the Fire of the Phoenix, you now work for me and it would be remiss of me not to include you. And Sascha will need someone to carry the supplies."

Drakon strapped himself into the harness, saluted at the dragons, blew a kiss to Sascha, and flew off.

Fifteen minutes later Sascha had given everyone a summary of their conversation with Atticus and what Atticus had said to her when they were alone. She opened the little red box and took out the tubes. "Do you think there's any way we can get this antidote reproduced, Marco?"

"I'm sure I can organize that. I'll ask the scientists who work in the laboratories at my headquarters. Does it save people from being killed by the weapons?"

"Atticus didn't know. He said it hadn't been tested."

"It's good to at least have a starting point, and to know about the side effects of the weapons. Speaking of the weapons, can I have a look at the map Atticus gave you?"

"Here it is," Sascha said as she pulled a piece of paper from her jeans pocket and handed it to him.

Marco snorted. "And where are these supplies I'm supposed to carry?"

Sascha pointed to the cave entrance. "They're in the two bags over there." Sascha waited until Marco picked up the bags and opened them.

"There are a lot in here," Marco said. "And they are tiny."

"I know this sounds bad after what Drakon said earlier," Sascha said, "but do you mind if I leave the supplies with you,

Marco? I need to meet with Athena, Zeus, and the girls' parents now."

"I'm happy to do that for you, Sascha. It's only Drakon I don't like ordering me around."

Sascha smiled. "You hide your dislike very well, Marco."

"Ha, ha! By the way, we're meeting Chiane and Isabella tonight, after the first sun has set. Will you be back by then?"

Sascha's stomach clenched. Her gut was warning her about this meeting. She wasn't convinced that it wasn't some sort of plot, perhaps to get rid of Marco. But they were going to find out soon enough.

"Yes, I'll be back. Where are we meeting?"

"I'll meet you at your chambers and we can leave from there. And bring a cloak. It might be worth hiding our identities when we're inside the Awakening headquarters."

Marco is worried about this meeting, too. He isn't stupid. He knows how much we're risking.

Sascha climbed onto Soleil's shoulders and strapped herself into the harness as Marco walked over to her.

"Sascha, I know we have to talk things through, but I wanted to say I'm sorry. I will do whatever I need to do, so that we can stay together."

"We both said things we shouldn't have," Sascha replied. "But perhaps it was good we did. We obviously need to talk. See you tonight."

"Sascha and Soleil, before you go," Kalurth called out. "I found out how to save pyrans from being sent to the fifth dimension."

"Oh, Kalurth, you're a true friend," Sascha said. "What did you find?"

"Pyrans must be bonded to their masters—a rather obvious point. Once they have been bonded, if they find a mate, and have children, both pyrans can bond to either master."

"So if Fenix and Soleil became mates and had children," Sascha said, "Fenix could choose to be bonded to me?"

"Yes," Kalurth said. "But if you're worried about Drakon sending Fenix to the fifth dimension soon, they might need to . . . work fast."

Sascha chuckled. "That's a good way of describing it, Kalurth. But I doubt Soleil will consider it work."

Kalurth laughed. "Maybe not."

"I don't appreciate the jokes," Soleil snapped. "Anyway, why would I want to partner with her?"

"To save her?" Sascha said. "Give her a chance, Soleil. Despite what you say, I know you love her. So now we have the answer. All we need is Fenix. And then I'll be a grandma to baby Soleils. . . ."

Soleil clicked his beak. "Sascha!"

"I hope Fenix returns soon," Kalurth said. "Especially now there is a way to save her."

∽

* EARTH

Sascha repositioned herself on Soleil's shoulders as they flew out of the dragons' cave, across the pebbled pathway, and over the lattice fence toward Zeus's cave in the Fire of the Phoenix headquarters. When Soleil landed at the mouth of the cave Sascha undid the harness and clambered down. She took a deep breath.

What are Athena and Zeus going to say when they find out I'm alone?

Four pyrans stood at the entrance to the cave. Two of them were stunning, their feathers colored with the seven colors of the rainbow. They stood tall and proud and were fitted with an elaborate golden harness. Everything about them told a story of wealth. The other two were the exact opposite. A dirty, mud-brown color, they were hunkered down, watching everything that moved, as if they were constantly on the lookout for any signs of danger.

"Soleil, look at those two poor brown creatures. While I'm inside talking to Athena and Zeus, talk to the pyrans. See what you can find out about Lee's and Ella's parents."

"I doubt they will say much," Soleil said. "I wouldn't."

"I doubt the ones with the gold harness will, but the drabber looking creatures might."

Sascha walked into the cave. Standing near the entrance to the squad bay were two couples. It was easy to recognize Lee's parents. They were both tall, distinguished, with curly raven-colored hair. Her mother was dressed in an elegant navy and white pantsuit and navy heeled boots. Her father was dressed in golden chain armor, as if he was here to fight a battle.

Ella's parents were nothing like her. They were a short, squat couple with dirty, mousy-colored hair. Their clothes were stained and creased and looked like they hadn't been washed in weeks.

How could these two be Ella's parents?

"Where is our daughter?" Ella's father snarled. "She was supposed to be coming with you."

Sascha cleared her throat. "The girls have decided against coming to today's meeting. Anyway, I thought you had been told that Ella has already returned to Earth."

"That's a lie," Ella's mother spat. "She's here all right. We know it. But that's okay. We'll just make our decision without her."

"The only one making any decisions here will be my father," a voice said from the cave entrance.

Sascha turned toward the voice. "Athena," she said nodding in acknowledgment.

"That's not acceptable," Ella's mother spat. "We have come

here to have our daughter sent back to Earth, permanently. This meeting must go ahead, with or without her."

"I never said the meeting wouldn't go ahead," Athena said as she moved toward the creek at the back of the cave. "I simply said, you will not be making any decisions. Zeus is the only one who will be doing that."

The air around them hummed and seconds later Zeus appeared next to Athena. "Let's get things moving. I don't have all day."

"Father," Athena said. "We were just talking about you."

"If you're Zeus"—Ella's mother stabbed a finger in Sascha's direction—"tell this woman to bring our daughter here. She was told she had to bring them."

"No, she wasn't," Athena said. "She was told to remind them of the meeting. Whether they attended or not was up to them."

"Athena, why aren't the girls here?" Zeus asked.

"Athena, may I have permission to address Zeus?" Sascha asked.

"Father?" Athena asked as she smothered a smirk.

Zeus lifted his chin high and smiled at Athena. "She is learning. Yes, tell her she can address me."

Athena nodded her head at Sascha. Sascha moved toward Zeus and bowed her head. "My Lord, I will keep this short but let me start by updating you on what is at stake today."

When Sascha had finished telling Zeus about Laela and the sacrifices being made at the temple, she stepped back.

"So who is this Laela?" Ella's father snarled. "And why should our daughters have to pay the price for Sascha's mistakes?"

"Shush," Athena whispered.

"I'm not going to—"

"You'll do exactly as my daughter has told you to do," Zeus growled. "Shut up, mortal."

"Father," Athena warned.

"Sascha," Zeus said, "am I correct in thinking that you only want this thing to be postponed, not canceled?"

"Yes, My Lord."

Zeus turned toward Lee's parents. "And what say you in all of this, mortals?"

Lee's father coughed. "My Lord, we want our daughter safe. There is much she doesn't understand or remember. And as highlighted by Sascha, there is much danger for them on Eratus. We think the best thing is for Lee to be sent back to Earth."

Sascha could feel the fury building inside her. How could they have so little idea of what it is they were saying? "My Lord—"

"Sascha you've been doing well up until now," Zeus said. "Wait until I address you."

Sascha clenched her jaw to bite back her response. Looking after the girls' interests was more important than her pride.

"Now, Sascha," Zeus said, "what is it you wish to say?"

"My Lord, I know from firsthand experience that running away from something doesn't make the problem go away. Instead you end up being forced to fight a battle you're unprepared to fight. If the girls are sent to Earth, Laela will still hunt for them. Except they won't know of the dangers she presents so Laela will have a greater chance of fooling them into building their powers, becoming as powerful as they need to be so she can then sacrifice them to the Ancients."

"What a load of dragon dung," Ella's mother said. "Sascha was safe enough on Earth."

"No, she wasn't," a voice said from the mouth of the cave. They all turned to see Lee, Ella, and Kira standing next to each other. Lee and Ella refused to look at their parents.

"My Lord," Ella said. "I'm asking for the freedom to make my own life choices, not have them dictated by others."

"And that is my request as well," Lee said.

Zeus turned to Kira. "The same for you, Kira?"

"Yes."

"And do any of you wish to return to Earth?"

"No," they said in unison.

"And do you wish to have your powers activated?"

"Yes," Ella answered, "and our memories returned."

"No," Sascha said. "Girls please don't—"

"But we ask, My Lord," Ella continued, "that we do this after the battle with Laela is over. But before the battle with the Ancients. We wish to be by Sascha's side when it is time for her to battle the Ancients and free Eratus from their threat. We believe that is our purpose."

Zeus nodded.

"The girls have no idea what their purpose is," Ella's father said. "We refuse to allow their request to stand."

"You have no choice," Zeus said. "Need I point out Lee and Ella are eighteen years old?"

"We always have a choice," Lee's father answered.

The sound of heavy boots on gravel thundered along the pathway outside the cave. A small army of soldiers marched into the cave. They were dressed in polished silver-plated armor engraved with a trident emblem. Ella's father pointed at Ella and the soldiers gripped their shields in their right hands and positioned themselves in a circle around the three girls with the shields in front of them.

"Sascha," Ella cried. "Help us!"

"Athena," Sascha called out. "The girls came here in good faith despite being terrified of what might happen. We owe them our protection."

A soft click of a weapon came from the left of the cave. Sascha turned to see Lee's father armed with a bow and arrow while Ella's father was armed with a staff and they were pointing their weapons directly at her.

"My Lord," Lee's father called out. "I'm sure you recognize Apollo's golden bow. This weapon has the power to kill a god, so imagine what it would do to a mortal. If you want to save her you will let us leave with the girls. For the sake of our lands, we will not permit them to regain their memories or their powers."

"They're only mortals," Ella's father said. "Let us go with the girls and we will never trouble you or Athena again."

"Zeus," Sascha pleaded, "please do not let them take the girls."

The cave fell silent as everyone's attention was on Zeus.

Zeus stood silently as he drew himself up to his full height and opened his hand. A jagged lightning bolt appeared in his palm, and he wrapped his hand around it. "This is my court, my home. No mortal comes into my home and threatens me or those who are under my protection."

"We're not picking a fight with you, My Lord," Lee's father said. "Our fight is with Sascha."

"You have drawn your weapons in my court. Sascha is under my protection. I am Zeus, God of the Sky, Ruler of Olympus. I will not stand for this outrage." He raised his arm above his head, his hand gripping the lightning bolt. In a powerful throw, he released the large white bolt so that it pierced the ground between Sascha and Lee and Ella's fathers. The cave exploded in a blast of white light that filled the cave. Thunder shook the ground. Sascha heard someone screaming, but the explosion had left her blinded and she couldn't see what was happening around her. The stench of burned hair and charcoal filled the air.

"Soleil, protect the girls," Sascha called out.

"The girls are safe," Soleil said. "Athena protected them."

Sascha frantically rubbed her eyes. "And you will be okay,

too," Athena said. "You were too close to the lightning. Take your hands away from your eyes but keep them closed." Sascha felt a soft breath of air on her face. "Now open them."

Sascha flicked her eyes open. She could see.

"What did you do?" Sascha asked.

"Oh, we gods always have a few tricks up our sleeve."

Zeus was standing in front of the soldiers as they stood openmouthed, staring at the mound of ash in front of them. One of the soldiers squatted and picked up a handful of ash. "Our shields . . ."

"Do you still wish to battle me?" Zeus asked.

The men dropped to their knees in submission. "No, My Lord."

Lee and Ella stood with Kira. They still refused to look at their parents.

Zeus turned away from the soldiers to face the two fathers. He glanced at the bow and staff which were now dust on the ground. "Consider yourselves lucky I decided to let you keep your lives. You have your daughters to thank for that. They would find it hard to forgive a god who killed their parents in front of them. But next time, you won't be so lucky. Mortals will try to interfere in the plans of the gods, but the heavens will never let a mortal win."

Sascha's heart skipped a beat.

Those words Zeus used, they were the same words the child had said in her nightmare. She shook her head in an attempt to shake away the fuzziness from Zeus's attack.

I need to talk to Athena.

"Now, back to what we are really here for." Zeus's voice boomed across the cave. "Lee, Ella, and Kira. I, Zeus, God of the Sky, Ruler of Olympus, permit you three mortals to have your memories and powers returned to you at a time of your choosing. Let no god stand in your way."

A boom of thunder exploded above them.

Zeus glanced toward the roof of the cave. "It has been recorded. No one can stop it now." He turned to Athena. "It's time for me to leave. You know what needs to be done now."

"Yes, Father."

There was a thunderous crack, a flash of white, and Zeus was gone.

Athena turned to Lee's and Ella's parents. "Take your soldiers and leave. Now! If I ever hear of you interfering in the girls' lives again, the price you will pay will be far greater than anything you can imagine."

"You have no idea what you have done," Lee's father muttered.

After the group had left, Athena turned to the girls. "Return to your home and let us have no more talk of you joining Laela."

"Yes, Athena," they said bowing before her.

"Come and see us soon, Sascha," Ella said.

"I will. And make sure you keep your defensive shield in place," Sascha said. "Keep safe. If Laela shows herself—"

"We will get a message to you," Ella said.

Sascha smiled as she nodded in acknowledgment. "Thank you, Ella."

Once they were gone, Sascha turned to Athena. "We need to talk. There are two things I need to tell you. Firstly, Drakon and I met with Atticus."

"And . . ."

"He said he still has questions about Drakon. He would like some more time to form his assessment, but he said you should go and see him if you needed an answer before the council meeting."

"How did Drakon react to destroying the weapons?"

"He said he wanted to help, but Atticus thought Drakon might have another agenda."

"Perhaps I'll go and see Atticus," Athena said.

Sascha retrieved the red box from her pocket. "And he gave me this. He said it has all the evidence you need to prove your case at the council meeting."

"What's the evidence?"

"I know he's included the three missing pages from the chronicle. He said they prove Ares has been involved from the beginning."

Athena opened the box. She picked up the pages and skimmed through them. "This is . . . this is perfect."

"There's something else in there, too," Sascha said.

Athena retrieve several sheets of paper, opened them up and read them. "You'll never guess what they are, Sascha. They're instructions that Ares sent to Hephaestus about building the weapons."

"No!" Sascha smirked. "This council meeting is going to be one hell of a meeting. Athena, there's one thing I wanted to ask you. In my dream, the child used the same phrase Zeus just used: 'Mortals will try to interfere in the plans of the gods, but the heavens will never let a mortal win.' Is it some kind of a mantra?"

"To be honest, Sascha, I haven't thought about it much, other than it being something Father says. Are you thinking your dreams are being influenced by a god?"

"Well, the gods have certainly played a large part in everything that's happened until now, so I guess it wouldn't be surprising."

"But it would be worrying," Athena said. "The work Owain is doing may shed some light on exactly what is going on. We need to know who the true enemy is. But to help Owain we must destroy those weapons destroyed."

"We're working on a plan to do just that," Sascha said. "I'd better leave now but I'll let you know how it goes."

Sascha walked toward Soleil. "Let's go back to the castle. We have a job to do. Did the pyrans tell you anything?"

"Both of the brown ones warned me," Soleil said. "Told me the parents wouldn't accept today's judgment."

"But Athena threatened them . . . ," Sascha said.

"Whoever or whatever is controlling the parents is evidently much more terrifying than Athena."

THE AWAKENING HEADQUARTERS

ERATUS

*a*n icy chill blew across the paddocks as Marco and Sascha followed Chiane and Isabella to the headquarters of the Awakening. Marco was pleased he and Sascha were back on speaking terms but they still had a lot to work out. He had been terrified she was going to cancel the wedding. It was clear to him that despite the gut-wrenching worry he felt every time she went away on one of her trips, life would be pointless without her.

"When we get inside, Sascha, let me do the talking," Marco said. "Your voice is too easy to identify. It's bad enough that Chiane and Isabella know you're a part of this. We don't want anyone else knowing."

"I'm sure yours would be just as easily identified," Sascha said.

"I'll change it so that it's not."

"I could do that, too," Sascha said.

"Please, Sascha. Let me do this."

Sascha shrugged. "Okay."

Marco and Sascha pulled their hoods lower over their heads as they followed Chiane and Isabella into a stone corridor that was filled with the stench of rotten leaves and brackish water. What little light there was in the oppressive darkness was provided by a few burning torches. Sascha squealed the first couple of times as screeching rats skittered across the floor, but it wasn't long before she adapted to the noises of the rats and the way they would race across in front of her.

"Chiane, where are you taking us?" Marco asked.

"I'm taking you to the guard who cleaned up after the disaster in Laboratory One. He is petrified Drakon will punish him if he finds out who was responsible for telling us about what happened here, but I've promised we will protect him. Anything he tells us stays as a secret until we work out what we're going to do."

"Agreed," Marco said. "Tell me, where is this laboratory?"

"It's deep in the dungeons," Chiane replied.

They arrived at the bottom of a set of stairs and walked toward a pair of solid metal doors. Chiane came to a stop at the doors and turned and looked back into the darkness. Isabella took her place next to him and they stood in silence for a time until, eventually, Isabella nodded in the direction of a shadow that was moving toward them.

Marco's heart was in his mouth. He prayed that this wasn't a trap and that the person arriving wasn't Drakon, or his soldiers coming to arrest them for treason. But he needn't have worried. The man who was racing from one shadow to the next was a skinny, skittish man whose gaze bounced around the room. Marco did a double-take when he could see the man clearly. He moved closer to Chiane. "He's the one Zabir caught at the furnace," Marco whispered.

"Yes."

"How come he's working here as a guard? He was a soldier."

"Drakon had told me to kill him," Chiane said. "He didn't

believe my soldier would keep his mouth shut, and it was in Drakon's interests to keep the storm season a secret for as long he could. But I refused to kill him. Instead I found him a job down here. Soldier, tell these people what you told me."

"Sir, I owe you, but I'm afraid. How can I be sure what I say doesn't lead to my death or even worse?"

"You have to trust me," Chiane said. "Have I ever betrayed you?"

"No, sir."

The soldier turned toward Marco. "The Prince . . . I mean, the Sire . . . conducted an experiment on a group of test subjects captured by Reya. He had found some ancient weapons and wanted to see what they did. It was a disaster and everyone watching the experiment was forced to flee." The soldier turned and looked at the metal door. "After the disaster, they locked this place down and Sire pulled me aside. He asked me to detonate the tags of all the test subjects, even those who had survived the experiment. He told me it was a kindness, and at the time I believed him. But since then I haven't been able to free myself from the guilt of knowing that when I pushed those buttons I was killing people whose only crime was to have been captured by Reya."

"Did he say why he killed them?" Marco asked.

"No. But I believe it was because he didn't want to leave any evidence of what happened here. Detonating the tags was an effective way of doing that."

"But he left the guards alive," Marco said.

"Everyone is too scared to speak up because they are all involved. They are all guilty of kidnapping and tagging hundreds of innocent people. And torture is a daily event. I've only just arrived here. I'm the only one who is prepared to say anything."

"Does anyone else know you're telling us about this?" Marco asked.

The soldier gave a vigorous shake of his head. "No, no way. I would be dead if they did." He glanced at Chiane. "Or worse . . ."

"Where are these test subjects," Marco said. "I need to see them. And I need to see where these weapons are."

The soldier's gaze darted around the room. "I can show you the feeding cage for one of the laboratories where there are tagged subjects put aside as they wait for the next experiment. The boxes of weapons are stacked along one of the walls in the laboratory next door to the feeding cage. I can take you there."

"Feeding cage?" Marco curled his lip. "What a revolting term."

"It's where the subjects are placed when they're waiting to be used in the next experiment."

"I realized what it meant," Marco spat. "What I struggle to accept is that this has been going on for months, right under our noses."

"Who's there?" a voice called out.

"Quiet everyone," Isabella said. "Move farther into the darkness."

Warm air wafted around them.

"They shouldn't see us now," Isabella whispered.

"I said, who's there?" the voice called out again.

"What is it, Max?" another voice said.

The owner of the second voice moved into the light of one of the torches. It was one of the guards. Marco recognized his face but didn't know his name. They all stood as far back in the shadows as they could, trusting Isabella's magic to conceal them. Marco's heart pounded in his chest.

"I could have sworn I heard voices here," Max said as he squinted into the darkness.

"Let's hope there are no survivors locked in there," the other guard said. "C'mon Max, let's get out of here. This place gives me the creeps."

Max took one last look. "Perhaps you're right."

Marco gave a sigh of relief when Max followed the other guard away.

"So where is this feeding cage and laboratory you were talking about?" Marco whispered. "Let's have a look and get the hell out of here."

"This way," the soldier said. They walked up a couple of flights of stairs and arrived in a narrow passageway. They walked quickly and silently toward a broad metal door. "When I open the door, we'll go down one flight of stairs and you'll be able to see one of the feeding cages. Each of the subjects is banded and tagged according to some sort of rating system devised by Reya. They won't be able to see you but please don't say anything. They will be able to hear you. If we're found—"

"We'll all be hung for treason if we're found," Chiane said. "Of course we'll be quiet."

The soldier nodded once in acknowledgment. "Then I'll take you to next door to the back entrance of the laboratory. You'll see the weapons there."

The soldier opened the door and walked down the stairs to a tinted glass window. He stood aside so that Marco and Sascha could see inside.

Marco stepped forward first and looked in through the window. There were at least a couple of hundred people in a room that would normally only fit about fifty. In the corner of the room was a makeshift toilet. The people looked as if they had been starved and their clothes were rags. He put up his arm to block Sascha from seeing but she pushed his arm aside and moved forward. She covered her mouth with her hand to muffle her gasp. Sascha shook her head in disbelief before she turned to face Marco. "We have to save them," she mouthed.

"I know," Marco whispered.

The soldier tapped Marco's shoulder and pointed to another door. They followed.

In the room beyond was a glass wall through which they could see into a pristine-looking laboratory. Crates stamped with the symbol of a circled V stood along the walls of the room.

"The weapons are inside those crates," the soldier whispered.

Marco and Sascha stared at the crates. Sascha grabbed his arm. "That symbol," she whispered. "It's the symbol I saw in my dream."

Marco glanced a second time at the symbol.

Surely there's no connection between Jenny, Vonn, and the weapons?

Voices sounded not far from them. "Let's go," the soldier whispered. "Before anyone finds us."

It took less time to get out of the building than it did to get in. As they stood outside in the cool air, they struggled to speak as they tried to come to grips with what it was they had seen.

"How long have these people been here?" Marco finally asked.

"Months," the soldier replied.

Marco glanced at the white shock on Sascha's face. "Do they receive any food?" Marco asked. "They were nothing but skin and bone."

"Enough to keep them alive but they can't afford to feed them too much. It might raise questions about where all the food has gone. The soldier turned to Chiane. "I had better go. Lieutenant General Chiane, you will come and get me?"

Chiane nodded. "Yes. Early tomorrow morning, before the first sun rises."

Once the soldier had left Sascha pushed back her hood. "We need to save these poor people. That was—"

"I agree," Marco said.

"Now do you see why Drakon can't be High King?" Chiane said. "He hasn't given these people a second thought?"

"Chiane, why are you coming forward now?" Sascha asked. "You've known about this all along. You're hardly innocent in all of this."

"Neither Isabella nor I are innocent. To be honest, if Drakon wasn't going to be the next High King, I don't know if we would have ever come forward. We were too afraid of what Drakon would do to us. All along we've hoped someone would find out and stop it all. But when we heard that he was to be the next High King . . . we couldn't let it happen."

"Why was he holding all these people here?" Sascha asked. "What was the point?"

Chiane glanced at Isabella before turning to face Sascha. "Reya used to boast about the subjects they had captured to test the ancient weapons on. They didn't know how the weapons worked so they needed a larger number of people in case experiments failed. Every one of those people is tagged so that if they try to escape the tag will be exploded, killing them instantly. To rescue them we will need to work out how to remove the tags."

"Everything that's happened here is—is because of those weapons?" Sascha stammered.

"Yes. Drakon is a brutal man," Isabella said. "There's so much people don't know about him. They don't know what he's capable of. My parents were test subjects in that experiment we told you about. They died in absolute terror and all I did was stand there and watch."

"I'm so sorry, Isabella," Sascha said.

"I am to blame for their deaths. I had feelings for Drakon and so I stayed here, in the hope that he and I . . . well, I think you know what I'm talking about. I've had to grow up here. My parents followed me because they hadn't heard from me and now they're dead. I know who Drakon is now. To have a man like that as our leader . . ." Isabella shuddered. "We cannot stay so Chiane and I will be leaving early tomorrow morning."

Chiane put his arm around Isabella's shoulders. "And there's something else you should know about Drakon. You might not have noticed but he wears an armband. That band protects him from the voices of the Ancients. Since he killed his true father, they own him, so watch your back. Do you really want a creature who is controlled by the Ancients as our High King?"

THE POWER OF THE ANCIENT VOICES

ERATUS

*D*rakon enjoyed reminding Marco who it was he now worked for. When Sascha realized who held all the power, perhaps she would see that it was him she should be with.

I'd give anything to know what it was they were fighting about. It might come in handy.

Drakon ambled into his war room. He glanced over at the bloody remains of a mess of rats in the corner of the room. His dragons, having evidently finished their dinner, had now settled down for the night.

He shifted his gaze slightly and noted that Athena's armband still rested on top of the cupboard next to where the dragons slept.

I have to decide what I'm going to do with that.

He clapped his hands softly so as not to wake his pets and the lights in the overhead beams started to glow. Atticus had lost his kingdom because he had relied on manticores. Drakon wouldn't make the same mistake. He relied on fire dragons—creatures unparalleled in their intelligence, swiftness, and brutality.

"Mirror, display the map I showed you yesterday."

A soft blue glow surrounded the war table. Shapes emerged from the table as the map Atticus had given them came to life as a three-dimensional representation of the planet of Eratus. Drakon searched for the symbols that would show where the weapons were hidden. There were thirteen sites in all, and none of them were within the areas that would be protected by the defensive shields the kingdoms had been building. That was good news. If he had been given this map years ago, he would already know everything about the weapons that he needed to know.

He took a step away from the map and walked out onto the balcony.

Am I doing the right thing in helping Sascha to destroy the crates of weapons at each of these sites? Am I stupid to rely on the vials? But I only need the vials to do what I need to do. I don't need the crates. And it is critical that everyone, including the Ancients, believe the weapons no longer exists. So supporting Sascha does seem to be the sensible thing to do.

He walked over to the cupboard where the fire dragons slept and pushed a panel on the top shelf. The cupboard moved aside.

I am already High King. The rest will fall into place when the time is right.

He waved his arm in an arc to dispel the magic that protected the wall and then pressed the fifth stone down from the ceiling to reveal the alcove in which he had hidden the vials. He reached into the pocket of his jacket and removed the supplies he had stolen from the bundle in Atticus's room. He put them in the alcove, pressed the stone again and then cast a protection spell. Finally, he pushed the panel on the top shelf on the cupboard to return it to its original position. He rubbed his hands with pleasure.

Everything I need to change my life for good is now hidden in that alcove.

Drakon frowned when he noticed that Athena's armband was still sitting on top of the cupboard. He had meant to hide it away. "Damn it. I'll deal with the band after I've spoken to Chiane and the Archmage."

He crossed the room and pulled the door open. "Guard," he barked at the young man who stood outside the door. "Get me Chiane."

"Yes, Sire," the guard said saluting.

Drakon turned away and shut the door behind him. As he did so, a burst of red light exploded in front of him, its pulsating glow filling the room. As Drakon stepped back from the table, his hand dropped to the hilt of his dagger.

Sokentash. Why do the gods keep appearing where they're not wanted? What do I say about my visit to Atticus?

"Hello, Drakon," Ares said.

Drakon dipped his head in acknowledgment and watched as Ares pace the floor.

Kalamar raised his head. He sat up and slowly rested back on his haunches.

Ares glanced at Kalamar. "I hear you went on an expedition today, Drakon."

Drakon flexed his fingers over the hilt of his dagger. "What are you talking about Ares?"

Ares is different. He's angry. Kalamar senses the difference, too.

"Drakon, don't play games with me. I'm the master of games. You're only a novice."

"Why should I tell you anything, Ares? How many times have you tried to kill me?"

Ares stopped pacing and studied him. "Kill you?"

"Didn't you tell me to open the crates with the weapons when I located them? You knew the weapons would kill me."

"And yet, here you are, alive."

"Only because I didn't do what you told me to do. How many times have I saved myself by doing the opposite of what you say?"

Ares stalked slowly toward Drakon. A soft roar rumbled in Kalamar's chest. "You . . . are challenging me, Drakon?"

"I'm not a fool, Ares. I would hardly challenge a god, but I won't work with one either."

"And you appear to think you have a choice in this?" Ares said.

"You want me to claim you as my god," Drakon snapped. "Athena wants me to claim her as my god. I choose neither."

Ares stopped several inches from Drakon. "You are too vulnerable to be acting bravely. Anyway, you already serve me."

Drakon's blood chilled. "In what way do I serve you?"

Ares turned to Kalamar. He waved his hand in an arc and Kalamar fell silent. Drakon's eyes narrowed. His dragons weren't moving, frozen midmovement.

"Kalamar!" Drakon called out. "Ares, what have you—"

"You have more important things to worry about. Now, where was I? Oh, that's right. You wanted to know how you serve me. That's easy. You serve the leaders I have chosen to rule Eratus." He leaned over and touched one finger to the armband Drakon was wearing. The band shattered at his touch.

A sharp, screeching pain sliced through Drakon's head, bringing him to his knees.

"You remember my friends, don't you, Drakon?" Ares asked as he circled Drakon. "I shall leave you to them. They know what is expected of you."

A loud clap of thunder reverberated around the war room as Ares disappeared.

"You're back," the familiar voice said. "I trust you will do what you're told to do this time."

"I won't . . ." The pain increased and Drakon gripped his head in his hands.

"You know how this goes, Drakon," the voice continued. "The longer you take to agree, the worse the pain will get."

Drakon screamed as the pain continued to build. "Stop," he called out.

"Do you agree to do as we tell you?"

Drakon could see Athena's armband. It wasn't so very far away. All he needed to do . . . As Drakon reached for the band the pain intensified. He gripped his head in his hands in an effort to ease the pain.

"Do you agree?" the voice said again.

Drakon stared up at the armband. It was so close. All he needed was a break in the pain. "Yes," Drakon said, "I agree."

A chained fist banged on the door. The door opened and Chiane's head appeared in the gap. "You asked for me?" Chiane said.

"Chiane," Drakon pleaded. "Help me."

Chiane's gaze fell on Drakon's shattered armband. He glanced around the room and then stepped in and closed the door behind him. Chiane edged closer to Kalamar. He smiled when he realized none of the dragons were moving. He prodded them. "Fascinating. It's like they are frozen in time. I guess you can't tell me how it happened. Your band has been destroyed, so I imagine you're in a great deal of pain." Chiane stood over the fragmented remains of the band. "It would have taken a lot of power to smash that into tiny pieces. Has Ares been here?"

"Help me, Chiane." Drakon pointed to Athena's armband. "Put it on my arm. Please." Drakon screamed again. The pressure was like that of a vice, and it continued to increase. He was sure his skull was about to crack.

"You won't win," the voice said. "But I must confess this

Chiane interests me. Your pain doesn't seem to concern him. I don't think he wants to help you after all."

"Athena's band," Drakon repeated. "Chiane, please. It's over there."

Chiane turned to look where Drakon was pointing. "I could use it to bribe you into giving me the role of General as you promised me all that time ago but I don't think so." He walked over to the cupboard and pocketed the armband. "I won't help you hide anymore." He walked back to the door, opened it, and strode away.

THE AKHULT

ERATUS

$\mathcal{M}$arco needed fresh air. He stepped out onto the ramparts and looked up into the sky. It would be morning soon. Sascha had finally fallen asleep but his mind couldn't seem to stop churning over what they found in the cave and what Chiane had said. Their first reaction was to have nothing to do with Drakon anymore but that wasn't going to be possible unless they could remove him from the role of High King. Sascha seemed to think once she had told Athena what had happened there wouldn't be a problem, but nothing was ever that simple.

The map Atticus had given Sascha showed that they would need to destroy the weapons at thirteen different sites, but that didn't include the weapons hidden in the Awakening headquarters. Neither he nor Sascha knew how they were going to deal with that. As for the other sites, Marco would need to work out a way to convince Drakon that he and Zabir were the right ones to set the explosives and the treatments.

Drakon's men could be given the task of ensuring the villages' defensive shields were activated. Now that the portals were closed, the telepaths should have advised the villagers what to do. But there was always a chance that something would go wrong, and that was something they couldn't afford if they were going to destroy the weapons. Marco sighed.

Why does everything involving Drakon have to be so difficult?

A bloodcurdling howl echoed around the grounds. Marco stepped closer to the arrow loops to see if he could spot any creatures in the forest that surrounded the castle walls. The shields would stop any creatures from getting in, and they hadn't seen the third moon, so the akhult wouldn't be here for a few weeks yet. Time was still on their side. The clouds were heavy in the sky and he could only just see the glow of the two moons, but there were only two. It was when he was close to the western towers he noticed the third faint glow low on the horizon.

The third moon. The season of the three moons is here, weeks ahead of time.

He raced down the stairs toward Zabir's quarters. He should be back by now. He needed to know what Zabir had found when he last checked in with each of the kingdoms. And he needed to talk to Drakon.

As he arrived at the bottom of the stairs, he looked over at the castle's main gates. He gasped. The gates were open. And standing in the space between the open gates was the leader of the akhult. His yellow eyes glistened as he stared at Marco.

Marco froze.

Who the hell left the gates open? And how did . . .

He glanced up at the sky. He'd missed it.

How could I have not noticed? The shield has been deactivated.

Marco's gaze bounced around the castle grounds.

Where is that creature's pack? Please Athena, don't let them be in here already.

"Shit!"

The creature snarled, its white teeth gleaming in the moonlight. It lifted its front paw and took a step toward Marco.

Marco's hand reached for his blade. It wasn't there. He was unarmed. The gates though . . . he had to close the gates. "Where are the bloody guards?" he cursed.

He knew he should yell for the guards but feared that the noise might set the creature off.

The horn. At Unidern, the horn sent the creature away. Maybe if I could find something like that . . .

"The memorial bell in the tavern garden?" he muttered. "I don't even know if it works."

He maintained eye contact with the creature as he moved slowly toward the bell. As his hand reached for the bell, the creature sniffed the air. It stepped farther into the castle grounds.

It's now or never.

He dived for the bell, reached for the rope, and pulled. The piercing sound of the bell reverberated off the castle walls. Shouts echoed from the guards' sleeping quarters. Help was on its way.

The creature stopped and shook its head vigorously as if the sound had hurt it. But it didn't take long to recover.

"Uh-oh. Maybe that wasn't such a clever idea." The creature roared and launched itself in Marco's direction.

A yell came from behind him. It was Zabir's voice. "Archers, fire."

Flaming arrows began to rain down upon the akhult. They bounced uselessly off the creature's protection. The akhult shook itself and gave an ear-piercing howl. Other howls joined in. Marco bolted for the gates.

"Close the gates!" he screamed. "This creature has friends."

As Marco arrived at the gates the horn he had heard at

Unidern echoed in the air around him. The akhult ignored the horn, its full focus on Marco. The horn sounded again. Still the creature ignored the sound.

"Marco," Soleil screeched, "I'm coming."

"No," Marco yelled. "Stay where you are."

But he was too late. In a desperate effort to protect Marco, Soleil raced, all claws and beak, at the akhult.

"No, Soleil!" Marco screamed. "It's got protection. You don't."

The akhult raised its massive paw and with one loud thwack sent Soleil spinning to the ground. It moved with surprising speed and stood over Soleil. As it opened its jaws ready to destroy him a loud shriek distracted it.

"Fenix," Marco yelled. "Soleil, get the hell out of there. Fenix, you stupid bird, leave it. The creature will kill you."

Fenix dived for the creature's eyes. She was mere feet away when the akhult turned toward her and sliced at her with its claws. Fenix screamed in pain as she was sent flying to the ground.

The akhult abandoned Soleil and stalked toward Fenix as the horn sounded a third time. This time the creature sniffed the air, then turned away from Fenix, leaped into the air, shimmered and disappeared.

"Quickly," Marco screamed. "Help me close these bloody gates."

Within moments there was a squad of men all forcing the castle gates closed.

When the gates were shut, they rested against them while they regained their breath.

Marco pushed himself upright. "Zabir," he said. "Find out who the hell was responsible for leaving these gates open and bring them to me. Now!"

"Yes, Colonel."

"And activate the shield! Right now. Do you hear me?"

"Yes, Colonel." Zabir hurried away.

Marco turned to the nearest soldier. "Get me the High King, and you," he said pointing at another soldier, "bring me Sascha."

"I need a healer," Marco screamed out as he raced toward Fenix who was still lying on the ground where she had fallen.

"I have one coming," a soldier replied.

Marco squatted next to Fenix, stroking her feathers as he waited for the healer and Sascha to arrive. Soleil called out softly to Fenix, a soft sad sound. He lay on the ground next to her, his beak touching hers.

"She'll be okay, Soleil," Marco said. "She'll be okay." He heard footsteps as Sascha raced down the castle stairs toward Fenix, the healer not far behind her.

"Marco, what happened?"

"I have no idea, Sascha. All I know is that we've been making sure that the villages are protected from the akhult and I find our gates have been left open and our shield is down. We nearly had the akhult in here with us."

"But how—"

The healer crouched down next to Fenix and began to examine her. "Sascha, Marco. Fenix will be okay. She's got a few nasty wounds, but nothing we can't fix. I've given her a strong sedative. When she wakes, she will feel a lot better. It's fortunate that pyrans are immune to akhult poison."

"Sascha," Soleil cried out.

"The healer said she will be okay, Soleil. Why don't you stay with her in the sick bay, look after her."

"I will," Soleil said.

Soleil, Sascha and Marco were watching Fenix being placed into a carrier so she could be moved to a healing room for treatment when Zabir raced up to Marco.

"Marco, you'll never believe this, but it was Drakon who turned the shield off and left the gates open."

"That's impossible," Marco blurted. "He wouldn't do that."

"We have witnesses," Zabir said. "There is no doubt."

"Why didn't these witnesses tell anyone what Drakon had done?" Marco asked.

"He had used some sort of magic to paralyze them," Zabir replied. "We had to get a couple of our mages to release them from the spell."

"So why didn't Drakon kill them if he knew they had witnessed what he had done," Sascha asked. "Why paralyze them?"

"He would have had a reason," Marco said. "Drakon always has a reason for things he does."

FENIX AND THE SEARCH FOR THE
WEAPONS SITES

ERATUS

*a*s Sascha strode toward the castle's sick bay she glanced over at the balcony to Drakon's chambers. Knowing Drakon had left the castle gave them the perfect opportunity to clean out the Awakening headquarters. The guards were imprisoned, and the test subjects were undergoing an intensive care program. Once her and Marco had carried out the instructions given by Atticus, and destroyed the weapons, they could then worry about how they would deal with Drakon—if he returned. Connell would have to be advised of what had happened, once he was well enough. And Owain—Sascha wondered whether Owain would ever return to the role of High King?

Sascha walked into the sick bay and squatted next to the healer in front of a temporary nest he had made for Fenix. The nest smelled of pine, cinnamon, and the minty aroma of selecine, a strange combination.

"How is the patient?" Sascha asked.

The healer pushed himself up with a grunt. "Fenix will be as good as new. I'll keep her in sick bay for observation but all she needs is time."

He turned to Soleil. "That pyran must think a lot of you to take on an akhult to save you. I don't know that my pyran would do the same for her partner."

"Stupid, damn female," Soleil snapped. "No sense."

"Um," Sascha said stroking her chin, "Soleil, I recall Marco mentioning you flying in to save him from the akhult. Is that any different?"

The healer chuckled. "Sascha, can I speak to you for a moment?"

"Of course. Is it about those poor people we released?"

"Yes," the healer said. Most of them will recover but we're not sure how to release the tags and the guards aren't talking. The good thing is we have managed to lock down the machine they've been using to detonate the tags. The guards are worried about what Drakon will say when he returns. Not to mention what he will do."

"*If* he returns," Sascha said. "I'll be talking to Athena as soon as I can. I'm sure she'll help us. But whatever happens, I'm happy to take full responsibility for this. There's no way we could allow those people to live like that. Allowing it to continue would make us as bad as Drakon's followers."

"What will we do about the tags?"

"I will talk to Marco about it. One of his people must be able to work out a way we can release these tags."

The healer fidgeted with the stethoscope around his neck. "Actually, there are two people who have offered to help— Chiane and Isabella. They were planning to leave this morning but when they heard Drakon had gone . . . well, now they want to stay. And they want to help with the victims if you agree to it. They've offered to help in any way they can with the tags."

Sascha scratched her head. "I'm happy for them to help you with the tags. But I don't want them to be involved in the care of the victims. I need to put the victims' needs first and I need to assess how they react to Chiane and Isabella before I let the victims come into contact with them. But feel free to conscript others to help you if you need it. If those two do find a way to release the tags and free those people, I am sure that will go a long way to help repair . . . relationships."

"I'll let them know, Sascha."

"Thanks, Healer."

The healer glanced back at Soleil and Fenix. "I'll leave you with these two but remember to close my door when you leave."

"Absolutely," Sascha said. "I'll only be a minute." She turned back to Soleil who had curled himself into a ball and was resting next to Fenix.

"I'll leave you here to guard Fenix, Soleil. Marco and I will set up the explosions, and the treatments, and be back before the evening."

"You can't go to Brun without me," Soleil said. "You need me."

"We're leaving Brun until tomorrow. You should be free to come with us by then. And we can get Rusty to help protect Fenix while we're gone."

"I'm glad she'll have Rusty with her."

"And you'll have to wear the same leathers the war pyrans do," Sascha said.

"That is totally unnecessary," Soleil replied.

Sascha crossed her arms across her chest. "Without the leathers, you're not coming with me."

Soleil clicked his beak at her. "Okay, I'll do it. But I still think it's an overreaction. Anyway, I want to say something before you go. I've already said this to Fenix, but I thought I should tell you as well. This may sound wrong, but I don't care what Fenix did. She risked her life to save me—again. I know deep down she would never mean to harm us so whatever she may have done was because she had no choice."

Sascha let her arms drop by her side as she stared at Soleil. "Where is Soleil. What have you done with my Soleil?"

Soleil clicked his beak at her. "I really do not like your sense of humor, Sascha."

Sascha chuckled as she picked up her satchel. "We'll be back before evening. Okay?"

"Okay," Soleil replied.

Sascha walked to the transporter in the corner of the healer's room, reached out, and touched it. Seconds later she arrived in the training grounds in the courtyard.

Marco had spread Atticus's map out on a large wooden table and was now deep in conversation with Zabir. Sascha moved to Marco's side and put her hand on his shoulder. He reached up absently to pat her hand as he studied the map.

"There are thirteen sites, Sascha," Marco said. "Zabir and I were discussing how we would tackle this. As time is running out we thought we would divide the soldiers into three or four groups so they can move quickly."

"Good idea," Sascha said. "But can I make one suggestion?"

Marco took a step away from the table and faced her. "Fire away. What's your idea?"

"I thought we could all go to the first site. If we follow the instructions Atticus gave us, everyone will see exactly what needs to be done. Then we can split up and do the rest."

"That makes sense," Marco said. "Let's make the first one the cache south of Blencalgo. Zabir, would you organize the men?"

"Yes, Colonel."

"And would you talk to the guards about deactivating the shield when it's time for us to leave?" Marco asked.

"That's all done. They will deactivate it long enough for us to fly out and then they will reactivate it as soon as we're in the sky."

Marco smiled. "Good. Thanks, Zabir."

Zabir saluted Marco and strode away to organize the men.

"Marco, what's happened about the weapons stored in the Awakening headquarters?" Sascha asked.

"Zabir organized for all the weapon crates to be stored in that laboratory the soldier took us to. When we return, we'll set up the explosives in there, and in the area Drakon had locked down after the failed experiment. That will be the final step in clearing out the Awakening headquarters."

Sascha moved closer to Atticus's map and trailed her fingers across it. "Why do you think in my dream I saw the child sitting on a box with the circled V symbol?"

"Didn't you say the child was gloating?" Marco asked.

Sascha nodded. "Yes, it was."

"I think that whatever or whoever is influencing your dreams doesn't think we will succeed in destroying the weapons. It clearly doesn't know that Atticus conceived of a way to destroy them."

Sascha studied Marco. "Do you think Jenny or Eham have anything to do with the weapons?"

"After everything they have done to help our cause," Marco said, "I don't think there's any way they could be connected."

Sascha sighed. "I hope you're right." She glanced at the soldiers and mages as they completed their final preparations for the trip to the sites. "It's not a stupid idea to drag all the groups to Blencalgo, is it? I mean we could test out Atticus's instructions at the Awakening headquarters."

"We could use the Awakening headquarters as our pilot site, except for the fact that we can't show them how to use the autobot or how to translate the symbols on the map we're working from."

"True," Sascha said. "I guess we're ready to go then?"

"Yes. You and I are taking the lead pyrans."

"It will be strange to fly a creature that isn't Soleil," Sascha paused. "This will be my first flight without him."

"I hadn't thought about that, but you're right. Apart from flying Kalurth when you were with Drakon."

"Marco," Sascha warned. "Changing the subject . . . Can I get a copy of the map?"

"Of course, I've made copies for each of the groups. Here is yours." Marco took a sheet of paper off the table and handed it to her. As she reached for the map he pulled her to him and kissed her. It was a soft, slow kiss. Her heart beat faster and her breathing started to deepen as she felt her body respond to his gentle touch. The world started to disappear as he pulled her even closer to him. "I'm sorry," he mumbled. "I shouldn't have said what I said."

The words broke the trance long enough to give her time to remember where they were. She pulled back and put her hands on his chest. "I don't think now is the right time for this conversation."

"Perhaps when we return?" he purred.

"Only if you behave," she said fluttering her lashes at him and stepping back. She didn't dare look up to see who had seen the kiss, but she could feel a warmth flush her cheeks at the possibility the entire group was watching.

Marco put his arm around her waist and guided her to the front of the group. "Here is the pyran you will be riding. He's one of my favorites."

"He's beautiful," Sascha said as she stroked his neck.

"Everyone mount," Marco called out.

Sascha climbed up onto the pyran and placed the map in her jacket pocket.

Minutes later Marco raised his right arm and waved it forward. "Let's fly."

The pyrans leaped skyward, and there was a soft hum as

the shield above them disappeared. Marco and Sascha circled above the castle grounds and watched as the vibrant blue shield flickered back into place. Sascha caught a movement out of the corner of her eye. A flash of gold headed west.

Soleil? I could have sworn I saw Soleil. But that's impossible. He's with Fenix.

They turned away from the castle and headed southwest toward Blencalgo. They flew over a mountain range and barren fields. The food would have been stored in silos under the shields, supplying the people with food until the end of the storm season. Sascha took out the map and studied it. She recognized a spot a mile past the base of the mountain range. "The location should be close." She pointed at a landmark below them. "The map shows that diamond-shaped field that's down there."

"Let's land then," Marco said.

Several minutes later they landed in the middle of the diamond and climbed down from their pyrans.

"What's next?" Marco asked.

"It shows a cave with a flame and a snake's head," Sascha said.

Zabir pointed twenty yards west of where they were standing. "There's a cave over there. Do you think that could be it?"

"Let's have a look," Sascha said.

A few minutes later they arrived outside the cave.

"Uh-oh. There are a hell of a lot of snakes . . . Look!" Zabir shone his torch into the cave and thousands of eyes glowed in the light. "The floor is covered with them." Zabir shivered. "If there's one thing that terrifies me, it's snakes."

"I'll use fire to clear a path," Sascha said. "We'll be fine. Marco, what do you think about only taking the group leaders into the cave with us? The others can wait here. I'd hate for anyone to get hurt."

"I think the ones who are staying behind will be happy with that idea," Zabir said.

It only took a few weak fire spells to clear a path in the cave, although it didn't seem to kill off the snakes, which instead regenerated, multiplying their numbers. Sascha dug into her satchel and retrieved one of the autobots Atticus gave her. It buzzed and a little green light on the side of it lit up. She rested it on the palm of her hand. It levitated for a few seconds and spun around several times. Then having decided on a direction it headed deeper into the cave.

"Keep that fire going, Sascha," Zabir said as he glanced nervously at the growing numbers of snakes.

They had only traveled one hundred yards into the cave when the autobot stopped and moved toward the wall to their right. It played a short tune consisting of three notes and then repeated the tune several times. A door in the side wall slid open and the autobot returned to Sascha. Once she held it in her hand the green light flicked off. She pocketed it and they all passed through the doorway. Along the far wall in the room they had entered was a large number of crates marked with the circled V symbol.

"We found it," Zabir said.

"Okay," Marco said as he put Atticus's instructions onto one of the crates. "Let's follow this step by step and see how easy it is to do."

It took nearly ten minutes to set everything up, including the beacon, but the instructions were clear and easy to follow. "Does everyone feel comfortable that they can do this on their own?" Sascha asked.

"It's very easy," Zabir said. "Atticus has done a good job." There was a murmur of approval.

"Good," Sascha said. "We can now do the rest of the sites."

With the help from a few more fireballs they made their way back out of the cave.

"The map you have been given provides all the details you need," Sascha said to the group leaders. "And you can each take an autobot with you. You must use it in exactly the same way I did. Let it sit in the palm of your hand. It will show you where the weapons are."

"And remember," Marco said, "the symbol marked on the map shows the creature you must fight. Don't try to clear them out altogether. I don't even know if that's possible. Just clear out what you need to do to get the job done."

There was another murmur of approval.

"So how do you want to distribute the workload, Marco?" Sascha asked.

"As we have to set the explosives for the weapons at the main site in Brun tomorrow, you and I will deal with the sites in the Kingdom of Lios today. Zabir, you take care of the sites in the Kingdom of Breyth, and Rohan you will take care of the sites in the Kingdom of Tasuna. Crestwell, you take care of the Kingdom of Brun, but leave the main site for Sascha and I to do tomorrow. Is everyone clear on where they're going and what they have to do?"

"Yes, Colonel," they replied.

"Good," Marco said. "Now, make sure you fly everywhere. With the season of the three moons upon us, walking is too dangerous. And make sure you give any akhult or ice ghouls a wide berth. Everyone is to report back to the main tavern by the time the second sun has set today. No excuses. We need to know everyone is safe and the tasks have been completed."

"Yes, Colonel," they said in unison.

They all climbed back onto their pyrans and flew off to the kingdoms they had been assigned. "Sascha," Marco said, "our next stop is Sleeping Hideout, then Silverkeep. Keep an eye out for any akhult."

RELIEF FROM THE VOICES

ERATUS

*D*rakon had no idea where he was. Since the Ancients had taken control everything had become a blur. As he crouched in the corner of the cold, dark room, another wave of an intense, scorching pain slashed its way through his head. He tried to flex his neck and shoulders to ease the throbbing headache that followed but all that succeeded in doing was making him feel nauseous. The Ancients kept speaking to him, but Drakon refused to listen.

As the pain continued to build, so did the nausea. He tried to breathe slowly to stop himself from vomiting but was instead forced to crawl to the opposite corner of the room where he again attempted to empty his already empty stomach. The stench of vomit was overwhelming, and it seemed there was no escape.

He needed to use his mind to push the pain aside, to be strong. "You will not win this," Drakon screamed out to the voices. "I'll make you pay."

A high-pitched cackle echoed around him. "We will win, Drakon. I can assure you we will win."

The heat in his body increased and kept increasing. He

was sure he was going to combust. He had to wait it out, wait for the heat to ease. "Where is your courage you creatures of the dark?" he called out. "Face me. Fight me in person."

He heard someone scream. It took him a moment to realize it was him. And then it came: another bout of hot, searing pain followed by the relief of nothing but blackness.

It was the freezing pain in his hands and feet that brought him back to consciousness. The heat in his body had completely disappeared. He rubbed his hands and feet to try to ease the pain, to warm them, but it seemed like even his blood was slowly but surely turning to ice. And all the time the only thing he could hear were the voices of the Ancients talking to him.

"Drakon, you've done well," one of the voices said. "Don't you think my idea was clever? If Marco and Sascha decide to recheck their work, they won't even think of checking inside the treatment boxes. It wouldn't occur to them that the boxes might be empty. And you were able to sabotage three sites. That's more than we hoped." The voice chuckled.

Drakon closed his eyes. He had tried to fight back but it was when the pain was at its worst that they seemed to take control. He tried to bring back the darkness so that he had time to plan, time to work out how he was going to escape. These were the creatures he needed to destroy with the weapons, but he had no idea how to do that. He couldn't give up. They were not going to get the better of him.

"We know you're in pain, Drakon, but you don't need to be," the voice continued. "We want you on our side. Allow us to help you. Become one of us and you will have the power you have always wanted. People will tremble at the sound of your name."

Drakon shook his head. Tears rolled down his cheeks. "No, I won't become an Ancient. I would rather die instead."

The voice tutted. "We can't let you die. We need you. We will leave you here for now. You're safe in this room. Rest and think about what we said. We offer you freedom from the pain and more power than you've ever dreamed of. We will return for you later, when we are ready for you to perform your next task."

What I wouldn't give to be free from this pain.

Soft music drifted around him—haunting, gentle sounds. A misty figure appeared in the distance. It moved closer and started to take shape. It was a woman with olive skin, flowing dark brown hair, and sparkling gray eyes. She was dressed in a gown of white and gold. "Did you say you would give anything to get rid of the pain?"

"Of all the gods, it is you who shows up, Athena?"

"I will help you, but in return you will need to help me."

Drakon was weak; the pain had sapped all his strength. "What is it you want from me, Athena?"

"I will give you my band, and the pain will stop. And Ares will not be able to touch you. But I need you to help Sascha and destroy the weapons."

"Chiane stole the band. I don't have it anymore."

"I'm the one who made it. Do you really think that's a problem for me?"

"And that's all you want?" Drakon asked.

"Yes, that's it. The people of Eratus will owe you if you help them."

I don't need those crates of weapons. Not if it gives me the freedom to finally carry out my plans.

Drakon leaned over and vomited again as the pain in his head worsened. After a moment Drakon had composed himself enough to speak. "I will help Sascha."

An armband appeared in the palm of his hand. It was

engraved with the images of an olive tree and an owl. He put it on and the pain disappeared instantly.

I am free. And soon I will destroy the creatures that have tortured me. I will be no one's slave.

"Thank you, Athena," Drakon said. "I will remember what you did for me today."

"I know you will," Athena said.

Kalamar—what happened to Kalamar?

"I had been hoping . . . I don't suppose you know where my fire dragons are?"

"How do you think I found you?" Athena said. "They're outside waiting for you. Kalamar will take you to a place where you can rest. There's no point in going back to the castle. You wouldn't be accepted there."

"Why not?"

"They know what you did to those poor people in the laboratory, and then when you left the castle grounds you left the shield down and the front gates open. They were nearly victims of an attack by the akhult."

"I didn't know what I was doing when I left. I'm sorry I put the castle in danger."

"And the people in the laboratory?" Athena asked.

"I don't want to lie to you, Athena, but if I admit to it, you will remove this band."

"I won't. And I'm grateful you didn't lie to me about it. When all of this is over, you and I will need to talk about how much Ares was involved in all of this. You can have tonight to rest and recover with your dragons but early tomorrow you must join Sascha at the site in Brun early tomorrow morning. She will be there to unlock the key to the underground city where the weapons are stored. She can't do it without you."

"I'm assuming Sascha knows what I did?"

"She does."

"Will she accept my help if I turn up at Brun?"

"She needs you, so she won't have a choice. Now go and see to your dragons. I would get out of here as soon as I could if I were you. It won't be long before the Ancients realize why they can't sense you anymore."

Drakon staggered out of the cave, his hand raised to cover his eyes from the bright sun. A loud, sharp call echoed above him. Then came a squeal of delight as a whoosh of wings and warm air whipped around him. The fire dragons twirled in the air before landing neatly on the ground not far from where he stood.

Drakon was surprised with the tears that filled his eyes. "Kalamar," he whispered. "You didn't give up on me."

Kalamar trotted up to him and rested his head on Drakon's shoulder. "You truly are my friend, Kalamar." Kalamar knelt down in front of him so that Drakon could climb onto his shoulders. "I'm sorry to make you carry me, Kalamar. You are not a beast of burden. You are more than that."

Kalamar nudged him with his nose, helping Drakon up onto his shoulders.

Drakon stroked his neck. "You don't have a harness my friend, so fly slowly for me. I'm weak and can't hold on."

Kalamar gave a soft warble before leaping into the air. The other fire dragons followed close behind him. With the warmth of Kalamar's body and the gentle rhythm of his wings soothing him, it wasn't long before Drakon fell asleep.

JENNY

ERATUS

*T*he tavern wasn't as noisy as Sascha had expected it to be. Inside were a couple of small groups of people having drinks before making their way home and a few couples having their evening meal. Sascha was the first one of Marco's group to arrive there. She decided to go to Marco's room. It would be nice to surprise him.

She walked up the stairs, knocked on the door and then opened it. She froze when she saw the child playing on the lounge with Jenny. When the child turned toward her, Sascha felt the blood drain from her body. It was Vonn. Jenny twisted around and stared wide-eyed at Sascha for a moment before leaping to her feet and standing in between Sascha and the child.

"Sa—Sascha," she stammered.

"Rusty! Vonn called out as a brown-and-white streak raced out from an adjoining room.

Sascha watched as Rusty leaped onto Vonn, pinning him to the lounge and licking him all over the face. Vonn giggled and pulled her closer to him in a cuddle.

"No," Jenny called out to Rusty. "Down."

Rusty stopped, twisted her head to study Jenny, then jumped down from the lounge and sat in front of it facing Sascha. She whined and wagged her tail slowly.

"Rusty and Vonn have become friends," Jenny said. "She seems to have become very protective of him."

"Jenny," Eham's voiced called out from the adjoining room, "is Rusty with you?"

"Umm, yes, she is."

"What's wrong with you, girl?" Eham said as he walked into the room. He stopped at the doorway when he saw Sascha. "Ah," he said as he stared at Sascha. "I see you've met Vonn. You must be wondering what we're doing in Marco's apartment. He was letting us—"

Jenny cut him off. "He wanted you and I to meet, Sascha, and this seemed the best place."

Sascha's voice still hadn't returned.

"Sascha," Jenny pleaded, "please say something."

Sascha watched as Vonn pushed himself closer to Rusty. The dog positioned herself so that she was directly in front of him, her back resting against his legs and her head still tilted to the side as she studied Sascha. "I need to talk to you alone, Jenny. Is it possible for Eham to take Vonn so that we can go downstairs and get a drink?"

"Yes, sure," Jenny said as she watched Sascha's every move. "Eham?"

Eham stepped forward. "Vonn, you come with me. Rusty, do you want to come and play?"

Rusty stood but her focus was still on Sascha.

"Mummy?" Vonn whispered.

"It's all right, honey. You go with grandpa. Mummy will be back soon."

Sascha squatted and called to Rusty. "Come here, girl."

As Rusty bounced over to Sascha like a newborn lamb,

Sascha couldn't help but laugh. She gave her a big hug. "You go with Vonn and Eham."

"Rusty," Eham called. Rusty turned and raced into the room after Sascha heard Vonn's infectious giggle through the open door.

Sascha turned and led the way down to the tavern.

She raised her hand at the tavern keeper and signaled for two drinks before leading the way to one of the corner tables. She noticed that some of the others from Marco's group of soldiers had arrived and were busy ordering drinks. Zabir was one of them. He waved at Sascha. "Come and join us."

"I'll be there soon. Would you mind telling Marco I'm having a quick drink with Jenny?"

"Sure thing," he replied.

Their drinks arrived as they took their seats.

Jenny took a sip of her drink and then rested it on the table as she gripped it with both hands. "I won't tell a lie. I'm terrified of how this is all going to play out, Sascha."

"A lot has happened lately, Jenny. And I've found out some things about who I used to be that has left me feeling rather gutted. So I'm not surprised that you are struggling with this. But we need to be honest. That is our only way forward."

"I agree," Jenny said. "Ask me what you want to know."

"Who is Vonn's father?"

"His name is Wiskari."

Sascha relaxed back into her chair and breathed a sigh of relief. She flexed the muscles in her neck and shoulders to ease the tension. She picked up her ale and had a couple of mouthfuls, giving herself time to compose herself. "You're sure his name was Wiskari?"

"Yes. He had a twin brother who was an Ancient. But

Wiskari was only a Master. He gave me the most wonderful gift—Vonn."

"Are you able to tell me what happened, Jenny?"

"Yes. I thought you would want to know." Jenny took a deep breath. "After you were sent to Earth, Laela sort of adopted me. She promised me the world. I can honestly say that at that time I loved her. I was so grateful to her for taking me under her wing, training me, guiding me. For my fifteenth birthday, Laela took me to the temple in Brun. She told me she wanted to give me a gift that she couldn't give to any of the other girls because they weren't . . . special like me."

Jenny gripped the glass in her hands as she stared into the drink. "She told me that to claim the gift I was going to have to be brave. And I was determined to prove to her that I was brave and that I deserved the gift she was going to give me. She took me to a large cave with onyx walls that shone like glass and told me to sit on the edge of a large stone stage while she changed. While I was waiting for her, all I could do was stare at the long, thin, black table next to me. It was covered with skulls and these sharp . . . weapons."

"You must have been terrified," Sascha said.

Jenny wiped a tear away with the back of her hand, took another sip of her drink, and continued. "I was so scared and I kept biting the inside of my mouth to stop myself from crying or telling her I had changed my mind. It wasn't long before Laela returned, dressed in a purple robe. Moments later this creature dressed in a long flowing red cloak came in. He was followed by these insects the size of large dogs. The insects came up to me. One leaped onto my chest, holding me in place, while the other two spat out these strands of sticky thread that wrapped around my hands and feet. I couldn't move. The red-cloaked creature walked toward the long thin table and grabbed a knife. I was sure he wanted to kill me so I tried so hard to free myself from the thread, but I couldn't. But instead of killing me he used the knife to prod the mark on my arm. He watched as the magic flared. Then he made this strange clicking sound and left."

Jenny gulped and took several breaths to calm herself.

Sascha put her hand on Jenny's arm. "Are you okay to go on? I need to know what happened but I'm so sorry you have to relive all of this."

"I have . . . visions, Sascha. I know how important it is you know the truth." Jenny glanced at the stairs that led to Marco's room. "Anyway, after the creature left, Laela raced over to me and released me from the thread. She said that he had accepted me. I didn't know what that meant, but I knew that I didn't want to be accepted. I tried to push her over and run away. That made her really angry with me, so she locked me in a room and told me I had to wait there until I could be cleansed for the Leader of the Ancients.

"I cried until I had no more tears. But then this soft voice came to me and told me that he was going to help. Someone unlocked the door and a man walked in. I'll never forget him. He looked like a god. He glowed. And he looked . . . he looked just like Vonn. He cast a magic spell over us and told me not to be afraid, that the others wouldn't see us. He took me by the hand and led me out of the temple to a golden pyran. Together the two of us flew to the most beautiful spot I've ever seen. The greenery, the colorful flowers and the rain-bow-colored exotic creatures—it was breathtaking. He looked after me for the next few weeks and one day he said he had to go away but would be back that night. He was true to his word; he came back before the second sun set. He told me Laela was looking for me and the only way he could protect me was if he was the one to give me a gift. That way the Ancient would no longer want me. He explained it wouldn't be the same as with the Ancient. When the Ancients consume you they force you to . . . " Jenny was quiet for a moment as she fingered the edge of the table in front of her. "Wiskari promised me he wouldn't have sex with me. He said he would use the magic of the goddess, Bendis. He then took me to Eham and asked him to protect me. Which Eham did, and has done ever since."

The both of them sat in silence as they stared into their drinks. Sascha leaned over and gave Jenny a hug. "Again, I'm so sorry you had to go through that."

"It turned out really well for me," Jenny said. "I got Vonn and I was given an opportunity to see a caring side of my grandfather I never knew he had."

Athena was right. The child is Wiskari's. The nightmare can't be true.

Jenny cleared her throat. "I need to know, Sascha. Are my visions true? Do you want to kill him? My Vonn?"

"Before I was taken by Laela, I would never have believed your story. I wouldn't have believed that I could have been so naive to have let all of that happen under my nose. I know the truth now. I do accept his father is Wiskari so he is safe from me. But I still think Vonn is in danger. After we have dealt with these weapons we all need to get together and decide how to deal with the real threat."

Sascha glanced at Jenny. Her head was in her hands and her shoulders were shaking. "Jenny, are you okay?"

Jenny nodded, sat back, and wiped her face with her hands as she took a deep breath. "I can't believe it's over. I've been so afraid of what would happen when you returned to Eratus and regained your memory, and now it's over."

Sascha's eyes stung. She leaned over and pulled Jenny into another hug. "Let's consider this a fresh start . . . for the both of us."

"I can live with that," Jenny said. She grinned and for the first time Sascha had realized just how pretty Jenny was. And to think she and Laela had given this young girl so much grief.

"I have to ask," Sascha said. "If you were so afraid of me, why did you come and work for me? Why not stay as far away from me as you could?"

"It was Connell who convinced me to work for you. He told me you had changed, that when the time came, you would understand. And I believed him."

"Connell convinced you." Sascha shook her head in disbelief. "Wow, I never expected that." She put her hand on Jenny's arm. "Jenny, I'm so sorry for not being there to protect you. Can you forgive me?"

Jenny covered Sascha's hand with her own. "There's nothing to forgive. I've been blessed, truly blessed, and I'm grateful."

When Jenny removed her hand from Sascha's, Sascha sat back in her chair. "There is one more question I need to ask you. Do you know anything about these ancient weapons? In my dream, I saw Vonn and a silver box inscribed with the same design that is marked on the weapon crates. I'm trying to work out what it all means."

Jenny shook her head. "No, I don't. But I have seen the crates at the Awakening headquarters. None of them were silver. Why do you think the box that appeared in your dream was a silver one?"

Sascha sighed. "It's a good question. Unfortunately, I have no idea. I guess it won't matter soon anyway because tomorrow, when we get back from Brun, we will be destroying all the weapons."

"There you are, Sascha," Marco's voice called out. "Our meeting is about to begin. Can you join us?" He sidled up to the table, his glance bouncing between Jenny and Sascha.

"You go," Jenny said. "You have work to do. After the

weapons have been taken care of we can talk again. And I believe we have a wedding to attend, if I'm invited?"

"Of course you're invited, Jenny. I'd be honored to have you, Eham, and Vonn there. Kira and the girls are organizing the whole thing. I believe we're now having the wedding at Aynor's Stone. But don't worry, the place has changed so much that you won't recognize it. There's nothing left that might remind you of Laela."

"We accept your invitation," Jenny said, pushing herself out of her chair. "Now I'd better go and see what my son and his great-grandfather are up to."

Marco watched Jenny as she walked away. "You two have sorted everything out?"

"Yes, we have. You are right. Vonn is a beautiful child and Jenny is lovely. I need to start putting my past behind me and create a new future, one in which I learn from everything that has happened before."

Marco put his arm around her shoulders and led her to the other side of the room to join the others. "And some more good news. Everyone is back and we had complete success."

"That is wonderful. Have the weapon crates in the Awakening headquarters been taken care of as well?" Sascha asked.

"Yes, everything has been done. Now all we need to do is deal with the temple in Brun tomorrow."

"And we need to check in on Soleil and Fenix," Sascha said.

TIME TO HEAL

ERATUS

*D*rakon woke to the soft rumbling of water as the first sun edged past the horizon. He yawned and pushed himself up from the grassy surface he'd been sleeping on. The air was foul with vomit and unwashed bodies. He raised his arm and realized the smell was coming from him. He would have to clean himself up before he met Sascha.

The lagoon was filled with glistening fish. Leafy shrubs covered in red, purple and yellow blossoms grew along the edge of the waters, and birds screeched at one another as they dived in and out of the trees. A sweet citrus and honey smell travelling on the breeze reminded Drakon of his hunger.

Where am I? And how did I get here? The last thing I remember is climbing onto Kalamar.

A squeal of delight sounded in the sky above him and he glanced up to see the fire dragons soaring upward along the air currents and then twirling as they dived back down. He smiled. He couldn't remember seeing his creatures this happy before.

"Good morning, my pets," he called out.

Kalamar answered with a soft chatter as he soared into the air and circled the lagoon.

I must find something to eat.

The branches of the trees were heavy with fruit, or what he hoped was fruit. He walked over to the nearest bush and plucked some berries that looked like cherry fruits from its branches. He held them up to his nose and sniffed them. He shrugged. They didn't smell poisonous. He popped a couple in his mouth and delighted in the sweet, juicy flesh. They tasted like the nectar of the gods. Assuming they were safe, he'd have the rest of them later.

Drakon took off his clothes and washed them in the lagoon before hanging them over the branches of a tree to dry. Then he dived into the clear lagoon waters. As he raised his arms to flick his wet hair off his face he caught the glimpse of gold—Athena's armband. He studied it as he ran his finger across the engraved picture of the olive tree and owl. It was very similar to the last one, the only difference being a thin red line that circled the band. He had forgotten what sort of a relief it was to put the band on and shut out the voices and the pain. But he couldn't depend on always having it so he needed to destroy the creatures the armband protected him from. And Chiane would pay for taking the band and leaving him to the Ancients.

There will be time to think about that later.

He took a deep breath and let his muscles relax as his mind went over everything that had happened in the last couple of days. Athena had told him he wouldn't be able to return to the castle, but he was the High King of Eratus and the castle was his home. He might need to stay away for a week or two, but he would return. He debated whether he should retrieve the vials and supplies from his war room in the meantime but decided against it. The magic would protect them until he returned.

He grabbed a handful of sand and gave himself a good scrub. After he had rinsed off the sand, he collected his clothing, which was almost dry, and then dressed. For a time he sat on a stone edge overlooking the lagoon. He watched as his pets darted in and out of the trees feasting on the little creatures that lived in them.

He was preparing to call Kalamar down when he remembered what the Ancients had said to him. He had helped them to disarm three of the sites. He tried to remember the names of those sites or how he had disarmed them. But his memories of those times were fuzzy. He rapped his knuckles on his forehead as he tried to think.

Remember! I have to remember! I cannot allow the Ancients to gain control over any of the weapons.

He remembered that the Ancients had wanted him to remove the treatments from the boxes and destroy them. But he hadn't done that. He had only removed the wires.

"So once I remember the sites it should be easy enough to fix," he muttered. "Maybe I'll remember something when Sascha shows me the map."

The only problem was time. Did they have enough time to undo the damage he had done?

He needed to leave for Brun but before he did that he needed to get some water and a cloth or something to clean the door to the site just in case it was covered with blood like the one on Earth had been. Once he had gathered what he needed, he called out to Kalamar.

"Kalamar, we need to go. Leave your family here for now. We have work to do."

Kalamar twirled around and landed on the ground next to him. He kneeled before Drakon making it easier for him to climb onto his shoulders. When Drakon was seated he rested his hands on Kalamar's back and gripped the dragon's sides with his knees and ankles.

"Kalamar, remember I don't have a harness so fly carefully."

Kalamar gave a soft warble before leaping into the air and heading in the direction of Brun.

ERATUS: BRUN

As they flew over the site in Brun Drakon searched for any signs of activity, any signs Sascha had arrived. But there was nothing. He decided to find the best spot to wait for her and it wasn't long before he found the perfect vantage point on one of the cliff tops which overlooked the area.

I'll wait for her here.

It was strangely comforting to know that to access the weapons at this site they needed each other. It was almost as if the fates were trying to tell them they were meant to be together. But he couldn't help feeling on edge when he knew that if he was to destroy the weapons, as he had promised Athena, he was going to have to suck up his pride and ask Sascha for her help. But he had seen what those weapons could do and there was no way he would ever let the Ancients get their hands on them. After everything they had done to him, he would not let them win.

When Kalamar had landed, he slid down from his shoulders and prepared to wait.

FENIX

ERATUS

*S*ascha massaged the knot in her stomach to ease the pain.

The thought of going to Brun is affecting me more than I thought it would. And I have no idea how we're going to do this without Drakon. Atticus said it would take both of us to do what we need to do.

"Come on, sleepyhead," Marco called out from the bathroom. "It's nearly time to leave for Brun. I've had my shower. It's your turn."

Sascha grunted as she pushed herself up and swung her legs off the bed. Last night, she'd organized practical winter leathers for the trip and laid them out on the bench at the end of her bed. She stood and padded over to the bathroom. She looked around her. "Where's my vimberry, Marco?" she called out. "The least you could have done is get that ready for me."

"I did. It's on the cupboard next to the shower."

"Oops, so it is. Thank you. Before we leave we need to check in with the healer and see how Fenix is doing. And Soleil is insistent on coming with us to Brun."

"It seems everyone wants to come on this adventure," Marco said. "Bibacr said he would meet us there. It seems he wants to be a part of it too. I must admit that I won't rest easy until we get this one done."

Fifteen minutes later they were walking out of her chambers and heading toward sick bay. The healer was waiting for them at the door.

Sascha hesitated. "It's not bad news, is it?"

"Everything is better than expected. It seems the two creatures have had good news but they won't say anything to me until they've talked to you. To be honest, their sweet nothings are driving me around the bend. I'm glad Fenix will be out of here by the end of the day."

Marco chuckled. "Sweet nothings? Since when does Soleil say anything sweet?"

Sascha nudged Marco with her elbow. "Since Soleil has realized he's in love with Fenix. And it's about time." Sascha strode into the healer's room to find Soleil and Fenix sitting up and waiting for her and Marco. "The healer has accused you both of being nice to each other. Is that true?"

"Yes," Soleil said. "We have agreed to put the past in the past and start afresh. Fenix had told me she would never sacrifice what we have for Drakon and I believe her. But that's not the best thing."

Sascha smiled as she glanced at Marco. "So what is the best thing?"

Soleil stuck his chest out. "I have a son and a daughter. Fenix didn't tell me before because she didn't want to force me to be her partner."

Sascha stared openmouthed at them. "You have what?"

"But that's still not the best thing."

"This seems to be a gift that keeps on giving," Marco muttered.

"Because we had the children after you and I were bonded..."

"No," Sascha spluttered. "That means that she and I..."

"Yes," Soleil said, clicking his beak. "The three of us are already bonded."

Marco pulled one of the healer's chairs closer to the pyrans so he could sit down. "So even if Drakon tries to send her to the fifth dimension—"

"Or dies," Soleil muttered.

"She's sa—safe," Sascha stammered. "She's safe and she can stay with us."

Soleil grinned. "Yes, she can."

"And you're sure?" Marco asked.

"I wasn't sure," Soleil said. "So when you headed off for Blencalgo, I took off to see Athena. She contacted Kalurth, and Kalurth confirmed it."

Sascha raced over and hugged them. "That is wonderful news, truly wonderful news. We have to celebrate."

"When we get back from Brun," Soleil said, "Fenix and I thought the four of us could go somewhere and formalize the bonding in our own private ceremony."

"What a fabulous idea," Sascha said. "An absolutely fabulous idea."

Soleil stood. "I guess we'd better go then."

"Why don't you stay here with Fenix?" Sascha said. "One of the war pyrans can take me."

"No. You're not going back to Brun without me."

"Marco, are you able to get someone to organize a set of pyran leathers for Soleil?" Sascha asked.

"I still think it's overkill," Soleil said. "But I agreed to it so I'll do it."

"Come with me, Soleil," Marco said, "and I'll get someone to organize the leathers. I'll also get Rusty too. She can stay with Fenix. I won't be long, Sasch."

Sascha nodded. "Okay." After Soleil and Marco had left Sascha turned to Fenix. "I'm so happy for you, Fenix. It's been a long time but I'm glad it's worked out. One day you'll have to tell me the story about your children and I would love to hear all about how you and Soleil met."

"I will," Fenix said. "Promise me you'll look after him for me. It would be too cruel if I lost him now."

"Of course I'll look after him. He's a father now. He has obligations to fulfill."

Fenix chuckled. "Yes, he does."

∼

ERATUS

Sascha, Marco, and the five mages flew over Blister Barrens, past the mountain range toward the Brun site. As they were nearing the cliffs that overlooked the site they could see a couple of figures on the cliff's edge.

"Is that Kalamar I can see down there?" Marco asked as they circled the area.

"Yes," Soleil snapped. "And I don't believe it but Drakon is there with him."

"Boys, we need to be gracious. Atticus believed it would take both of us to open this site, so let's be grateful he turned up today. I know I am."

"We need to deal with him before we go down to the site," Marco said.

"Let's land where we had planned to," Sascha replied. "I'm sure Drakon will join us. He hasn't come all this way to avoid us."

When they landed at a spot below the clifftop Drakon was spotted, they slid down from their pyrans and waited for Drakon to arrive.

Moments later Drakon landed not far from where they

were, and before Sascha had a chance to say anything, Marco had stormed over to him.

"What the hell were you doing when you left the castle's shield down and the gates open? Do you know how many lives your carelessness could have cost?"

Kalamar stood straighter and fixed his gaze on Marco as Drakon held his hands up in surrender. "Marco, I apologize. I wasn't at my best. Things haven't been . . . right since we got back from seeing Atticus. Especially after Ares' surprise visit."

"Ares?" Sascha asked as she joined them. "I guess he knew about the visit to Atticus then?"

Drakon nodded and rubbed the armband he was wearing.

"We know all about the armband," Marco snarled. "You kept so many secrets from us. So many horrific secrets."

"How did—" Drakon shook his head. "Anyway, it doesn't matter. Ares knew about the band, too. He destroyed the one I was wearing which meant the Ancients had me under their control. They had a task for me to do, and it seems I did it."

"What did they want you to do?" Sascha asked.

Drakon stroked Kalamar's neck. "Do you mind if we talk about that after we have opened this site?"

"Oh, and we will talk about it," Marco said taking a step toward Drakon. "And if it's the last thing I do, I will make sure you pay for what you have done."

Drakon laughed. "I'm struggling to see that happening, Marco—Ever."

"You two, that's enough," Sascha snapped. "Drakon, where did that armband you're wearing come from?"

"Athena gave it to me. Kalamar found her, told her what had happened and she came to rescue me."

"Athena?" Marco asked. "Why would she save you?"

Drakon winked at Marco. "Apparently, I still have my uses. Perhaps she's also worried what damage I would do if I gave in to the voices and became an Ancient. And speaking of damage, are the other people you brought with you the mages I asked for?"

"Yes," Sascha answered. "They're excellent craftsmen. We're lucky to have them." Sascha glanced at the messy state of Drakon's clothes. "It's not like you to look such a mess, Drakon. Are you okay to do this?"

"A mess?" Drakon smirked. "I'll have you know these clothes were freshly laundered only this morning. But in truth, you needed me to help, so here I am."

"Thank you," she said. "We both need each other if we're going to do this."

"I've always said we'd make a good team." Drakon glanced over at Marco and chuckled at the fury on Marco's face.

"Marco, I thought you said Bibacr was going to be here," Sascha said.

"He said he would be. It's unlike him to be late. Maybe something has happened."

"I hope he's okay." Sascha cast a final glance around the area before retrieving the map from the pocket of her leathers. She proceeded to study it. "There's supposed to be a cave to the right of where we're standing now, but I didn't see anything when we were flying over the site."

"Atticus asked you if you knew what to do when an object is hidden in magic's shadow," Drakon said.

"That's right. He did. Let's get as close as we can to where we think the cave is and I'll cast the spell and see what happens."

They walked two hundred feet to the east and then fifty feet to the north.

"According to the map this is the right spot," Sascha said. "Let's try the spell and see what happens."

"Let us see behind magic's shadow
As all magical protections forgo

The powers of green ice, red fire, and dark magic
As I order, let it be so."

Nothing happened.

"I think I saw something shimmer over there," Soleil said directing their gaze to a spot farther to the east. "Why don't we try there?"

They followed Soleil until they reached the spot where he had seen the shimmer. "It might not be it but it's worth a try, Sascha," he said.

She recited the spell a second time and this time the scene in front of them dissolved. In its place stood the entrance to a cave.

Marco picked Sascha up in a hug and swung her around. "You did it. You did it." He kissed her smack on the lips and then placed her back on the ground.

Sascha laughed. "So that's all a girl has to do to get a kiss from you?"

"I'm a lot easier to please," Drakon said.

"Pipe down, Drakon," Marco said.

Drakon's voice chilled. "Don't forget who you're talking to, Marco. No one tells a High King to . . . *pipe down."*

"But a High King doesn't abandon his kingdom to the akhult and paralyze the only witnesses to his crimes."

Drakon raised an eyebrow as he studied Marco. "Paralyzes—what are you talking about Marco? I didn't—"

"That's enough, you two," Sascha said. "We have a job to do. There's a skull and crossbones on the map. What creature do you think that represents?"

"Pit hounds," Drakon answered. "Or destruction by fire. If you try to open the entrance to the site incorrectly you get attacked by pit hounds. If you try to open the trapdoor leading to the underground city without following the appropriate steps of the ritual, you get destroyed by fire."

"Right," Sascha said. "Nothing to worry about then?"

Drakon smirked. "That's right. Nothing to worry about. The good news is, if it's the same method to open this site as it is to open the one on Earth, I know what to do."

"And if it isn't?" Marco asked.

"If it isn't, we're in a lot of trouble."

They walked into the cave and up to a sealed stone door.

"Now what?" Sascha asked.

Drakon rubbed his hand over a patch of stone beside the door to reveal five orbs. "They look as if they're the same colors as the ones on Earth. One red orb and one white. Two blue ones, one with a faded symbol engraved into the stone surface below it. The final orb is black."

"Are they definitely the same colors as the ones you found on Earth?" Sascha asked.

Drakon nodded. "We need to press these orbs in the right order. And if luck is still on our side, there will be four elements engraved into the middle of the door, which I will reveal by one of my many magical talents. If we get all this right, we're in."

"And if we get it wrong, we're attacked by pit hounds?" Marco asked.

"Yes. But surely a brave warrior like you, Marco, isn't afraid of a few pit hounds. Before I do anything…" Drakon retrieved a parcel wrapped in wide leaves from a pocket inside his jacket. "I have to clean the surface. The magic won't work if the surface is too filthy."

"You're kidding me," Marco said. "The magic won't work because it's too dirty?"

Drakon chuckled. "Of course you wouldn't understand, Marco. I forgot that you still have a lot to learn about the more technical aspects of magic. But to make it simple for you, layers of dirt can hide magical elements. Magic is an exact science. It's not like swinging a sword and hoping you hit something."

"Drakon," Sascha warned.

Drakon bowed before her and gave a flourishing sweep with one hand. "I apologize, My Lady."

"Get to it then," Marco said. "Time is not on our side."

"I know," Drakon muttered. "Believe me I know."

Drakon unwrapped the leaves. Inside the parcel was a shirt that had been torn into shreds and soaked into water. "I used the leaves to stop the shirt from drying out."

"Please, Drakon," Marco said. "We don't have time for science lessons."

Once Drakon had cleaned the door he stood back and stretched his sore muscles. He grinned. "I can feel the magic now." Drakon flexed his fingers and took a step back.

"There's a secret here I know, element of air, the secret show."

Four symbols—the symbols of fire, earth, water and air—shimmered in the center of the door.

Drakon chuckled. "It is the same, exactly the same."

He pressed the elements as the magic lit each one up in turn. He did the same with the orbs. When the last two orbs lit up, he hesitated. "This would have to be the same too, wouldn't it?"

"What's wrong?" Sascha asked.

"I only press one of these two orbs. Last time I pressed the white orb. I'm hoping this is the same."

"And if it isn't?"

"We'd better be prepared to fight pit hounds."

Marco drew his sword. "Let's get this over and done with."

"My thoughts exactly," Drakon said.

"Hey." Marco pointed to the door. "The glow has disappeared."

"Damn it," Drakon said. "It's all timed. I took too long. I need to do it again."

Drakon repeated the process and it came down to the last two orbs. He moved his hand to the white orb and was about to press down on it when he changed his mind at the last second and pressed the black one.

"What did you do that for?" Sascha asked. "Why did you change?"

"I had a sudden feeling. . . ."

Everything had fallen silent.

"Did it work?" Marco asked.

A grinding sound reverberated below them. Moments later, the large stone door started to move. "It worked," Sascha said. "Good on you, Drakon. It worked."

As they stepped into the cave a wave of musty air wafted around them. A misty figure whipped past them and flew into the cave.

"What the hell was that," Marco said.

"Bibacr, is that you?" Sascha called out. There was no response. "I could have sworn it was Bibacr." Sascha withdrew the autobot from her satchel and put it on the palm of her hand. The light on it flicked green as it turned around several times before it decided on a direction and took off. "Come on, everyone. Let's go."

"What is that thing, Sascha?" Drakon asked.

"It senses the magic of the weapons."

"Did you get it from Atticus?"

Sascha hesitated and then nodded. "Yes, I did."

"He obviously didn't trust me to have it. Maybe he knew what was going to happen to me."

"You don't think he really knew, do you?" Sascha asked. "He would have warned one of us."

"Would he?" Drakon asked.

The autobot was moving quickly, so they abandoned the conversation to race after it. When the autobot stopped, they were in a large auditorium lined with seats. At one end of the auditorium was a stage.

"Everything is so similar to the site on Earth," Drakon said. "But it's strange . . ."

"What's strange?" Sascha asked.

"Who lit the torches?" Drakon asked. "This cave has been sealed for centuries and yet the torches are lit."

"Bibacr light torches," a voice said from the shadows.

"Bibacr," Sascha cried out as she raced toward the spindly creature. "I thought it was you. Why didn't you talk to us?"

Bibacr peeked at Drakon. "Bibacr worried about Sascha and Soleil. Bibacr came to stop Ancients."

"The Ancients are here?" Drakon asked.

"Bibacr know Ancients want to escape when door to city is opened. Bibacr not let Ancients escape." He giggled. "Bibacr lock them in."

Sascha turned to Drakon. "Did you see any Ancients in the site on Earth?"

"I think our focus should be on opening this site and destroying the weapons?" Drakon said. "Not what happened on Earth. We don't have a lot of time."

Sascha glanced at Drakon and then turned back to Bibacr. "How will you lock them in, Bibacr?"

"Bibacr go first when door to underground city is open. Bibacr lock Ancients in city."

"Okay," Sascha said. "You can go first. But we will help you."

Bibacr gave a vigorous shake to his head. "Bibacr do this on his own. Bibacr not need help."

"You trust this creature of darkness?" Drakon asked. "He might be leading us all into a trap."

"Bibacr Sascha's friend," Bibacr growled. "Bibacr help Sascha."

"Let's not argue. Drakon, it's over to you to open the door

to the underground city. Then we can plant the explosives, the beacon, and the treatment, and get out of here."

Drakon walked up onto the stage of the auditorium and found the same five-pointed star. "I would advise that everyone watch from up here while the mages and I open the door. If we fail a massive fire ball will flash through that area down there. Nothing could survive it."

Everyone shuffled up onto the stage. As Drakon moved to the middle of a five-pointed star engraved into the stage's floor, Kalamar emitted a soft warble and flew down to perch on the back of one of the seats not far from where they all stood. Sascha glimpsed a smile on Drakon's face as he looked over at Kalamar

Should I be worried? Is there something going on here that I can't see?

"Mages, take your positions on the star. Stand next to the element you are strongest in."

The mages positioned themselves around the engraving. Drakon glanced around him to make sure everyone was ready as he retrieved his bollock dagger. He tapped the bottom of the pommel three times. The blade glowed and the pommel extended as the blade changed to the color of ice.

"I never realized his dagger was a staff," Marco said. "That man seems to be full of surprises."

When the room fell silent, Drakon spoke again. "Drink your vials, and focus your powers. When I say so, direct your powers to the top of my staff."

"As you command," the mages answered in unison.

The mages retrieved their vials, drank them down, and placed the empty vials in their cloak pockets. They lifted their staffs toward the roof of the cave as they chanted. Colored lights spilled into the air above them, forming luminous arcs of red, green, gold, orange, and blue.

Standing with his feet planted firmly apart, Drakon drank

the contents of his vial, closed his eyes, and raised his staff. After a minute, he opened his eyes and concentrated on the lights. "Now!" he yelled. The mages slowly lowered their magic until it touched his staff. When all colors were touching the top of his staff, Drakon twirled it, blending the colors together until they formed a perfect white light. In one quick movement, he lowered the staff with a sharp thump onto the tile below his feet.

This time the magic didn't flash; instead, the room went quiet. Too quiet.

"Damn," Drakon muttered.

Sascha watched as Drakon glanced at his armband.

"This band is different," he said. "Why didn't I think of that before."

Sascha looked at Marco, unsure of what to do. Should they run, or—

The ground shook and the tile Drakon was standing on rumbled as it moved aside. Drakon jumped off it as a set of stairs leading down into the bowels of the cave appeared in the newly formed opening.

Drakon breathed a sigh of relief. "It's okay," he called out. "It worked."

"Thank Athena," Marco muttered.

Sascha walked to the top of the stairs. "Bibacr, you go first."

"Sascha wait until Bibacr say it's safe."

"Yes, we'll wait."

As Bibacr raced down the stairs, the torches flickered into life, making it easy to see the path they were to take.

Moments later Bibacr called out to them. "Sascha follow now."

When they arrived at the bottom of the stairs, they stared around in awe. They were surrounded by a small, perfectly preserved but uninhabited city.

"What an exceptional place," Marco said as he strolled toward the closest building.

"Marco not go into the city," Bibacr called out. "Bibacr put up magic door to lock in Ancients. Ancients asleep at the moment."

"Asleep?" Marco repeated.

Bibacr nodded. "Ancients not wake or their powers and memories return."

Marco stopped where he was. "Sorry, Bibacr. I won't go any farther. This place. It truly is something to see."

Sascha scanned the cavern and spotted a familiar sight near the far wall. "The crates of weapons are over there," she said. "Let's do what we have to do and get out of here."

"And then, Sascha," Drakon said, "can I talk to you? I need your help with something. I'm afraid there's something else we need to do before we're finished."

CONFESSION

ERATUS

*D*rakon stood at the entrance to the cave as he waited for the others to finish off placing the explosives and the treatments. He didn't understand how the beacon system worked, but Atticus had seemed certain it would advise them of their success or failure in destroying the weapons. His stomach churned.

I only hope Atticus isn't betraying us, too.

In the cave Bibacr had said something that had given him an idea on how to sort out his issue with remembering the sites he sabotaged. But would it work?

I will have to be strong. But I cannot and will not allow the Ancients to control me. That is too bitter a pill to swallow.

Sascha arrived and strode over to Drakon. She stood in front of him, her arms crossed and her foot tapping the ground. "Out with it, Drakon. Before the others get here. What's happened?"

"I might know how to fix it, but I will need your help."

"Fix what?"

"Ares destroyed my armband because he wanted me to

work for him, or more accurately, he wanted me to serve the ones he referred to as the new rulers of Eratus. The Ancients."

"What did he want you to do?"

"The Ancients want to use the weapons to help them regain control of Eratus. I was sent to destroy the treatments you had installed—well, at least destroy the treatments at three of the sites. I don't think they believe they need any more than three sites."

"And did you?"

"I can't remember. It's all fuzzy. I do remember fighting the instructions, trying to find another way of doing what they wanted done. And I also remember thinking that I wanted to be able to fix it if I was ever freed from their control."

Sascha turned her back on Drakon. He watched her shoulders rise and fall as she breathed out the stress of what he had just told her.

"I don't think I removed the treatments," Drakon said. "I'm sure that all I did was undo the wires. Which means all we need to do is attach them again."

Sascha turned back to face him. "Which sites?"

Drakon gave a frustrated sigh. "I can't remember which sites. But Bibacr gave me an idea. If we take this armband off me, the voices will return, and, with any luck, so will the memories."

Feet crunched on gravel as the others arrived to join them.

"And when were you going to tell the rest of us what you did, Drakon?" Marco asked as he moved closer to Sascha.

"How much of what I said did you hear, Marco?"

"Enough to know we have a huge problem."

"I want to fix what I did," Drakon said. "And I believe the

only hope we have is if someone removes my band. But if you agree to that, I need Sascha and the mages to bind me with magic. If I had black lyrium I would take that. But all I can hope is that the magic of Sascha and the mages is enough to hold me."

"I don't understand why we need all that protection," Sascha said.

"You have no idea what the Ancients are capable of, Sascha, or, how powerful I am without the band. I turned off the defensive shield without anyone even registering it was no longer on. I opened the gates to the castle on my own and I even dismantled the magical shields that your people erected to protect the sites with the weapons. What sort of magic do you think that would take?"

"Drakon, what is your plan?" Sascha asked.

"You and the mages bind me. You or Marco would need to remove my armband and ask me which sites I visited. And then," he said, taking a deep breath, "I'm trusting you to put the armband back on."

"What happens if we don't put the band on?" Marco asked.

"Then I want you to kill me. It's better for me to die now than be a pawn in a game I can't win."

"A pawn in a game you can't win," Marco repeated. "That sounds like a fitting punishment to me."

~

ERATUS

The cool winds whipped around them as Sascha and the mages circled Drakon. Marco stood next to him, ready to remove the band when Sascha instructed him to do so.

Drakon took a deep breath and exhaled slowly as he tried

to manage the fear that was building inside him. What if the magic didn't hold? What if they couldn't stop him and the Ancients forced him to kill Sascha? They hated her.

But I have no choice. I have to do this. I will protect Sascha with every grain of magic I have left.

"Are you ready, Drakon?" Sascha asked.

"Yes, I'm ready." He closed his eyes as he sensed the golden magic wind itself around him. He allowed his mind to calm. The world around him vanished and was replaced by mists and dark clouds. He walked through them as he searched for where he was supposed to go.

Where is the pain?

The mists parted and he could see the skeleton of Demipos lying on the ground in front of him. "What is going on here? Have I been tricked?"

The ground around the skeleton was covered with ash and bone and a faint, slightly metallic odor filled the air.

"It's time for you to fulfill your destiny," a raspy voice said to him. "And what better place to do that than where it all started."

The voices, they're here. But there is no pain. Where is the pain?

The mists parted and Drakon saw four creatures with long, emaciated frames, three times his height, sitting on their thrones. They looked down at him. In the middle of the four thrones was a fifth throne. The fifth throne was empty.

"You're—you're here," Drakon stammered. "And there is no pain."

"Of course we're here, Drakon," the voice continued. "There's no pain, because this time you won't be leaving. You did accept the invitation to become one of us."

I didn't . . .

"All you needed was time. You had Athena's band, yet you willingly took it off. You made it easy for us to perform the magical transformation on you by asking the mages to bind you. You have been very obliging."

I didn't . . .

The creatures laughed and then the voice continued. "Together we will rule over Eratus, as we should have been doing for centuries. Athena should have never stopped us, but she will pay the price for her betrayal. In a few minutes, your transformation will begin and you will become who you were always meant to be."

"What sites did you visit?" Marco's voice echoed around him.

Drakon shook his head. "What did you . . ."

"What sites did you visit?" Marco's voice repeated.

A sharp, screeching pain sliced through Drakon's head, bringing him to his knees. "You will not answer the question," the voice said. "You will do what you are told. It is you who chose this path. You cannot undo destiny."

"Sascha, it's not working," Marco's voice called out.

"Repeat the question one more time," Sascha answered.

Sascha's voice was like a cool cloth to his head, easing his pain. He couldn't let her down.

"What sites did you visit?" Marco snapped.

"Do not answer them," the voice screamed at him.

"I remember," Drakon said. "I know the answer. Kilmarnock, Dalhurst, and Skystead." A bolt of pain slashed through him. His heart pounded in his chest. The winds that whipped around him felt like they were made of acid and every breath of it burned.

"Quickly," Sascha's voice called out. "Put the band on, we're losing him."

Drakon glared at the creatures who were now on their feet, moving toward him, their limbs swayed with every movement. They were giggling and speaking to each other in a language he couldn't understand.

If only I had one of those vials with me. . . . That's it. That's how I can finally free myself.

Everything went black as the pain disappeared and Drakon allowed himself to collapse onto the ground.

ERATUS

"Drakon?" It was Sascha's voice.

I made it! And I finally know how I can free myself.

"Drakon, can you hear me?"

"Yes," Drakon drawled. His tongue refused to work properly. His mouth was as dry as a desert.

"Water, I need some water."

Somebody lifted his head and a cool sweet liquid was poured into his mouth. He was in heaven. A heartbreaking cry floated on the air around him.

"He's alive, Kalamar," Sascha said. "Come and look for yourself."

Drakon smiled at the wet snuffling sound close to his ear as Kalamar's head nudged him.

"Kalamar," Drakon croaked. "I'm fine, my pet."

Kalamar gave him another, slightly firmer, nudge before lying down on the ground next to him.

Drakon opened his eyes to see that Sascha was holding him in her arms as she sat cross-legged on the ground.

"You saved me, Sascha."

"Drakon, you saved so many innocent lives today. Marco and three of the mages have already left for the three sites. They will fix the treatments so that everything works. The question for you and me to resolve is where you stay during the season of the three moons. It's not really possible for you to be High King. If something happened and you lost the band, the Ancients would gain control of the throne."

"Sascha, as much as I want to do whatever pleases you, it is Athena who decides who becomes High King. Not you."

"Drakon, I thought you would—"

Drakon pushed himself out of Sascha's arms and up onto his feet. The horizon tilted at a weird angle and the ground swirled around his feet as he tried to force his hollow legs to keep him upright.

"You thought I would give up the one thing I've wanted all my life—the throne."

"Drakon, please. This is your chance to make things right."

"I won't give up the throne, Sascha, even for you." Drakon felt his heart break. She would come to realize he was right. She had to.

He reached down to help Sascha stand, but she waved his hand away.

"Drakon, we can't let you back into the castle."

He watched, confused, as Sascha nodded at the mages. She turned away from him and began to walk toward Soleil.

Kalamar screamed but it was too late. Circles of yellow light shimmered around Drakon. He couldn't move. He wanted to call for Sascha, tell her to undo the magic, release him, but he couldn't speak. He saw Kalamar hunker down ready to attack but then stopped, a roar rumbling deep in his chest.

"Well isn't this a lovely sight," a silvery voice called out from behind him. "The package I'm here for is wrapped and ready for me to take."

Drakon watched as the color drained from Sascha's face. "Hello, Laela," she said.

"Laela?" Drakon tried to move but he felt as if he were buried in wet sand. He had to help Sascha. Laela couldn't take her again.

Laela chuckled. "Hello, Sascha. It feels like it's been ages.

We must do vimberry sometime and catch up. And believe me, we will catch up. But today you and I have to put our differences aside. Hades has sent me here for Drakon. Something about him trying to change his destiny. And here he is. Prepackaged and ready for transportation. This is too easy."

She wants me. Not Sascha. There's no way I'm going with her.

He tried to call out to Sascha, to say anything, but he had no voice.

"I won't let you take him, Laela," Sascha said. "This won't be as easy as you first thought. Haven't you noticed the mages?"

"Are you sure they're with you, Sascha?"

Sascha shook her head. "The mages have matured a lot since you've left. They no longer owe you any allegiance."

Laela cackled. "You really are just as naive as you were the day I met you. Excuse me for a minute." She retrieved a wand from a pocket inside her shirt and extended it. She circled the wand in the air and a soft whirring sound echoed around them as a large circle of spinning air opened. "There," Laela said, stepping back and placing her hands on her hips to examine her work. "It won't be long before it's completely open."

"Not this again. Laela, you've tried this before and it didn't work. It won't work this time either."

"I've always loved challenges," Laela said. She smiled at the mages. "And I do have Graven and Sinarka to help me."

The two mages faced Sascha, brought their hands together, and bowed their heads for a brief second. They let their hands fall to their sides and then rested their right hands on their staffs before starting to walk slowly in Laela's direction.

"May Athena guide your magic," Sascha said.

Laela sniggered. "I've stolen two of your mages and all

you do is give them Athena's blessing? I thought you cared a lot more than that about your own people."

"Nothing is ever what it seems, Laela."

The mages stopped about twenty feet from Laela.

Laela sighed. "I'll never understand you, Sascha. Mages, bring Drakon here. I'll keep guard so Sascha or that creature of hers don't do anything."

Sascha, don't let her take me.

He had to stop this from happening, but he couldn't.

The mages were looking at Drakon when Kalamar flew into action. A high-pitched screech echoed around them, followed by a blood-chilling scream as Kalamar dropped to the ground. Laela stood in front of the portal, a smile on her face and blood on the blade in her hand.

"Surely that's not the best you can do, Sascha."

The air was filled with screams that ripped at Drakon's heart. Kalamar lay writhing in agony on the ground, blood pooling around him.

No! Kalamar! Athena save my creature.

Drakon tried again to scream out to Sascha, ask her to help Kalamar but his voice was silent. He had to help Kalamar. He had to do something.

"Mages, I told you to bring Drakon here. And make it fast. The portal is closing."

The mages glanced at Sascha, who nodded.

Together they lifted their staffs and created a swirling vortex of air. They flicked their hands and sent the whirlwind toward Laela. The winds plucked a screaming Laela from the ground and carried her into the portal. The portal closed and Laela was gone.

In the ensuing silence, Kalamar's cries seemed louder and more desperate.

"Mages, release Drakon," Sascha called out.

Free from the spell, Drakon half-raced, half-stumbled over to Kalamar. "No, not Kalamar. Sascha, please help him."

"Mages, the selecine," Sascha ordered. "Quickly."

Sascha raced over and squatted next to Kalamar as the mages arrived with the selecine. They handed it to her and she slathered Kalamar's wounds with it. The creature's cries started to quieten. "I can help Kalamar in the same way I helped Soleil, but he won't be able to fly anywhere, not for now."

"We need to get him under cover," Drakon said. "He can't stay out here in the open."

"The only place here is the cave where the weapons are," Sascha said.

"Well, we'll take him there. If you follow the instructions Atticus gave you on how to destroy the weapons, the cave should be safe enough for us."

"Us?" Sascha repeated.

"Kalamar and me. I'm not leaving him here alone."

"Why not? He has a better chance of survival than you do."

"Would you leave Soleil?"

Sascha shook her head.

"Kalamar is the one creature that never abandoned me, never gave up. I will not leave him."

"Moments ago, you were determined to keep the throne. Is it even possible that you would give that up for your fire dragon?"

"I am only giving up the fight for now. The throne is mine. I will be coming to take what's mine when the time is right. But for now, Kalamar must come first."

Sascha shook her head. "You will need to protect yourself with some magical barrier, at least until the weapons are destroyed. We will send you supplies, enough for the both of you."

"We will only need supplies until he can fly. Then I plan on taking him to join his family. That's where we will stay until the end of the storm season. The only matter that remains is for you to flick the switch and destroy the weapons. Let's hope the magical shields that secure the area with the weapons are sufficient. I guess I'll be the first person to know if they don't work."

DESTRUCTION OF THE WEAPONS

ERATUS

The three moons were full, providing Sascha plenty of light as she paced along the ramparts. She kept checking the horizon, looking for any sign of the pyrans. The soldiers had told her that Marco had collected three of his men on the way to the sites so that they could help him protect the mages.

If he has his soldiers and the mages, he has to be okay. But he should be back by now.

Drakon and Kalamar were as well supplied, and protected, as they could be, especially considering where they were staying. There would come a time when everyone would have to agree on a strategy to deal with Drakon but that would be a fight for another day. For now she had work to do. Once Marco returned, the two of them would join the rest of the group in the tavern. There she would collect everyone's codes and enter them into the SAWA40 application. Then they could finally destroy the weapons.

"Where the hell is he?" she snapped. "He's taking longer to do the three sites than we took to do the twelve."

"Flyers coming this way," a soldier called out.

Sascha squinted as she searched for the flyers. Her heart was in her mouth.

Please let it be Marco.

"They're ours," the guard called out as he deactivated the shield. Sascha tore off down the stairs and watched as the pyrans landed.

There were seven pyrans but she could only see six riders. The seventh pyran was riderless.

Who didn't make it?

Sascha studied the men as they clambered off their pyrans. Their shoulders were slumped, and they dragged their gear behind them. They were exhausted and while they glanced in her direction none of them were prepared to meet her eyes. For a moment she forgot to breathe. She could see Zabir, Rohan, Crestwell, and the three mages.

Where the hell is Marco?

"Marco," she whimpered. "No." She shook her head slowly. "Please Athena. Don't let anything have happened to Marco."

"Are you looking for me?" a deep husky voice said behind her.

"Marco!" Sascha screamed as she whipped around and threw herself into his arms. "You made it. You're safe."

"Of course I made it. You've promised me a . . . . reward . . . . tonight for being a good boy, if you remember. There's no way I'm missing out on that."

Sascha pushed herself away from him and whacked him across the arm with all her strength. "How come you weren't on your pyran with the others?"

Marco rubbed his arm and chuckled. "I had to talk to one of the guards, so my pyran dropped me off on the roof of the western tower."

"You had me worried, you great big oaf."

"Well maybe tonight you can show me just how worried

you were," he said wrapping his arms around her. She snuggled into him. Sascha felt the strong beat of his heart as she rested her head on his chest. She was so grateful he was alive.

"You were able to fix the damage Drakon did?"

"Yes. We double-checked everything, and the mages have sealed the weapons areas, as well as the caves. Everything should be good now. If this all works."

A knot formed in Sascha's stomach. "I have to admit it will be a huge relief when this part is over."

"I agree." After a minute Marco released her. "I told the others we'd meet them in the tavern in fifteen minutes. Let's get the computer and then we can finish this bloody nightmare off. Let's kill us some weapons."

Sascha laughed. "That sounds like a good plan to me."

"What happened with Drakon?" Marco asked.

"It's a long story. I'll tell you everything later, but for now he's hunkered down in the cave at Brun nursing a badly wounded Kalamar."

"You left him at the weapons site after everything he's done?"

"I know what you're thinking. It's the same thing I thought, but we had no choice. I'm hoping I don't regret my decision."

"What if he does something to sabotage the destruction of the weapons at that site?" Drakon asked.

"I guess we'll know soon," Sascha said. "SAWA40 will tell us. And as far as his crimes are concerned, one way or another he will pay. I'm sure Athena will see to that."

"Athena is the one who helped him escape, and gave him her band," Marco said.

"That was to help us destroy the weapons. And if he betrays her . . . . "

"You have more faith in how this is all going to work out than I do, Sasch?" Marco said.

Sascha sighed. "Let's talk about it later. We've other things to focus on now."

Five minutes later they were walking into the tavern with the computer.

"Drinks are already on the table," Zabir said. "We're desperate to see if we succeeded so come on, you two."

" 'You two' . . . what happened to 'Colonel'?" Marco laughed. "No respect." He pulled out a chair for Sascha and one for himself.

Sascha mouthed her thanks to Marco as she sat. "Okay, this is the moment we've been waiting for," she said. "Can I have everyone's codes?"

Once she had the codes she turned on the computer and opened the application. Sascha wiped her hands on her jacket, picked up her prumble ale, and swilled it down. She held the empty glass up to Marco. "I need another one."

Marco grinned as he signaled the tavern keeper for a top up.

It only took her a few minutes to type in all the codes. "Okay, that's done," Sascha said. "Now the instructions say I have to press the green light for the weapons and then seven seconds later, the blue light for the treatments. You would think there would be some counter on this supposedly powerful computer, but there isn't. Who will be my counter?"

"I will," Zabir said.

"Okay. Start counting aloud the moment I press the green light."

"Will do," Zabir said.

"Everyone ready?" Sascha asked, glancing at the expectant faces seated around the table.

"Let's do this," Marco replied.

Sascha took a deep breath. "Clicking the green light on . . . now."

Zabir began to count aloud. "One, two, three, four, five, six, SEVEN!"

Sascha pressed the blue light and every pair of eyes was drawn to the computer's black screen. The name SAWA40 flickered at the top of the screen, but there was nothing else.

"How long would it take for it to register if it was successful or not?" Zabir asked.

"I don't know," Sascha said. "I didn't think of asking that question."

They all continued to stare at the computer screen while they sipped nervously at their drinks.

After five minutes, there was still no action. The screen remained black.

"Maybe the application doesn't work," Crestwell said.

"Take it easy, Crestwell," Marco said. "When the explosions happen it would have to—"

The computer beeped. "Look," Sascha exclaimed. "It's working." Blue text started to flick up on the screen.

"What does it say?" Marco asked.

Sascha smiled. "Awakening HQ, successful."

The table brimmed with excitement as everyone started to realize what they had achieved.

"It's working," Marco sighed. "It's actually working."

"There's more," Sascha said. "Blencalgo, successful; Freehaven, successful; Whitebone, successful." The names flooded in, then stopped.

"How many names are there?" Marco asked.

Sascha counted, then recounted. "Thirteen."

"That's it," Marco said. "There were only thirteen sites."

"The thirteen sites didn't include the Awakening headquarters."

"Damn. You're right. Which one is missing?"

Sascha paused for a moment, chewing her lip. "Brun. Brun is the only one missing. But surely he wouldn't—"

The SAWA40 beeped. "Brun, successful."

The table erupted as everyone jumped up to hug each other and congratulate Marco and Sascha.

Zabir raised his glass. "Let's make a toast, to the best Colonel of the Fire of the Phoenix and the best leader of the Four Sisters. To Marco and Sascha."

"Hear, hear." There was a murmur of agreement as glasses clinked together.

After a few minutes Sascha left the group and walked outside into the cool night air. Two of the moons were high in the sky while the third still rested on the horizon.

There's one more matter to sort out before I can relax. I need to do what Atticus didn't and make sure the explosions really did work and the weapons were destroyed.

"What are you doing out here, Sascha?" Marco's voice sounded behind her. "Are you thinking about Drakon?"

"No," Sascha said. "When Atticus tried to destroy the weapons last time, his greatest regret was not checking to see if everything worked as he had expected it to. We cannot make the same mistake."

"What are you saying, Sasch?"

"I need to check that the weapons really were destroyed. I thought about inspecting the Awakening headquarters, but it's too close—and it's under our shield. If the treatment hasn't worked . . ."

"It could be catastrophic," Marco said.

"Exactly."

Marco stood silently as he stared at the memorial bell in the tavern gardens. "What did you want to do?"

Sascha knew Marco wasn't going to be happy with her idea, but it made sense. She stood tall as she turned to face Marco. "I want to check the site in Brun."

Marco scrubbed his face with his hands. "Is it the weapons you're worried about or Drakon?"

"Brun is the only site where there is a witness to what happened when we released the explosions and the treatments."

Marco put his hand on Sascha's shoulder. "Sascha, you do realize that if the magical barriers didn't keep the explosions and weapons contained, then Drakon will be dead?"

"If the barriers didn't work then our problem is bigger than Drakon's death," Sascha replied.

Marco lifted his hand from her shoulder and trailed his fingers down the side of her face. "Well, I'm coming with you."

Soleil dropped down from the edge of the tavern roof. "And so am I."

"I want to do this alone," Sascha said. "It's easier for one person to—"

Marco shook his head. "You can't keep us here. And we're not letting you go on your own."

"Soleil, you're a father. You need to stay and look after your family."

"You heard Marco, Sascha. We won't let you go alone. And if we die, Fenix will kill you."

Sascha chuckled. "That makes no sense, Soleil."

"When did you want to do it?" Marco asked.

Sascha listened to the raucous, happy hollers coming from the tavern. "Now. Let's get this over with. We could be back within a couple of hours." She nodded at the tavern. "And none of them will be any the wiser."

Marco stepped past Sascha as he headed toward the tavern door. "I should tell Zabir."

Sascha took a step forward and grabbed his arm. "Let's tell them when it's all over."

Marco stopped walking and glanced back at Sascha. "We need to let someone know what we're doing."

"I will tell Bibacr when I see him," Sascha said. "I'll also leave a note for the girls. Zabir deserves a break. Anyway, apart from that, he's had too much to drink to be useful."

"I'll let the soldiers know we're leaving for a couple of hours," Marco said. "They need to manage the security around the shield. Are you sure a couple of hours will be sufficient time, Sascha?"

"It shouldn't take any longer than that. We're just checking in on things. We don't have to do anything—at least, I hope not."

"I'll collect my blades," Marco said. "It might be worth you doing the same. My blades reacted to the akhult when Zabir and I were in Unidern. That means the creatures are connected to dark magic."

"Which means the Blades of Light could come in handy?" Sascha said.

"Yes, they could."

"Would you take Soleil with you, Marco, and organize another set of leathers for him?"

"I don't need leathers," Soleil snapped.

"You're the one who warned me about what Fenix would do to me if something happened to you. I don't think I can afford to take that chance, now, can I?"

Soleil clicked his beak at her.

Sascha watched Marco and Soleil leave. She had to find Bibacr and make sure the barrier he had set was still in place. The last thing she wanted was for them to be attacked by the Ancients while they were down there. "Athena protect us. I can't lose these two. Not now."

∼

THEY ARRIVED in Brun and circled above the cave. The moonlight reflected off a magical blue barrier that covered the entire area. Underneath the barrier Sascha could see that the electrical forcefield they had set up in front of the entrance to the cave was still in place.

"That blue barrier is intriguing," Sascha said. "Drakon must have wanted extra protection."

As they moved closer to get a better look, they saw a horde of akhult lurking two hundred yards or so from the blue barrier.

Marco took his glove off, licked his index finger and raised it in the air. "Drakon would have been protecting himself from the akhult. The good news is that the winds are blowing away from the creatures. At least the winds won't carry our scent to them. If we fly in quietly we should be able to get in and out of the cave without them knowing."

As they landed in front of the blue barrier Sascha studied it. "It looks like Drakon has used air magic to create this, so I should be able to destroy it using fire magic."

Marco glanced in the direction of the akhult. "Can you do it quietly?"

"Seriously, Marco?"

"Do you think Drakon put this barrier up because the protection around the weapons was destroyed in the explosions?" Soleil asked.

"What do you mean?" Marco asked.

"He might have been worried about the weapons escaping and killing everyone."

Marco laughed and then quickly covered his hand with his mouth. "Sorry, that slipped out before I could stop it. Soleil, do you think it would even occur to Drakon to save others?"

"He did put himself at risk to look after Kalamar," Soleil snapped.

"Marco and Soleil, soon you won't have to worry about my magic attracting the akhult. Keep up that fighting and you'll be the ones attracting them."

She was reluctant to admit it, but she had thought the same thing Soleil had. It was easier to ignore when it had been just a thought, but now that Soleil had voiced her fear, it seemed so much more terrifying. "Soleil has a point, which means that we need to be prepared. If the weapons did escape, then we have a real problem—and so do those akhult."

"It is ironic to think that this land could be free of akhult if we kept the weapons we are so desperate to destroy," Marco said.

"This land would also be free of us, our protectors, and anyone else who carries the genetic mix those weapons destroy."

"I was only thinking aloud," Marco said.

Sascha raised her hands and pictured fire. As the fire came to life and flowed between the palms of her hands, she manipulated it to form a ball. Using all her strength, she threw it toward the barrier. The barrier shook under the impact of the fire, but didn't disappear.

"It looks like this might take a few attempts to destroy," Sascha said. She raised her hands and created another, larger ball of fire. After several more fireballs, the barrier finally flickered and then disappeared.

"Yes," Sascha said. "It's done."

Sascha walked back to Soleil and took her blades out of the satchel attached to his harness. "Soleil, you and the war pyran stand watch. Warn us the moment it looks like the akhult are heading our way. Are you ready, Marco?"

Marco nodded.

Sascha walked toward the electrical forcefield. When she was only several feet away she cast a spell to shut it down. She moved toward the cave and took a step inside. She placed her blades in her jacket pocket as she stared into the darkness. "Where are all the torches?"

Marco joined Sascha and put his arm around her waist. "Maybe the torches have run out of oil? If we take it slowly and light the torches as we go, we should be OK."

"That's not the point, Marco. We set up a site for Drakon and Kalamar about two hundred feet ahead. We should see the light from their camp or that of the barrier he set up to protect them."

"That is strange," Marco said. "Let's make a move and see if we can find the two of them."

It didn't take long to find the site that had been set up for Drakon. "It's strange," Sascha muttered. "The supplies are still here but Drakon and Kalamar have disappeared." Goose bumps raced across Sascha's skin. "What could have happened to them?"

"Perhaps Kalamar carried Drakon somewhere else," Marco said.

"He couldn't have. Kalamar was badly wounded by Laela's blade. It was touch and go whether he would survive. There's no way he could have flown anywhere."

"Maybe they've moved farther into the cave?" Marco said. "They could have gone to the underground city?"

"I don't see how Drakon could have helped Kalamar to move that far when it took the mages, myself, and Drakon to carry Kalamar to here. I guess there is a possibility the barrier around the weapons was destroyed and the weapons killed Drakon."

"Let's go and inspect the barrier you set up around the weapons then," Marco said.

They arrived at the auditorium a few minutes later and looked around. There was no sign of Drakon or Kalamar. They moved toward the staircase leading down to the under-ground city and after lighting the first couple of torches, made their way down the icy, slippery stairs.

Their sense of awe as they arrived at the bottom of the

stairs was as powerful as it had been the first time they had seen the underground city. Marco ambled closer to the buildings nearest to him but he obviously remembered Bibacr's warning because he was careful not to go too close. "Sascha, did you talk to Bibacr about the barrier he put around the city?"

"Yes, he said the barrier would still be in place. He told me to remind you that you're not allowed to go exploring the city."

Marco smiled. "I'm not that silly. As long as the Ancients stay asleep I'll be happy."

"Hopefully we'll be out of here soon."

"It looks like Drakon's not here either." Marco pointed at the place where the crates of weapons had once stood. "But your barrier survived."

"Which means Drakon and Kalamar couldn't have been killed by the weapons." Sascha shrugged her shoulders and sighed with frustration. "I have no idea where they could be."

Sascha moved forward to look through the barrier. Broken crates scattered the ground and scorch marks could be seen on the floor and up the wall. On the floor, blinking green, was the beacon.

"Didn't you say that if the beacon is green, that's a good sign?" Marco asked.

"That's what Atticus said, but he also said the report had to come back successful."

"Which is what happened," Marco said.

"Yes. So all the signs of success are there. But to be on the safe side, I'll cast a protective spell at the top of the stairs before removing the barrier around the area where the weapons were."

"Don't you trust Atticus?" Marco asked.

"I do. Well, I think I do. But we need to make sure that the weapons were destroyed. We can't take any chances. If I'm wrong and the weapons are still active, the protective spell will stop the weapons from going any further." She walked to the top of the stairs and cast the spell.

"With the powers of green ice, red fire, and dark magic
Cover this entrance with a magical fabric
And using the powers of magic's shadow
Prevent any enemy from leaving this borough."

Sascha walked back down the stairs. As she arrived at the bottom, Marco walked up to her and pulled her into a hug. He brushed his lips against hers and Sascha felt her body respond. She groaned and moved into him as she deepened the kiss. Desire flooded through her and the world around her disappeared.

"Sascha," a voice called out, "are you okay?"

It took Sascha a moment to realize who it was that was talking.

"Sascha?" Soleil called out again.

Sascha put her hand on Marco's chest and gently pushed him away, breaking the spell.

"Soleil," she answered. "Yes, I'm fine." Sascha smiled as Marco groaned and shook his head.

"Tell Soleil he has very bad timing," Marco whispered.

Sascha grinned at Marco. "Soleil, there's something I need to tell you. I have put a barrier across the top of the stairs to the city. Marco and I are going to bring down the barrier that is protecting the area where the weapons were."

"I have a bad feeling about this, Sascha."

"I trust Atticus, Soleil," Sascha said. "And as far as I can see, the destruction of the weapons was a complete success."

"Please be careful, Sascha."

"We will. It's unlikely, but if something does happen and you're worried—and this is really important—fly back to the castle and tell Bibacr. He will help you. He will know what to do."

"Sascha, you can't—"

"Trust me, Soleil. Please."

"Well, you don't have long," Soleil said. "The akhult are looking restless."

Sascha turned to Marco. "Soleil said we don't have long. Are you ready to do this?"

He leaned over and grabbed her hand. "Yes, I'm ready. Let's do this so we can go back home."

She glanced at the barrier they created to trap the explosions and the weapons and took a deep breath. "It's now or never.

Let us see behind magic's shadow
As all magical protections forgo
The powers of green ice, red fire, and dark magic
As I order, let it be so."

The barrier disappeared.

They moved toward the broken crates. "I know the weapon is a fine dust," Sascha said, "but I don't know how to tell if it's here or not, other than us disappearing."

"From what Chiane said, it was quick," Marco said.

They inspected the crates. There was no sign of any dust. The place was clear. Sascha looked down at the beacon with its blinking green light and smiled.

"We have done it, Marco. We have honestly done it. The weapons have been destroyed."

Marco picked her up and swung her around. "We have a lot to celebrate. Let's go home."

Sascha removed the barrier across the top of the stairs and Marco raced up the stairs ahead of her. As Sascha was about to follow him she heard whispers echoing in the air behind her. They sounded as if they were coming from deep within the city. The whispers grew louder and the pitch rose higher and higher as the voices grew more excited. But then, as suddenly as they had started, they stopped.

"Sascha, are you coming?" Marco called out.

"Marco, did you hear those voices?"

"What voices?"

"You didn't hear anything?" Sascha asked.

"Nothing."

She glanced around her. "It was probably just my imagination. Give me a minute, I'll meet you at the top of the stairs."

"Okay. But be quick. We need to get out of here."

The mark on Sascha's hand started to tingle, then burn. When she looked down, she saw the blades in her pocket glowing. She lifted her head and shivered as a child's laughter reverberated off the stone walls of the buildings that stood in front of her. She wanted nothing more than to run up the stairs and race home, but she forced herself to stay where she was. She needed to find the child. She moved toward the buildings.

He sat on the porch of a small, insignificant house. On the table next to him was a silver box inscribed with a circled V. He laughed. "Mortals will try to interfere in the plans of the gods, but the heavens will never let a mortal win."

Sascha put her hand into the pocket of her jacket and retrieved the blades. She grasped the tips of the blades between her thumb and fingers, bent her wrist back toward her forearm, swung her arm forward, and released the blades.

The blades spun in circles, becoming brighter and brighter the faster they spun. The explosion came without warning, and as the flames subsided, the blades dropped to the floor with a soft thud.

"That's not possible," Sascha muttered. "The blades can't be destroyed."

The child roared with laughter. "You will learn, Sascha. You will learn." He shimmered and then disappeared.

Sascha raced to where her blades had dropped to the ground and picked them up. The metal was black, and the design engraved into them had been obliterated.

"Sascha," Marco yelled as he came up behind her, breathing heavily. "What happened? Are you okay?"

"It was the—the child," Sascha stammered. She pointed toward the porch where she had seen him. "Marco, the child was over there on that porch. I tried to kill him with the blades." She looked at the blackened blades resting in her palms. "And this is what happened to them."

"How did—I didn't think it was possible to destroy those blades."

"Neither did I," Sascha said. "So now what?"

"Let's go home. You can talk to Athena. I'm sure there is a way to heal them. After all, didn't Atticus say you would need them one more time?"

Yes, yes, he did. But I can't use them like this."

"We will work this out together, Sascha."

"Marco! Sascha! We'd better get out of here," Soleil called out. "The akhult are on the move."

"Come on, Sascha. Let's get out of here." Marco grabbed hold of her hand and pulled her towards the stairs.

On their way out, Sascha put a barrier across the entrance to the city and a second barrier across the entrance to the cave. If the child was still in that city, perhaps she's locked him in there. She glanced down at the blades.

I wonder if there is a way to heal them? Marco seems to think there is.

She shook her head. She was too tired to work it out now. They needed to get home.

~

AFTER THEY ARRIVED BACK at the castle, Sascha sent Soleil to join Fenix while she and Marco walked back to the tavern to join the revelers. Everyone was still there, a bit worse for wear but still going strong.

After telling everyone the good news, that the weapons had indeed been destroyed, and joining them for another couple of drinks, Sascha and Marco walked back outside.

"So I wonder what happened to Drakon?" Marco said.

"I wonder if they're still alive," Sascha replied. "After everything we went through together, it's hard to think of it ending with them just disappearing."

Marco pulled Sascha into his arms and she rested back against him. They stood that way for several minutes as they listened to the happy hollers coming from the tavern and the sounds of the creatures of the night. "We will work with Athena to sort out what happened to your blades," Marco said. "Try to put them out of your mind for tonight."

"I will. There's nothing I can do about it now. And, anyway, I wasn't sure how I felt about having them."

"We will go and visit Connell tomorrow," Marco said. "The healer says his recovery has been quite remarkable. He should be the next High King now that Drakon is out of the picture, assuming Owain doesn't make a surprise return. But the next thing we should focus on is our wedding."

Sascha smiled. She knew Kira would be working hard to organize the perfect wedding. "The girls will be looking forward to it. They'll have gone overboard, of course."

"And we'll enjoy every moment of it," Marco said. "But there is one more thing we need to discuss. I believe you promised me some time alone with you tonight."

Sascha laughed as she took his hand. "And, as you said, we have a lot to celebrate," she said as she dragged him toward her chambers.

EPILOGUE

*S*ascha took Marco by the hand and led him into her chambers. The filtered glow of the three moons was the only source of light, and a cool, peppermint-scented breeze drifted in through the open balcony doors. When Sascha started to move toward the balcony, Marco stopped and pulled her to him. He turned her around to face him, cupped her chin in one hand and brushed his lips against hers. A flash of pleasure sizzled through her. She couldn't stop the moan when he pulled away, dropped his hands to her waist and studied her. She felt his warm breath on her face as she breathed in his unique scent of citrus, spices and sweet wood.

"I love you, Sascha. I know we've had a few . . . arguments, but I love you and I cannot imagine my life without you in it."

Sascha snuggled into him. "I love you too, Marco." They stood that way for a few moments before she added, "And you do know the only reason we have arguments is because you're way too stubborn."

Marco snorted. "I'm stubborn? That's rich coming from—"

Sascha pushed herself away from him, reached a hand up to his collar and pulled him down to her. She kissed him, gently at first and seconds later she deepened the kiss. When he groaned and pulled her closer, she stepped back out of his reach and smirked. "Now, what were you saying?"

"Saying? I wasn't saying anything, you tease."

Sascha laughed.

Marco entwined his fingers in hers and led her out to the balcony. A burning candle sat on a small table covered with a black silk cloth, its honey scent filling the balcony. A huge bunch of red roses tied with a black silk ribbon and finished with a large red plush heart lay beside the candle. A bottle of Dom Perignon in an ice bucket, two champagne flutes edged with gold was placed next to the roses. Resting against the stem of the flutes was a card on which the words 'Will you marry me?' were written in big black letters. The final, and smallest, object on the table was a black box, the lid of which had been left open to show off a ring set with sparkling diamonds the color of Soleil.

"Marco, this is just . . . " She pushed back the tears. "This is beautiful." She turned to him. "But I already said I would marry you. You didn't need to do all this."

Marco walked over to the table, lifted the bottle and released the cork with a loud pop. He poured some champagne into the glasses and walked toward Sascha with the glasses in his hands. "I know you did, but I thought we could do with a fresh start."

He handed Sascha a glass and then swallowed several mouthfuls of his before putting his glass on the table, removing the ring from the box and kneeling before Sascha. "Sascha Morgan, would you do me the honor of becoming my wife?"

Sascha covered her mouth with her hand to stop herself squealing like an excited schoolgirl. Tears rolled down her face. "Yes," she said. "Yes."

Marco slid the ring onto her finger and stood before her. He leaned down and their mouths touched. She tasted the champagne on his lips as he brushed his lips against hers. She wanted him with every beat of her heart. He took a step back, lifted her hand, turned it over and kissed the palm of her hand. "I was worried you would say no."

"Of course I wouldn't say no, Marco. I love you, and besides I couldn't resist the diamonds." She chuckled as Marco raised his eyebrows at her. Sascha took her hand out of his and twisted her hand back and forth as she studied the ring. The diamonds reflected the moonlight and sparkled like the stars in the night sky. "It is a beautiful ring, Marco. Where did you get it? And where did you get the roses and the champagne? They don't have roses or champagne on Eratus."

"The ring is from a little place in the village at Aynor's Stone. As for the roses and champagne, well, I do have part ownership of a coffee shop back on Earth. I asked Mike— you remember the guy who owns the other half of the coffee shop?"

"Yes, I remember him."

"He organized it for me so all I had to do was collect everything from him."

"So it looks like I have to thank Mike too?"

"Not the way you thanked me," Marco said.

Sascha fluttered her lashes. "Spoilsport. He *is* young . . . and good-looking."

Marco grinned. He picked his glass up from the table, drank the rest of his champagne down in a couple of mouthfuls, then topped both of their glasses up and put the bottle back on the table. "Let's toast to new beginnings," he said.

They clinked their glasses together before sipping at their champagne. Sascha sighed as she walked to the balcony rim and leaned against it, still staring at the twinkling diamonds as they gleamed in the moonlight.

The night was quiet aside from the crashing of the sea as it pounded against the shoreline. The energy of the ocean seemed to reverberate in the air around them. There was magic in the air – she could feel its warm touch, taste its sweetness. She glanced over at Marco as he stood beside her and watched him gulp down his champagne again.

"Marco, that's not how you drink champagne. It should be savored and enjoyed."

"There's something else I'd rather savor and enjoy right now," he said. Marco moved closer and stood behind her, resting his chin on her head. His touch burned. She felt his arms slide around her waist. Their bodies fitted together perfectly.

As Marco put his hands on Sascha's shoulders and turned her around to face him, a crack of thunder reverberated through the night sky. Trailing her fingers down the side of his face, she looked up into his eyes and saw her own hunger reflected in them. The mark on her hand warmed as the storm around them started to build. The strength of the winds increased, and she felt the magic and power of the ocean build as the waves crashed against the shoreline with increasing intensity.

Marco took a step back and pulled her into the room. As they stood by the bed, she watched him step out of his jeans and pull his shirt off over his head, flicking each item of clothing aside. His lean, muscled body glinted in the filtered moonlight.

He took her in his arms and lowered her gently onto the silk sheets. Another boom of thunder crashed around them as he lay down beside her. Marco kissed each button on her shirt before undoing it and then helped her to free herself from her shirt and jeans. His touch was soft as he trailed his hand across the delicate skin of her neck and shoulders, resting it on the curve of her breast. Desire crashed through her. She craved his touch, yearned to feel his skin against hers. He stared into her eyes for a moment before kissing her neck, her shoulders and moving down to her waist. She groaned as his lips assaulted her body, leaving trails of fire and ice.

The boom of the storm had changed to the beat of a drum, filling the room around them. Muted voices began chanting, calling to her to satisfy her desires. Instead of being afraid of the voices, they vibrated in her blood, reassuring her.

She called out as her body responded to him, arching her back so she could move even closer. She was consumed with the mindless wonder of being so close to someone who belonged to her, someone who loved her, truly loved her. The powers crashed around them as they moved together as one, filled with a desperate desire that consumed them both. She could hear Marco calling her name.

"I love you, Sascha. I will never lose you. Never." They took each other to the brink and together tipped over the edge into the darkness.

IT WAS the hooting of an owl that woke her. Moonlight was shining in through the window as she turned to face Marco. He was still asleep beside her, the sheet down around his waist. She itched to run her hands over his broad shoulders, through his dark shoulder-length hair. Soon they would be married, and she knew that life with him would never be dull.

She lay back and stared at the ceiling beams, breathing in the familiar smell of honey-wood, pine, and cinnamon. The storm was over and the night was quiet once again.

The owl hooted again and Sascha sat up, searching for the source of the sound. She recoiled when she saw the dark figure sitting on the window ledge. Its hand reached out and stroked a glossy, ebony-colored owl that sat next to it.

"Rest easy, Sascha. Enjoy your time with Marco…for as long as you have him. There is much in store for you, and you should treasure every moment you have with him."

"What the—who the hell are you?" Sascha whispered, not wanting to wake Marco.

The figure laughed. She recognized that laugh. Where had she heard it before?

"You will find out soon enough. I wish you good night."

The figure vanished along with the owl.

Sascha glanced back at Marco. He was still asleep. She trailed her fingers across his muscled back. She always knew that what lay ahead would mean change, but she was determined not to lose Marco. Not now, not after everything they had been through. And with him by her side, she knew she could face anything. She lay down and snuggled against him. With Marco, she could face whatever was in store for her.

INDEX ON TERMS AND CHARACTERS IN THE STORY

An aid in pronouncing the names/titles in this novel.

- **ALEX** – (Pronounced Al-ex) Marco's brother.
- **ARES** – (Pronounced Ar-eez) God of War.
- **ATHENA** – (Pronounced Ath-een-a) Goddess of Wisdom
- **ATTICUS** – (Pronounced At-i-kus) High King of Eratus.
- **BENDIS** – (Pronounced Ben-diss) Fertility Goddess.
- **BIBACR** – (Pronounced Bib-a-car) A gibleree.
- **BRONTU** – (Pronounced Bron-too) A tall ashberry-skinned worker from the Kingdom of Breyth.
- **BREYTH** – (Pronounced Brair-th) One of the Kingdoms in Eratus.
- **CHIANE** – (Pronounced Chee-ann) Lieutenant General working for Drakon.
- **CIARA** – (Pronounced See-r-a) A healer and maid for Sascha.

- **CONNELL** – (Pronounced Kon-il) Adopted son of the High King of Eratus.
- **CRESTWELL** – (Pronounced Crest-well) Soldier in the Fire of the Phoenix forces (Marco's army).
- **CRUDOURAKS** – (Pronounced Kroo-door-aks) Creatures that protect the entrance to the High King's meeting place at Ocean's Mouth.
- **CRYPTO** – (Pronounced (Krip-tow) The brother of Atticus.
- **CRYSTAL** – (Pronounced Kris-tal) The Mirror.
- **DEMIPOS** – (Pronounced Dem-ee-poss) Master that helped Athena stop ancient weapon attack.
- **DRAKON** – (Pronounced Dray-kon) Son of the High King of Eratus.
- **EHAM** – (Pronounced Ee-ham) Mage advisor to the Four Sisters.
- **ELLA** – (Pronounced El-a) Powerful enchantress, yet to discover her true magical powers.
- **FENIX** – (Pronounced Fee-nix) Drakon's pyran. She's in love with Soleil.
- **FIRE GODS** – Fire Priests in the Temple of Brun.
- **FOUR SISTERS** – Powerful female mages.
- **FRAN** – Maid in Marco's castle in Kilmarnock.
- **GIBLEREE** – (Pronounced Gib-al-ree) A creature, believed to be made from dark magic.
- **GEORGE** – Bonded pet of Connell.
- **GERAUD** – (Pronounced Jer-owd) Marco's father.
- **GRAVEN** – (Pronounced Gray-ven) Mage working for Sascha.
- **HUWEIN** – (Pronounced Hoo-wayne) Grandmaster in Magic, works closely with Raeshaan.
- **ISABELLA** – (Pronounced Iz-a-bell-a) Mage Isabella, was attracted to Drakon.

- **JABIT** – (Pronounced Ja-beet) Corporal Jabit, sent to the Ancient Weapons site on Earth.
- **JENNY** – Sascha's book keeper and granddaughter of Eham.
- **KALAMAR** – (Pronounced Kal-a-marr) Leader of Drakon's Fire Dragon. The dragons are from the Kingdom of Breyth. They're the smaller cousin to the dragons from the Kingdom of Brun.
- **KALURTH** – (Pronounced Kal-earth) Master Dragon from the Kingdom of Brun (Lives on Earth).
- **KAN** – (Pronounced Karn) Manticore protecting Atticus.
- **KEN** – Sascha's neighbor when she lived on Earth. She thought of him as a second father.
- **KIRA** – (Pronounced Kee-ra) Powerful Enchantress, yet to discover her true magical powers.
- **LAELA** – (Pronounced Lay-la) A powerful enchantress and ex-leader of the Four Sisters.
- **LEE** – (Pronounced Lee) Powerful Enchantress, yet to discover her true magical powers.
- **LEERON** – (Pronounced Lee-ron) Aide de camp for Atticus when he ruled as High King.
- **LEWIN** – (Pronounced (Loo-wen) Captain Lewin. Sent to the Ancient Weapons site on Earth.
- **MANTICORE** – (Pronounced Man-tee-core) Mythical creature with the body of a lion, wings of a dragon and tail of a scorpion.
- **MARCIE** – (Pronounced Mar-see) Vet in Sascha's business.
- **MARCO** – (Pronounced Mar-ko) Leader of the Fire of the Phoenix, connected to Sascha.

- **MIKE** – Part owner of Coffee shop on Earth. Shares ownership with Marco.
- **NADIYA** – (Pronounced Na-dee-ya) Powerful mage and eight year old girl captured by Laela.
- **NORI** – (Pronounced Noor-ee) Looks after pyrans and horses in Marco's castle.
- **NOVO** – Lieutenant General Novo in Drakon's army.
- **OWAIN** – (Pronounced O-wayne) High King of Eratus.
- **PAT** – Partner of Ken's. Besotted with Drakon.
- **PEALACK** – (Pronounced Peel-ak) Archmage Pealack. Responsible for creating armband for Drakon.
- **PIT HOUND** – A mythical beast that is said to be created from dark magic.
- **PYRAN** – (Pronounced Pie-ran) A bird, a larger version of the mythical creature called Phoenix.
- **RAESHAAN** – (Pronounced Ray-sharn) Master of Air Magic, and sister of the Healer.
- **REDHEAD** – Guard at temple in Brun. Worked for Laela.
- **REYA** – (Pronounced Ray-a) Drakon's ex-lover who attacked by Novo.
- **ROGER** – Sascha's accountant.
- **ROHAN** – (Pronounced Row-ann) Soldier in Fire of the Phoenix forces.
- **ROSETTA** – (Pronounced Row-zetta) Maid in Marco's Castle.
- **RUSTY** – (Pronounced Rus-tee) Ken and Sascha's favorite distraction.
- **SASCHA** – (Pronounced Sash-a) Adopted daughter of the High King of Eratus.

DID YOU ENJOY THIS BOOK?

Please consider leaving a review once you have read this book. Every review makes a difference and helps other readers discover our stories.

Once you have left a review, if you would like to join an exclusive team of readers who are sent an advance copy of my books, please email me at: anaya17.writer@gmail.com.

Should you wish to find out more about the author you can also go to the following social media sites:

Website: https://www.anayamacleod.com
Amazon Page:
https://www.amazon.com/author/anayamacleod

Facebook: https://www.facebook.com/anayabooks.
Twitter: https://twitter.com/macleodanaya
Instagram: https://Instagram.com/anaya_macleod_author

ALSO BY ANAYA MACLEOD

BOOK 1 - IN THE MOON'S SHADOW

**They stripped her of her magic, her memory, and her home.
Now, they want her help.**

Betrayed by her family, Sascha—the adopted daughter of the High
King of Eratus—has built a new life on Earth as a vet and foster
mom to three young orphaned girls. She has no memory of her life
on Eratus, only brutal nightmares of a past she can't remember.

Then her ex-lover Marco appears, asking for her help. An ancient
evil has been unleashed on Eratus, and only Sascha can stop it. The

fate of Earth and Eratus is at stake, and in order to save them, Sascha will need her memory and powers back. But they come at a price, and before long, Sascha realizes nothing is as it seems, and her family's secrets may be deadlier than the Ancient Masters she's supposed to destroy.

A fast-paced fantasy adventure filled with magic, mystery, and intrigue, *In the Moon's Shadow* is the first book in the exciting new Four Sisters series.

ESPECIALLY FOR YOU:

Grab a **Free Copy** of this book by clicking on this link:
http://anayamacleod.com/**free-book**/

FOR MORE DETAILS ON THE AUTHOR:

Website: https://www.anayamacleod.com

Amazon Page: https://www.amazon.com/author/anayamacleod

Facebook: https://www.facebook.com/anayabooks.

EXCLUSIVE OFFER TO NEW READERS

- Don't want to miss out on opportunities to grab any free novels or novellas?
- Don't want to miss out on chances to enter competitions which include giveaways?
- Don't want to miss out on receiving an advance copy of the next book in the series?

Click on the picture of Soleil (below) and he will fly you to my website.

Or **Visit**, *https://www.anayamacleod.com*

Have a look around and then **go to** my *Contact Page.*

Prepare for your next epic fantasy adventure.

SOLEIL

I am very conscious of your privacy and I promise not to spam you. I will only send you emails when special offers or exciting updates are available. For information about my privacy policy feel free to visit my website:

https://www.anayamacleod.com

ACKNOWLEDGMENTS

I would like to thank all those who have supported me in my endeavor to finally publish my second fiction novel. While this is very much the beginning of my journey, and I still have a lot to learn, I have been incredibly blessed to have been given so much support to get this far.

Thanks to my parents and my family, and a very special group of friends. They have kept me going and never allowed me to give up. I am grateful to have them in my life.

I would specifically like to mention those who were brave enough to read my unpolished manuscript, and who have given me invaluable feedback: Paquita Fadden, Michele George, Sarah Millin and Kristie Kirkwood.

Not to mention a very special group of fellow writers – the Infamous SLQs.

I would also like to thank my brilliant and very patient

editors: Tegan Holmberg (Sprout Editing Services); Susannah Noel (Noel Editorial); my talented cover designer, Angie Ayala; and my wonderfully creative map designer, Ren at Renflowergrapx.

SOLEIL'S WORDS ABOUT THE AUTHOR

Hi.

My name is Soleil.

I told Anaya she was supposed to write a bio about herself as an author on this page, but she doesn't like being the center of attention. She said she had a better idea. When she asked me to write about myself and introduce readers to my world, a planet which is fighting for its life, how could I say no?

For those who don't know me, I am a pyran, and I live on Eratus. Pyrans look similar to the birds of fire called the Phoenix, although we have a larger build. We come in all the colors of the rainbow. I have ochre-colored eyes and my feathers are a mixture of reds, greens and burnished gold.

Eratus is a planet that resides in a star system next to Earth's solar system. Our world is protected by a magical shield that works in much the same way as the atmosphere protects Earth. But our shield has an additional protection. It cloaks Eratus so that we remain invisible to all our enemies and even Earth's powerful telescopes can't locate us.

But in this isolation our corrupt have grown even more vile, our Gods have developed an insatiable dark lust which can only be sated by the spilled blood of our people. And once they have consumed Eratus they will be searching for another home to destroy. And their next target is Earth.

This is why my friends and I visited Anaya MacLeod late one winter's night. We are hoping that by sharing our stories with you, one day you may read them and see them for what they are. A warning.

My prayer to Athena is that you don't discover these stories before it is too late to save yourselves.

Soleil

www.ingramcontent.com/pod-product-compliance
Lightning Source LLC
Chambersburg PA
CBHW070825260626
47170CB00007B/2264